UNBRIDLED
MURDER

D0483515

The Carson Stables Mystery series by Leigh Hearon

Reining in Murder

Saddle Up for Murder

Unbridled Murder

UNBRIDLED MURDER

Leigh Hearon

Barbara,
Hope you
enjoy the latest
thrilling adventure!
Warmly,
Leigh

KENSINGTON BOOKS
http://www.kensingtonbooks.com

KENSINGTON BOOKS are published by

Kensington Publishing Corp.
119 West 40th Street
New York, NY 10018

All Kensington titles, imprints and distributed lines are available at special quantity discounts for bulk purchases for sales promotion, premiums, fund-raising, educational or institutional use. Special book excerpts or customized printings can also be created to fit specific needs. For details, write or phone the office of the Kensington Special Sales Manager: Kensington Publishing Corp., 119 West 40th Street, New York, NY, 10018. Attn. Special Sales Department. Phone: 1-800-221-2647.

Kensington and the K logo Reg. U.S. Pat. & TM Off.

ISBN-13: 978-1-4967-1408-4
ISBN-10: 1-4967-1408-3
First Kensington Mass Market Edition: January 2018

eISBN-13: 978-1-4967-1409-1
eISBN-10: 1-4967-1409-1
First Kensington Electronic Edition: January 2018

10 9 8 7 6 5 4 3 2 1

Printed in the United States of America

*For Eddie and Lefty, who crossed over to safety,
and for all of their compatriots
who have not.*

CHAPTER 1

Annie's face was infused with damp sweat. The bright fluorescent light overhead nearly blinded her, and it took all her willpower not to twist and squirm from its pitiless gaze. She scrunched her eyes and tried to breathe evenly. She vowed that she would not speak or cry out in pain, no matter what happened.

"Relax."

The word floated above her, and Annie wanted to kick the speaker. She didn't, and the speaker continued, in a gentle, soothing tone.

"If you squeeze your eyes like that, I can't do my job. And you do want beautiful eyebrows, don't you?"

Did she? Annie had never given much thought to her eyebrows. But apparently, her girlfriends had, and they had pretty much demanded that she *do something about them* before she saw that *fabulously handsome man* again.

Lisa Brunswell, one of Annie's newest friends and her very first stable assistant, was the most adamant. It probably was her age, Annie thought. Lisa was at least two decades younger than she was, the time when things like waxed eyebrows and silky-smooth skin still mattered. Annie was about to turn forty-four, and aside from slapping on a bit of moisturizer before bed— when she remembered—she didn't really think about her face. Her horses had never complained about her looks.

But then Marcus Colbert had entered her life, and everything had changed. Deliciously so.

And now here she was, lying on a massage table with her knees propped up and her hair pulled back into a plump white towel, and feeling extremely vulnerable. She'd felt more courage when she'd encountered a black bear on her property last autumn.

"Your skin might be a little red after the procedure, so we're doing the eyebrows first," the voice continued. "But by the time I've finished with your facial, you'll look perfectly normal. Radiant, in fact. Now, hold still, please. And relax the eyes. That's it."

Annie breathed out and thought, not for the first time, that Marcus had seemed to like her just fine when he had first met her. She'd been wearing dusty cowboy boots and faded jeans.

Two hours later, Annie had to admit she looked remarkably better than any time in recent memory. Her skin *was* glowing, and somehow her green eyes looked more vibrant when unruly eyebrows didn't take center stage. She'd initially squawked at the stylist's insistence on trimming her long, dark brown hair and could barely watch as four inches of it languidly slipped to the salon floor. But looking at herself in the mirror thirty minutes later, she realized the shorter length gave her hair more bounce and shape.

She felt beautiful but had no time to revel in her new stunning self. Annie was meeting Marcus at Port Chester's one French restaurant in two short hours, and she still had to go home to change and check on the horses before making the half-hour drive to the county's most populated—nearly nine thousand at the last census—metropolis.

She ducked out of the salon while stylists from every booth were still oohing and aahing about her transformation. Rushing straight into the sunlit world, Annie didn't see Deputy Tony Elizalde approach until he tapped her on her arm. Predictably, she shrieked, and reached into her saddlebag purse for her never-used can of Mace.

"Relax, Annie. It's me, Tony. Glad I caught you. Boy, you look different."

He was the second person who'd told her to relax today, and she was already tired of it.

"Try calling out my name next time. I respond to words."

"Didn't have time. You burst out of that salon like your hair was on fire. Looks nice, by the way. What's the hurry?"

As if Annie were going to say anything about her date with Marcus. She'd endured enough snide remarks from Tony about her budding relationship to share any new information now.

"Nothing. What's up?"

"I got a call from a buddy in eastern Washington this morning about a lead on some fine horses for sale."

"Thanks, I have all I can handle at the moment."

"Not you, Annie! For Travis's new farm, Alex's Place."

She squinted at Tony, who was standing right in front of the sun. "I thought we'd decided at the last board meeting that we were going to look for horses at our local rescue centers."

"We did, which is why I want to talk to you now. This is an opportunity to acquire good horses for all the right reasons. But it'll take time to explain. And my keen detecting mind tells me you don't have a lot of that right now."

"You got that right, Deputy. I'm booked for the rest of the day. But stop by the farm tomorrow, if that works."

"Will do. Morning okay?"

"Ah . . . let's make it early afternoon."

"Roger that."

Annie nodded at Tony, climbed into her F-250, and started to make an illegal U-turn to head out of town. Glancing in the rearview mirror, she saw Tony still looking at her, his hands on his hips, his expression amused. And curious. Well, he'd just have to stay curious, Annie thought. Although she had to admit she was a bit curious herself about Tony's new lead on adoptable horses. Her friend, Travis Latham, had recently acquired property to build a working farm for boys at risk. Tony and Annie, both members of the nonprofit board overseeing the project, had been tasked with acquiring horses.

Checking on her own horses was pretty much pro forma tonight. As she pulled into her stables, she saw Lisa's yellow VW bug already parked by the tack room and heard her friend humming inside. Annie nudged the door open and slithered inside.

"Wow! You cleaned up good!"

Annie grinned back at her friend, who was stuffing two massive flakes of Timothy into Trooper's hayrack. Trooper was a Thoroughbred and required more hay each day than her youngest horse, a fourteen-hand Saddlebred, consumed practically all week.

"Well, I did have a lot of help."

"And they sure knew what they were doing. You look incredible, Annie! Marcus is going to think he's met a totally new woman!"

Fat chance of that, Annie thought. Miracle workers might enhance her exterior, but she doubted anyone could change her personality, which had been described as stubborn, willful, and annoyingly averse to accepting advice. And those were her friends' opinions. At least everyone stipulated to her fine sense of humor.

"Are you set for tonight?" Annie asked anxiously. Lisa had been Annie's right-hand stable hand for nearly two months now and knew the horses' schedules, needs, and personalities almost as well as she did. But this was the first time Lisa was going to spend the night in her farmhouse, alone, unless you counted the dogs, Sasha and Wolf, and Max the kitten.

"Absolutely. The dogs and I are looking forward to staying up late watching zombie movies and eating all your popcorn. And I don't have to be back at my place until ten a.m. tomorrow, so I've got plenty of time to feed, muck, and make sure everything's set for tomorrow night."

Annie truly relaxed for the first time that day. She was certain everything would be fine and wondered why it had taken her so long to realize that, as her mother used to say, "many hands make light work." For fifteen years, as long as Annie had owned Carson Stables, she'd summarily dismissed any suggestion of bringing help on board, even while her herd grew, and her horse-training business became a demanding year-round job. When Sheriff Dan Stetson, a friend from high school and now a close colleague, had convinced her to invest in a flock of sheep to bring in wool income, she'd still managed to do everything herself. After all, she'd had her horses' help with herding and maintaining the flock's fence line.

But with the arrival of Trooper, her newest horse and a gift from Marcus, plus a sudden surge in income when Marcus had asked for her help in divesting his late wife's equine estate, there seemed no reason *not* to bring in someone to share the workload. Meeting Lisa a few months ago had been fortuitous, indeed.

"Thanks, Lisa. Well, I've got to go—I still have to dress." Annie grabbed her purse and started to jog toward her farmhouse, fifty feet away.

"Go for it, girl! What are you wearing? Something slinky and easy to slip out of, I hope! And don't forget your makeup!"

Laughter was the only answer her new stable hand was going to get.

Annie had never exactly understood what a "double take" was until she saw Marcus's reaction as she walked through the crowded restaurant toward his table.

At six-two, Marcus could stand up remarkably quickly—and elegantly. In his haste this time, however, he managed to bump his knees on the underside of the table, nearly upsetting the bottle of red wine that the waiter was just putting down. Marcus didn't seem to notice the waiter grab and steady the bottle. His eyes were entirely on Annie.

Unlike Lisa, he did not squeal with praise. He merely took her in, admiration and something a bit earthier gleaming out of his dark blue eyes. He held out his arms and Annie slid into them, mindful that other people were watching.

"You look good enough to eat," he murmured into her ear.

"Later. At the moment, the tablecloth looks appetizing. I'm starving."

He laughed and let her go. "Then let's get to it. I've perused the menu, and I believe there are several items that will tempt you."

The waiter poured a small dollop of wine into Marcus's glass, but Marcus merely gestured for the waiter to fill both goblets. He raised one and cocked it and his head toward Annie.

"To you, Annie, a woman of infinite surprises."

Annie smiled. They drank, and Annie felt the rich, warm liquid flow through her body. At that moment, she felt so happy that she could do nothing more than gaze at the man across from her. It seemed that her companion could only do the same.

Fortunately, a waiter came by to hand oversized menus to both of them discreetly. He apparently had the good sense to realize that this would not be the time to tell them about the specials.

Marcus glanced at the menu, then deliberately put it aside.

"Now then, you gorgeous creature, you, tell me everything that's happened since I last saw you. And don't leave anything out."

"And then Patricia showed me what dressage horses can really do, which has opened up a whole new market for Hilda's remaining horses."

By now, Annie had worked her way through two appetizers and a sizeable slice of prime rib. The waiter was impressed. If Marcus noticed that his dinner guest had outeaten him, he didn't show it. Annie's appetite was legendary among her friends, who wondered how a five-foot-eight woman managed to maintain a slim figure while ingesting practically everything in front of her.

"I can see I handed this job off to the right person."

"Well, I couldn't do it without Patricia's help. And I'm learning so much—that's the best part."

"I'm glad Hilda's horses are going to good homes." Hilda had been Marcus's wife, who had been savagely murdered almost six months before. To some, it might seem unseemly that Marcus appeared to be courting another woman so soon, but Annie knew that the long-distance marriage had been rocky for years, and on the verge of collapse when Hilda died. Of course, the timing of Hilda's death hadn't helped Marcus, who had initially been charged with his wife's murder. But that was all behind him now, and the equestrian center that Hilda had once reigned over would soon be known as Alex's Place, the nonprofit farm Tony had alluded to earlier.

The sun was still shining brightly when they emerged from the restaurant at eight o'clock. August truly was the perfect month, Annie thought, and not just because her birthday happened to fall in the middle of it. It was the consistently long, warm, sunny days, when Peninsula residents could forget about the rain that would soon fall and the short days ahead of them. Annie wished it could be August the whole year 'round. She suspected her herd felt similarly.

They strolled down toward the marina, arm in arm.

"Annie."

"Yes, Marcus?"

"I know your birthday is just around the corner. . . ."

"Don't remind me."

"I am reminding you. And I'm so sorry that I can't be here on the given day. These meetings in London were set up months ago, before I realized . . . well, before I knew . . ."

Annie laughed. "It's okay. Really. I don't think I've had a proper birthday celebration since I was twenty-one."

"Well, I promise you one when I get back. But I did want to give you a small token of my affection in advance, just so you'd know I hadn't forgotten this important occasion."

They had reached the main pier, a mass of wooden plank walkways that were surrounded by tourist shops and maritime stores. Marcus stopped in front of a tall bronze sculpture of two dolphins entwined together and reached into his inside blazer pocket.

Annie's heart began to thud against her rib cage. Her mind flashed onto what he might pull out. It couldn't possibly be a ring. Not at this early stage in the relationship, surely?

The piercing yelp of a police siren obliterated any thoughts she might have had. Both she and Marcus whirled around to see what heinous crime had brought the police so close to their own private zone. Annie watched a Suwana County Sheriff's Office patrol car lurch into a business-zone parking space beside them and two officers emerge, the vehicle's strobe lights still flashing.

"Annie! Where in the Sam Hill have you been? And what have you done to your hair?"

CHAPTER 2

Annie groaned. Trust good ol' Dan Stetson and his sidekick, Tony Elizalde, to break up a good party. The sheriff and deputy strode toward them, seemingly oblivious to the tender love scene that had been about to unfold.

"Marcus! Good to see you! Didn't realize you were in town!" Dan stuck out his hand, and Marcus grasped it warmly.

"I'm here just today, and heading back to California tomorrow."

"More of Hilda's business to wrap up, I suppose?"

"Something like that."

There was something in Marcus's tone that made Dan look quizzically at him, then Annie, then clear his throat in embarrassment.

"Yes. Well. That's good. But Tony and I have been

looking for Annie all evening." Wheeling toward her, he said petulantly, "You haven't answered your phone."

Annie dug into her purse and extracted her banged-up cell phone. She flipped open the top and looked askance at the list of missed phone calls on the screen.

"Sorry, Dan. It's been acting up for weeks now. I don't hear the calls and often can only salvage the messages days after they've been sent."

"I will attest to that," Marcus said drily. "She's a hard woman to find even when she's not riding one of her horses."

Annie was not amused by any of them. "Well, you've found me now," she said crossly. "What is so important that you need to put out an all-points bulletin?"

Dan put one of his enormous hands on Annie's arm. "Now, Annie, don't be getting cantankerous on us now. Especially when you look so pretty."

Annie glared at him, and Dan hastily resumed talking.

"Tony had a new idea about how to stock Travis's farm with horses and couldn't wait to tell you, could you, Tony?"

Annie glanced at the deputy. He looked about as happy at the way Dan's conversation was going as she was. She noticed he was holding a thick manila envelope in his hands, nervously turning it over and over again.

"What's the hurry, Tony? I thought we'd agreed to talk tomorrow afternoon."

Tony cleared his throat. "We did, Annie. But my timeline shifted, and I really need to clear it with you now."

Marcus glanced around the group.

"Why don't we go into that coffee shop across the

way to talk about it? The sun's going to go down in another fifteen minutes, and I have a feeling this conversation will take longer than that."

Dan immediately turned and made to set off, but
Tony shook his head slightly and cleared his throat.

"I don't think that's necessary, Dan. Why don't I just
give Annie the broad strokes and let her review what
I've brought, when she has time?"

Dan looked surprised. "Well, she'll have to do it
pretty darn quick, because as I understand it, you're
leaving tomorrow morning at oh-six hundred on your
buddy Rick's private plane. That doesn't give Annie
much time to weigh in."

Annie looked at her friend Tony with amusement.
*He knows this isn't exactly how Marcus and I intended to
spend our one precious evening together. Unlike Dan, the doo-
fus.*

"I'll be blunt, Annie. I'm suggesting that we first look
at horses that are bound for the slaughterhouse. A lot
of them end up in feedlots in eastern Washington before they're shipped out. After I talked to you, I learned
that transport's arriving any day now, maybe even tomorrow, at the Loman feedlot. There are a lot of young,
relatively healthy horses there that are ripe for training,
as well as a lot of seasoned horses that still have years of
riding left in them. But we have to act fast."

Annie's mouth was hanging open, not that she noticed or cared.

"Headed for the *slaughterhouse?* What are you talking
about, Tony? Equine slaughterhouses were outlawed almost a decade ago. They're not allowed anywhere in
the U.S., the last time I looked."

Tony sighed. "Yes, but you can still transport horses
to countries where slaughtering them for human consumption is still legal. Too many good horses end up on

transports to slaughterhouses in Canada or Mexico. I thought we could save a few."

Tears sprang into Annie's eyes, and she could feel a deep-burning rage begin to churn in her gut.

"That's deplorable! Of course let's save a few. Let's save as many as we can!"

She felt Marcus's hand on her arm, and looked down. Her hands were balled into fists. She slowly relaxed them.

"Sorry, Tony. I just had no idea. I . . . I know we've got a problem with too many unwanted horses, but the thought of killing them for food is just too . . ." Her voice wavered. She knew she was close to tears.

Tony thrust the manila envelope at her.

"Take this. It's a printout of all the horses currently up for sale in the feedlot I'm visiting tomorrow. You don't have to look at it now. I'll call you when I'm there and give you a rundown on what I see and we can discuss everything then. It'll be a pretty fast trip. All I'm hoping to do is zero in on the best horses we can save, make a deal with the feedlot owners, and come home. We can arrange for trailer transport from here. They'll have to be quarantined at first, of course."

Annie numbly took the envelope extended toward her.

"I'd really hoped that we could talk about this privately tomorrow. And I don't want to ruin your time with Marcus," Tony went on. "But I've got to get to eastern Washington before the transport vans do, and I wanted to consult with you—and Marcus—first. After all, you're both members of Travis's board, and you're our resident horse expert."

Annie half smiled at him.

"Thanks. Although I think Jessica ranks a bit higher than I do. Have you told her yet?"

"Our large-animal vet already has told me she'd be happy to thoroughly check any horses we buy. But she said we'd have to find separate accommodations for them for the first thirty days. Jessica can't risk bringing any new viruses or diseases into her own clinic."

"Understandable. I won't be able to board them at my stables for the same reason. But we'll find some place to quarantine them, I'm sure of it. How about Travis? How does he feel about this?"

"Just what you'd expect. He's totally on board. He's authorized me to bring back as many horses as I want."

Now Annie gave Tony a real smile. "I second that, Deputy. Go get 'em."

"Will do. But there's no need to look inside that envelope until I call tomorrow. In the meantime, Annie, my humble suggestion is to get a room."

And with that parting remark, Tony and Dan practically scuttled away, leaving Annie with a bright red face that lasted long after Dan's police vehicle headed out of town.

Marcus's gift to Annie was the latest smartphone. She didn't know if she was disappointed or thrilled at uncovering the box that bore the familiar logo. Not that Annie had even thought of the idea of marrying Marcus, or anyone, for that matter. But buying an expensive smartphone also would never have occurred to her. Paying someone to help muck the stalls was one thing. Spending money on a device that did everything except walk the dog was another.

"Do you like it?" Marcus asked anxiously. They were seated in the bar of Marcus's hotel, small snifters of brandy before them. Hordes of tourists were yakking it up in every available corner of the room. The noise level, bolstered by the high ceiling, was close to deafening, but Annie had tuned them all out. Her eyes eagerly took in all the brightly colored icons on the screen. She then gazed up at Marcus, beaming.

"It's beautiful. But you're going to have to teach me how to use it."

"With pleasure. I took the liberty of signing you up under my plan and playing with a few of the apps."

He looked a bit embarrassed as he admitted this.

"Like what?"

"Well, your list of contacts, for starters." Marcus punched an icon that looked like an address book and a list of familiar names came up.

"I notice your name tops the list."

"Only because my last name starts with C, and I couldn't think of anyone you knew whose name starts with A or B. Or C, for that matter, other than your own."

"Aha." Actually, there was one person whose name would supersede Marcus's—Lavender Carson, her nutty half sister. But so far, Annie had mentioned Lavender to Marcus only in passing and no opportunity for the twain to meet had occurred. *May it ever be so*, Annie fervently prayed to her Good Angel.

She glanced down at the list, and saw, in addition to Marcus's name, Dan, Tony, Jessica, and Travis—every board member of "Alex's Place," named for Travis Latham's late grandson.

"They were the only people whose phone numbers I knew," Marcus said sheepishly. "I do realize your circle of friends and acquaintances extends far beyond this small group. Let me teach you how to add them to your list of contacts. I know you're friends with Deputy Kim Williams, right? Let's use her as an example."

Annie put her hand over the screen and looked directly into Marcus's blue eyes.

"Marcus, this is the best gift I've ever received. Besides Trooper, of course. But doesn't your plane leave in just a few hours?" She tried her best to look seductive. "Isn't there anything else you'd like to . . . show me?"

Marcus nodded, a slow grin creasing his face. Annie slipped the phone into her purse and stood up from the table, cognizant that her blue dress clung quite closely to the contours of her body. She accepted the hotel key that Marcus handed her and, hand in hand, they walked toward the elevator.

CHAPTER 3

Annie smiled beatifically at every person she saw the next day, starting with the nice server who arrived at 7:30 AM with coffee and croissants. Her smile extended to all the people in the elevator with her on the ride down to the lobby, and continued as she walked down the street to the lot where her F-250 was lodged. Passersby might have described Annie as definitely having a spring in her step. In fact, it was all Annie could do to stop from skipping her way out of town and back to her stables. She couldn't remember being this happy, ever.

Marcus had left before dawn in order to catch his early morning flight back to San Jose. Before leaving, he had awakened her, gently, and bestowed on her such a long, lingering kiss that she'd wanted to grab his lapels and hold him in place. She resisted the urge, but he got the message.

"I'll be back before you know it" was his whispered good-bye. And then he gently shut the door behind him.

Marcus's kiss had made sleep impossible. So Annie snuggled up in a very large, very comfortable wingback chair in the hotel suite and thought about her wonderful and totally unpredictable new relationship.

Annie had wanted Marcus from the very moment she'd seen him, and she suspected his ardor for her hadn't been long in coming, either. During the first months after they'd met each other, circumstances, as well as geographic distance, had made it impossible for any relationship to develop, and while both had been acutely aware of how they'd felt about the other, there had been little either could do to hasten the process.

Now, however, the time was right for exploring just how well a Northwest horse gal and a California CEO of a multimillion-dollar software company could get along in a long-distance romance.

If Annie were perfectly honest with herself—which she tried to be, whenever possible—on the face of it, she and Marcus didn't have much in common. She compared their backgrounds in her mind's eye. Really, they could not have been more disparate. Annie had been raised by a single mother in a small, rural community, and had struggled for everything good in her life, from graduating from college to buying her first truck, then her ranch. Marcus hadn't talked much about his childhood, but he'd said enough for Annie to know he came from a wealthy, privileged family in the Bay Area. He'd undoubtedly had his own private struggles growing up, but they were not the same as Annie's.

And as far as professional paths, it didn't take a rocket scientist to figure out just how divergent Annie's and Marcus's careers really were. Annie spent most of her time with horses, and that was just fine by her. Horses had been her one constant solace growing up, and they would always be her constant companions in life. It was as simple as that. Marcus, on the other hand, was a corporate wizard, who knew how to foster innovation within his company and persuade investors to buy into it. He regularly spoke to the most powerful and successful CEOs in the world. Annie mostly spoke to horses, and she didn't usually use words.

And it wasn't just the fact that they pursued different careers. Neither of them knew the least bit about the other's chosen field. Marcus couldn't put a halter on a horse to save his life, and Annie wasn't sure she knew how to turn on her new smartphone.

And then there were their lifestyles. Annie pulled on a pair of Levi's every morning. Marcus put on an Armani suit. Annie lived in a 1930s farmhouse that didn't have a dishwasher and not nearly enough closet space for even her meager wardrobe. Marcus lived in a home Annie could only imagine, and she suspected it wasn't his only one. After all, Hilda had had her own McMansion right here in Suwana County.

Thinking about everything they didn't share was starting to give her a headache. So she turned her mind to the one thing that she and Marcus definitely had in common. And remembering what had occurred just a few hours ago was enough to wipe out all her nagging concerns and put one smug smile on her face, which had no intention of going away anytime soon.

By the time she arrived back home, it was late morning, and, thankfully, Lisa had already departed. Annie wasn't sure she could have handled the questions that Lisa was sure to pepper her with about her hot date with, as she called Marcus, "the sexy stallion from San

Jose." Her horses were far out in the pasture, enjoying the hot sun and warm grass. Her friend, Sarah, had mentioned coming over in late afternoon to pick up her Tennessee Walker, whom Annie been working with for the past four months, but that was many hours away.

For the first time that day, Annie wondered how Tony was getting along on his trip to the feedlot. She pulled out her old cell phone—which looked distinctly déclassé now—and flipped the cover. No message, but that hardly meant anything since the phone often delivered messages days after they were received. She realized she'd better figure out her new cell phone soon. Until it was up and running, no one knew her new phone number, which was amazingly easy to remember. She was convinced Marcus had played a part in making that happen.

Tucking the manila envelope Tony had given her into her overnight bag, she headed up the path to her farmhouse. There, on the top step, sat Hannah, looking exceptionally forlorn. The reason for the little girl's unhappiness was readily apparent. Her left arm was swathed in a bright pink plaster cast, which extended from her wrist to just below her elbow.

Annie quickly sprinted up the steps and sat down next to her.

"Oh, Hannah! What happened?"

"I broke my arm." That much was evident, but Annie said nothing. The despair in the child's voice was palpable.

"I'm so sorry. How did it happen?"

"Mr. Bo Jangles was chasing our kitten, and I fell over him. I put out my arm to break the fall, but it didn't help."

"Oh, dear. That must have hurt." Annie squelched her desire to ask if the kitten had survived the chase by a small Belgian Tervuren puppy.

"It did. A LOT. But Daddy said if I was brave and

didn't cry, he'd buy me new riding boots when the cast is gone."

"Wonderful! How long do you have to have this thing on?"

"Three weeks." Annie bit back a laugh. Hannah had made it sound as if were three years, although, to a just-turned-eight-year-old, three weeks probably did seem that long.

"Well, what are we going to do until then?" Annie was curious to see what the child would come up with.

"I don't know," Hannah said, spreading her short arms wide and nearly bonking Annie with her plastered arm in the process. "Mommy says I can't be around horses because if one bumped into my cast, my arm might get worse. I can watch them, but not touch." A long sigh followed.

This *was* tough, Annie realized. She fully understood why Judith Clare wouldn't want Hannah to risk being injured further, but she also knew that Hannah needed her horse fix just as much as she had when she was her age.

"Want to see a new present I got yesterday?"

"I guess."

Annie pulled out the smartphone from her saddle-bag purse.

"Ever seen one of these before?"

"Wow! How cool, Annie! My mom has one of these."

"Very cool, indeed. The only problem is I don't know how to turn it on."

Hannah grabbed the phone from Annie's hand with her one good arm and pressed a button on the top.

"You did charge this last night, didn't you?" she asked anxiously.

Amused, Annie nodded. Marcus had insisted, and had done the honors himself.

Instantly, Hannah's sad mood vanished. Annie was dumbfounded to learn that Hannah knew more about smartphone operations and apps than she probably ever would. After five minutes of watching Hannah's thumbs navigate at warp speed, Annie gently persuaded her to come inside and into a chair by her kitchen table. She let the little girl work her magic while she went about putting out milk and cookies. Even with a cast limiting her mobility, Hannah seemed remarkably proficient with Annie's new toy.

Two hours later, Hannah had shown Annie how to work all the features and insisted Annie try them herself to make sure she could use them. She also had told Annie she was perfectly fine to walk the quarter-mile path that separated their two homes—but Annie had insisted even more firmly that she would drive her. In just two hours, Annie had become far more conversant with her new phone than she'd ever expected and could hardly wait to call Marcus to tell him. However, the conversation she envisioned with him would not be suitable for small ears. Annie's decision to make sure Hannah was delivered safely and quickly home was not entirely altruistic.

"Remember what I told you about using the burst," Hannah instructed her as Annie dropped her off at her home. "And remember to send the photos we took today to my mom so she can put them on Facebook."

"I will, I will," replied Annie with good humor although she wasn't sure she knew how to upload the photos onto her old computer—yet. Hannah had shown her several amazing features of the phone's camera, including one that took rapid-fire images in a row. That, and the zoom lens, had enabled Hannah to take excellent shots of Annie's horses, which she naturally wanted to share.

She'd also taken great care with selecting Annie's

ring tone. Her first choice—a hip-hop jingle—had been quickly nixed. Hannah's second choice—a dog barking—had also been vetoed; Annie had explained that if her phone rang when her dogs were present, they might mistake it for a real dog and be confused. Hannah had understood that far more easily than she had Annie's disdain for hip-hop. They finally compromised on the sound of a rotary phone—something that Hannah had never seen, and took on faith had once existed.

It tickled Annie that someone a fraction of her age, and with the use of only one good arm, had managed to train her so well. Actually, when she thought about it, it was downright scary.

As she headed home, her smartphone gave off its new old-fashioned trill in her purse. Annie scrambled to find it. Who could possibly be calling her this soon? No one even knew her number yet. That was, no one except the person who'd given her the phone.

She expertly swiped open the screen and put the phone to her ear.

"Hello, darling," she heard Marcus say.

"Hello, darling back," she replied, as easily as if she'd been saying it all her life.

CHAPTER 4

On the heels of Marcus's call came one from Annie's
friend Sarah, which she took on her landline.

"I can come over now, Annie, but I'll only have time
to pick up Layla and write you a check. If you can wait
until tomorrow, I'll have more time for a visit, and besides bringing my checkbook, I can corral Samantha
Higgins, who's offered to bring a thermos of her fa-
mous dirty martinis."

"Come tomorrow," Annie promptly replied. "It's always
great to see Sam, and it'll give me one more chance to
work with Layla. And I never refuse one of Sam's exotic
concoctions."

It also would give her a chance to review the packet
that Tony had given her. A little advance preparation
couldn't hurt, if she still had time. It was now 2:00 P.M.,
and she expected his call at any moment.

She settled on her back porch with a glass of iced tea in one hand and Tony's packet in the other. After a long swallow, she ripped open the manila envelope and pulled out a stapled set of papers. The first sheet held the ominous heading, *Kill Pen Horses*. Below and on the following pages were photos and descriptions of all the horses currently in line for the slaughterhouse unless they were adopted out. Annie began to read.

Twenty minutes later, she was practically in tears. How could anyone willingly give over these animals to a kill pen, knowing their eventual destination and fate? Every horse she read about deserved a second chance at life. She glanced down at the page flipped open on her knee. So many were so young! It seemed impossible that any owner would truncate a horse's life when it hadn't even begun to live it. And the older ones seemed to have been discarded for the slightest of reasons—a racehorse too old now for the track, a trail horse for a closed-down summer camp, a broodmare who didn't produce enough foals—the reasons went on and on, and Annie did not understand a single one. She was looking at horses that had done their best for their owners and now were not going to enjoy a pleasant retirement but instead be loaded onto a trailer and delivered to a frightening, turbulent house of death. What was wrong with people? What was wrong with the world?

She thought back to her own horses. All of them, with the exception of Trooper, had been rescued as well. If she had not stepped in when she had, what would have happened to them? She shuddered and refused to think about it anymore.

As if on cue, Tony's number appeared on the screen of her old cell phone, now carelessly cast aside. Blowing her nose thoroughly, Annie answered his call.

"Annie, you there?"

"I am indeed," she replied, trying to sound perky and normal. "What's the news from eastern Washington?"

"Let me tell you, Annie, this has not been a fun trip." She swallowed hard.

"I've just finished reading the descriptions of the horses up for sale. You do realize, of course, that we have to buy them all." Annie said this in a half-joking manner, but Tony knew that she meant every word.

"I wish we could. The feedlot conditions here are pretty grim. The couple who run it are a couple of snakes. The horses you're looking at represent the cream of the crop. Here, I'm seeing the lame and crippled ones, the horses with injuries, the ones that no one will ever buy and are doomed already. Nicest thing for them would be to put them out of their misery in a humane way. It's just criminal what's going to happen to these poor beasts."

"Stop it, Tony. I've already used up one box of Kleenex. I'm sorry you've had to witness all this. I'm the lucky one. All I have to do is look at pretty pictures and descriptions. Where do you stand now, as far as selection?"

It sounded coldhearted even to talk about the feedlot horses this way, but it was exactly what she and Tony were doing—deciding the fate of a herd of horses, nearly all of whom should live.

Tony sighed. "Here's my best wisdom. There's a yearling, a liver chestnut quarter horse that's halter broke and has a terrific personality, really people-oriented, which is what we want. He's still a stallion, so Jessica would have to fix that. He's on page two, third one down, on the list I gave you."

"I noticed him. Sounds perfect." *But then, they all do.*

"Next is farther down that same page, a bay broodmare, trail experience, about fifteen years old, looks rock solid."

Annie gave the description a cursory glance. "Let's take her."

"And then, on the next page, there's a mustang mix. He's gelded, probably three or four years old, behaves well with others. I just latched onto him, thought he'd be a good work project."

"I'm sold."

"And finally, on the last page, there's a bay mare, probably a Morgan, who was used for hunting trips. She's somewhere shy of twenty, looks in excellent condition. She's only been here a day or two."

"Then let's spring her."

"Total for all four horses is two thousand two hundred and twenty-six dollars."

"A bargain."

"It's calculated by their total weight. It's what the feedlot owners would get if they sold them for horse meat. At the moment, that's sixty-five cents per pound."

Annie's throat closed up so tightly that she couldn't speak.

Annie thought Samantha's dirty martinis couldn't arrive soon enough. The next day, she diligently worked one last time with Layla, and was hosing her down by the round pen when Sarah arrived with her horse trailer.

"Come look at your beauty while she's still clean," Annie called over to Sarah. "I definitely feel a roll coming on."

"Oh, what the heck," Sarah said. "It'll save me from having to give her fly spray today."

There were many reasons why horses like to get

down on the ground and roll, and one of them was
using dirt as a shield from pesky mites.

"You are such an indulgent parent. Don't go spoiling
her, now, just because she's coming home."

"I'll try. But I don't promise you I'll succeed."

As predicted, once Annie released her halter, Layla
knelt on her front knees, rolled over twice thoroughly
in each direction, stood up, and gave her body a massive
shake that extended through her entire spine and scattered dust and dirt far and wide. Annie tossed her a
flake of orchard grass and left her in the round pen. She
fully intended to enjoy her time with her friend as they
sipped Samantha's signature drink. Sam swore her martinis didn't depend on the brand of gin or vermouth—
it was the olive brine she used, and so far, she refused to
reveal the brand name.

It was hot, in the mid-eighties, rare for the Pacific
Northwest, even in the thick of summer. Annie had a
feeling a martini at four o'clock in the afternoon would
go straight to her head. She didn't care. Her meager
education yesterday into the world of kill pens had un-
nerved her more than she'd thought. Annie had done
her best to put it out of her mind. She'd fed her horses,
then herself, and picked a mind-numbing movie to distract her. But just as the credits were rolling, Tony had
called again, ostensibly to report that he'd met with the
feedlot owners and completed the sale. But it had been
clear other things were on his mind. He'd also sounded
bone weary.

"I'm telling you, doing anything in this town takes a
SEAL team," he'd groused to Annie. "People don't show
up on time, no one knows where they are, when they'll be
back, no one wants to tell you anything. I'm just trying to
make a simple business transaction, and it's turned into
a small nightmare."

"Why, Tony? What happened?"

"Oh, at the eleventh hour, when I was about to put more than two thousand smackers into this cretin's hands, he backed out."

"*WHAT?*"

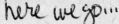 *here we go...*

Sasha had jumped from where she'd been sleeping on Annie's living room rug. Wolf, a few feet away, hadn't moved. He was used to his mistress's periodic outbursts.

"Don't worry, he backed in again, but a little more cash had to exchange hands before he let it happen. And, by the way, the brains behind this operation is the wife. He's the front person, but she's the powerhouse. I'm sure this last-minute snafu was all her idea. Probably happens to every person who wants to save a horse. Anyway, I now have a receipt and their promise, for what it's worth, that the horses will be sequestered in a separate paddock until our transport van comes for them. And by the way, Annie, it can't come too fast. I don't trust these people. We've got to get them out of here as soon as possible."

"I'll call Jessica tomorrow and see what we can arrange."

"Thanks. And while you're at it, don't forget that we need a safe place to board them for the next month or so. Preferably one that's close to you, me, and Jessica."

"I'll put out all the feelers I can. I'm seeing a horse owner who lives on the other side of the water tomorrow. She may know of a place or two that I've never heard of. It wouldn't be ideal, having to cross the Worden State Bridge every time we want to visit, but it would only be for a month or two."

"I appreciate that, Annie. I'm getting out of this hellhole as fast as I can. Rick's gone back already—he had some kind of family emergency. But he lined me up with a local flyer here who says he can take me back tomorrow afternoon. If it's not too late, I'll come by and show you more up-to-date photos of Travis's new horses."

"Great, Tony. Just give me a call on my new smartphone as soon as you know when you're going to touch down."

"A smartphone? You? You're coming out of the dark ages at last?"

"If you must know, it was a gift. And I'm already taking photos with it."

"Hah! This I have to see. I'm surprised you can turn it on."

"Well, Hannah helped."

"Ah, that explains it. Which reminds me—I met a couple of kids over here that would make even you think about embracing motherhood."

"You're delusional. Get some sleep."

They'd clicked off at the same time, but at least, that time, the conversation had ended with laughter on both ends.

Now, at five o'clock the next day, Annie was still laughing, this time over Samantha's impression of a particularly snotty parent of one of her young riders. Samantha's stables catered to children, and for this brave act Annie held her in awe. She preferred clients who were adults, and dropped off their horses at her barn and returned when training was done.

Samantha continued her story. "So Lori comes right up to me, and says, 'No child of mine is going to lug that big saddle back to the tack room. She could get permanent back problems from all that lifting!' " Samantha imitated the woman's voice to roars of laughter from her appreciative audience.

"Speaking of lifting, have you seen her lately?" Sarah chimed in. "You notice how her eyes have that wide-open, surprised look? What do you want to bet she's had some heavy lifting herself?"

"Hmmm . . . I think you're right," Sam said. "She's always so obnoxious that I try to avoid looking at her. It doesn't help that she's the kind of mother who insists on 'fully participating' in her child's every activity. It drives me batty."

"So what did you tell Lori?" Annie asked. She was curious to see how other people solved people problems. She knew how she would have handled it—she would have told the woman to take her attitude and never darken her doorway again.

"I told her that the saddle only weighed seven pounds, which probably is less than the knapsack Brandi lugs to school every day. I told her to weigh her daughter's knapsack and if it weighed less than seven pounds, I'd haul the saddle myself."

"Did the mother ever complain again?" Annie had to know.

"Nope. And Brandi is hauling around her little saddle just fine, with one big smile on her face."

What a great response, Annie thought. Maybe she could learn a thing or two about how to get along with difficult people from her friends. Or, she could simply do what she'd been doing all her lifetime: hang out with horses.

She heard her smartphone ring and looked around for it, shading her eyes with her hand. She found it on the table, where the martini glasses had been deposited. Whatever liquid any of them still held was quickly evaporating in the hot sun. She scrambled to her feet and grabbed the phone when she recognized Dan Stetson's number on the screen.

"Excuse me, ladies," Annie said. "Official business

that will only take a moment." Sarah and Sam vaguely waved their arms in her direction and continued their conversation. She sprinted toward her home, where reception was best, passing Layla on the way. Layla was now contentedly eating grass under Annie's biggest apple tree. The round pen was great for work but provided no shade.

She swiped the screen on Dan's fourth ring.

"Is Tony back?" She assumed that was why the sheriff was calling her.

"Annie." Dan's voice was uncharacteristically low, and she sensed he wasn't quite in control of his emotions.

"Yes, Dan?" she asked quietly.

"I have bad news. Very bad news. The private plane—" Dan's voice broke. He waited a few moments and began again, in a steadier voice. "The airplane bringing Tony home went down this afternoon somewhere around the Snoqualmie Pass. Looks like a fire may have broken out in flight. We're not sure. The plane crashed nose first in a forested area. If it wasn't on fire before, it was as soon as it hit the ground."

Annie had unconsciously put her hand over her mouth while Dan was talking. Now she took it away. She knew the answer to the question she was about to ask, but she had to ask, anyway.

"Any survivors?"

"None. Tony is gone, Annie. He's dead."

CHAPTER 5

It was impossible to absorb the enormity of Dan's news. She slowly walked back to her friends, tears streaming down her face. Sarah and Sam jumped to their feet and embraced her. Annie wasn't much of a touchy-feely kind of person, but today she allowed the two women to enfold her without question. Her brain still couldn't quite believe that what Dan had said was true. It seemed too horrible to fit into any reality that Annie could fathom.

The next two days were a blur.

She took care of her horses and her sheep, in a numb, sleep-deprived state because sleep was often impossible. She was vaguely aware that Lisa and others were pitching in as well, and was grateful for their help, even if it often was only expressed with a tired smile. Most of the time, she camped out at the Suwana County

Sheriff's Office, which predictably had become the hub for information.

The news of Tony's death quickly spread throughout Suwana County and beyond. The deputy had been a beloved member of the sheriff's office for more than a decade, and Annie knew that Dan had always considered him heir apparent to his position as sheriff, when the time was right. And there was no doubt in Annie's mind that Tony would have been easily elected. He was known for his cool, calm ability to defuse potentially explosive confrontations and for always being fair. Annie could remember a number of occasions where Tony had deftly resolved situations that could have erupted into real violence. Even habitual residents of the county jail would admit that Tony was one of the few deputies they could trust to keep his word.

The local newspaper dedicated the entire front section to the life and times of Tony Elizalde, small-town boy made good. Media from Seattle and other major cities rolled in to get sound bites from the residents who knew him, although no one from the immediate family agreed to make a statement.

Tony's parents, predictably, were devastated by the news. Annie, Dan, and Deputy Kim Williams visited them, but there was nothing they could do or say that seemed to diminish their raw and all-consuming grief over the tragic loss of their eldest son. Tony had been their pride and joy, the first of their six children to graduate from college, and his sudden death left a gaping chasm in their lives that could never be filled.

Tony's siblings seemed similarly stunned by their brother's death.

"Did you know he put me and my sisters through college?" Carlos was the next eldest son in the Elizalde clan, and now the unspoken head of the family. "Tony had this great job, see, but he never thought about buying a fancy car or a house or taking a big vacation. He put all his money back into his family. He said we were the best investment he could make. We couldn't wait for him to marry and have children so we could start giving back to his new family all the love he'd given us."

Annie realized she'd had no idea how pivotal Tony had been in so many people's lives. It stunned her to see how much Tony's kindness and thoughtful nature had touched others.

The funeral was planned for Sunday, August 7. It would be a closed-casket ceremony. The medical examiner who'd performed the autopsy had merely told the family that Tony unquestionably had died instantly, as soon as the airplane hit the ground. Dan and Annie got a much fuller and more gruesome picture of what had happened.

"We found soot in his airways," Dr. Kate Mulligan announced to Dan and Annie, who were seated in Dan's office and talking to the medical examiner on speakerphone. "That's proof positive that Mr. Elizalde was alive and breathing when the fire started in the cockpit. The same goes for the pilot."

Both Annie and Dan winced.

"But what I told the parents was the truth," she continued. "Not many people survive a crash in a Cessna 180, especially when it nose-dives into the ground at a high rate of speed. Both men suffered substantial thermal burns while still alive. But in the end, there wasn't much time left for either man to suffer—a minute or two at the most."

Annie excused herself from the conversation. She already knew more than she really cared to know about how Tony had died. Representatives from both the Snoqualmie police and fire departments had been more than accommodating as far as sharing information. Of course, their reports only covered what they had seen and done at the crash scene, after the fact. But according to several eyewitnesses, the crisis in the air had begun just as the plane crested the Snoqualmie ski lodge. In August, the lodge was well populated with tourists and employees, and so there was a dizzying array of statements from people who claimed they had seen exactly what had happened.

Annie, Dan, and Kim had pored through the statements on Friday morning, as soon as they'd landed in Dan's e-mail in-box.

The one thing every witness agreed on was that they'd heard the Cessna before they'd actually seen it.

The clouds rolled in all morning, wrote one witness. *By one o'clock, the mountains had disappeared behind one massive cloud bank. My wife was complaining about the lousy weather and wanted to leave. We were outside on our deck discussing it when we heard the sound of a plane overhead. When it emerged from the clouds, you could tell something was wrong. It wasn't flying straight like you normally see. It was listing a bit to the left and losing altitude.*

Other people claimed they had seen a fire inside the cockpit as the plane descended.

I remember hearing the plane first, then seeing it come out of the clouds. But the engine sounded different—it was sputtering and coughing, like it was dying, wrote another witness. *Then the engine just sputtered to a stop. All I saw was the plane dropping pretty rapidly toward us. I saw a flash of light in the cockpit and thought, that plane's on fire! For a moment, I thought it was going to crash into the lodge. But it zoomed past it and over the parking lot and out into the forest. We all heard the crash. The noise was terrible.*

One witness, a hiker, had actually seen the crash.

I was at a trailhead about five hundred feet away when I saw a plane on fire coming by me, was the hiker's blunt description. *Clouds of black smoke were trailing out in back and it looked like it was going a million miles an hour from where I was standing. The wings scraped off the branches of at least four old-growth trees before the nose hit the ground. And then it just exploded. The flames went up nearly as high as the trees. I took off running for the lodge. I could feel the heat from the fire from where I'd been standing.*

When they were done reading, Dan, Annie, and Kim stared at each other in numb silence. Every statement made Tony's death more real—and more puzzling. The medical examiner's latest pronouncement confirmed that the fire had started on board and in midair, and several witnesses thought this, too. Now, the question Annie and everyone else around the table were asking themselves was *why? Why did the plane catch on fire at all? And how?*

According to fire department reports, little remained of the Cessna. It had taken only twenty minutes to put out the blaze, but the damage had been done and judging by the photos they'd sent Dan, it was extensive. The landing gear was gone, presumably ripped off when the Cessna met the forest floor. Both wings had broken off, and the nose of the plane looked like that of a pugilist who'd just lost his last fight. The propeller was twisted beyond repair. Because the fire had started in the cockpit, the instrument panel was one black, sooty mess, and all the wires attached behind the dashboard were charred and broken. According to Dan, it would take a forensic expert to determine which wires were damaged in the fire and which might have been tampered with, if that, in fact, was the source for the fire. As he explained to Annie, the fire could have been caused by any number of reasons, some perfectly innocent and others less so.

The National Transportation Safety Board was now on the job, but getting updates from this organization was like pulling teeth, Dan said.

"They'll take their own sweet time getting back to us," he grumbled. "By the time they get around to telling us what caused the fire, I'll be retired. The only thing they'll tell me is it's a 'hull loss accident,' which I take to mean that plane will never fly again."

Annie wanted to remind Dan that it had only been two days since the crash but resisted the urge. She intuitively knew that any federal agency involved in oversight of plane crashes would not be inclined to give out information prematurely, especially if criminal intent was involved. And Annie suspected it was.

"Have you talked to Tony's buddy Rick yet?" she asked the sheriff. "Maybe he can pull some strings."

"He'll be here in an hour. Stick around if you want. Kim's off to see the folks. I'll fill her in later."

Annie had only met Rick once before, at Tony's thirtieth birthday party. The man who entered the sheriff's office on that afternoon held no resemblance to the jocular and gregarious guy who only a few years ago had regaled the audience with Tony's high-school hijinks. Now he was pale and somber, and obviously wracked with guilt.

"I'll never forgive myself for not sticking around and taking him home," he told Dan in a hoarse voice. "It was my kid's soccer game, that's all, the first of the season. The guys at the community airport recommended Danny Trevor, and when I talked to him on the phone, he seemed perfectly capable. More than capable, in fact. Said he'd been a commercial pilot for nearly twenty years, some Asian airline that flew to Thailand, Japan, I don't know. But he made trips across the globe, for God's sake. How could he go down on a puddle jumper?"

Rick already had done all the due diligence he could from his end. Unfortunately, it still didn't explain why a fire should have erupted in the plane a half hour after takeoff.

"As soon as I got the news, I called the ground crew at county airport," Rick told Annie and Dan. "They were as shocked as anyone. Trevor was a frequent flyer, had a good reputation as a pilot, and had built a brisk business ferrying hunters and fishers back and forth across the mountains. Never had a problem with his aircraft before. His annual inspection was coming up in the next few months, but the guys said he always inspected the plane before loading up."

"Why didn't he radio for help?" Annie asked. It seemed the most obvious question.

Rick smiled patiently at her. "Probably wouldn't have done much good if he had," he said gently, "but the fact was, he didn't have any contact with air traffic control on this flight."

"What the hell? Had his radio gone out?" This came from Dan.

"I guess that's something the NTSB's figuring out right now. But the truth is he didn't need to be in contact with anyone. The flight from Loman to the Port Chester International Airport takes a little over an hour, and in weather like this, there's no need for him to be flying IFR."

"IFR? What in the Sam Hill is that?"

"Sorry, instrument flight rules. Generally speaking, airplanes like a Cessna 180 can fly two ways—by visual flight rules, or VFR, or instrument flight rules, IFR. VFR is perfectly fine when the weather's good, the view is unobstructed, and there's little or no competing air traffic. If a pilot chooses this route, he doesn't have to do much except check his plane and take off. He's not required to file a flight plan. He's not required to stay in touch with ATC—" Seeing the quizzical look in Annie's eyes, Rick paused, and continued, "Air traffic control, and he doesn't even have to follow a predefined flight plan. He can literally wing it."

Annie and Dan digested this information for a moment. Then Dan demanded, "How about that cloud cover over Snoqualmie? Shouldn't he have checked weather conditions over the mountains before he took off?'

Rick paused. "Yes and no. I chose to fly IFR going over with Tony the day before, and the pass was as clear as could be. I could have flown VFR—I just tend to be careful. Plus, I like having contact with ATC. Just makes me feel a bit safer. We don't know if Trevor checked the weather in the mountain passes before taking off. But even if he did, it might have shown the same blue sky as I encountered twenty-four hours before. The weather's a bit unpredictable in that part of the sky, and cloud banks have been known to come in unexpectedly."

"Well, he should have known that," Annie said bitterly. "If he's as good a pilot as everyone says he is, I mean *was*, he should have anticipated that."

"Yes, but . . ."

"And why do you say even if he had contact with air control, it wouldn't have made any difference?

"Because, Ms. Carson, even though Trevor was flying in a dense cloud bank, chances were very good that he'd have come out of it all right. He knew the terrain, and he wasn't going to fly without clear visual cues for

very long. It's unlikely he would have flown the plane
into a mountain.

He smiled sadly at both of his listeners.

"The real question is why a Cessna 180, even one flying in a cloud bank, should suddenly catch on fire.
That's what caused the plane to crash. Trevor might
have cut a few corners, but unless he lit a cigarette in
the cockpit or he or the ground crew didn't properly
check out the plane before it took off, it was sabotaged.
And that means someone wanted to kill Danny Trevor,
my good friend Tony Elizalde, or both."

Dan and Annie sat silently in his office long after
Rick had left, until the sun finally began to make its de-
scent into the western skies. They'd also learned from
Rick that the Cessna 180 had nothing like the black box
found on commercial jets. That knowledge, along with
the absence of radio communication, was downright
depressing. Although neither of them said it, they were
thinking the same thing: that whatever Tony and Trevor
might have said as flames erupted in the Cessna's cockpit
and the plane plummeted toward the earth would forever be unknown. Unless the NTSB unearthed a clue—a
smoking gun—in the rubble, the reason Tony died
might have died with him.

CHAPTER 6

Driving home that night, Annie made a decision. Nothing would bring back Tony Elizalde; he was beyond saving. But there were four horses in the Loman feedlot, already bought and paid for, that could be saved. She silently vowed that she would oversee their transport back to the Peninsula if she had to bring them back herself. No one, or nothing, would dissuade her.

Her smartphone buzzed and she glanced down at the screen, an act that seemed like second nature to her now. Travis Latham's name appeared, and she felt a rush of guilt, realizing that she had yet to talk to her old friend following the news of Tony's death. She let it go to voicemail. She'd call him later, when she had a glass of Glenlivet in one hand. Pulling into her long, sloping driveway, she noticed that Lisa, who had become an in-dispensable rock in her and her horses' lives, was already here, feeding the horses without waiting to be asked. It was time to tell her just how appreciated she was—and to ask for a favor.

The smell of horses, hay, and saddle leather engulfed Annie as she entered the stalls. It acted as an instant balm, as did the appearance of her dependable stable assistant.

Lisa was combing Trooper's tail in his stall, while he munched on hay from his rack. The Thoroughbred was accommodating that way. A few months ago, he'd come from the racetrack, where he had undoubtedly been groomed on a regular basis, but perhaps not with the love and care that the women in his life now bestowed.

"I don't know what I'd do without you," Annie said simply as she walked toward Trooper's stall.

Lisa turned toward her and smiled. "Being here makes me happy. It feels good to be around your horses."

Annie slipped into the stall and stroked Trooper's mane. "I can't tell you how delighted I am to hear that because I need to ask another favor of you now."

Lisa's eyes sparkled. Annie suspected for a horse-crazy just-turned-twenty-one-year-old, working at her stables probably seemed like the ultimate dream job.

"I need to make some calls first. But if things go as I hope they do, I'll need you to stay here and take full care of the horses for a few days, maybe as many as three or four. The sheep will need feeding, as well. I'll leave you Sasha so you have some company and protection. Can you do all that for me? I realize it's pretty short notice."

"No problem. Hunter's so low-maintenance now that it's easy to come here and help out. I still can't thank you enough for saving his life last spring."

When Annie had first met Lisa, her quarter horse, Hunter, had been chronically colicking. Annie had diagnosed the issue and convinced Lisa's vet to treat Hunter accordingly. She realized she was now a bit of a heroine in Lisa's eyes. The thought was not entirely displeasing.

"Take the day off tomorrow, Lisa. I can handle the horse chores. The only thing that's going on is Tony's funeral, and that's in the afternoon. But be prepared to move in on Monday morning. I don't know how long I'll be away. I hope it's only for a few days. But you might have to stick around a bit longer."

There were so many people Annie had spoken to in the past few days that she didn't even know, and so many people that she hadn't and desperately wanted to.

Marcus was a prime example. Her last conversation with him had been on Wednesday, three full days ago, when she'd proudly regaled him with her new prowess as a smartphone user. On Thursday morning, Marcus had flown to London on business and she knew his return date was at least a week away.

She'd found a text from him on her phone on Friday morning:

Dan just shared the devastating news about Tony. Will call as soon as I can—8-hour time difference makes it a bit challenging. Hope you're getting the answers I know you need. Keep your chin up. Love, Marcus.

Annie dutifully sent a text back to Marcus, assuring him she was fine. It was her first text, ever, and Annie discovered she did not much like the process. Hannah had taught her how to use the microphone to dictate texts, but the icon now proved elusive, and she was in no mood for another tutorial. She painstakingly pecked out her brief reply and hoped that Marcus would call, and soon.

He did not. And Annie had been so consumed with finding out the whys and wherefores of the plane crash that by the time she tumbled into bed at night, she had no energy to speak to anyone. Consequently, while she'd met and talked to at least fifteen members of the Elizalde clan and shared condolences and memories of Tony with nearly every deputy on the Suwana County payroll, she still hadn't talked with the people she knew and liked most.

Pouring herself a generous shot of Glenlivet, she settled into her most comfortable chair and picked up her new cell. She had a pile of people to talk to and started with Travis Latham, with whom she'd established a fast friendship earlier this year, despite an age difference of at least forty years.

Travis was one of the county's most distinguished citizens, who now was in charge of repurposing Hilda Colbert's equestrian property as a place where boys at risk might make a new start. He'd named it "Alex's Place" after his grandson, who had died at the hand of juvenile bullies several years before. Despite a gruff exterior, Travis was one of the kindest and most empathetic people Annie had ever met. Sasha, her Belgian Tervuren pup, adored him, and Annie had promised Travis the pup was his after her training as a companion dog was complete. Years before, Travis had suffered a stroke, from which he had mostly recovered. Still, he was now in his eighties and lived alone by choice. Annie had decided early in their friendship that he needed a dog, and so far Travis had not said no.

"Hold on, Annie, I'm just making a cup of hot chocolate," he told her when she called his home landline. She could hear the sounds of someone working in the kitchen and patiently waited while she stroked Sasha, now at her feet. A few minutes later, Travis picked up the phone.

"How are you doing, dear girl?" he asked. Annie felt tears prick at the corner of her eyes. Trust Travis to inquire about her well-being first instead of plunging into the awful news at hand.

"I'm fine," she said, her voice quavering a bit. She willed herself to snap out of it. "I've been hanging out at the sheriff's office waiting for news. None of it has been very good, I'm afraid. We still don't know what caused the crash. Or if it was intentional, which is what I care about."

"You, Dan, and most everyone I've spoken to, including myself," Travis replied. "The chances of a Cessna catching fire on a routine flight are just too extraordinary. If it was due to mechanical failure, my money's on someone's deliberately making it so."

"Great minds think alike," Annie said gloomily. "But I think we've gotten all we can out of the eastern Washington cop shop. You probably know that both the FAA and NTSB are looking into it now. Although the chance of either agency telling us what they've found from the debris is probably nil."

"Look at you, rattling off those acronyms. I'm impressed."

"Yes, and just ask me about the difference between VFR and IFR. My education has grown by leaps and bounds."

"I can tell. But, Annie, it's not like you just to sit back and say you've obtained all the information that's available. I know Dan's fuming over his inability to contribute to the investigation, but he's law enforcement and obliged to work within the confines of the territory allotted to him. You're not. I'm surprised you're not calling from the local airport right now, telling me the results of your interrogation of the maintenance crew."

Annie laughed, and her chest suddenly seemed to lose some of its heaviness. It had been the first time she'd laughed in days—she hadn't since Sam's impression of her student rider's obnoxious mother.

"You know me so well," she admitted to her friend. "That's exactly what I'd like to do right now. Someone's got to know what happened after the Cessna took off. And actually, making a trip to eastern Washington is one of the reasons I called. I'm assuming that Tony filled you in on the horses he and I selected?"

"He did, indeed. In fact, I believe he called me right after hanging up with you. He sounded quite excited about the prospect of acquiring them and, more to the point, delivering them from their alternative fate."

"Did he tell you about the feedlot owners almost pulling out of the deal at the last minute?"

"No, Tony didn't mention that. He probably wanted to spare my aging heart. What happened?"

"It appears they tried to wrangle more money out of him and won. There really wasn't much choice."

"Those scurrilous dogs. I suspect they make more money out of bleeding-heart horse rescuers like us than they do from the meat factory."

"I'm sure you're right. Anyway, I'm concerned that three days have passed since Tony bought the horses, and I haven't made any progress in securing transportation for them. Tony said the feedlot owners promised to keep them apart from the rest of the doomed herd, but I don't know how long that promise stands."

"You're absolutely right, Annie. We've got to get those horses back without further delay. Do you know of anyone who could bring them here? As I understand it, there are specialized haulers for this type of thing. Something to do with not spreading diseases."

Annie sighed. "The problem is, we don't know what these horses are carrying until Jessica examines them.

A regular commercial hauler probably doesn't want to risk passing on a respiratory disease to his next load of horses. But I can certainly check out the possibilities."

"That's good, Annie, but frankly, I'd feel a lot better if you were there to personally oversee their delivery. I believe that's what you and Tony were expecting to do right about now."

"Well, I'm glad to hear you say that, Travis, because that's exactly what I was going to propose. And just in case finding a transporter proves difficult, I thought I'd haul a trailer myself, just to make sure the job gets done. I've only got a three-load slant myself, but Jessica's got larger trailers, and I'm sure she'd let me borrow one for the trip."

"What about the cross-contamination issue?"

"If I do end up using it, I promise to thoroughly sanitize it after the horses get here. Which brings up another issue. We need to find a place to quarantine them."

"Ah, yes. I remember Tony's mentioning that as well."

She sighed again. "I feel so remiss. I promised Tony I'd get on this right away, then . . ." Her throat tightened, and she swallowed hard.

"Annie, Annie. Only a few days have passed since we received the dreadful news. You're on top of it now. When do you expect to leave? And will you need any money? The coffers of Alex's Place are quite full, you know, thanks to your very good-hearted boyfriend."

She was glad Travis could not see her blush. "I'll be fine, Travis. I've got my credit card, and I'll bring as much cash as the ATM will allow. I think it's better that I pay now and the organization reimburses me when the job is done."

"If you're sure."

"I'm sure."

"Then go get 'em, Annie, and if you dig up any clues about the plane crash, please keep me in the loop."

"I will. Promise."

Annie reflected upon hanging up that she'd used the same words—"go get 'em"—with Tony on the advent of his departure to eastern Washington. She hoped that her return from across the mountains would not end as badly as his had.

But then, she was driving.

Annie's next call was to Jessica Flynn, who, she was embarrassed to discover, was already asleep.

"Sorry, Annie," Jessica yawned into the phone. "I have to get up at four o'clock tomorrow. My one clinic worker is on vacation this week, and yours truly is in charge of cleaning the stalls. And right now I have a full house. It kills me to go to bed when the sun's still up, but there you have it."

"I'm so sorry, Jessica. Do you want me to call tomorrow?"

"Nonsense. Have you called to talk about Tony? What awful news. I still can't believe it."

"Neither can I." Although after reading the witness statements and police and fire reports, not to mention looking at the hundreds of photos taken at the crash scene, Annie's hold on her fantasy that it had all just been a bad dream was rapidly slipping. But there was no reason to share what she knew with Jessica.

"Look, Jessica, Tony's death has been a shock to all of us. So much, in fact, that I, for one, completely forgot about the fate of the four horses Tony rescued up in Loman three days ago. Tony made it sound as if they might be carted off to the slaughterhouse any day now, and when I last talked with him, he wasn't at all confident the feedlot owners would keep their promise of separating them from the others. I'm terrified that they've been taken already."

"What do you need from me?"

Jessica may have been half-asleep, but she had no problem understanding that Annie needed help.

"I need a trailer. I'd prefer to have a commercial outfit do the job, but I'm concerned about getting the horses out of there as quickly as possible, and I may not find another hauler in time. You know my trailer's a stall short. Can I borrow one of yours?"

"Absolutely. Since my clinic is full, I won't need my four-stall to haul any horses, and you're welcome to it. When are you planning on leaving?"

"Monday morning, early."

"Well, you know what time I get up. You're welcome anytime."

"Thanks, Jessica. And, there's one more thing—"

"What, you want a thermos and bag of hot doughnuts to come with the trailer?"

Annie laughed for the second time that evening. It felt good.

"I haven't had the time or energy to find a place to quarantine the horses after I arrive."

"Leave that to me. Since I'll be overseeing their care, I'll want it someplace close to my own. You go rescue the horses, and I'll find a place where they can temporarily stay."

"You're wonderful."

"I know. My new mule tells me all the time."

Annie was acutely aware that Tony's funeral was the next day. It would be the third service of its kind that she had attended this year, but the others had not filled her with quite as much dread as this one. On the two previous occasions, she'd barely known the deceased. This time, she would be at the funeral of a very good, longtime friend. She knew it would be a long, emotional afternoon and wasn't sure she'd be able to keep herself together. She also knew practically nothing about the Roman Catholic faith and was afraid she'd make some ritualistic gaffe.

Perhaps she could at least mitigate the chances of that occurring, she thought, and picked up her phone at once to consult with another octogenarian friend, Martha Sanderson.

"Wear black, dear, and just watch what everyone else does," Martha had counseled her. "There will be a lot of kneeling, and you should, too. But you don't need to try to cross yourself when you see others doing so, and you really shouldn't take communion, if it's offered."

"Are you planning on attending?" Annie couldn't imagine anyone *not* going, but wanted reassurance.

"Of course, dear. Lavender and I plan on being there early, and we'll save you a seat if you want. The church is sure to be packed to the rafters."

As much as Annie would have loved to sit by Martha and take her cues from her—even if it meant her half sister Lavender would be seated on the other side—she regretfully declined. She knew that she would be expected to join Travis, Dan, and other law enforcement officers. She'd known Tony through his work on the force, and most recently, for his contribution to Travis's organization. She needed to be counted among his many friends and colleagues in those arenas.

* * *

The last phone call was the hardest, but it had to be made. She found the Loman feedlot listed on the Washington State Department of Agriculture Web page, confirming it was duly licensed and open for business. The owners' names weren't listed, but their phone number was. Annie took her last sip of Glenlivet and punched in the number on her phone.

The string of rings went on for an interminably long time, without a voice message encouraging the caller to leave a number. Just when Annie was about to give up, a woman's voice answered.

"Yes?" She sounded angry.

"This is Annie Carson. I'm calling from the Olympic Peninsula in reference to four horses recently purchased by Tony Elizalde on behalf of . . ."

"I got 'em. Someone was supposed to pick them up a few days ago."

Not bloody likely, thought Annie. *They were just purchased a few days ago.*

"Yes, I know. You may have heard that Mr. Elizalde was killed in a plane crash the day after he executed the sale."

"I did. Danny Trevor will be sorely missed."

As will Tony Elizalde, you old cow, Annie inwardly seethed.

"Well, it's taken us a bit longer than we expected to round up transportation, considering Mr. Elizalde also just *died.*"

"Well, they're here. But if you don't pick 'em up soon, they won't be much longer. When are you planning to have them hauled out?"

"Tuesday is the earliest I can be there."

"Tuesday, you say? Well, I can hold 'em until then, but it'll cost you."

Of course it will. "That's fine. I'm happy to pay for their feed and board until I take possession." Normally,

Annie disdained people who made a point of saying they "owned" or "possessed" any equine. As far as she was concerned, her horses owned her, rather than the other way around. At the moment, however, it seemed best to use a word that this harpy could understand.

"All right then. What's your name?"

"Annie Carson. Let me give you my cell number in case you need it."

"I got it. It came up on my screen."

"Great. And, uh, your name is . . . ?"

"Myrna. See you on Tuesday. Don't come before two. That's when we feed. Before that, the lot is restricted to sellers, and no one else is welcome."

"All right, Myrna. I'll see you at two on Tuesday."

The conversation abruptly ended.

Annie found that her hands were shaking. She slowly got up, put her tumbler in the sink, and saw Wolf by her woodstove, inquisitively looking at her. She bent down to scratch behind his ears.

"Well, this is your lucky day, Wolf. You're about to embark on an exciting road trip."

His prompt bark assured Annie that her stalwart companion was already packed and ready to go.

Memories

CHAPTER 7

Monday, August 8

By seven o'clock, Annie was on the road to eastern Washington, with Wolf riding shotgun. She'd hurriedly packed the night before and arisen before daybreak. After writing a detailed note of instructions for Lisa—who she realized probably didn't need any reminders—she fed the horses and turned them out to pasture. Unlike Annie, the horses did not grumble at being roused at such an unseemly hour. The dawn showed all the promise of another glorious August day, as well as a hot one, and Annie suspected her herd was happy to be out on the grass while it still held dew and the air was still cool.

She pulled into Jessica's clinic on her way out of town, and was greeted by a long whinny from Jessica's latest equine acquisition, Mollie the Mule.

"And top of the morning to you, too," Annie replied,

clambering down from her truck after Wolf, who had deftly leapt over her, strictly against orders.

Jessica had her four-stall trailer ready for hookup in front of her clinic.

"Since we don't know how big these horses really are, I'm giving you the straight-load," Jessica informed her. "It's longer that the slant, but it's all-aluminum construction."

Annie nodded appreciatively. Slant loads could cramp large-size horses if filled to capacity. Her F-250 could handle the weight of all four rescues, but she'd take all the help she could get. Even with an all-aluminum rig, the return trip would be slow going.

"In case you encounter a problem loading, there's a front-load ramp as well as one in the rear," Jessica went on, pointing out this feature.

Now that was a break, Annie thought. She didn't know if any of the horses had been hauled anywhere—except to the feedlot. She hoped they'd be easy to load without a hissy fit about their next-door neighbor, but you never knew.

Jessica opened the rear doors to show the stall areas. "They should be fine for the ride home. Floor mats are three-quarters of an inch thick, there's a pop-up roof vent for each horse, and the bulkhead window in front has front opening windows, as well."

The weather in Loman was in the high nineties, according to Annie's new phone, and adequate ventilation inside the trailer was key. Jessica had it covered.

Annie's vet now opened the small door to the "dressing room," a small space tucked in front of the right-front wheel where most horse owners stored tack, hay, and shavings. Annie stared in amazement.

"I've given you two bales of orchard, which probably

is what they've been eating, two sets of hay nets, halters because I doubt any came with them, and a couple of bags of shavings."

"You've thought of everything."

"Tried to. I knew you'd bring your own medical kit, but I put in my emergency one, as well. You've got bute, antibiotics, meds for ulcers, bandages, stethoscope, everything I thought you might need when you get there."

"Thanks, Jessica." Annie felt overwhelmed by her vet's generosity—and perspicacity. She'd never thought of bringing extra halters.

When both women had checked and double-checked each lock and latch, Jessica handed Annie a piece of paper.

"I did a bit of research this morning," she told Annie. "There are a lot of horse rescuers where you're headed, some with excellent reputations, others, not so much. I've put down the names of two people I trust. Naturally, they're women—"

"Of course."

"And they've been doing this for years. They know all the feedlot owners in eastern Washington and how to work horse deals without handing out bribes."

"You've got to be kidding!" Annie was horrified.

"Well, I'm speaking metaphorically. At least, pretty much. The horse-rescue business in the Northwest is a mixed bag. Motives aren't always clear. Most organizations are just trying to do the right thing, but there have been a few horror stories in recent years of so-called rescuers flipping the horses and selling to another kill pen. I've heard of other outfits that sell rescues at exorbitant prices and profit just as much as the feedlot owners. Don't automatically assume everyone who says they want to save the horses has the horses' best interests at heart. The two women I'm putting you in touch with are solid. That is, to the best of my knowledge."

Annie thanked Jessica and climbed into her truck. In truth, she felt a lot less certain about her ability to perform what she'd set out to do. But there was no turning back now. Tony would want her to carry on. And her conscience demanded that she finish his job.

"Call me once you've seen the horses," Jessica called up to her in the cab. "And if there's anything I can do from here, just let me know. "

"Just find a place where I can park them upon return, and I'll be forever grateful," Annie said, and flashed her friend a smile as she slowly pulled out of the clinic's circular drive. She sounded more confident than she felt.

She'd calculated a six-hour drive to Loman, which, according to Google Maps, was somewhere northeast of Moses Lake, and had filled her CD player with her favorite country western albums to keep her company along the way. But she didn't dare risk the distraction of music now. Traffic at the height of summer took all her attention, at least while she was in urban territory.

She'd decided to drive around the Peninsula rather than take a ferry into Seattle to join up with I-90E, the highway that would lead her closest to her destination. Ferries were crowded this time of year, and Annie didn't want to wait in line. She also didn't want to pay the exorbitant fee for transporting an oversized vehicle on water. Besides, Seattle traffic was daunting at the best of times. Instead, she wended her way to Tacoma, crossing the Tacoma Narrows Bridge, a mile-long suspension bridge that Annie never forgot, at least when she was on it, had been turned asunder in a freak windstorm back in 1940, months after it had been built. She knew the replacement bridge was aerodynamically designed to prevent another collapse, but stuck to the middle lane where she could pretend she had blinders on and willed herself not to look down.

Once she'd navigated Tacoma and turned off on Highway 18, she relaxed and settled in for the long drive ahead. It was a familiar path; Annie had graduated from Central Washington University in Ellensburg more than twenty years before and the route hadn't changed all that much, although North Bend, to her astonishment, was no longer a hick town but a major suburban draw, with a shopping mall whose square footage Annie couldn't begin to fathom.

Normally, she would have enjoyed climbing the switchbacks that led up to Snoqualmie Pass, known for its ski runs in the winter and as a vast recreational area in the summer. But with a twenty-eight-foot trailer behind her, she was constantly shifting gears and pulling into turnouts to let less encumbered vehicles pass. And, more to the point, she was heading straight to the place where Tony Elizalde had perished. As her truck and trailer slowly chugged up the mountain pass, her sense of dread increased proportionally with the altitude. She needed a break but couldn't bear stopping at the summit. As it was, she still noticed detour signs on the highway berms approaching the lodge. Nope, she'd keep rolling until she reached more neutral ground.

About a half hour outside Ellensburg, she pulled off at a rest area with a dog run and used the restroom. It was now eleven o'clock, and the sun was high in the sky. She knew the temperature would be fifteen degrees higher when she hit the valley below. She remembered what it had been like during her college years, when students wore shorts and sported flip-flops until mid-October, when the weather suddenly changed and fall and winter quickly merged into one long, cold, and often snowy season.

"Ready for some grub?" she asked her blue heeler. The answer was an enthusiastic yes. She set out his bowls, and Wolf dived in. In about the same record time as Wolf, Annie demolished a ham-and-cheese sandwich she'd made that morning. Glancing around, she soaked in the rich green tapestry surrounding her. It wasn't the thick, dense forest of the Olympic Peninsula, where Douglas fir and cedars dominated the landscape, but the forests of ponderosa and lodgepole pines were equally impressive, she thought.

After a prolonged game of fetch, Annie headed out again. Wolf had been excellent company so far, wide-awake and alert throughout the drive. But now, he decided a postprandial nap was in order, and he leapt into the extended cab to take a snooze.

"Really, Wolf," Annie observed. "Others of us might like to take naps, too, you know, but we *can't*. That's fine, you just have a nice rest. I'll let you know when we hit Ellensburg, and you can take the wheel."

She pushed the PLAY button, and Alan Jackson's greatest hits began to play. As the strains of "Don't Rock the Jukebox" filled the cab, she thought about Tony's funeral, only twenty-four hours ago. Most of the service had baffled her; the prayers had been different from the ones she was used to, and while the other Catholics had seemed quite at home, knowing how to respond, when to kneel, and when to cross themselves, Annie had found it a continual guessing game and had finally given up trying to play along. So, she'd noticed, had most of the Suwana County deputies sitting beside her, although Dan had managed to stand up when required. She suspected that if his colossal knees had ever hit the kneeler, he'd never have been able to get up.

What had been predictable was the outpouring of emotion. There had not been a dry eye in the house, as Father Connors went on at length about Tony's life and the treasures that awaited him in heaven. When it was finally over, she'd been ready to flee. Then she'd looked at Dan and known she couldn't take the easy way out. Annie had quietly stood by as the sheriff stoically responded to every person who approached him during the reception, and they'd remained in the hall until the last guest had departed. After another half hour sharing reminiscences with the Elizalde family, Dan and Annie had finally escaped to the parking lot, where their vehicles had been close to the only ones left. She had been thoroughly exhausted and grateful beyond words that Lisa had ignored her instructions and fed the horses that evening. It was all she'd been able to do to pack and fall into bed.

Annie knew that Dan would still be fielding calls from local citizens and media and trying to wangle more information from the NTSB in the weeks ahead. In contrast, she had been able to get out of Dodge for a few days to save four rescue horses from a kill pen in eastern Washington. Annie was sure she had the better deal.

As they zoomed by the few exits for Ellensburg, Annie gave a short wave to her alma mater and yelled out the window, "Go Wildcats!" She glanced at her interior mirror. Wolf was still fast asleep.

"Lucky dog," she muttered. By her calculations, she was now a bit more than two hours out from her destination. She leaned back and concentrated on what Alan Jackson had to sing about love gone wrong.

Thirty miles past Moses Lake, she saw her exit. Putting on her turn signal, she made a slow, hard left and began driving due north. Now she was in real farm country, not whizzing along on a freeway with fruit and vegetable stands beckoning along the way. She was on a two-lane country road, and her more sedate traveling speed succeeded in rousing her dog. Wolf leapt into the front seat and sat straight up, tongue out, eager to take in the new territory. Annie ruffled his neck. If there ever was a dog that could remind you that life was just one big adventure, Wolf was it.

Almost an hour later, she had crisscrossed so many country lanes that she had no idea where she was headed. But the little blue ball on her smartphone assured her she was on the right path, and she had no choice but to follow its course. Just when she was about to give up and pull into a gas station for directions—assuming she could find one—she saw a sign for Loman, announcing it was four miles ahead. She gave a sigh of relief and mentally began to steel herself for the next part of her trip.

She was prepared for a small town, but Loman rivaled even her own small town of Oyster Bay as far as size. The main street consisted of four short blocks and one traffic light by the cop shop. Most of the retail signs were in Spanish. The closest thing to a restaurant she saw were a couple of taco trailers, and judging by the deserted streets, neither had many customers. True, she had arrived in town during the worst heat of the day. Maybe everyone was inside taking siestas. Annie was more than ready for a nap herself, but she knew she had no time for such a luxury. Her meeting with Myrna was in twenty-four hours, and she wanted to be thoroughly conversant with the lay of the land before that encounter occurred.

She looked around for a motel, and cursed herself for not scouting out possible places to stay before she'd left. She'd assumed that there would be at least a couple of local motels in town. It would be a major inconvenience if she had to trek back to the freeway to find accommodations. As she recalled, the last major exit was at least forty miles away.

Well, it was time to gas up, anyway. She pulled into the town's one gas station, and a small Hispanic man ran out, window cleaner in hand. Annie was already climbing out of her truck, but the man waved her back. An oppressive wave of heat enveloped her outside, and she hastily hopped back in the truck, where the remnants of air-conditioning still lingered.

¡Yo puedo hacer eso!

I can do that. Yes, you can, Annie thought, but in Washington State, people usually pumped their own gas. It's only when you hit Oregon that you usually got the royal treatment with a real live gas attendant.

"*Nosotros bombardeamos todo el gas aquí,*" he said proudly.

Annie nodded. She'd only understood a few words, but enough to know that he was in charge, and she was the customer.

As if to prove his point, the man began vigorously scrubbing Annie's windshield, which admittedly reflected about three hundred miles' worth of bug splatter. Annie decided if washing windows and pumping gas provided one more job in this godforsaken town, she sure wasn't going to make a fuss, even if it raised the cost of gas a few pennies. Besides, who wanted to stand outside in that heat? It was killing her.

Having made Annie's windshield sparkle again, the man moved around to the pump. He extracted the nozzle and gave a questioning wave with it toward the octane selections.

Annie pushed down her passenger window, pointed to the one for regular, and released the gas-cap button from inside the truck. The man smiled and commenced with his work. Annie smiled back at him. She could get used to this kind of treatment, even if she couldn't get used to the heat.

After the transaction was completed, she waved good-bye to her cheerful attendant and drove one short block to a corner market. Inside, she bought a Pepsi for herself and a large bottle of cold water for Wolf. Spanish was the primary language spoken here, as well, and Annie wasn't sure hers was adequate for the questions she had. She stationed herself under the store's meager eave, reckoning she wouldn't die of heatstroke for at least five minutes. Then she reached into her pocket and extracted both her phone and the paper Jessica had given her. She dialed the first number on the list. It was for Maria Hernandez, and Annie prayed that Ms. Hernandez spoke English.

She did. And she was delighted to hear from Annie. Jessica had called her this morning to tell her to expect Annie's call. Where was she staying? Ah, Maria said with an amused laugh, you thought Loman might actually have lodgings for visitors. As Annie had feared, no such luck.

"No one ever comes to Loman," she told Annie. "It dried up years ago, around the time cattle driving did. You'll find decent motels in Browning, eight miles east of there. That's close to where I live. The feedlot is between the two towns. You'll actually pass it on your way here. But don't stop—the owners have camcorders stationed at the entrance and at every gate, and they're the kind of people who shoot first and ask questions later. Jessica said you've got an appointment for tomorrow at two. That's perfect; it's the one time each day the horses and livestock get any attention, not to mention feed. We should get in without a problem."

Annie absorbed all this information without comment. She felt as if she were at the edge of a foreign country and was being told by the nice border guard that she had to obey all rules absolutely, or she would not be allowed inside. Going along docilely simply because someone said she had to was not something Annie did easily, or often. But she obviously was in no position to argue any of Maria's points. She was simply grateful that Maria was there to explain how things were done.

"I'm assuming I won't have trouble getting a room in Browning?" she asked. "I did bring my dog."

Maria laughed again. It was a low, gentle laugh that Annie liked. "Browning isn't exactly a destination among summer tourists. And neither motel's going to object to your dog, although you'll probably have to put down a deposit for damages."

"Fine." Annie was relieved that she and Wolf wouldn't be bunking tonight in the truck. "As I'm sure Jessica's told you, I have a four-stall with me, but if you know of a professional hauler who can do the transport, I'd just as soon hire their services."

"Sadly, I don't. There are only two haulers around here who will transport dirty horses, and they're both booked way in advance. Bringing your own trailer was the right thing to do."

Well, at least that issue is resolved, Annie thought.

"But you've got my full services while you're here," Maria went on. "I know Myrna and George all too well, and will go with you tomorrow to make sure they don't pull any fast ones. And I'd love to get together with you tonight, just to talk, but my two sons both have Little League games, and I can't miss them play. I'd suggest you come along, but you're probably beat from the drive, and you've got a long return trip ahead of you."

Annie silently blessed Maria for giving her an out. Watching kids play baseball for hours on end was about as appealing to her as watching grass grow.

"I could use a relaxing evening and an early bed."

"There should be a few restaurants in town that won't give you food poisoning. I'd stay away from the bars. They're pretty rowdy and testosterone-ridden."

"I shall avoid them like the plague. What time should we get together tomorrow?"

"Let's meet up at noon for lunch at the local diner, then we'll go out to the feedlot. As I understand it, the horses are paid for, so all we need to do is to load and go."

"That's the plan."

"Then let's do it, Annie. Let's get it done."

CHAPTER 8

Browning was a sight better than Loman. Annie counted four stoplights through town, caught a glimpse of a regular IGA market, and, as Maria had promised, identified two motels, each flanking one end of town. She chose one at random. She was tired, and even Wolf looked as if he needed a place to call home for the night.

She was surprised at the size of her accommodations, especially since it had cost all of eighty-eight dollars, pet deposit included. The place obviously catered to long-distance truckers. In addition to a bedroom and bath, the room included a small kitchenette with a microwave, a small refrigerator, a four-burner electric range, and a sparse set of dishes. There was even a small sitting area in front of an old-fashioned TV. All the walls and most of the furniture were constructed out of knotty pine.

All in all, it wasn't a bad place to crash for a night, she decided.

"We provide free Internet," the clerk explained to her, "but not cable. That leaves you with three working stations, all local. But most people watch movies on their tablets these days, anyway." Annie didn't own a tablet but seldom watched television, so this was not a hardship. She realized the desk clerk was the first white person she'd seen since she'd veered off the freeway. And he was definitely white—his bright orange hair guaranteed a perpetually white skin.

After freshening up in the small but efficient bath-room, she decided to take a walk down the main street. It was now nearly four in the afternoon, and the sun, while still shining brightly, wasn't pulsating with quite as much heat as it had a few hours ago. Wolf had regained his usual enthusiasm for whatever his mistress had in mind, and after carefully locking the room with her one key, she set out to size up the town.

The bars Maria had warned her against entering ap-peared to be the main attractions. All were dimly lit and so Annie could not see inside, had she wanted to. She concentrated instead of what interested her most at the moment—food. The sandwich she'd consumed five hours ago was a distant memory, and her stomach was reminding her of its lack of nourishment with conspic-uous rumbles.

Several taco trailers, which might have tempted Annie, were shuttered and closed for the day. So was a diner that catered only to breakfast and lunch customers. Annie made a note of it for tomorrow; she suspected it would be where she and Maria met before going to the feedlot to load up. At the far end of town, she saw a steak house, but noticed that it was attached to a bar that looked as sleazy as the ones she'd already passed. The situation was getting serious. If Annie was unable to satisfy her appetite soon, she envisioned raiding the nearest gas station mart and being forced to dine on a couple of hot dogs.

Telling Wolf to stay, she entered the IGA, where a bitter blast of air-conditioning instantly brought goose bumps to her arms. Why couldn't grocery stores ever get it right? Didn't they realize freezing temperatures were not conducive to desultory shopping? She picked up a bag of chips she knew her half sister would thoroughly disapprove of and one pale ale, icy cold. She'd decided to stow these in her mini refrigerator for later. It appeared that more driving would be required in order to slake her hunger. But Annie decided that if any more driving were required, it would be without the trailer.

The desk clerk highly recommended the steak house at the end of town, but Annie regretfully told him she was a vegetarian and didn't eat meat. This was an outright lie, as anyone who had ever shared a meal with Annie knew full well. But just in case the clerk's father-in-law owned the restaurant, she didn't want to offend him unnecessarily.

"Well, there's a café about twelve miles down the road that's open for dinner," the clerk said doubtfully. "They do serve meat, but you probably could get a grilled cheese or veggie burger there. It's right before you get to the rez. If you hit the rez, you've gone too far, and there's nothing in there that'll feed you."

"Great. What's the name of the café?" Annie asked.

"Cattle Rustler Café. Just keep heading north out of town. You can't miss it."

* * *

Annie felt as if she and Wolf were practically sailing down the road without the trailer impacting their speed or maneuverability. She was now in desert country, where scraggy brush intermittently dotted the brown, dusty ground, but no sign of green lingered. Annie imagined the wildlife that managed to survive within it—snakes and lizards mostly, she thought, and perhaps the occasional marmot. She was certain coyotes roamed the hills at night. They were a constant presence in her own pastures, and the prime reason her donkey, Trotter, was stationed with her flock of sheep right now. Most coyotes knew better to enter a pasture armed with a donkey or a mule in attendance. Those who didn't learned quickly—if they survived the quick kick to the head that was sure to come.

Occasionally, Annie saw a small herd of horses standing along a fence line parallel to the road. She wondered what they were used for and how they were fed. Any grass that might have been there had long since been eaten or had withered by late spring. She could see no apparent water source. She was suddenly grateful for the rain that pelted down on her side of the mountains for months on end. It ensured her well was full and that her rotated pastures offered good grass nearly all year long.

She had not noticed the entrance to the feedlot on her way to Browning, and for that, she was thankful. She'd been so intent on getting to her destination and securing a room for the night that she'd barely glanced at the many private roads leading to ranches and farms on either side of her. Evidently, the feedlot didn't publicize its location very prominently—probably a wise decision, she realized, considering how many people abhorred its existence and practices toward horses. She would see the feedlot soon enough and already felt that she couldn't wait to see the back of it.

An adobe building appeared ahead on the right. Annie glanced at her odometer and knew it had to be the café the clerk had mentioned. It was, and it was open. *Thank the Lord*, Annie thought, as she got out of her truck. Below the hand-painted restaurant sign was another: LAST FOOD FOR THE NEXT 100 MILES. STOP NOW OR YOU'LL BE HUNGRY!

The food was superb and so was the service, the latter, Annie suspected, because Wolf was such a hit with the owner and the few patrons.

"I've never seen such a well-behaved heeler in my life," declared the woman who took her order. "How did you train him so good? By the way, I'm Mindy, the owner, chef, waitperson, and chief bottle washer of this place."

"Wolf's a very exceptional animal," Annie explained, trying to sound modest and not quite succeeding. "He's quite attuned to people and what they want, aren't you, boy?"

"Well, he deserves an extra special treat for being such a good dog and sitting here so quietly without begging," Mindy said. "Mind if I bring out a steak bone or two for him to gnaw on?"

Annie did not, and Wolf was gracious enough to take his treats out back, where he could gnaw away to his heart's content. There were some areas of Wolf's behavior, Annie explained, such as demolishing bones, which really needed be done outdoors.

"What brings you here?" Mindy asked pleasantly as she rang up Annie's tab a half hour later. "Don't see many visitors here, even in summer."

"This is just a stopover. I'm headed to Spokane to visit a friend." Even without Jessica's cautionary words ringing in her ears, Annie had no intention of telling Mindy or anyone she didn't know what her intentions were. She suspected that many ranchers had little or no issue with rounding up unwanted horses and selling them for slaughter. She'd seen enough of the country-side to intuit this. The horses she'd seen on the way to the café had looked about as prized and well-tended as a flock of sheep or herd of cattle, and might be valued as little as livestock. She couldn't be sure, of course, but she was taking no chances.

"You own horses?"

Annie momentarily froze. Did Mindy suspect her real reason for being here? She smiled, and hoped it looked natural.

"Matter of fact, I do. Five of them. Plus a donkey to watch my sheep."

"Thought so by the trailer hitch on your truck. Where do you live when you're not on the road visiting friends?"

Observant little minx, isn't she? Annie thought. *And a nosy one.*

"My home's on the Olympic Peninsula. A place that gets a lot more rain than you probably do."

"And a lot less snow." Mindy chuckled. "Well, if you're a horse person, you really ought to check out the wild horses on the rez just ahead when you're passing through. Although if you're heading out in the morning, you won't see as much as you would now. It's quite a sight to see them galloping below the ridge. They're protected by tribal law, of course, so roam free."

Annie knew the average life span of a horse that "roamed free" was considerably less than a domesti-cated one, but the chance to see a wild herd at sunset intrigued her.

"Thanks, Mindy, I think I'll do that. Where would I

get the best view? I assume no one from the tribal police is going to hassle me."

"Naw, naw. No one's going to bother you. Just keep heading out east, and take the third road to the left. You'll follow a long, winding road for a couple of miles. Stop at the crest, and you should get a fine view from anywhere up there. Got a camera?"

Annie grinned and pulled out her smartphone. "My new trusty friend."

"Enjoy yourself. What you're watching won't be around much longer."

"What do you mean?"

"The tribe thinks there are too many horses on their land. Claim they harm the vegetation and water sources. Now they've got federal funding to help pay for reducing the herd. It's a shame, isn't it? The animal they used to revere is now rounded up and destroyed."

Annie decided she could trust Mindy, after all.

"It's a terrible shame. I wish there was a better solution."

"Honey, so do I. Well, enjoy the sight while you can. What you're seeing is a dying breed."

Annie followed Mindy's directions to the letter. The road leading up to the ridge was a tad too precipitous for her comfort level, but Annie persisted. To call the road two-way would be presumptuous, and she hoped she'd not encounter any vehicle wending its way down. The drop-off was about as sheer as any Annie had ever encountered, and there were no guardrails in sight.

She finally emerged on a small plateau overlooking a deep canyon and turned off the ignition, careful to put the parking brake on. Stepping outside the truck, she slammed her door shut and was aware of the absolute silence that reigned in this elevated clime. Except for the flutter of a very faint breeze and the sound of her footsteps crunching on dusty gravel, there were no other sounds. She felt absolutely alone.

Then she felt the horses through the soles of her boots. It was an almost infinitesimal tremor, but she knew it was real. Wolf sensed it, too. He stood alert on all four paws and made an inquisitive sound in his throat. Annie walked quietly to the lip of the plateau and scanned the vast valley below. She saw nothing for a minute or two. Then, all of a sudden, the herd was upon her, racing from the east across the landscape below. There must have been more than a hundred, she thought, although it was impossible to count. The horses were traveling so fast that their shapes blurred together. Dust swirled around them, so while Annie knew they were in a flat-out gallop, she could barely see their feet move, they were traveling so fast. Annie observed one black horse—undoubtedly a stallion—leading the herd. As the stream of horses rushed by, she noticed a number of foals in the back, clinging close to their mothers and doing an admirable job of keeping up with the adults that preceded them. She watched the herd disappear into the valley and listened as the sound of their hooves gradually faded away. She stood still long after they were gone. She knew she'd witnessed the most magnificent display of strength and power she ever hoped to see. It was as if in a few short minutes she had seen the embodiment of all that was good and great about the horse, the magnificent animal that so many people wanted to destroy.

"Run while you can," she murmured. "Run while you can."

She was so intent with her thoughts that she never noticed the two pairs of eyes carefully watching her from behind a rock.

CHAPTER 9

TUESDAY, AUGUST 9

Annie was in a panic. She'd awakened the next morning with Maria's words ringing in her ears: "As I understand it, the horses are paid for, so all we need to do is to load and go."

Yes, they were, but what proof did she have? Sure, she'd talked with Myrna and the crotchety old woman had seemed to accept that Annie was a colleague of the late Tony Elizalde. But they hadn't talked much about money. Tony had told Annie he'd demanded a receipt, but where was it now? Probably reduced to ashes in that unholy conflagration near Snoqualmie Pass. If Myrna was an honest businesswoman—and that Annie doubted—all should go as planned. If she wasn't, Annie might be asked to fork over another sizeable payment. Right now all she had three hundred dollars in cash to cover the horses' so-called care and feeding for the past six days. Would that be enough? As Annie recalled, Myrna had warned,

"It'll cost you." But how much? Perhaps she should have accepted Travis's offer of up-front money, just to be on the safe side. Well, it was too late now.

She checked out of the motel, hitched the trailer back to her truck, and was waiting inside the Browning café by 11:30 AM. She'd skipped breakfast at the motel—Wolf's dog food looked more appetizing than what she'd seen on the breakfast bar—and gratefully accepted a cup of coffee from the waitress now. Maria arrived fifteen minutes later. Annie recognized her as if she had known her all her life—she had the air of a confident horsewoman as well as someone who was comfortable with her place in the world. She wore a bright turquoise blouse, around which a multicolored scarf was draped, while bold silver bracelets jangled against her warm brown skin. Her long black hair was tied back but still graced the small of her back. She was beautiful, Annie thought, and wondered why she could never achieve this aura of femininity, no matter how hard she tried. Well, the truth was she didn't try very often. Maybe that was the problem.

Annie rose to greet Maria, who enveloped her in a soft hug. Surprised, Annie responded in kind. Maybe it was the ordeal of the last week that was making her all mushy. Whatever it was, Annie was not averse to the change she saw slowly emerging within her.

"I hope you haven't been waiting long," Maria said, sitting down with a flourish.

"Not at all. Just stocking up on good coffee that was sadly deficient at my motel this morning."

"I'm not surprised. I hope you slept well?"

"Like a lamb. Not a lot of traffic comes through here to disturb your sleep."

Maria laughed. "Ain't that the truth."

They spent the next few minutes perusing the menu.

Annie had already decided on huevos rancheros, and
Maria chose a Cobb salad. Preliminaries over, Maria
rested her elbows on the table and leaned in toward her
guest.

"So, Annie. Have you ever been to a feedlot before?"

"This is my maiden voyage."

"Let me take the liberty of telling you what to expect.
It can be a bit daunting the first time."

This was precisely what Annie was afraid of. "I'm all
ears," she said bravely.

"You have to remember that George and Myrna consider horses part of the food chain—and no higher up
that chain than livestock. I'd like to think it's the only
way they can live with what they do, although that's
probably giving them too much credit. And they care
for them accordingly.

"Annie, you're going to see horses who are significantly
underweight, whose hooves haven't been touched in a
year, and many that have untended injuries. It'll break
your heart. The feedlot owners will patch them up as
much as they can. They're not totally inhuman, but
their care is only predicated on the animal's being well
enough to ship by the time transport arrives to take
them to the slaughterhouse. They're actually fed rather
well, and when you think about it, it makes sense. The
more weight that goes in the transport vans, the more
money they make. But be prepared to see some horses
that are in terrible physical states. For them, at least
their suffering is finite although the road to death is
still a long and traumatic one."

Annie slowly nodded. Her appetite was quickly fading.

"You'll also see a lot of horses that look perfectly
healthy, such as the four Tony and you picked out and
purchased. But you're only taking four, not forty, and that

will break your heart, too, because you know that, through no fault of their own, they're being sacrificed for easy money.

"What I'm saying is that it's difficult for anyone who loves horses to visit a feedlot and not be affected by what they see, hear, and smell. There's no way I can adequately prepare you for the experience, but I do want you to walk in there with your eyes open and knowing what to expect."

To her extreme embarrassment, Annie realized that she was starting to cry.

Maria put her arm on Annie's. "It's okay to be upset, Annie. We all cry. And then we wipe our tears and try to save as many as we can."

Their food arrived. Annie fumbled with her napkin to wipe her eyes. She wasn't sure she could eat.

"How do you do it?" she asked Maria. It was an open-ended question, but Maria knew exactly what Annie was asking.

"It took me years to be able to go to Myrna's place and not curl up in a ball afterwards and weep," she replied. "It gets easier over time. But I will tell you that witnessing the relentless selling of horses for slaughter also makes you more determined to stop the cycle. It becomes your life work."

"But it seems so hopeless."

Maria nodded. "It does. Which is why we can never lose hope. And there is some cause to think things will get better. Right now, the Washington legislature is discussing a bill that would make transporting horses for human consumption illegal in our state."

Annie looked up. This was the first thing Maria had said that was not profoundly depressing.

Maria smiled and put down her fork. "The House bill under discussion is partly based on the grounds that horses are not part of the human food chain, and it's impossible to humanely slaughter horses in the way it's done now. But that's not the real selling point of this bill. It's the very reasonable fact that it's impossible to track the medical histories of the vast majority of these horses, and so the meat itself is questionable and unsafe to eat."

"Ah, yes," Annie said bitterly. "Appeal to the consumers' concerns, not the horses'."

"We'll use any argument necessary if it helps pass that bill."

Annie managed to make a dent in her breakfast before Maria looked at her watch and informed her that it was time to leave.

"There's one more thing to keep in mind," she said, as they exited the small café. "George and Myrna aren't complete demons. They do take adequate care of the horses that come to them, and as I said, they feed them well. If they weren't operating the Loman feedlot, someone else would. You have to remember that they're only one small part of the problem."

"And that is?"

"Too many horses, Annie, and too many people who think horses are disposable, from racetrack owners to backyard breeders. And yet we keep breeding them. There are many toxic cycles at work when it comes to unwanted horses, and we have to break *all* of them, not just one or two, if horses are ever to be truly safe."

Annie followed Maria, who drove a beat-up Toyota pickup that Annie pegged as her primary farm truck. As they headed back toward Loman, Annie thought about her own horses, all of which had come to her because they were unwanted by their previous owners. Even Trooper's life had hung in the balance while Hilda Colbert was alive, since she had been convinced that an injury had impacted the horse's ability to perform in the riding arena. People were nuts, Annie thought. There should be a test for horse owners. But deep down, she knew Maria was right. There were simply too many horses and way too few dedicated owners.

The road leading into the Loman feedlot was nondescript, to say the least. Annie never would have found it on her own, and she was glad that Maria was leading, and for more reasons than merely her navigational acumen.

She followed Maria's pickup for another mile and watched it turn right again and stop in front of an electric gate. She watched Maria roll down her window, push a button, and wait. After a few seconds, the gate slowly opened, and the Toyota, followed by Annie's F-250 and trailer, entered. On the right was a huge circular paddock packed with horses. Annie took her cue from Maria and parked underneath a row of aspens adjacent to the paddock. She noticed that there was no source of shade in the horses' pen.

Maria walked over to a short, scrawny woman, who was gesticulating to another woman who loomed over her. The smaller woman had a baseball cap on, and a few strands of grey hair poked out underneath it. The cut seemed to resemble a boy's. The woman she was addressing was dressed in riding breeches and a sleeveless shirt. Annie assumed that the small, craggy woman was Myrna, but she couldn't fathom who the other woman might be. She looked totally incongruous in this setting. Annie imagined her on the back of a Hanoverian in a dressage arena, perhaps being schooled by her friend Patricia Winters, the operations manager for Running Track Farms, a rehab/boarding facility for premier sports horses. Patricia was also an instructor in dressage, something Annie knew nothing about. She had a feeling that the tall, elegant woman in front of her probably did.

She decided to double-check the latches and locks on the trailer rather than crash what obviously was a private matter, but as she started to turn back, she saw Maria gesture to her. Reluctantly, Annie slowly walked up to the group, where a heated conversation was taking place.

"He just doesn't fit my daughter's riding needs right now," the tall woman was patiently telling the woman Annie assumed was Myrna.

"Well, that's fine and dandy, but as I've told you, I've got a full lot."

"You can squeeze him in."

"No, I can't. Until the transport comes, I don't have any more room."

"It's just one horse."

"And that's one horse too many."

"Please."

Myrna glared at the woman. Finally, she said, "I can only give you a hundred dollars for him."

"Fine."

"All right. Let's see what you've brought."

Annie watched as the woman strode back to her own trailer, a six-stall deluxe model, and one that Annie was sure offered air-conditioning. The woman pulled up the handle to unlock the rear door and disappeared. She emerged a minute later leading a tall, chestnut Thoroughbred who looked at least four hundred pounds underweight by Annie's reckoning. The horse looked a bit dazed, as if he wasn't sure where he was or why he was here.

Buddy, you don't want to know, thought Annie.

The horse delicately stepped down the ramp and docilely followed the woman. Myrna gave the Thoroughbred a quick once-over.

"He's a bit skinny," she said disapprovingly. "I don't have much time to fatten him up."

The woman said nothing but simply handed over the lead rope to Myrna.

"Come to my office, and I'll pay you," the feedlot owner said grudgingly.

"His name's Eddie. He just doesn't fit my daughter's riding program right now," the woman repeated.

Annie stared at Maria, who was looking back at her. When Myrna and her customer were out of earshot, Maria said in a low voice, "And this is how feedlots are filled."

Annie wanted to kill the woman. But she didn't have time. It appeared that Eddie's own life was now on the line. Myrna had unlocked one of the paddock gates and was leading the Thoroughbred in. She undid his halter and without a backward glance, left and refastened the gate. Annie was aghast. She could see the lot contained at least fifty horses, several of which were stallions. She couldn't imagine what was going to happen to this lovely Thoroughbred once the other horses realized a new lodger had entered their midst. And that would be any second now. She ran to the paddock to observe more closely.

"Easy, Annie," she heard Maria say behind her. "This happens all the time. He'll learn to adjust."

Learn to adjust? Annie watched in horror as one after another male horses lunged menacingly at the Thoroughbred, then bit, kicked, and aggressively chased him away. Myrna must have just finished feeding because most of the horses had their heads through livestock feeding grates and were eating hay strewn outside. But that didn't stop most horses from taking a break to tell the newcomer that he was now the new bottom of the herd. Annie watched the Thoroughbred duck and weave and try to escape the increasing crowd of horses intent on making his lowly status stick.

Annie could barely stand to watch. She knew there was nothing she could do.

Once Eddie's transaction was complete, Maria and Annie approached Myrna as soon as she emerged from her office. As Annie had feared, new obstacles quickly rose to the surface. Myrna insisted that Annie had promised to show up the day before, and it took all of Annie's self-control not to argue the point.

"Well, she's here, now, Myrna, and ready to take them all off your hands," Maria told her. Her tone was light, without a whiff of rancor. Annie decided to let her new friend do all the talking. Maria was doing much better than she could have managed.

"Well, now there's a problem," snapped Myrna.

"What's that, Myrna?" Maria asked, her tone still pleasant.

"One of 'em's blowing green snot. Can't transport him now."

"You think it's strangles?" Annie couldn't help joining in. Strangles was a virus that attacked the upper respiratory tract. Swollen lymph nodes were a common symptom, and if the virus caused an airway obstruction, it could prove fatal. Strangles also was highly contagious.

"Could be. But whether it is or it isn't, I don't let unhealthy horses travel. It's a rule."

Annie wanted to laugh, and it wouldn't have been pretty. None of the horses in the feedlot were healthy, no matter how well they may have looked. How could they be? Too many horses were crammed together and no one knew their backgrounds or health status. Their environment reeked of fear and confusion, and there was constant cutthroat competition for food. With no trained vet tech on site, it was no wonder diseases spread among them. It would be a miracle if any of the horses weren't sick.

"But you can take the other three. I've put the mustang in a separate pen. When he's better, you can come collect him."

Annie started to speak again, but Maria was ahead of her.

"I appreciate your concern, Myrna, but frankly, if one horse has strangles, the others are likely to develop it over the next few days as well. Annie's come a long way to haul the horses, and it would be a hardship to make the trip over the mountains again. They're all heading straight to her equine vet and will be quarantined, right, Annie?"

Annie nodded her assent.

"We'll accept the risk that one horse has strangles and all the horses may be infected. And we're prepared to take them right now."

The undulating waves of heat were making Annie feel faint. She desperately wanted to flee to the closest form of shade. She wondered how the horses stood it. She'd noticed deep sweat marks encircling the Thoroughbred's mane when he'd first entered the pen. It appeared shade had not been part of his lifestyle with his previous owner, either. But escape was not possible now. And so Annie stood silently as perspiration dripped off her face and through her shirt.

Myrna squinted at Maria. "I'll have to ask George."

"Fine, Myrna. Where is he?"

"Off-site. He'll be back tonight. If he says okay, then you can pick them up tomorrow, first thing. I won't be here, but George will. It's my banking day."

"Thank you, Myrna. Okay if Annie and I just take a quick look at her horses before we go?"

"All right. But you know the rules. No photos. No feeding. And no amateur vet care. George'll take care of that when he gets back."

"We understand. I'll call you later, Myrna, to see if George agrees with us."

"Suit yourself."

Myrna turned and headed back to her office. Maria and Annie began to walk down the aisle that separated the sick horses from those in the large paddock.

It was the longest, most painful journey Annie could ever remember making.

CHAPTER 10

As Maria had predicted, Myrna reported that George had given the okay to pick up the horses the next day.

"Telling us George had to approve was just a ruse," she told Annie on the phone later that night. "As far as I can tell, George's responsibilities extend to throwing hay at the horses and making sure the Bobcat is gassed, greased, and lubricated. Myrna's the control freak in the family. George probably just ducks for cover."

"I hope Myrna doesn't try to pull any more stunts tomorrow," Annie replied. "I can't wait to load up and hit the road again. I just wish I could take Eddie with me."

"I know. He's not going to have an easy time in there."

Whenever Annie started to think about Eddie, her heart started to ache. She willed herself to concentrate on the task at hand.

Before leaving the feedlot yesterday, Annie had suggested to Maria that she square up with Myrna now and get a receipt, so there would be no more hiccups the next morning. Annie had now seen Myrna in action and what she'd seen had not inspired confidence in an easy departure. Maria had readily agreed, and with her help, Annie had ended up giving Myrna half her cash instead of all of it. When Annie had asked for a written receipt, Myrna had hemmed and hawed, but finally scribbled one in pencil on the back of an old envelope. She'd assured Annie that if George let her haul out tomorrow, he'd help her load, although Annie wasn't at all sure she wanted his help. Maria, to Annie's regret, would not be there when the horses made their walk to freedom. She held a part-time job at her sons' elementary school and was on deck tomorrow morning at 7 AM sharp.

"Someone's got to pay for those Little League uniforms," she cheerfully explained to Annie. "And believe me, it's not their father." Annie demurred from asking any further questions. She'd assumed Maria was a single mother, although how she managed to look so fabulous and well rested was beyond Annie's ken.

"Call me when once you're on the road," Maria urged her. "I need to know you got off all right. And call me once they're settled."

"I will." Annie hesitated, then forged ahead with a question that had been nagging at her. "Maria, before Tony took off for eastern Washington, he told me a buddy of his had alerted him to horses for sale in the Loman feedlot. You wouldn't happen to know who that was, do you?"

"You're speaking to her. Tony and I went way back. His sisters and I met when we all won leadership scholarships in high school. We met in Bellevue at a conference. Tony showed up for the final award ceremony, and we just clicked. It was our mutual love for horses, you know."

"Did you ever think of dating him?"

"Did I ever! But he was there, and I'm here, and our lives just never crossed to make that happen. But he was a good friend as long as I knew him. I know his death hit his family hard. I'll miss him, Annie, but my work keeps me focused."

"So it was your Facebook page that we used to select the horses?"

"Sure was. I go out to the feedlot once a week to take photos of any new arrivals and post the ones that look most adoptable."

"Be sure to get Eddie's good side when you take photos of him this week. And give him a carrot for me."

"Will do. Although Eddie may not know what a carrot is."

Once more, Annie's heart inwardly keened, and she quickly ended the call. She'd checked back into her motel and spent the long summer evening setting up the trailer so all it needed was four horses and a key in the ignition in order to make a quick getaway. As she filled and hung Jessica's hay bags, spread shavings on the floor, and double-checked each window and vent, she marveled at how neat and tidy everything was, inside and outside the trailer. Jessica's standards for maintaining her veterinary vehicles were exemplary, and Annie blessed her for it.

She called Jessica when she was satisfied the job was done. Annie still didn't know precisely where she was delivering the horses when she landed on the Peninsula tomorrow afternoon.

Jessica was none too pleased when she learned one of the horses might be in the early stages of a strangles virus.

"I didn't feel I had much of a choice, Jessica," Annie said a bit testily. "If I leave him, the feedlot owner probably will find room for him on the transport. As far as I know, I may be seeing the van rolling in while I'm driving out."

Myrna had been conspicuously coy when Annie had asked when the transport was due to arrive. She guessed the feedlot owner held this information close to her chest for good reason. Annie could envision angry protests in front of the feedlot if the date the horses were loaded for the slaughterhouse was made public. But not knowing how much time Eddie and the other horses had before their fates were sealed was making Annie's stomach tie up in knots.

"I understand," Jessica said, although Annie could tell she was still not comfortable with the news. "The place where they'll be quarantined is a large ranch about eight miles from my clinic. It belongs to one of my clients, and he's doing me an extreme favor. I'm sure he'll be as thrilled as I am to know a small strangles epidemic may erupt on his property."

Annie fleetingly wondered whether, in fact, she should just take the three and return for the mustang. Then again, the little horse hadn't looked that sick. Not that lack of symptoms told the whole story.

"In theory, it should be fine," Jessica said thoughtfully. "There are twenty horses already stabled there, but your four will be housed a half mile away, in the original stalls. When my client bought the ranch five years ago, he overhauled the place and constructed an indoor arena with closed-in stalls around it. You'll use the old entrance and the bunch from the feedlot shouldn't have any contact with the other horses. I've checked out the old stalls, and they'll be fine. Each has a run-in, and there's a common paddock area with tons of grass and plenty of shade. I agree, the damage is done—by now, they're either infected with strangles or not, although traveling side by side for six hours pretty much guarantees it."

"If it's any consolation, the mustang's lymph nodes felt perfectly normal. He may just have a runny nose. I couldn't take his temp, though. The owner frowns on anyone practicing medicine except her husband, who I'm sure is a trained and licensed veterinarian."

"What's his name? I'll check him out."

"Just kidding, Jessica. I can guarantee you that no one with a veterinary license has been at the feedlot for a long time, if ever. Ditto for a farrier."

"Well, just get them home safely. I'll be waiting at the ranch for you. Let me give you the address. You've probably passed right by it a million times."

The next morning, Annie could hear trouble as soon as she turned onto the dusty road that led to the feedlot. High-pitched squeals and whinnies of terror flooded her ears, and she craned her neck to the right, trying to see what danger was threatening the horses. But she was a hundred yards too soon to see the feedlot, or anything around it.

Then rage poured through her. It had to be the transport van. It had arrived even earlier than she had, although Annie's watch told her it was just shy of 8:00 AM, and she was right on schedule. But it seemed Myrna had had another plan in mind. *Not while I'm driving this trailer,* Annie thought angrily. *Those horses are coming with ME.*

Annie instinctively stepped on the gas pedal and quickly discovered this was not a good idea. Behind her, the trailer began to rock from side to side, and Annie compensated by gently compressing the brake to get it back on track. She maintained this safe but steady speed as she approached the electronic gate. To her surprise, it was already wide open. She drove straight through, her eyes frantically scanning the property for the van of death. It had to be much larger than what she was driving.

There was none. But what had assaulted her senses a mile back was overpowering here. The horses in the pen were frantic, racing around in frenzy and trying to escape. Many were rearing and pawing the sky, only to land solidly on their front hooves and lunge off at a gallop. The noise, agitation, whirlwind of hooves, and smell of fear had turned the paddock into a scene of utter mayhem.

"Stay," she ordered Wolf. She didn't want his herding instincts to kick in now; it was far too dangerous for the heeler to be anywhere near the pen. In one fluid motion, she turned off the ignition and leapt out her truck. Racing over to the paddock, she saw a bright yellow Kubota parked at a strange angle in the aisle. The back was filled with hay, and she thought she saw a bale in the front loader. As she neared it, she realized the engine was still running. That was odd, because she was sure no one was in the driver's seat. Annie slowed down to a jog and stepped in front of the farm vehicle. And then she froze.

Just inside the paddock, where the horses usually bent through tight bars to get their daily ration of hay, was a body, or what was left of one. Annie could see two steel-toed work boots in the rubble, but beyond that, the body was wholly unrecognizable. Two horses were systematically pounding on the bloody mess in front of them, rearing up and coming down with the full force of their front hooves. Whose body was it? Could it be George? Maybe. Whoever it was, he was being torn asunder. And judging by the ferocity of the attack from on high, the horses knew exactly what they were doing.

For once, Annie's trusty smartphone failed to work. The little bars Hannah had informed her told her how much reception she had were now one thin flat line. Cursing, she ran over to Myrna's office, a rundown doublewide trailer with a television satellite dish perched on top. She tugged on the front door, but it refused to open. She ran around to the back but saw no other entrance. She scanned the ground in front of her and picked up a large rock, then jogged back to the entrance. Heaving the stone with all her might, she managed to break one of the small glass panes in the upper part of the front door.

Dashing back to the truck, she grabbed two socks out of her overnight bag and wrapped her hand and upper arm in them. She gingerly placed her swathed hand through the broken pane and after a brief search, found and flipped the dead bolt on the other side. She was in.

Fortunately, Myrna still believed in landlines. She'd have to out here in the sticks, where reception was zilch. Annie picked up the phone and punched 9-1-1. Two minutes later, she hung up the phone and sank wearily into one of the office's plastic chairs. She put her head in her hands. If Tony had thought his trip was one long list of unmitigated disasters, her trip was rapidly catching up. At least she was still alive. For now.

Annie had been assured that deputies from the sheriff's office were on their way, but she was taking no chances. Unless the riot in the paddock was squelched in short order, real damage could be done. More to the point, many of the horses would figure out that they could clear the five-foot chain-link fence that girded the paddock. She didn't want to think about the injuries the horses might have already incurred, and immediately thought of Eddie. She hadn't seen him in the commotion. And what about the other three horses? Where were they? She assumed the mustang was safe, since he was in quarantine, and knew the other three were allegedly sequestered, but until the horses settled, no one was safe, including her, should she be so foolhardy as to enter the pen.

Annie knew the smell and sight of death was a major reason the horses were acting so crazed now—that, and perhaps the violence that had preceded it. As prey animals, horses were constantly on the lookout for any danger to their existence. They knew something had died violently, and that had put them on high alert. But instead of fleeing, as any horse would, these animals were forced to remain in a cage along with the dead, and it was driving them crazy.

She decided she would have to remove the body. Only if she rid the paddock of the source of death did she have a chance in hell of calming the herd. Technically, she knew, this would be tampering with evidence. Annie had tampered with evidence once before in a murder investigation, and rather cavalierly. She wasn't proud of it now and didn't want to do it again. But unless she did something, a precipitous situation might spill over into disaster. And she had no assurance that the law enforcement officials on their way would do anything to mitigate the horses' anxiety.

At least she could try to preserve the scene. After all, now she had a camera with her at all times. She'd forgotten about it two nights ago. She'd been so mesmerized by the sight of horses running free that it had never occurred to her to try to take photos. And if she had, she'd have had to do it by using what Hannah called the "burst," which took rapid-fire photos to capture anything in motion.

It was precisely what she needed now. She pulled it out and walked back toward the pen. Fortunately, the two horses in front had ceased their merciless pummeling and now were uneasily pacing up and down the fence line. She took as many photos as she could of the body, the scene, and the surroundings. And wondered how she was going to remove a body from a pen with fifty unpredictable horses inside.

CHAPTER II

Fortunately, Annie was spared from coming up with an answer. As if on cue, three county patrol vehicles barreled through the open gate, strobe lights flashing, but thankfully, without the wail of sirens in their wake. Before she could move, three officers had surrounded her. The largest, a man in a Stetson that Dan would have coveted, spoke first.

"You the one who reported the accident?"

Annie found her mouth was exceptionally dry. She nodded.

"Name?"

"Annie Carson." She watched as an ambulance pulled in behind the police cars, and several medics spilled out. The last two were hauling a stretcher. *Lots of luck,* Annie thought.

The man in the Stetson snapped his fingers in front of her. "Ms. Carson? Pay attention."

Her eyes reverted back to his. They were a dark, steely grey, all business, and, she thought, they showed not a shred of compassion.

"I arrived at eight o'clock to pick up four horses," she began.

"We'll get your statement later. Right now, just answer my questions. Did you know the deceased?"

A laugh started to burble up in Annie's chest. She fought it down.

"I have no idea who's in that pen."

"If you don't know who it is, why were you here?"

"As I said, I came to pick up four horses. I dealt only with Myrna, and I'd only met her yesterday, when I came by to settle up." She glanced over to the horse pen, where several paramedics crouched down by the body. "If that's her husband, George, I never met him. He wasn't on the property when I was here. At least, that's what Myrna told me."

There. That was short and sweet.

"And you saw nothing suspicious when you arrived?"

Of course I did, you idiot. "I heard the horses raising a ruckus almost as soon as I turned off the highway. I knew something was wrong right away."

"And what did you do?"

"The gate was open, so I drove in." Annie wondered what she would have done if the gate had been closed. Clear it with a single bound, she hoped. "The horses were going nuts. I ran over to the Kubota and saw . . . saw the body. I broke into the office to call 9-1-1. I couldn't get any reception from my phone."

Annie decided to say nothing about seeing two horses stomp the body into smithereens. It was pretty self-evident what had happened, anyway.

A deputy approached them. "Sheriff, there ain't nothin' we can do for old George over there. But the horses are pretty restless. I'm not sure how we're going to get him out without causing a stampede."

The sheriff paused, and then spoke directly to Annie. "Wait over there. We'll get your statement when we're through here."

"Mind if I get my dog? He's been in my truck the entire time."

"Roll down your windows, but keep your mutt inside. We don't need any more help right now."

Oh, yes, you do, thought Annie. So far, she'd seen no one who looked as if he had the slightest idea how to calm the horses. And the onrush of a half dozen more people into the horses' territory was doing nothing to assuage their fears.

The sheriff turned back to the deputy, and Annie took this as her cue to leave. She walked over to the truck, made sure Wolf was all right, and inserted a bowl of water into the extended cab. At least he was in the shade, which, even at this early hour, was essential to his well-being. Wolf was eager to join his mistress, but Annie firmly told him to stay. She regretted not having him by her side. She would have welcomed his company.

She watched the sheriff stride back to his car, pull out his radio mic, and speak into it. It was impossible to hear the conversation, but by the length of it, Annie assumed that the process of extricating George's body was going to be difficult and prolonged. She sighed, and discreetly walked over to the far side of the pen, wondering if she'd see the three horses that should have been on the road with her by now. Myrna had promised they'd be separated, but Annie didn't trust that she'd followed through. Almost immediately she saw Eddie, standing in a far corner. His prominent ribs made him stand out compared to the other horses. He looked more banged up than he had the day before. Annie could see several new bite marks on his flanks, and he looked positively haggard. She wondered if he'd eaten at all since being tossed into the pen yesterday afternoon.

The other horses were still a blur of legs as they paced and erratically charged within the confines of the pen, all the while emitting shrill, worried cries. Annie struggled to see the identifying marks of the Morgan, yearling, and bay mare she'd met yesterday afternoon with Maria. It was impossible, she decided, and perhaps they were, in fact, in another paddock farther away. She started to walk up the aisle to ensure she was correct but was soon informed by a deputy that going farther was not allowed right now. Annie thought of arguing the point, but resisted the urge. She was a stranger in a strange town and knew that any debate would be of no value. As much as Sheriff Dan Stetson routinely annoyed her, she desperately wished she could speak with him now.

Walking back to her truck, she saw another vehicle approach the feedlot entrance—a pickup truck, judging by the amount of dust it created. As it turned the corner toward the gate, she recognized the sea-foam-green color of Maria's Toyota. Her heart rose. Curbing her desire to run out to greet her new friend, she waited for the pickup to enter the compound, then walked up to the driver's window. She noticed that Maria had to roll it down—the truck was that old.

"Boy, am I glad to see you," she said when Maria had completed the task.

"Are you all right?" Maria asked anxiously.

"A lot better than George," Annie answered. "Not to mention all those half-crazed horses you see in there."

"I heard about it on the police scanner at school. I

figured you and the horses needed me more than thirty fourth-graders. Besides, they can read on their own. I should know—I tutored most of them last year."

"I can't tell you how glad I am to see you," Annie repeated. "But I should warn you—there's a big nasty sheriff in there who may not be happy you're here."

"Harlin?" Maria snorted. "I tutor his kids. He'll be delighted to see me."

Annie ducked her head in mock acceptance and took her hands off the door. "This I've got to see."

To Annie's surprise, the sheriff greeted Maria with more than a modicum of warmth, and gave her carte blanche to separate the horses into adjoining, albeit, smaller paddocks and to feed them. Perhaps it was the fact that Maria had mingled with most of these horses before, Annie thought, or that Maria was just a natural horse whisperer. Whatever it was, she obviously knew what she was doing. Using nothing more than a lead rope as a directional, she herded the horses down the aisle to paddocks at the other end of the property, where they quickly regained their composure. Annie tried to help, but she realized that Maria was fully capable of doing the job alone.

"There," Maria said, panting a little, as she closed the paddock gate on the last delivery. "Now let's get them fed."

Annie was delighted to help. The Kubota was not available, since it was now in evidence, but Maria's battered pickup worked just fine. The two women stacked the bed high with hay and generously distributed it among the paddocks. As Annie feared, Eddie was not getting anywhere near the piles; every time he approached a group of horses, he was roughly chased away.

"I can't stand this anymore," Annie told Maria. "Let's

put Eddie in with my three." Maria looked up in surprise. "Are you thinking of taking him, as well?"

Annie hadn't thought about it until now. She'd only been intent on making sure Eddie was fed. But she realized she had come to that decision. "Yes, I am," she said firmly. "I don't know when, but Eddie's coming home with me."

Maria grinned. "Stick around, Annie, and we might find another trailer-full of new playmates for you to haul."

Annie was afraid she was right.

Eddie fared much better in the smaller group. Even the yearling, which technically was still a stallion, did not give the Thoroughbred any grief. True, Eddie was at least twice the size of the yearling, but Annie noticed that the Morgan and bay, both mares, seemed to have the yearling in check already, and he probably didn't want to push his luck.

The mustang's nose was still running, but Annie rechecked his lymph nodes, and they continued to show no signs of swelling. She wished she could take the horse's temperature, then realized no one was around to stop her.

"Where's Myrna?" she asked Maria.

Maria paused mid-throw of a large flake of Timothy in Eddie's direction.

"Good question. Where, indeed?"

"She said this was her banking day, but surely she must have heard the news about George by now."

The women glanced down the aisle toward the now-empty paddock. The ambulance had departed, and it looked as if the sheriff and his deputies were about to leave, as well.

Glancing at her watch, Annie saw that it was high noon. Prolonged distance from the crime scene had reignited her appetite. But first she had to have a little chat with the sheriff. This was his party, not hers. And she wanted to get the show on the road. As it was, she figured she wouldn't arrive on the Peninsula until close to sunset. She needed to call Jessica and tell her about the revision in plans.

"Let's go talk to Harlin and get his permission to leave," Maria said firmly, as if reading Annie's thoughts.

"Fine with me. Sorry about George, but I've got horses to haul."

They found the sheriff by his county vehicle, scribbling in a notebook.

"Harlin?" Maria said as they approached him. "Where's Myrna?"

Harlin looked up. "You done settling the horses?"

"Yes, and I'd like to know if anyone's going to feed them tonight. Or would you like me to come back?" Maria's tone clearly showed her displeasure at having her question ignored.

"Might be a good idea to check on them for a few days."

"Why? Is Myrna so prostrate with grief she's unable to perform this chore?"

Annie, no stranger to sarcasm herself, could hear it loud and clear in Maria's response.

"Don't know. We can't find her. Yet."

Maria paused. "You know, I just assumed that George consumed one too many beers for breakfast, fell off his Kubota, and the rest is history. Am I missing something here?"

The sheriff carefully closed his notebook. "George got a thirty-thirty slug in his back. That's why he slipped off the Bobcat."

Annie felt a tingle go down her spine. So George had been shot. Murdered. And she had arrived perhaps mere minutes after the shot had been fired.

"We'll be wanting your statement now, Ms. Carson. So if you'll be so kind as to get in the backseat of my vehicle, I will personally escort you to the precinct for an interview."

"Hold on, Harlin," Maria exclaimed. "Annie showed up after the fact. I'm sure she's happy to write out a statement. Is a formal interview really necessary?"

The sheriff nodded toward Annie's truck, where Annie could see Wolf sitting up in the backseat, wondering why he'd been abandoned for so long.

"We noticed you carry a thirty-thirty in your rig, Ms. Carson. When was the last time you used it?"

All of a sudden, Annie felt dizzy. When had she last fired her rifle? Her mind went blank.

"I think last fall. I was chasing a black bear off my property."

"Then you won't mind if we test it, do you?"

"No, not at all." She stumbled over the words. Her heart was beating like a jackrabbit. *For heaven's sake,* Annie thought crossly, *I'm completely innocent. Why am I acting like I'm not?*

"Good. As far as those horses you planned on hauling, well, that'll have to wait. The feedlot's a crime scene now. And until we've got this all sorted out, it'll stay that way. Goes for you, too. You're not leaving town right yet, either. Not until we talk to the last person who saw George alive."

"But the last person to see George alive would be his killer!" The words burst out of Annie before she had time to think.

"Exactly what I mean. Step inside, Ms. Carson." And with that, the sheriff opened his rear passenger door.

CHAPTER 12

WEDNESDAY AFTERNOON, AUGUST 10

The gunshot-residue test had been the final straw for Annie.

She'd endured nearly three hours of questioning. But when she was asked if she would submit her hands to this test, she'd nearly done what infuriated Sheriff Stetson every time it occurred in his jurisdiction—told this hayseed sheriff she wanted to lawyer up. The problem was the only attorney she knew was James Fenton, retained by Marcus Colbert for corporate work. True, after Marcus had been arrested for his wife's murder, James Fenton had flown in, given an impressive court speech, and succeeded in getting Marcus out of jail on bail, but that's as far as his work as a criminal defense attorney had extended. Besides, Annie had the distinct feeling that James Fenton didn't like her very much. Their few conversations had been superficial at best, and the attorney always seemed to want to end the call as quickly as possible.

So Annie submitted to the test. She was still trying to wipe her hands clean when she emerged into the sheriff's office reception area at five o'clock. Maria, bless her heart, had been patiently waiting there with Wolf by her side.

Wolf leapt into Annie's arms—a definite no-no, but Annie didn't care—as Maria stood up, watching the blue heeler lick Annie's face exuberantly.

"I'm so sorry this happened to you, Annie," she said. "You're living proof that no good deed goes unpunished."

Annie managed a half laugh. "Well, I just hope the sheriff is reviewing the surveillance cameras you talked about, so I'm eliminated from the list of suspects."

"I'm sure he will. And in the meantime, I'll be sure to tell him what I think of the way he treats people who are just trying to help the horses. I don't know who killed George, but believe me, the number of people who wanted him dead stretches from here to Pasco. Scratching you off the list will be the easiest part of his job."

"I hope you're right," Annie replied, extricating Wolf's paws from her shoulders. "I feel as if I'm in a bad Western. I've been ordered not to leave town until the sheriff tells me I can go. Please don't take this personally, but I'd really like nothing better to do than go home with a full trailer and Wolf by my side." She looked down contentedly at Wolf, who was gazing up at her with adoring eyes.

"I hear you. I got a friend to drive your rig back to the motel. Let me drop you off there so you can freshen up."

Annie had given Maria her keys before she'd begun

her escorted ride to the sheriff's office. She'd been most concerned about Wolf, who'd been stuck in the truck far too long, no matter how well he could control his bladder. He looked fine now, she observed, and was reeking of hamburger. Annie suspected her blue heeler had recently devoured one of his favorite meals—a Big Mac, no onions.

As Maria pulled into the now-familiar motel, she turned to her. "Annie, there's one thing you should know."

Annie watched Maria put her truck in park and inwardly sighed. She just wanted to be alone, but Maria had been nothing but kind. So she leaned back and smiled. "Shoot."

"You asked about Tony yesterday. I wasn't quite truthful about our relationship." For the first time, Maria looked something less than at ease.

"The truth is, he spent the night with me when he was up here last Wednesday. He'd checked into a motel—the other one in town, and we met for a beer. One thing led to another. . . ." She spread her hands as if to complete the sentence.

"Say no more. It's none of my business." In truth, Annie was distinctly tickled. She was glad that Tony had had a romantic encounter the day before he died. *Everyone should be so lucky,* she thought.

"We had a relationship like that. We didn't see each other often, but when we did, sparks would fly, and we'd usually end up in bed together." Now Maria was positively blushing, which was hard to do over her warm brown skin.

"Maria, for heaven's sake. You were both consenting adults and, I might add, single. I think it's great that you and Tony had a thing going, even if it was long-distance.

It must not have been easy. I have a long-distance relationship myself."

Annie couldn't believe she'd just admitted this. She'd hardly admitted it to herself.

"He was so excited about the boys' ranch that you and your friends are creating," Maria went on. "It's all he could talk about."

Annie's heart plunged again. Once more, she was reminded that she would never see or talk to Tony again. "His death was tragic," she said simply. "But I'm glad he had you in his life up to the very last day."

"Thanks, Annie. Now I'll leave you alone. I'm sure you're dying to take a bath. And I'm picking you up at seven o'clock. It's high time we did something to cheer you up, and I've got just the thing."

With those enigmatic words, Maria gave her one of her usual bright smiles and waved good-bye. Annie and Wolf turned and headed to the office of the Browning Motel. She noticed that its façade was becoming less enticing the longer she remained in this dusty old town.

"You're checking in *again?*"

The desk clerk looked at Annie with amusement. Annie did not smile back. She was not amused. She was not happy at all.

"Yes, and I don't know precisely when I'll be leaving," she answered grumpily. "Is there a weekly rate?"

The clerk looked surprised. "Browning doesn't usually hold that much appeal for our visitors. Most of 'em arrive in the evening and leave before dawn. Let me check with the owner." He disappeared behind a cloth curtain.

Annie sighed and flopped down in a chair. She picked

up a magazine extolling the amazing recreational opportunities in the area, flipped through it, and tossed it aside. All she wanted to do was go home. With four horses and Wolf. Not to mention take a long, cold shower, and not necessarily in that order.

The clerk reappeared. "We can give you a weekly rate of five hundred dollars. That's a savings of a little more than a hundred dollars."

"Swell." She reached for the registration form, but the clerk deftly took it away.

"That's all right, Ms. Carson. We've got it all on file. All we need is your credit card."

Annie pried it out of her wallet and handed it over. The clerk must have gone to charm school because he politely refrained from asking Annie what fascinating business in their metropolis had prolonged her stay.

A cold shower, followed by a cold pale ale, which had been purchased two days ago but was lying in wait in Annie's cooler for just such an occasion, made her feel much better. Wrapping her wet hair in the threadbare cloth the Browning Motel called a towel, she sprawled on her bed and called the only law enforcement official she ever wanted to talk to again.

Dan picked up on the first ring.

"Annie! Why in the Sam Hill haven't you called by now?"

"Gee, I missed you, too, Dan. And I would have called earlier, but I just finished being interrogated by your comrades in Browning. I'm pretty sure I'm their number-one murder suspect, but I don't think they'll hang me until sundown."

"Spare me the sarcasm. I know all about it. I just got off the phone with Sheriff Mullin."

"I told him to call you about a million times. I told him to call you while I was being interrogated."

"Interviewed."

"Interrogated. It's all on tape. You'll see."

She could hear Dan sigh. "Annie, you can't blame the man for doing his job. You were found at the scene, and your rifle is the same make as the one that killed the man. It sounded pretty gruesome."

"It was. And I understand the guy's wanting to test my Winchester. Even though I was the one who was thoughtful enough to alert nine-one-one about the body in the first place."

"Killers have been known to do it before."

"And stick around? For three hours?"

"Well, not usually, no."

"Besides, it was all so unnecessary. The place is staged with surveillance cameras everywhere. If Sheriff Mullin really wanted to find out what happened, why wasn't he reviewing those instead of interrogating me?"

"I'm sure he is, right now. But don't be surprised if they don't reveal anything."

"What are you talking about? A murder takes place right in front of a feedlot pen with several cameras overhead, and you're not going to see anything?"

"The digital recording might reveal the man being shot and the time, but I doubt the killer put himself in the picture."

Annie thought about this. "Well, at least it would take me out of the equation. The desk clerk can verify when I checked out."

"Look, Annie, I don't think you have to worry about being a suspect anymore. After my conversation with Mullin, I'm fairly certain he believes you were there for exactly the reason you gave, to load four nags and hightail it back to the Peninsula. But depending on what the autopsy report says, the time of death may be so close in time to your arrival that a good prosecutor could persuade a jury otherwise."

Now that was chilling.

"And another thing, Annie. I talked with the NSTB yesterday, and they've recovered remnants of an explosive in the crash. There's bomb residue all over what used to be the dashboard. The FBI has K-9 units out right now looking for a trigger device."

An icy-cold bead of perspiration slid down Annie's back, and it wasn't from her recent shower.

"What are you telling me, Dan?"

"That the Cessna was rigged to blow up in midair. Tony's death, not to mention the death of the pilot, is now classified as a homicide. Possibly an act of terrorism. Mullin doesn't know if there's a connection, but he's strongly considering the idea that whoever killed the feedlot owner did it as an act of revenge. Apparently you did a pretty good job of convincing Mullin how close you and Tony were. That gives you a very strong motive. Add to that your thirty-thirty and being at the scene of the crime moments after it occurred, and you really can't blame the guy for wanting to wipe your hands for gunshot residue. Although that probably was just for show. Two hours of bucking hay probably removed any traces."

"Dan! I didn't shoot the guy!"

"Sorry, Annie. Just thinking like a cop. Nothing personal."

For once, Annie ended the call before the sheriff had time to hang up.

After talking to Dan, Tony's death no longer seemed a mere tragedy. As she'd suspected all along, it was an out-and-out horrific crime. She wished she could talk to

Marcus. There was so much to catch up on, and she admitted she wanted to hear a voice that would sympathize with her, not simply recite all the reasons she was a viable suspect. It was now six o'clock in the evening—2 AM Marcus's time. She decided to settle for a short text to bring him up to speed. As she pushed SEND, she had a small, slightly guilt-tinged feeling that Marcus would soon be calling her, no matter what the time difference was in London.

Then she remembered Lisa, who was back at her ranch, expecting Annie to roll in with a mission-accomplished wave any moment now. She rapidly punched in her stable hand's number. It went to voice mail. Damn! She called the landline in the tack room and received a cheery "Carson Stables" response after the second ring.

"Lisa! It's me, Annie. How are you?"

"They're fine, everyone's fine. Are you still on the road?"

Like every good horsewoman, Lisa had known full well that any question about her well-being actually referred to the horses in her care, and she'd responded appropriately.

Thank God for that. Annie didn't think she could have held it together if there had been any scent of a crisis at home.

"Unfortunately, no. Believe it or not, I'm still in Browning. There's been a murder"—Annie could hear Lisa gasp in the background—"and I happened to show up right after it happened. The whole feedlot is closed down until the cops have it figured out. Since I'm such an important witness, I can't leave just yet, either. Can you stay at the farm a few more days? If not, I understand." Annie crossed her fingers and shut her eyes. She wasn't sure who else she could call upon.

"No problem," Lisa promptly responded, and Annie

let out her breath. "I just got hired as a barista in Port Chester, but the job won't start until next week, and anyway, I made sure my hours wouldn't interfere with the ones at your place. I'm happy to stay on as long as you need me. How are the horses?"

Annie knew Lisa was referring to the rescues she'd hoped to bring back today.

"They're surviving, although the mustang has a respiratory issue, or worse, and is separated from the rest of the herd. It probably isn't going to hurt that he's by himself a few days longer. Jessica wasn't too happy knowing that I'd planned to transport them all together."

"Yes, but if you don't, who knows what'll happen to the poor boy. The alternative is too terrible to think about."

Well said, little Grasshopper, Annie thought smugly. Without trying, she was successfully training Lisa to think just the way she did. Which was the right way, of course, at least pertaining to all things equine.

"I'm glad you agree. I'm hoping it won't be more than a day or two before that happens. I'll keep you posted every day I'm still here in this godforsaken place. And, oh, Lisa, would you mind calling Jessica and telling her I've been delayed? Tell her I'll call her tomorrow as soon as I've got the latest update. And tell her I'm sorry she made the trip out to her client's ranch for nothing— that's where they'll be staying while they're in quarantine. But you might say that the mustang is looking better." This wasn't exactly the truth, but Annie wanted no more guff from Jessica about taking the mustang with her.

"Will do. Would you like to say hello to Sasha?"

Sasha obediently barked and howled as soon as she heard Annie's voice, which caused Wolf to bark and howl as well, within the confines of her motel room.

Annie was glad that no one else seemed to be staying at the place and, if they were, that they would check in late and check out early.

Annie's last call of the evening came just as she was about to walk outside with Wolf to wait for Maria to pick her up. The number that appeared on her cell was from California, but she didn't recognize it as Marcus's. She swiped her screen and answered.

"Annie Carson."

"Miss Carson? This is Felipe, Mr. Colbert's assistant. Mr. Colbert has asked me to deliver a message."

Annie closed the motel-room door and leaned against it, all attention. "Yes?"

"Mr. Colbert wants you to know that he will be flying to Loman on his private jet on Sunday. He said that you were not to talk to anyone else from the sheriff's office until he arrives, and if anyone persists in trying, to contact him immediately, no matter what time. Mr. Colbert was very insistent that you understand and agree to this."

"Please tell Marcus I hear him loud and clear."

"Great. I'll tell him. Mr. Colbert also wanted you to know that he's sorry he won't be able to join you before Sunday, but he's trying to rearrange his schedule now to see if it can be earlier."

Annie felt a warm glow spread throughout her. Somebody cared for her. Somebody was determined that she wasn't going to be set up for a crime she hadn't committed. But then, who would know better than Marcus what that felt like? He'd lived through the same experience just a few months before.

"Thank you, Felipe. And please tell Mr. Colbert that I am very grateful for his help."

"Will do. He also said he would try to call you tomorrow, and to not get mad, but to remember to keep your cell phone fully charged."

Annie marveled. *The power of a single text message,* she thought, as she stepped outside and into Maria's waiting pickup truck.

CHAPTER 13

Maria seemed to know exactly where she was going, and Annie was not in a mood to ask where that might be. She was getting out of the dreary little town, and that was all that mattered. Maria's pickup also was headed in the opposite direction of the murder scene. That helped, marginally. Try as she might, Annie could not erase the scene of the chaotic feedlot from her mind. The sight and smell and sounds of the horses' confusion and terror this morning would not leave her. Curiously, she realized she was not half as upset to recall the sodden mess that had once been Myrna's husband. It was the horses' heartbreaking circumstances and their utter bewilderment at the violence that had occurred within their bleak sphere that depressed her now.

A phrase floated into her brain: "He needed killing." It was a pronouncement Annie had heard in many an old Western, and it came unannounced to her now. Perhaps George's death qualified as this form of rough justice. She really didn't care. All she knew was she hadn't done the deed, and she had no idea who had.

She tried to shift her mind to the scenery but saw merely the same sparse, dry tumbleweed that had surrounded her on the way to the Cattle Rustler Café. Had she really made that drive only two days before? It now seemed a lifetime ago. She longed to get back to the lush green landscape of the Olympic Peninsula. She was missing too many precious summer days in the environment she loved most.

"A penny for your thoughts." Maria's words intermingled with the squeaks and groans of the ancient pickup as it bounced along an unpaved and untended country road.

"Oh, nothing much," Annie replied without thinking. Then, after a pause, she decided to voice what truly was on her mind.

"You were right. Going to the feedlot was intense sensory overload. It would have been even if I hadn't come across George's body. I really don't know how you do it."

Maria didn't explain. She merely said, "Well, now you're going to see something completely different. And it will make you very happy."

"Is food involved?" Annie was acutely aware that she had never had lunch. She'd been so busy answering questions in the sheriff's office, where most of her responses had been a simple "I don't know," that for once, her stomach had not protested the absence of its usual midday meal. Until now.

"There's a burrito trailer just ahead. We'll stop there."

Annie had never eaten at one, although the small

aluminum trucks offering Mexican fare had peppered every small town through which she'd recently traveled. She found her burrito to be surprisingly good, and ample enough to satisfy even her thriving appetite. It was difficult to share her bounty with Wolf, who, she reminded herself, had inhaled his dinner before they'd left the motel.

"Where are we going?" Annie finally asked, wiping her mouth with a paper napkin. She was feeling much better.

"I want to show you an animal sanctuary a friend of mine runs," Maria said. "It's about fifteen miles north of here. Olivia owns a thirty-five-acre plat, and she's developed quite the menagerie over the past decade. She runs it with the help of volunteers, mostly teenagers. It's a bit like the ranch you're involved in creating. The kids aren't necessarily juvies in trouble, but there's no doubt that working for Olivia helps keep them focused and less likely to get into trouble."

"Good for her. It'll be interesting to see how someone else does it." Annie had never thought of Travis's ranch as a sanctuary, but now she realized that was exactly what he was creating—a sanctuary not only for the boys who would live there but also for the animals they cared for.

"Olivia and I have worked together for about a decade now," Maria went on. "We found each other, predictably, through the feedlot circuit. She's bailed out plenty of horses from the Loman pen, particularly ones who are in foal or who have recently given birth."

Once again, Annie felt a sharp pain rip through her. "In foal? The feedlot buys horses that are in utero?"

Maria turned and gave her a sad smile. "'Fraid so. And if the mares drop before the transport arrives, the foal stays behind, even if it's still nursing."

Was there no end to the horror of feedlot practices? Annie found she had no words to express what she felt. She was simply glad that people like Maria and Olivia existed to help mitigate the cruelty of feedlot owners. And the people who sold their horses to them, she reminded herself. She still couldn't get over the nonchalant attitude with which the woman had off-loaded Eddie, and her obvious lack of care before dumping him at the feedlot. The Thoroughbred was seriously underweight, Annie knew, and his hooves looked as if they'd been neglected for years. Now that she'd internally committed to taking him, she couldn't wait to get him back on track—although she vowed a racetrack was one thing Eddie would never see again.

The two women bounced along in companionable silence for the remainder of the ride. Twilight was coming, and faster here than on her own side of the mountains. Maria switched on her headlights.

"We're almost there," she told Annie, who nodded.

A quarter mile later, Maria peeled off onto a side road as nondescript as the one that led to the feedlot. It took them up to a long, steep drive with switchbacks almost as precarious as the ones Annie had encountered on the reservation. Finally, they came to a ten-foot farm gate. Annie offered to get out to open it, and unhitched it before Maria slowly drove in. Wolf, naturally, had jumped out to help. She reattached the chain and waited for Maria to climb out of her truck. There was a mishmash of farm buildings in front of her, but because of the quick arrival of dusk, it was difficult to see what they were used for, or who might be inside. A minute later, a lean, tall woman emerged from within the labyrinth. Her hair was as long as Maria's, only a shimmering golden color that illuminated her face in the fading light. She reminded Annie a bit of an angel in a Nativity scene.

"Maria, you made it." The woman warmly embraced Annie's companion, then turned to her. The angelic look was gone, and in its place was a face creased with lines from years of working outside in sun as well as cold. Yet it was still surrounded by that mane of golden hair, and it was a kind face, Annie decided, one that suggested a highly empathetic nature.

"You must be Annie," the woman said, extending her hand. "Welcome to the menagerie."

Olivia had encouraged her to stroll around at her leisure while she and Maria caught up. As Annie wandered from paddock to paddock, she thought "menagerie" was the perfect description for what she saw before her. Horses, pigs, goats, donkeys, dogs, and cats roamed everywhere—in paddocks, pastures, and all places in between. She saw an old, half-blind white horse sharing space with donkeys that couldn't have been more than six months old. While the donkeys rushed up for the carrots she held out for them, the white horse held court in the center, with all the dignity of a revered old warrior. In one of the lower pastures, she watched a herd of yearlings cavort with each other as the last bits of sun dipped over the distant mountains.

In the field above lay another pasture in which horses of every shape, size, and color ate from a communal trough of hay. By the hay shed stood an old donkey, munching on a stack of orchard hay he'd found and claimed as his own, while chickens ran around his hooves. Everywhere she went, she saw pygmy goats inquisitively exploring nooks and crannies, occasionally ducking inside a pasture or paddock to the complete equanimity of any other animal who happened to be there.

And there was one small animal Annie was particularly

taken with—a little black-and-white miniature horse named Sassafras. It was an apt name, Annie thought. Sassafras had a shock of black mane that reminded her of Sid Vicious, and she watched with amusement as the mini strutted her way around the farm, paying no attention to any animal she encountered, and looking as if all this were a great kingdom that belonged to her.

An hour later, her tour complete, Annie knew just how much she'd needed to see this place after the horrors of the feedlot. She was grateful for Maria's prescience in making the journey here. Not everyone was as heartless as George and Myrna and Eddie's last owner. There were just as many—she hoped—helping the forgotten and unwanted animals. And here, at least, they were safe in what was truly a peaceable animal kingdom.

She wandered over to where Maria and Olivia were in deep conversation. She hoped she was not disturbing them, but Maria waved her over enthusiastically.

"We were just talking about when we could deworm them all," she said. "It's an all-day extravaganza."

"I'll bet," Annie replied, flopping down on a hay bale. "How many horses do you actually have here?" She'd tried to take a headcount, but it was impossible to catch them all.

"At the moment, I think about thirty-one," Olivia said. "Or is it thirty-two? Somewhere around there."

"The yearlings you see in the lower pasture were all born here," Maria said. "They're the ones who are most adoptable, although most of them are only halter-trained at the moment. They'll need to go to homes where we can be sure they get good training."

"How do you do it?" Annie asked Olivia. She realized she seemed to ask the same question of every animal rescuer she met. "How do you find the time to feed all of them?" Annie knew exactly how long it took to care for her own five horses and donkey, and she had help. She couldn't imagine getting up every morning and facing this lot. By the time she'd finished feeding the breakfast meal, it would be time to start prepping the one in the evening.

"I've got plenty of volunteer help," Olivia said simply. "Somehow, it just seems to all get done."

Annie still had her doubts, but every animal on the place looked healthy, well fed, and undeniably content. She concluded she was in the company of extraordinary women with superpowers. There was no other plausible explanation.

"Enough shop talk," Maria said firmly. "Olivia, what do you make of George's death? And you know that Myrna's missing in action."

"This requires a bottle of wine. Hold on, I'll be right back."

Olivia disappeared into her home, just a few yards away.

Annie looked at Maria with a half smile. "You know, for a moment, I'd forgotten all about the feedlot."

"I'm sorry, Annie. That was thoughtless of me. We don't have to talk about it."

"Actually, I'd like to know more. I know absolutely nothing about this couple other than the few things you and Tony mentioned. If I'm going to be a suspect, I might as well know more about the person I supposedly killed."

"Stop with the suspect label."

"No, seriously. Tell me about this charming couple. And let me know who you think really did it."

Annie spoke half-jokingly, but her request was serious. She knew better than to share Dan's staggering news that a timed bomb had been found in the airplane wreckage. And while she'd never give Dan or Sheriff Mullin the satisfaction of knowing so, she, too, suspected there was a connection among the deaths of George, Tony, and the pilot of the downed aircraft. If she knew who wanted to kill George, it might lead her to finding justice for Tony.

Olivia returned with a bottle of Chardonnay and three plastic cups.

"I'm a staunch advocate of twist-off wine caps," she announced as she poured liberally from the bottle. "It makes life so much easier."

The other women assented and raised their cups toward the stars now overhead.

"To the horses," Olivia said.

"To the horses," Annie and Maria solemnly repeated, and then Annie added, "And Tony." Olivia and Maria silently nodded.

The wine was chilled, and if not the vintage Marcus might have ordered off a sommelier's list, it had the same effect. By the time the second glasses were consumed, the three women were thick in conversation about the strange and terrible lives of the feedlot owners.

"George was always just a good ol' boy," Maria told the group. "His daddy had a feedlot for steers, and George always knew he'd inherit the place. And the old man was all right. There were plenty of feedlots in the area that collected horses for slaughter, but George's dad's wasn't one of them. He always said he wouldn't sully his feedlot with horses. Loved them too much. He'd grown up near the Lakota Sioux tribes, who truly honor the horse and are absolutely opposed to the idea of slaughtering them for human consumption."

"They've even filed federal lawsuits to try to stop it," Maria chimed in.

"So what happened?" This came from Annie.

"George met Myrna," Olivia said glumly. "George's father had been gone five years, and he had the business. Myrna came to town from—was it Idaho, Maria? Or Wyoming?"

"Idaho," Maria said firmly, finishing a large mouthful of wine. "Although we never learned much about her background."

"Except it was obvious that she was mean as a snake," Olivia chimed in. "Within a year, she'd married George and convinced him that the feedlot would be three times as profitable if they took in horses. George caved in, just like that."

"So why wasn't Myrna killed instead of George?" It seemed obvious to Annie that Myrna was the real villain in this tale.

"Good question," Maria replied. "George never really cottoned to buying horses for slaughter. And while he was never a teetotaler, over the years he became a quiet, steady drunk. Probably was the only way he could live with himself."

"So what you said to the sheriff about George's having one too many beers at breakfast was true?"

"George would chug a beer before he had a shower. That is, if he showered. It's why Myrna confined him to the simple stuff at the end—feeding and maintaining the horses and steers before they were shipped off. He wasn't really safe to drive at any speed. The Kubota was about the only vehicle he could handle without endangering others."

"Do you think Myrna killed him?"

"No reason to," Olivia said promptly. "He was her chore boy. It's hard to find people to work on a feedlot that sells horses for human consumption. As pitiful as he was, he would have been hard to replace."

"Maybe Myrna's chopped up in a million places and lying in a ditch somewhere, too," Maria said dreamily.

"You are terrible," Olivia said severely, although Annie doubted she meant the sentiment. "But it is odd, her not showing up. Especially since the transport van is due to arrive. It's not like Myrna not to be right on top of things, even with her husband gone."

"Well, I still think she did it and is hiding out in Idaho as we speak. She's probably holed up on the Snake River, communing with her reptilian friends. In any case, I'm now in charge of feeding and caring for the horses until such time as Myrna reappears," Maria told her friend. "I got the official okay from Sheriff Mullin. Which means Annie and I can sneak in and give them all the medical attention they've been missing. That is, if you're willing, Annie."

"Of course," Annie replied although she knew the horses would only receive this care until they were shipped. Once more, her mood plummeted. She decided to get back to George's death, a subject that was infinitely more gratifying to think about, even if she was a suspect.

"So if it wasn't Myrna, who do you think did it?"

Olivia and Maria looked at each other.

"I can think of about a hundred people in the county who wouldn't miss George and had the means and opportunity," Olivia mused. "How about you, Maria?"

"At least. And if you expand that list to every horse person in the tristate area who's ever looked at my feedlot photos and realized what George and Myrna were up to, I'd say that list could quadruple, easily."

"Yup." Olivia finished her wine with a deft swig. "I'd say George's fan club is about as small as Danny Trevor's. We've lost two men in the past week, and the only ones who'll ever mourn them are their mothers. Or possibly not."

Annie sat up straight, confused. "Why? What? What was so bad about Danny Trevor? I thought he was just a local pilot." Annie glanced over at Maria, who seemed as perplexed as she was.

"Me, too. What's his story?"

"Didn't you know, Maria? Last year, Trevor signed a contract with the rez. He was hired to fly over tribal lands to locate wild herds. Once he'd pinpointed their feeding areas, the natives would swoop in on ATVs and round them up. Most of the horses ended up in the Loman feedlot."

"You're kidding!" Maria looked stunned. "I had no idea."

"Well, I sure did," Olivia said coolly. "Every month, like clockwork, I'd hear that old airplane overhead on its way to the rez. I considered it as kind of a preset alarm. I knew I'd be wrangling with Myrna over a bunch of pregnant mares in the next week or two." She nodded toward the lower pasture. "All the yearlings over there? Their mamas came from the rez, every one. If killing Trevor keeps even one foal from losing its mother, I'd say his death was worth the price of the bullet."

The ride home was long and mostly silent. Both women were lost in their thoughts, but Annie suspected she and Maria were wondering the same thing. When Tony got into the plane with Danny Trevor, had he known he was flying with one of the bad guys? And, more to the point, who exactly had been the intended victim—Tony, the horse rescuer, or Trevor, the horse ambusher?

There was no doubt in Annie's mind. Someone in this desolate country was out to kill every key player in the horse-slaughter business.

CHAPTER 14

Annie's new nighttime ritual was washing out socks, underwear, and blouses in her motel bathtub. It wasn't ideal, but it was the best she could do. She thought wryly that on Sunday Marcus would see a far different person from the one he'd seen the last time he'd set eyes on her. The glam was gone, and in its place was the same country cowgirl he'd always known, smelling of horses, saddle leather, and the great outdoors. She kept reminding herself this was what had attracted Marcus to her in the first place.

Marcus had called her early that morning while she was trying to pry open a small plastic container that held one packet each of sugar, sweetener, fake cream, and a thin red wand to stir it all in. Annie wasn't sure she wanted any of these substances in her coffee, and judging by the resilience of the plastic bag, she wasn't sure she was going to gain access to it anytime soon. She was trying to decide whether bad coffee would be better with or without it when her cell phone lit up from its place on the nightstand. She leapt for it, the weighty issue forgotten.

"Annie, I hope I didn't awaken you." Marcus's deep, resonant voice filled her ear. It was the best wake-up call she could imagine, and she promptly told him so.

"Whew. It's two in the afternoon here, and I'm just finishing a late lunch with a client. I go back into the fray in a half hour but was hoping to catch you before I did. Your text message was, how shall I put it, rather provocative."

"Really?" Annie's surprise was genuine.

"Really. Let me refresh your memory. 'Trapped in eastern Washington for now. Feedlot owner was murdered Wednesday and I'm the prime suspect. Will fill you in when you call. Wolf is OK.'"

Oh, yes, that text. Annie vaguely remembered feeling that perhaps she'd overdone the melodrama just a bit at the time she'd sent it. But then, dammit, she'd wanted to talk to the man. Besides, everything she'd texted was true.

"I was delighted to hear that Wolf was in good health," Marcus went on dryly, "although what I really wanted to know was how you were faring. I envisioned you locked up in some rural jail and the lynching party outside the door. Fortunately, a phone call to Dan assuaged those fears, but I'm still very concerned about your situation."

As only Marcus would be. After all, he'd been in a rural jail not long ago.

"Well, when I talked with Dan, he made the evidence against me sound pretty convincing. Although he did say he'd done his best to assure the local sheriff I was here just to pick up Travis's horses and wasn't the murdering kind."

"Yes, I got the same assurance, but with all due respect to Dan, it's not enough. You need an attorney, and I've taken the liberty of hiring one for you."

"Are you sure that's necessary? And you don't have to do that. I can pay for one."

"Too late, Annie. I've just wired a retainer to Alvin Gilman, although you'll need to meet with him to sign the contract so he officially will be your attorney of record."

"Alvin? People are still named Alvin these days?"

"Apparently they are if they're born and raised in Duncan, which is Alvin's story. He has a good reputation for criminal defense, and in any event, he'll have to do for now. I'm not going to rest easy until I know you're represented by counsel."

Annie still wasn't sure this was necessary. After all, if one rural sheriff endorsed your good character to another rural sheriff, wasn't that enough? She intuited it probably was not.

"Thank you, Marcus. You're going to have to stop being such a wonderful guy. Although I really don't want you to."

Marcus laughed a rich, deep laugh that she loved to hear. "I think this will all blow over, but we can't just assume that simply because we know you're innocent. Let me give you Gilman's number so you can arrange a time to meet. But, Annie, make it today, all right? And text me afterwards, so I know it's done. I really can't concentrate on business until I know Gilman is covering your back."

"Promise. I'm going out to the feedlot in an hour or so to help Maria feed the horses—she's my contact here, and was Tony's, too—but then I'll drive to Duncan and meet with the guy."

"Are you sure you should be going to the feedlot

right now? After all, it was a crime scene two days ago. And why do you have to feed?"

"The wife of the deceased is missing. Personally, my money's on her as the killer, but in the meantime, fifty horses need to be fed. Anyway, as I recall, I took you to a crime scene not too long ago, and that was mere moments after you'd been sprung from jail."

"Touché. All right, Annie, but be careful, and make sure Maria can vouch for you the entire time. I wish I could be there sooner than Sunday, but right now, I just can't seem to find a way."

"I'll be fine."

The call ended ten minutes later, and after Annie had said good-bye, she realized she *was* fine. Just fine. And she decided drinking black coffee at least once in her lifetime wouldn't kill her.

Ten hours after dropping her off the night before, Maria's pickup rolled into Annie's motel's parking lot once more. Annie already was waiting outside and gratefully accepted the tall latte Maria quietly passed to her. They drove to the feedlot in silence, content to listen to the patter of news from a local radio station. Today, Maria had chosen to wear shorts with her cowboy boots, while Annie, confined to the only pair of jeans she'd worn all week, sported the one sleeveless shirt she'd tossed in her overnight bag days ago. Even at seven o'clock in the morning, the sun baked hotter here than it ever did on the Peninsula.

Fifty restless, nickering horses greeted them upon arrival, and there was no sign of any other human on the property. The two women got down to business. Annie couldn't remember ever working as hard as she did that morning, except for the early days on her ranch, and she had been fifteen years younger then. She flung so many mounds of hay and orchard grass into each paddock that they soon resembled haystacks in a Monet painting. And because there was enough to share, the usual internecine fighting over food was replaced by the steady chomp-chomp of hungry horses. Annie then joined Maria at the "sick bay," where the most infirm horses were quarantined. She calmly served as Maria's vet tech, handing her bandages, salves, and vet wrap, and taking temperatures upon direction. Some of the horses looked beyond hope, but Maria determinedly ministered to all of them. It was hard to look at some of the wounds many had suffered, and Annie wondered whether they had come at the hands of humans, hooves, or the barbed wire that the local farmers seemed to prefer over electric string. Barbed wire certainly was cheaper.

The last task of the morning was to dump, clean, and refill every water trough on the place. It was difficult to tell when, or if, this had last been done. It was backbreaking work, and by eleven o'clock, sweat was pouring down Annie's face and under her clothes, making rivulets in the dust that had settled over her flushed cheeks.

Annie's one comfort was noticing that all the horses seemed less distressed and anxious than they had under George and Myrna's care. And the little mustang, still in solitary, had ceased blowing snot and looked infinitely more alert.

"Soon, buddy, soon," Annie murmured to him as she slipped him a carrot. "You'll be out of this hellhole very soon."

She hoped she was right. If Myrna's surveillance cameras had been turned on the day before, surely by

now the sheriff's office had reviewed what had had re-
corded and with any luck, unearthed a clue that would
convince Sheriff Mullin she was innocent. and free to go.

    With the horses.

    Maria brought her back to her motel at noon. After a
quick lunch at the local taco stand, Annie was on the
road again, this time headed due east, toward the small
town of Duncan. She realized she was on a road she'd
never traveled before. She'd headed north to the reservation and south to the feedlot, and traversed the small
square blocks of Browning proper too many times to
count, but this was a new path, one that meandered by
a small river for a short while and provided the first welcome scenery in several days. Even Wolf seemed to appreciate the new landscape. Rolling along at seventy
miles an hour, she glimpsed a sign for the county airport. This must be the place where Tony had landed
and where he'd departed on his ill-fated trip home—
just one week ago today. She thought back to Travis's
remark about interrogating the airport employees. It
wasn't a bad idea even though she suspected FAA inves-
tigators had done exactly that by now. She was less sure
that Myrna was behind the plane crash, but feeding fifty
horses twice a day wasn't going to give her much time to
probe that theory.

    The sign for Gilman Law Offices was prominently
displayed in the front yard of a small house right in the
heart of downtown. The house was painted sky blue
with white trim and looked large enough to serve as
both home to the Gilman family and office for the
attorney-at-law. After responding to the sign next to
the doorbell—IT'S OPEN—COME ON IN—she discovered
she was right. Shoes of persons much younger than she

lay strewn on the hardwood floor, and a row of different-sized bike helmets was neatly arrayed on a nearby coat-rack. A door farther back opened, and a tall man in his late thirties quickly walked out. He had to be at least six-four, Annie thought. He had the physique of a pro basket-ball player, not a criminal defense attorney, and Annie suspected he still managed a pickup game after closing shop each night.

"Annie? I'm Al Gilman. It's a pleasure to meet you . . . and your dog," he said, glancing down at Wolf, who was politely standing next to his mistress. Thanks for making the drive over."

During the hour drive to Duncan, Annie had been glad for the chance to think mindlessly for once. Now that she was here, she had to focus again on the un-comfortable fact in front of her—that being in the right place at the wrong time had somehow made her a mur-der suspect in the eyes of the law. She reluctantly con-ceded that she needed the attorney looming over her right now. She was glad that he'd at least dropped the old-fashioned part of his first name.

Alvin Gilman made Annie feel right at home—espe-cially since she could hear the pounding footsteps of children running upstairs and squeals of laughter. It was in stark contrast to the room into which he'd ush-ered her and Wolf. Everything was in dark oak—the walls, the desk, the swivel chair behind it, as well as the floor-to-ceiling library bookcases packed with ancient law books that looked in danger of crumbling if dis-turbed from their perch. The only incongruous part of the room was a basketball hoop pegged to the back of the office door. A certificate for Most Valuable Player from Georgetown discreetly hung on the rear wall.

"Excuse the twins." He grinned at Annie. "They've just turned five and are still enjoying the remnants of a neighborhood birthday party yesterday. I think they found the leftover party favors."

Annie smiled politely. She didn't have children so she couldn't respond with the empathy of a fellow parent who had gone through the same experience. The absence of children in her life wasn't a conscious choice; she'd just never been in a relationship during those critical childbearing years when having one might have been possible and desired. Besides, there was Hannah, the best surrogate child a person could possibly have. Hannah went home at night to her own family.

"Let me see if I've got the picture right," Alvin went on. "I understand you've lost a close friend recently."

Annie nodded, feeling sudden tears prick her eyes.

"And, as I understand it, his death now looks like it might have been the result of foul play."

Annie nodded again, slowly feeling her equilibrium return.

"And now that you've come to finish your friend's job, which is to transport four horses back to your own county, another murder has occurred. And the sheriff is toying with you, making you an unlikely suspect in that death."

Toying was precisely the right word, Annie thought.

"It's ridiculous. I happened to show up just after George—the feedlot owner, the guy who was killed— had been shot. Simply because I happen to carry a rifle the same caliber as the one that killed him and was at the scene around the time he was shot, I've been named the person most likely to do the job."

As she described the scenario, Annie realized just how easily someone might come to the same conclusion. Maybe having an attorney wasn't such a bad idea, after all.

Alvin nodded thoughtfully back at her.

"But there are several mitigating factors, are there not? A gun test should easily rule out your rifle as the one used in the crime, correct? And you have no apparent motive. As I understand it, you'd never even met the man, only his wife."

"Who's missing," Annie added angrily, "and probably is the one who pulled the trigger herself."

"Let's not worry about solving the murder. That's the sheriff's job. Let's just concentrate on keeping you out of Sheriff Mullin's crosshairs."

Hearing this, Annie sat up a bit straighter. "Why? What's his reputation?"

"He's a good ol' boy. Never lost an election in twenty-five years. Mostly handles domestics and DUIs and the occasional break-in. When something like this comes along, Sheriff Mullin gets all excited. In his rush to judgment, he sometimes makes a few errors. About five years ago, he bungled a major homicide when his boys got too rough on a suspect and the confession was thrown out of court. He's not likely to repeat that experience, but he's not going to let another murder go unsolved."

Annie could think of another sheriff who was prone to making snap decisions about suspects but said nothing. Dan happened to be her friend, as flawed as his judgment had sometimes been.

"Let's start from the beginning. Why don't you tell me exactly what happened, from the time your friend flew here to pick out the horses until now? I'll just take notes; we won't tape-record anything. You know everything you tell me is confidential. No one else will ever know what you've told me. But I need the truth in order to do my job."

Just in case I decide to confess to murder, Annie thought, but she knew that she was simply getting the attorney's standard line to new clients.

When she was done with her recitation, Alvin leaned back in his chair, put his fingers together, and looked at her critically.

"I really don't think you have much to worry about," he finally said. "But until we hear it from the sheriff's mouth, I think it's best that we go over a few ground rules. If anyone from the sheriff's office, the press, or just a friend asks you to talk about the case, refuse. Do not say one word about the case or discuss your peripheral involvement in it. If someone insists—such as one of the sheriff's over-exuberant deputies—politely refer them to me. The only thing you need to tell them is that you're represented by counsel and hand them one of my cards."

He leaned forward, plucked a half dozen from a card holder on his desk, and passed them over to Annie, who put them in her purse. She noticed that the card was printed in both English and Spanish.

"I'll be in touch with the sheriff and the local prosecutor tomorrow morning to try to find out where you actually stand as a suspect. I'll let you know what I find out as soon as I do. In the meantime, don't hesitate to call me if you have any questions or if any new incident occurs that makes you nervous."

"Like what? Another death?"

"Anything. If you get the sense you're being followed, or someone keeps pressuring you to talk. Anything at all."

"I'm friends with the sheriff back in Suwana County. Does this mean I can't talk to him about George's murder, or Tony's death?"

"I'm afraid so. You wouldn't want to make your buddy the sheriff an involuntary witness to something you discussed, would you?"

Perish the thought. Dan would kill her. Then she remembered an item she'd brought specifically to share with Alvin, and dug into her saddlebag purse to find it now.

"I have something for you that might help. It's a receipt I demanded from Myrna on Tuesday, the day before I was supposed to haul out. She was charging me for care and feeding until the very last minute. Technically, I guess I still owe her money."

Annie brought out the envelope upon which Myrna had scratched out, in pencil, the amount due and then PAID IN CASH in capital letters below.

"Great. Having a paper trail will help establish your bona fides. Not many murderers insist on receipts from the wife of the person they intend to kill the next day."

"It's all yours."

"Thanks, but let me make you a copy. You never know; Myrna might reappear, and you'll need it to renegotiate the terms of the horses' release."

He was right. Annie waited patiently as Alvin left the room. She thought he easily could have put a small copier in the office, but then, it would have clashed with the dark oak paneling and décor. She glanced around and noticed that Alvin Gilman was admitted not only to practice law in the state of Washington, but also to argue cases in the Ninth Circuit Court of Appeals and the U.S. Supreme Court. She fervently hoped her case would go away before that was required.

Alvin stepped back into the room and handed her a Xeroxed copy of the receipt, front and back.

"Mr. Gilman, may I tell you what I really want?"

"Please."

"I just want to go home with my dog and four horses."

"I'll do my best to make that happen."

As Annie started the hour-long journey back to Browning, her mind no longer was on the scenery. She was thinking about the return address she'd seen on the envelope that Myrna had turned into a receipt. The sender of the letter was the local tribal council; the return address was printed right on the envelope, and the postmark was Monday, August 8, the day Annie had arrived in the area. But what intrigued her most was the PERSONAL AND CONFIDENTIAL in big block letters underneath the names of the recipients, George and Myrna Fullman. What secrets did the local tribe and the feedlot owners share? Did they have to do with Danny Trevor and his death?

She'd just been told to let the sheriff handle the feedlot owner's murder investigation. That was fine and dandy, but the connection between the tribe and the Fullmans was one piece of information she intended to ferret out herself. As she settled back for the drive, she recalled the electrifying sight of wild horses racing across tribal lands. They thought they were headed to a place of safety. Little did they know that the big steel bird that circled overhead would ultimately betray them all.

CHAPTER 15

Lost in thought, Annie didn't hear her cell phone ringing until it flipped over to voicemail. Sighing, she pulled over to the side of the road to find out who had called. She had yet to get an earpiece for the smartphone, and while she was under the watchful eye of Sheriff Mullin, she intended to obey every single traffic law she knew of.

"Hi, Annie. It's Maria. Hey, I've got an unexpected night off—the kids are with my mom for the evening. Want to meet up at the local tapas bar in Loman? A couple of friends are joining me, and you'll like them. They're all horse-crazy women. I'll probably get there about seven. Hope you can come!"

Maria rattled off the name and address of the bar and disconnected. Annie caught only the name but didn't take the time to listen to the message again. The truth was Annie had little desire for more socializing in eastern

Washington. She didn't go out often at home; she'd much rather spend the evening with her dogs, horses, and kitten. Here, however, Wolf was her only boon companion, and she could hardly expect him to keep her entertained in a pine-paneled motel room, as spacious as it might be. Anyway, how many tapas bars could Loman hold? She sighed again and decided to extend herself one more time. She reminded herself that Marcus's arrival was now only three days away. Maybe tomorrow she'd find a library or a good used bookstore to fill the time until he arrived.

She could have used a shower—she'd had time for only a quick wash-up before dashing off to Duncan— but the sun was already setting, and her watch informed her that with no stops she would land in Loman a little past seven. Poor Wolf. He'd miss dinner at his usual time. She'd have to make sure that there was tapas suitable for blue heelers, which, on reflection, probably was just about everything on the menu. She parked underneath a small bower of trees and rolled down the windows a good eight inches. Annie was fairly confident that Wolf wouldn't bound out and leave her for another woman, unless that woman tempted him with a large T-bone steak.

The tapas bar was easy to spot; Mexican music poured out of it onto the sidewalk. In fact, walking into the place, Annie thought it seemed more like a typical Mexican restaurant than a Spanish one. As far as she could tell, no one was drinking sangria. Most of the patrons were tippling Coronas or frosted margaritas. She espied Maria's long dark hair and saw her sitting at a large circular table in the front room with several other women around her. Annie's heart sank at the prospect of meeting more total strangers, but she smiled and wended her way toward them.

"Annie! So glad you could make it! Donny, this is Annie Carson. Annie, meet Donny. Donny's got eight horses, all of them rescues, and runs a year-round camp for kids with disabilities." Annie shook her hand, wondering if she could stand meeting one more woman with the drive and dedication of Mother Teresa. But she decided Donny looked nice enough even if she did more good acts than Annie was likely to achieve in her lifetime.

"And this is Connie." Maria gestured to a middle-aged woman whose bright red hair obviously was not her natural color. "She has only two horses, but she's still as crazy as the rest of us." Annie smiled again and sat down at the one empty chair, which, thankfully, Maria had saved next to her own. "And over there is Tinker, short for Tinkerbelle, which isn't her real name, but it's what everyone has called her since she was two." Tinker was a fine-boned, petite woman, whose eyes showed a fierce internal resolve. Annie wondered if her tiny size had contributed to that outward persona. She suspected Tinker could merely tell a rattlesnake to get lost, and it would immediately slither away.

"Nice to meet you," Annie shouted over the noise and hooked her purse over the arm of her chair.

"We've ordered a pitcher of margaritas," Maria explained. "It just seemed simpler."

Annie nodded her assent and wondered how tequila would sit with her. She'd last imbibed the substance when she was twenty-one, and the ensuing hangover still made her shudder.

"We were just taking a poll on Myrna," Connie shouted toward her. "Did she or didn't she?"

"Did or didn't do what?" Annie knew what she was asking, but wanted to hear it first.

"Kill George, of course! I'm betting she did. Everyone knew she was having an affair. George probably found out and Myrna decided to shut him up for good."

Annie turned to Maria and looked quizzically at her. This was the first time she'd ever heard this tantalizing bit of gossip. It was difficult to think of Myrna having an affair with anyone. It was less difficult to think of her killing her drunk of a husband.

"Oh, that rumor's been floating around for years," Maria said, laughing. "It may have been a loveless marriage, but I doubt Myrna had the time to have a fling. Or the stamina."

"You'd be surprised what older women can do," Donny said ominously. "Six weeks after my grandma went into a retirement home, she up and married the guy in the room next door. I'll bet even Myrna would still be happy to get a little on the side."

"Maybe so, but why bother to kill George?" This came from Tinker, barely visible in her chair in the corner. "Even if he knew about the affair, he wouldn't do anything about it. Doesn't have the backbone."

Annie was beginning to find the conversation a bit distasteful even though she, too, wondered if Myrna had been complicit in George's demise. As his surviving spouse, she was the obvious suspect. Particularly since she'd been AWOL since yesterday morning. But the conversation was dangerously crossing into off-limits territory, according to her new attorney.

Fortunately, the subject was changed.

"I think we could load up all the horses in the feedlot while Myrna's still gone and take them away." Donny looked as if she was ready to execute this plan at a moment's notice.

"I think that's called horse stealing," said Tinker.

"Are you sure, Tinker? I'd call it horse rescuing."

"It's a nice thought," Maria chimed in. "I wish we could do it."

Annie decided to remove Myrna from the conversation altogether.

"How are the horses? Do you need my help tomorrow morning with feeding?" Annie had assumed this was her new schedule until further notice.

Maria shook her head. "Not necessary. Tinker and Connie have offered to help, and Donny's going to come out on Sunday."

Annie felt instant relief flood through her, quickly followed by a touch of guilt. She should be helping out, at least taking care of the four animals she planned to take, plus Eddie, but frankly she wasn't sure how many more visits to the feedlot she could handle. It was such a heart-crushing experience, and she realized seeing the horses' plight, day after day, was becoming more difficult, not easier, to absorb.

"You sure?" Annie asked gamely.

"Positive. Eddie's now permanently in the paddock with your three and is doing fine. And the mustang is right next to them. We'll keep your horses safe and happy and make sure they're ready to travel as soon as you get the word."

"Thanks, Maria. I really appreciate it. But if you need help, please let me know. I'm just hanging out and don't have much to do. You're the ones with jobs and families to juggle."

"Maria's the pro," Donny told Annie. "This woman can keep more balls in the air than anyone I know. Yesterday she jump-started my car at dawn before taking off for . . ."

"Stop, Donny," Maria interrupted. She was laughing, Annie noticed, but she also seemed intent on curtailing her friend's flow of conversation. "You'd do the same for me."

"Well, I would if I knew how to jump-start a car. That's the problem."

"You picked up my kids from school yesterday. And babysat them all last night. Now that was helpful."

Annie remembered that Maria had patiently waited for her at the sheriff's office yesterday afternoon. She'd forgotten all about the fact that Maria had two young sons who might need their mother's attention. The only thing Annie never forgot was to feed her horses.

The pitcher of margaritas arrived and Maria, obviously the alpha mare in this female herd, served up.

"Ah . . ." Connie sighed contentedly. "Nothing like a cold margarita on a hot summer day."

A chorus of agreement followed Connie around the table.

"Which one of you is Annie?"

The words were harsh and accusatory and brought the group instantly to attention. Annie turned to where she'd heard the deep male voice, which was somewhere from behind Maria. A big, burly man stood behind her friend, glaring at the group of women. Annie was momentarily mesmerized by the sheer size of the man's gut, which stuck so far out it was in danger of touching the back of Maria's head. A belt buckle was barely visible somewhere south of its lowest point, and Annie wondered when gravity would take its toll. She looked up toward the man's tanned and weather-beaten face. Deep furrows were etched into his forehead, which somehow only emphasized the meanness in his eyes. They were black, Annie thought with astonishment. She'd never seen eyes so dark—or so angry.

And he'd asked for her.

Annie slowly stood up and turned around to face the man.

"My name is Annie," she said. Her voice sounded far steadier than she felt.

"You the gal who killed George Fullman?"

Annie's heart suddenly pounded. She was aware that other men were quietly gathering around the spokesman.

"No, I'm the woman who found his body. I don't know who killed Mr. Fullman."

"That's not what the sheriff says."

One part of Annie's brain wildly reminded her that she was now talking about the case, which she'd been firmly admonished not to do. But there was no chance of getting out of this conversation. She wondered why she felt so light-headed. Perhaps she'd imbibed a bit more tequila than she'd thought.

"Really? He didn't say that to me."

"Well, maybe you ought to talk to him again."

Aha. This was Annie's cue, the one she'd just learned.

"Sorry," she said brightly. "No can do. But my attorney will be happy to talk to the sheriff."

There was a brief silence. The leader appeared flummoxed, unsure of what to say next. Annie glanced around and weighed her options. She had none. All the convenient exit doors were blocked by the mob in front of her and other patrons.

"Let me tell you something, *Annie.*" The man made her name sound like a piece of disgusting garbage. "We've just about had it up to here with all you liberal dope-smoking freaks coming in here to 'save' our horses. You spread lies. You tell the media how bad we are, when all we're doing is what we've been doing for the last hundred years. So why don't you just pack up and go home where you can hug a tree or something? You're not welcome here."

Tinker stood up so fast her chair back clattered on the floor.

"Leave us alone, or we're calling the police."

The leader glanced at Tinker's diminutive stature, shook his head in exaggerated disbelief, and turned to face his compatriots.

"Hear that, boys? If we don't leave, she's going to call the po-lice."

The group laughed heartily.

"Why, there's no need for that, little missy. We got the po-lice right here, don't we, Ray?"

A man from the back slowly shouldered his way to the front. He didn't look happy at being called out in front of the group.

"This here's Ray Goddard," the big man said. "One of Browning's very own deputies. Ray, tell Miss Annie how we feel about her being in our town."

Ray was young and lanky, and looked a bit green around the mouth. Annie suspected he resented being called out to confront her.

"May I see your identification, please?" Tinker's question was politely stated, but with all the gravitas Annie knew she could muster.

Ray glared at the leader and dug his police identification out of his pocket.

Tinker and Annie both peered at it. It was Ray, all right, but he looked about sixteen years old. It must have been taken the day he'd graduated from the academy.

"Well, Ray, what do you have to say to Annie here?" Annie noticed the man appeared to enjoy goading the deputy as much as he did her.

"I know the sheriff has ordered you not to leave town," he began, a little uncertainly.

"See?" Annie turned to the leader and gave what she hoped was a dazzling smile. "I couldn't leave your charming city even if I wanted to!"

The group behind her shifted uneasily. Ray took a deep breath and spoke more forcefully. "But maybe you should take my friend's advice and leave. It might be safer. You might still have a truck to drive out in."

"That's right," the leader menacingly added. "Although she should be in jail right now for what she's done."

A Hispanic man in a white shirt and bow tie thrust his body into the mix.

"*Señores! Señores!* Stop badgering this young woman or I must ask you all to leave. Please! This is not good for the other patrons. Please, go to your tables and calm down."

It was all the encouragement Ray needed. He turned his back on Annie and started to move through the crowd. The leader gave Annie and Tinker one last glare, then grudgingly joined the rest of the men, who had chosen to follow the deputy. Annie watched the group slowly make its way back to the bar area in the next room. To her surprise, the men didn't stop but exited through the rear door. Annie fleetingly wondered whether they had paid their bar tabs before leaving.

Annie and her four new friends continued the party long after the sullen men had departed. The owner quickly brought over a fresh pitcher of margaritas and several delicious tapas.

"On the house," he assured the women. "Men like that are not welcome in my restaurant."

The conversation became more animated with every replenished glass. Tinker, despite her small stature, did a stunningly realistic rendition of the leader's bombastic stance and coarse talk. Everyone thought the way Annie had stood up to him showed incredible courage, and Annie found herself getting more compliments than she'd ever received in her life. Maria was adamant about filing a complaint with the sheriff's office about the unbecoming behavior of one of his deputies and would have queried all the patrons about what they'd seen and heard if the rest of the women hadn't convinced her that the owner's statement would do. At eleven o'clock, the ebullient group of women wandered out of the tapas bar and into the cool evening air.

As much as she tried to downplay the earlier ugly encounter, Annie knew that the threats that had been made against her tonight were real. She had no intention of letting down her guard as long as she was forced to stay in the vicinity. Giving in to heartfelt hugs from each of the women, she assured them all she would keep in touch, clasped the bag of tapas the owner had made up for her now very hungry dog, located her truck, and after carefully looking four ways, slowly made the drive from Loman back to Browning and her now-familiar motel.

Wolf had been granted the rare treat of consuming food inside the truck; it was so late that Annie didn't want to deprive him any longer. So the matter of cleaning up after her blue heeler's enthusiastic inhalation of yummy tapas made her unaware of what had happened in her absence. Wolf, who had jumped out upon their arrival, alerted her with his trademark growl that insinuated someone bad was in their territory.

She grabbed a flashlight out of her glove compartment and trained it on her dog. Wolf was standing at full alert in front of Jessica's horse trailer. Annie slowly moved the light across the body of the vehicle. Someone—in fact, probably several people—had taken baseball bats to the windows and aluminum siding. The formerly gleaming panels were now crunched and distorted from repeated blows. Whoever had done the damage was vicious. Every double-paned window spanning the length of the trailer had been smashed. Every one of the tires had been flattened.

Annie ran to the rear. The doors were gaping open; the cable lock that had secured them had been jaggedly sawn off and flung inside. Annie didn't want to look, but she forced herself to point the flashlight into the interior. It was strewn with garbage, obliterating all the clean shavings she'd scattered earlier. She nearly gagged from the stench.

Suddenly weary, Annie walked back to her truck and unlocked the toolbox bolted to the outside bed. She found a few bungee cords and another lock. Returning to the wreck of the trailer, she managed to secure the back doors, garbage still inside, so they could not be reopened. She then went to her truck to unbolt her trusty Winchester from the rifle stanchion inside the cab. The gun rack was empty. Damn! She'd forgotten—her Winchester was now in the hands of the sheriff's office for testing. Had the goons known that when they'd decided to destroy the horses' transport? Probably, if Ray Goddard was among them. Well, she had her own backup. She whistled for Wolf. He gave a small, inquisitive whine, but obediently trotted over to her side.

Cautiously, she approached the insubstantial door to

her motel room. Shining a light on her lock, she could see no perceptible damage, but that hardly gave her confidence. It would be child's play to jimmy the room lock without leaving any visible traces. But she couldn't stand outside forever. She quickly turned her room key in the lock, flung open the door, and flipped on the lights. Nothing. Everything in the room appeared intact, and a quick search showed that nobody else was there. Whoever had wreaked such terrible destruction on the trailer had not penetrated her temporary domicile. She should have been thankful for small blessings, but she was not. She was fuming.

It took Annie several hours to fall asleep that night, and when she did, she awakened at the slightest perceived noise. The images of the destroyed trailer kept flashing through her brain. The one that stood out among all others was that of the words scrawled in bright red paint along the side of the trailer: GO HOME.

At the moment, there was nothing Annie would have rather done.

CHAPTER 16

The trailer looked even worse by light of day. Annie slowly walked around the circumference, feeling more disheartened at every turn. The brake lights had been pulverized. The slides on the windows were mangled and wouldn't shut. The miscreants who'd done this hadn't even spared the dome light inside the trailer.

There was no doubt in Annie's mind who was responsible for this despicable act. The question was what to do about it. She hoped she could find a competent mechanic to examine the rig and determine the extent of the damage. At least then she'd know whether or not she could use it for transport, graffiti scrubbed off or not. But what was the point of reporting the vandalism to the police, when Annie was pretty sure Deputy Goddard had been part of the goon squad that had wielded the baseball bats so effectively? Would she simply be laughed out of the sheriff's office?

It was a question for Alvin Gilmore. He needed to know about the incident, and, for once, Annie was glad to let someone else decide how best to proceed. She pulled out her cell and Alvin's business card, punched in his number, and walked to the one side of the trailer the graffiti artists had missed.

"Are you all right?" was Alvin's first question. He'd picked up on the first ring and listened without interruption as Annie had described in detail the events of the night before, starting with the threats at the bar.

"I'm fine," she said, and heard a small sigh of relief on his end of the line. "But I wish I had my rifle right now. As you know, the sheriff removed it from my gun rack the day George Fullman was killed."

"Did you give it voluntarily?"

Annie paused. "Frankly, I didn't think I had much of a choice. But yes, I told him he could test it, and he gave me a receipt for it after he interrogated me."

Alvin Gilman, Annie was pleased to note, did not correct her use of the verb "interrogate."

"Well, you really didn't have much of a choice. If you'd refused, the sheriff would have gotten a search warrant for it. So you did the right thing."

"Now what should I do? Should I report the incident to the sheriff's office? Or should I just lick my wounds and look for a good mechanic?"

Merely licking her wounds was precisely what Annie did not want to do, nor did she think she could stand to do so, even if Alvin suggested this.

"God, no. You need to report this. If you haven't already, take detailed photos of all the damage. Talk to the night clerk and see if he or she heard anything. It would be awfully strange if they didn't. Although if the motel staff claims they heard nothing, we can assume they're either too scared to talk or have been paid off."

How reassuring, Annie thought.

"But let me make the first move. Neither the sheriff nor the prosecutor returned my phone calls from yesterday, but I'll make damn sure I get through this morning. Let me tell the sheriff first what's happened and what I think about citizens in his county terrorizing out-of-town visitors and destroying their property. At the same time, I'll try to get a bead on how seriously they actually consider you as a suspect and remind them they have no cause to keep you here. And I'll try to get your gun back. You have a legitimate need for protection right now."

"If Sheriff Mullin would just let me go home with the horses, it would solve a lot of problems."

"Yours, maybe. Not his. He's got two murders on his hands, and clearly doesn't have a clue as to where to look next. But letting his deputy play the bully is unacceptable. You've got a good basis for a lawsuit."

"I just want to go home. Preferably in the trailer I came with and an unscathed truck."

"I assume you've got insurance. Have you reported it to your insurance company yet?"

"It's not even mine. It belongs to my equine vet back in Suwana County. She is not going to be amused."

"Tell her she can sue, too. Just take photos, don't touch anything you don't have to, and wait for my text."

Annie set to work recording the damage. By now, she felt like a pro with the smartphone camera. To her secret pride, she'd also discovered the video record button and was able to take a short clip of the entire truck, both inside and out. Hannah would be so proud, she thought, as she zoomed in on the bags of garbage, now surrounded by swarms of hungry flies. Unfortunately, the steps to downloading the photos and video—not to mention the photos she'd taken at the feedlot two days earlier—still eluded her. She figured this task could wait until she had returned home and could summon the eight-year-old computing wizard to pay a call.

Alvin's text arrived just as she'd documented the last smashed window:

Sheriff has been properly rebuked. Promises to release rifle when you file report. Won't give test results, but you wouldn't get it back if it wasn't clean. I'm betting you'll get clearance to leave by EOD. Myrna's still a no-show and looking more viable every hour she's gone. IMO you can be polite and wait for his OK or go, as long as he has your contact info. Stay tuned, and stay safe. Alvin. P.S. You might think about changing motels.

Annie snorted. She could move to the other motel on the opposite end of town, but what was the point? Her F-250 would stick out just as much there as it did here. And she really didn't want to distance herself further from the feedlot. She'd been poised to rescue the horses ever since she'd arrived five long days ago, and as soon as she was given the okay by the almighty sheriff, she intended to be on the road.

Except now she had no way to transport the horses.

Telling Jessica that her new, beautiful horse trailer might be headed for the salvage yard was going to be tough. But at least the bad news could be delivered in an air-conditioned space. Wolf already was in her motel bedroom, tucked into a corner where he got the full strength of the portable unit.

"You always were a lot smarter than me," she told her blue heeler. "Move over. I need to make another phone call."

Jessica was surprisingly calm. "That's why I pay hideously high insurance premiums," she told Annie. "I'll file the claim today. Have you, by chance, taken any photos?" Jessica knew Annie's limited skill set with anything technical.

"Yes, but I have no idea how to get them out of my new phone."

"Let me teach you."

Annie was doubtful, but under Jessica's patient tutelage, starting with a lesson on how to put the call on speaker, she managed to forward the most graphic photos and the video to Jessica's email account.

"Okay, great, Annie," Jessica said a few minutes later. "Looks like they've all come through. Let's take a look at the damage."

Annie silently waited as Jessica began to look at the attached photos. The fury she'd expected to hear coming from her vet from the beginning now exploded in full force.

"Jesus God, Annie! What kind of monsters do they breed over in Loman? I can't believe what I'm seeing!"

"Actually, I'm in Browning, which is about fourteen miles away, but the emotional intelligence quotient is about the same, hovering somewhere between one and zero."

"I'm assuming the boys at the bar are responsible?"

"Either they did the damage or paid someone else to do it. But the time line's right. They slink out of the bar, I continue to party with my new friends and come back to the motel four hours later to find your lovely trailer smashed to smithereens."

"Well, the real question is the structural damage. Did you look underneath the body?"

"I took a quick look and, aside from the flattened tires, didn't notice anything out of whack. But I'll need to take it to a mechanic to make sure."

"Unbelievable. Make them scrub that tag off. Even if

it's headed to the junkyard, I don't want it to exist any longer than necessary."

"Will do. Do you have any preference where it's hauled? Not that we may have much of a choice. There seems to be one of everything here. One grocery store, one gas station, one barista stand. Browning doesn't seem to foster the kind of competition that we expect in America. There may be only one or two mechanics in the entire county. And, of course, we have to hope that they don't mind working for tree-hugging freaks like us."

Jessica sighed. "See what you can find, Annie. I'll ask my insurance company if they'd prefer the trailer just be hauled to the shop of their choice. But that puts you in a bind. You need a trailer to haul. And why aren't you back yet? Lisa phoned me a couple of days ago telling me you'd got involved in yet another murder and been detained. What's the hang-up?"

"Oh, nothing much. I'm still a suspect and have been told to hang around until my name is cleared."

"No, seriously. What's taking you so long?"

"I am serious. In fact, as Dan would say, I have officially lawyered up."

"Where's Marcus?"

"Jessica, as you know, I am an independent woman who does not rely on the kindness of others. At least, I used to be that woman. Marcus, bless his heart, is responsible for getting me legal counsel and has promised to rescue me on Sunday."

"Well, thank heaven for that. Do you think the second murder has anything to do with Tony's death?"

"Sorry, Jessica, I wish I could tell you what I think, but I can't. Lawyer's orders. I'll let you know if I find any reputable repair shops that can handle horse trailers. Text me the claim number when you get it. And by the way, my attorney said to tell you he thinks you have an excellent civil case."

"Against whom?"

"The lowlifes who did this to your trailer. Maybe the sheriff's office, as well, since one of them may be on the county payroll."

"This just gets worse and worse. Come home soon, Annie. I'm worried about you."

Predictably, the desk clerk claimed he'd been called away on a family emergency the previous evening and so had no idea that Ms. Carson's horse trailer had been vandalized. He was most sympathetic, and even went as far as suggesting that boys from a local reform school might be responsible.

"Why? Did I miss the report about a massive break-out on the news yesterday?" Annie didn't bother hiding her sarcasm. She was appalled by the clerk's clear allegiance with the thugs who were responsible for the mess she was in now.

"I'm just saying," the clerk replied, his eyes growing wide with feigned innocence. Annie was tempted to throw her room key in his face and tell him she'd take her business elsewhere. The problem was there weren't many other places she could go, and, she reminded herself, she'd have to find a way to take the trailer with her.

She grabbed a quick bite at her now-favorite taco stand. Her plan to walk to the sheriff's office was quickly nixed—it was midday, the sun was directly overhead, and no intelligent person would walk even a few blocks if an air-conditioned truck was available to them. Besides, she was restless after all the unpleasantness of this morning, and might want to drive somewhere. She put Wolf's dog food in a secure container in the truck bed and gestured for the blue heeler to jump in. He was thrilled to accept her invitation.

The sheriff's office was little larger than a corner market, Annie noticed with some disdain, and only a few county vehicles were parked in back. She pulled into one of two visitor's spots and left Wolf in the truck with the windows rolled down. Then she squared her shoulders and marched in.

"I'm here to make a report of vandalism," she coldly told the deputy on duty.

"Name?"

"Annie Carson."

"The sheriff's been expecting you. Thought you'd be here earlier. Have a seat, and I'll tell him you're here."

Annie declined to sit. Instead, she amused herself by reading the wanted posters tacked up on a bulletin board by the front desk. Even the women portrayed in the posters looked mean and ugly. She itched to have her .30-30 back in her possession.

That wish, at least, was fulfilled. A few minutes later, Sheriff Mullin walked into the reception area, holding her Winchester in his hand.

"Here you go, Ms. Carson," he said, handing it over to her. "Sounds like you may need this if you stay here much longer."

"Does this mean you're giving me permission to go?" Annie knew Alvin Gilman already had asked the same question, but perhaps in the last hour the sheriff had come to his senses.

"Not quite. We're still going through the surveillance tapes. Don't pack your bags yet."

"And meanwhile, I've got a severely damaged horse trailer to deal with." She was getting angry. The sheriff's nonchalant attitude about her situation was insufferable.

"So I hear. We're a bit busy today, but we'll try to send someone out to take a look at the trailer this afternoon. I understand you discovered the damage last night. Any particular reason why you decided to wait until today to report it?"

Annie ached to tell the sheriff exactly what she thought. She did not. That was what lawyers were for, she reminded herself.

"It was late, and difficult to see the full extent of the damage," she said tersely.

"I see. Any witnesses?"

"Isn't that your job, finding witnesses?"

"Just asking. I hear you were out having drinks with your lady friends earlier. We've got a strict DUI patrol out here on the weekends. Just a word to the wise."

Annie nodded but said nothing, vowing to herself she would not have so much as another sip of beer if she had to drive as much as a block.

"You might want to consider the company you keep. Stick with Maria—she's the only halfway sane female in the bunch."

Obviously, Deputy Goddard had reported back to the sheriff. So much for thinking there was only one bad apple in the bunch.

"She's a nut case when it comes to those feedlot horses," the sheriff continued, "but she knows what she's doing when it comes to teaching kids to read. Wish the school had enough money to take her back. Well, take an accident form with you and sit tight. As I said, I'll send out a deputy as soon as we can spare the man power."

"Just how many deputies do you have at your disposal, Sheriff?"

He paused, then gave her a small sardonic grin.
"Thirteen."

"Impressive."

"We've got a large territory to cover, Ms. Carson. We
need every deputy we got. Understood? As I said, we'll
get to your problem as soon as we can." He reached behind him and handed her a form.

Annie held out her hand stiffly, took the sheet of
paper, and turned to go. As she did so, a small, scrawny
woman rushed in the door and flew at Annie. She
reeked of booze, and waved one arm wildly in her direction.

"That's the woman! She killed my George! Arrest
her, Harlin! Don't let her get away with murder!"

Sheriff Mullin instantly inserted himself in front of
Annie and brought Myrna's hands down and behind
her back.

"Calm down, Myrna. Let's go someplace where you
can tell me all about it." The sheriff nodded toward
Annie. "You'd better go, Ms. Carson. But remember,
don't leave town just yet."

Annie numbly walked out of the building and back
to her truck. The full strength of the sun bore down on
her, crushing her energy and her spirits. She felt as if
she were in her own personal episode of *The Twilight
Zone,* stuck in a town that she could never leave. And
now Myrna Fullman was back in it. Maybe the woman
truly believed Annie had killed George. Or maybe she
was just trying to pin the blame on her to cover her own
tracks. Wherever the truth lay, one thing was certain.
Annie had just made an enemy, and one who con-
trolled the destiny of the horses Annie desperately
wished to take home.

CHAPTER 17

Annie had never been one to sit still for long, and waiting in her motel room for a deputy to show had gotten old, quickly. While she'd been with the sheriff, Jessica had texted her both the claim number and the name of her insurance agent. Annie had promptly filled out the incident report, making it clear that photos and a video of the damage would be forthcoming. She'd also exchanged texts with Lisa, who reported all the horses were healthy and frisky, and boy was it hot—the thermometer by the barn tipped past eighty degrees yesterday.

You don't know what hot is, Annie glumly texted back. **Can't wait to return to the Peninsula version**. But she was relieved to know all was well in her own horse world and that Lisa was more than content to continue her role as barn matron.

Now there was nothing to do except wait, which was

excruciating. She snagged a copy of the local newspaper, a weekly that reminded her of the one in her own hometown that reported mostly local news. George's death had made the front page, although the only photo was of a much younger George, taken somewhere other than the feedlot. She scanned the article for her name. Thankfully, it did not appear. Myrna was mentioned as George's wife, but nothing was said about her being a missing person. Annie figured she was one of the few people who knew the grieving widow had recently returned, alive and drunk. She noted with amusement that Sheriff Mullin had characterized the feedlot owner's death as "a tragic accident." Annie knew from Dan Stetson that what a sheriff fed the local press was often a cover for the real investigation being done.

Annie badly wanted to talk with Dan. She was well accustomed to sharing information and theories about cases with the sheriff, and she yearned to tell him her suspicions about Myrna and what she'd learned about the pilot, Danny Trevor—if he didn't already know. But she also knew that while she was still a suspect in George's death, any conversation she had with the Suwana County sheriff might make its way back to Sheriff Mullin. She hadn't trusted the local sheriff from the beginning, and she sure as hell didn't now, knowing that at least one of his deputies had been given carte blanche to harass suspects and destroy their property.

So when Dan called an hour into her impatient wait for a deputy to show, she picked up her cell with both relief and concern.

"I just got off the phone with Harlin Mullin," Dan said abruptly, without waiting for her opening greeting. "What's this I hear about Jessica's trailer being smashed up?"

Annie was silent.

"Annie? You there?"

The words came out in a rush.

"Dan, I can't talk to you. Marcus hired—I hired an attorney yesterday. He's told me not to talk about the case, not even with you—especially with you, because that might make you a witness later on. I'm sorry."

She stopped her flow of words, feeling terrible, as if somehow she'd betrayed their friendship.

Dan's response was uncharacteristically calm.

"Calm down, Annie. I'm not trying to sucker you into a confession to a murder I know you didn't commit. I just was checking in with Sheriff Mullin to make sure you were okay, and he told me that the horse trailer had been vandalized. We won't talk about anyone's dying, or how they might have died. I just want to know what happened to the damn trailer." As Dan spoke, his voice became louder and more emphatic. It was immensely cheering. Dan was acting more like his normal self.

"Okay, but you're not going to like it. A bunch of rednecks threatened me last night at a bar, and I'm sure they're behind the vandalism. One of them was a local deputy who reported back to Mullin, so he must be in on it, too. The trailer looks like a squashed tomato can. It could be totaled for all I know. My attorney read Mullin the riot act this morning, and at least I got my rifle back. Now I'm waiting for a deputy to show up to take a report on the trailer. I just hope it's not the same guy I saw last night. Oh—and Mullin's still not giving me permission to go."

A series of expletives exploded in her ear.

"I knew Mullin was running a bent operation." Dan's voice was ominously menacing. "And he's got no right to keep you there any longer. It's bull. You may have your Winchester back, but it still may not be enough to protect you from the sheriff's hoodlums. I want you to come back now, as in immediately. Screw Mullin. And forget the horses. We'll get 'em later."

"I can't do that, Dan. I just can't. If I don't take the horses with me, they'll be sent to slaughter, I know it. If the van comes, and I haven't taken them, Myrna will pocket the money we've given her and put them on the truck."

Another string of expletives ensued. Annie waited until it subsided and rushed on before she could give Dan a chance to speak.

"What I need most right now is a serviceable trailer. I don't know if Jessica's can be repaired in time to be of any use. Hell, I don't even know yet where to take it for repairs."

Annie was dangerously close to tears, but she willed herself not to give in. She'd never cried in front of the sheriff, and she intended to keep it that way.

"I can see I'm about as close to changing your mind as I've ever been, which is never," Dan grumbled into her ear. "Since you insist on being so pigheaded, here's what you need to do. Stop waiting for someone to show up for your report. They'll show up at nine o'clock tonight if they show up at all. If they do, don't expect them to be bringing a fingerprint kit or anything. My guess is they'll pick up your incident report, say thank you very much, and leave. It'll be a waste of time."

Annie felt better. At least she didn't have to sit around anymore. Wolf had assumed they were going on a road trip when he'd hopped into her truck, and she'd recognized his look of disappointment when they'd soon returned to the motel.

"And since you're so damn insistent on taking the horses with you, get on the horn and find a place where you can get the trailer examined," Dan continued. "Can it be towed?"

"My attorney told me not to touch anything. But all the tires are flat, so no, I can't haul it behind my rig. I've already called my roadside assistance club, and this is out of their league."

"Just as well. There might be damage to the under-carriage that would make it unsafe to pull even with a new set of tires. I wish to hell you weren't doing this alone, Annie. I've got half a mind to drive there tonight myself."

"I'll be fine, Dan. Marcus gets back from London to-morrow. He's planning on flying here on Sunday. If I can just get the trailer business sorted out by then, we should be ready to get out of Dodge on Monday."

"What does Marcus know about fixing horse trail-ers?"

"Nothing. But he's a pro at getting people to do what he asks."

"Sure looks like he's got you wrapped around his lit-tle finger. Or did I get that backwards?"

Annie laughed. She and Dan were talking like the old friends they were. And the subject of murder hadn't come up once.

She found what she needed at the local library, an old Carnegie building that she was pleased to notice was several times larger than the sheriff's digs. A polite young woman directed her to the reference works that might help, then stopped by the desk to whisper her own personal suggestion for finding a good mechanic.

"Have you contacted the local airport?" she whis-pered to Annie. "They've got several excellent mechanics on staff there and just might know who could work on your vehicle."

What an excellent suggestion, Annie thought, and told her so. And the librarian was right. The head of maintenance informed her he knew precisely who could handle the job, and at a fair price, too.

"But call the shop now," she was advised. "It's Friday, and if they're not busy, the crew may go home early. Tell them Dave from the airport told you to call."

She reached the owner of the repair shop just in time.

"Andy's Repair."

"Do you fix horse trailers?"

"Lady, we fix anything except broken hearts. Now what can I do for you?"

Annie explained and Andy, incredibly, was intrigued by the challenge.

"The problem is that I need to get the show on the road early next week. I'm picking up four horses, and this is the only hauling rig I have with me," she explained.

"Four horses, you say? Local seller, I assume?"

Last night's encounter at the bar had convinced Annie that not every person she met in eastern Washington held people who rescued feedlot horses in high regard. She decided to fib.

"Actually, the sellers aren't from here. They're in Ellensburg. I dropped off four horses in Spokane earlier in the week and plan to pick up four new ones on the way back. It's a pretty tight time frame."

"What needs fixing?"

Finessing the answer to that question was going to be a bit tricky. Annie took a deep breath and plunged in.

"Well, there was a bit of a party going on in the motel room next to mine last night. I complained about the noise, went out for dinner, and when I came back, found that my neighbors had taken a baseball bat to the trailer."

"Whoa."

"Yup, they really did a number on it. I think most of it is cosmetic, but I really don't know. I know all the lights got smashed. Insurance will cover most of it, although I'm happy to cover the cost of repair myself and get reimbursed later. It's more important to me that I can get back on the road on schedule."

"Does it need to be towed?"

"Sure does. All the tires are flat."

"I'm assuming you told the police about it?"

"Oh, yes," Annie said. "Problem was that the occupants of the room left after they were finished with the trailer."

"I'm sure the cops got their registrations from the front desk. Shouldn't take long to track them down."

"Absolutely. I'm sure the police will find them in no time."

Annie sighed. How had such a simple trip become so utterly convoluted? She was back at the motel, anxiously awaiting the arrival of a thirty-foot flatbed trailer to cart the trailer away and hopefully restore it to good health. She wanted to make this as easy as possible. She'd give Andy her credit card and if he was like most people, he would be happy to accept her story, do the work, and make a lot of money fast. She'd told the mechanic that she'd gladly pay rush rates, as long as the trailer was ready to go by Monday morning. Her biggest concern at the moment was that a deputy would show up just as the trailer was being loaded. She willed the police not to show, as Dan had predicted.

Even Andy was taken aback by the trailer's appearance.

"I've seen a lot of vandalism in my time, but this beats all," he told Annie. "Just exactly what did you say to those party animals to get them so ticked off?"

"Just to keep the noise level down," she replied. "I think alcohol was a factor in their reaction."

"I guess," Andy said doubtfully, but turned to the flatbed to lower the ramp.

To Annie's immense relief, the transfer was made without mishap and without the interference of any law enforcement.

"It doesn't have to look perfect," she assured Andy, as he was about to drive away. "It just has to run and be safe to drive on the freeway."

"Those must be expensive horses that you're hauling," Andy said admiringly. "I can't think of much cargo that's worth the time and money it's going to take to get this trailer in shape to haul again."

"Oh, yes," Annie told him. "These horses are priceless."

She really should call Maria, she thought, but nagging thoughts kept her from picking up her cell and bringing her up to speed. Most of her reticence came from the offhand remark Sheriff Mullin had made to her this morning. Annie interpreted it to mean Maria had once worked at the school but had been laid off, which entirely contradicted what she'd told Annie. She'd been so believable when she regretfully told her she couldn't be at the feedlot last Wednesday morning, when Annie had expected to load and haul the four horses back to the Olympic Peninsula. In fact, now that Annie remembered that conversation, she realized

Maria had actually told Annie when she was expected to be at school—something about 7 AM sharp. What was up with that? If Maria hadn't wanted to be at the feedlot that morning, why lie about it? It was no big deal.

Except that maybe it was. Annie now also remembered how Maria had cut off Donny when she'd started to share the story of how she'd jump-started her car that same morning, at "the crack of dawn," as she'd described it. She'd been about to say where Maria was headed but hadn't gotten the chance. Was that because she hadn't been headed toward school, as she'd told Annie? Or was Annie completely overreacting to a perfectly harmless conversation among friends?

Annie thought about all her encounters so far with the woman. She'd been extraordinarily helpful navigating the final negotiations over the horses, and Annie was impressed by her commitment to saving as many feedlot horses as she could. On the other hand, she'd appeared suspiciously quickly after George's death. And since Annie now assumed she hadn't been at school, Maria obviously had heard about George's death from some other source than the school's police scanner. That was, if she hadn't killed George herself, waited nearby for Annie, then the sheriff's office to show up, and returned on a ruse, but really to make sure no incriminating clue still remained. Dan Stetson had told her that killers sometimes did that.

Yet, she'd remained as long as Annie had, and even Dan thought that was highly unusual behavior for a killer. And she obviously had a good relationship with Harlin Mullin. But now that she knew more about the sheriff's dishonest character, was that a good thing? Who knew what the two of them might have plotted together.

But Maria was a good person, Annie's conscience kept telling her. She saved horses. She dedicated her life to finding homes for lost and forgotten horses that otherwise would end up on the table in France, Canada, or Mexico. Plus, she'd worked with George and Myrna Fullman for years. Why kill George now? And, frankly, why not kill Myrna instead? If Olivia and Maria could be believed, Myrna was the brains and power behind the operation, and killing her would go a lot further in potentially shutting down the feedlot business. Annie assumed that with Myrna's return, the feedlot would return to business as usual. Although she was highly curious about where Myrna had taken herself for two full days. Even Sheriff Mullin had to be suspicious about her unexplained absence from home. She hoped that the sheriff was now grilling Myrna in the same interview room she'd uncomfortably inhabited just a few days before.

But Maria's inconsistencies continued to nag at Annie. What else had Maria said to her—or not said? Well, she'd certainly seemed as surprised as Annie was to learn that Danny Trevor was a hired gun for the local tribe. How believable was that? Maria had been a fixture in the horse-rescue business for years. Surely she would know if Trevor was under contract to help round up wild horses on tribal lands. This was a small community, and Annie knew from personal experience that it was difficult, if not impossible, to keep news like that contained.

And finally, there was Tony. Maria had made a big deal out of confiding in Annie the true nature of their relationship, and Annie had accepted it, hook, line and sinker. But for someone who had carried on a long, al-

beit long-distance, relationship with a guy she supposedly was nuts about, Maria wasn't showing a lot of grief
or emotion over Tony's death. Of course, Maria still believed Tony had died in a tragic accident. Unlike Annie,
she didn't know that Trevor's airplane had been rigged
to explode. But still. Annie thought back to those first
horrible days following the news about the plane crash.
She could not recall seeing a card, a bouquet of flowers,
or even a simple phone message from Maria Hernandez
during that time. Annie was sure she hadn't attended
Tony's memorial service. She would have remembered
that.

Perhaps she should talk to Tony's sisters, who might
recall meeting Maria at the Bellevue conference for
gifted high school students so many years ago. But
then, if Maria and Tony had conducted a largely clan-
destine relationship, the fact that other family members
hadn't been privy to it might not mean a thing.

Annie realized she'd been tearing a flyer touting
pizza delivery in thirty minutes or less into little bits.
The fragments now littered the pale green carpet below
her, and she self-consciously started to pick them up. As
she did so, she noticed Wolf. He was looking at her with
deep concern in his big brown eyes. Wolf knew his mistress, and for Annie to sit around dejectedly was a clear
sign that the planets were misaligned in her private
world. He slowly rose to his feet from his new favorite
place by the air conditioner, padded over to her, and
whined politely for her attention.

She was putty in his hands. She was also tired beyond
measure of not getting the real answers to her questions. Perhaps she couldn't fathom the true nature of
Maria Hernandez, at least right now. But maybe she

could uncover the secret the local tribe had wanted to share only with George and Myrna Fullman a few days before George's death. She stood up decisively and grabbed her keys.

"C'mon, Wolf, let's go. We've already seen the nightlife in Loman. Let's take a walk on the wild side and see what it's like on the rez."

CHAPTER 18

As she drove along the country road heading east, Annie was glad neither Dan nor Marcus was around to tell her this was all a very bad idea. She had no intention of doing anything that would get her any more entangled in George's murder than she already was. After all, she wanted to go home on Monday, as soon as the trailer was roadworthy. But Olivia's story about Trevor's working for the tribe had piqued her interest, and she wanted to know more about the relationship between the natives who lived here and the feedlot owners. She didn't want to step on anyone's toes. She just wanted to understand.

Wolf's head was hanging out the passenger window, and Annie had a feeling this was the first time her dog had actually felt cool and comfortable all day. She ruffled his fur. She looked forward to taking him home, where, on a hot day, he could take a splash on the pond

on her property and find plenty of cool forest ground
to lie upon.

As she approached the Cattle Rustler Café, her stomach predictably reminded her she hadn't eaten in hours,
and Annie was tempted to stop. But the tedium of waiting around had taken up much of the sunlit day, and
Annie did not want to squander a second more than
she had to. She reached into her glove compartment
and found a power bar. Her health-conscious half sister
Lavender must have left it there, she thought. Well, it
wouldn't kill her to eat something that was good for
her—as long as she consumed a big, juicy hamburger
later.

The absence of real mountains on this trip seemed
incongruous to Annie, who had grown up with the
backdrop of the Olympic National Forest. Still, she enjoyed seeing the sun, now arcing over the western part
of the sky, cast its light on the hills and curves of the
land in front of her. She passed the road she'd taken to
get to the ridge above the wild horse run and decreased
her speed. She knew this was the witching hour for deer
and other animals and had no desire to encounter one
in the center of the road. Two miles in, she saw a highway sign for the tribal center up ahead. She slowed
down even more to accommodate any speed limits she
might not have seen in her hurry to get where she was
going. Remaining a law-abiding citizen was still prominent in her mind.

The town that greeted her was more dismal than the
one she'd left. A number of homemade signs heralded
the town limits: HUGS, NOT DRUGS, ALCOHOL FREE ZONE,
METH MEANS DEATH. Poverty draped this town like a worn,
flea-bitten blanket. Most of the residences were old, rusty,
unkempt singles and double-wides, set closely together
with no apparent property boundaries. The few yards in

front of the trailers were sparse patches of dirt dotted by broken and discarded plastic toys. There was not a blade of living grass in sight. Annie looked around for some semblance of industry. She found none. She saw a church, a trading store, and, in the middle of town, a tribal council house that undoubtedly had been built with federal funds and was the best maintained building she'd seen yet. The street running through the gauntlet of shanties and trailers was silent. No one was sitting outside, but then, there were no places to perch, as far as Annie could see. She saw no municipal park where children might play and dogs roam freely. It was a desolate and profoundly depressing way station, and Annie was beginning to regret her decision to come here.

Still, she had arrived and might as well make the best of it. She peered inside the smoky glass that covered the entryway to the council building. No one was inside. Well, what did she think? It was six o'clock on a Friday evening. Did she expect elders to be sitting around, waiting to answer her questions? She slowly turned and motioned for Wolf to return to the truck. This had been a wild goose chase. The only good it had accomplished was getting her outside the four walls of a too-familiar motel room.

"Can I help you?"

A young man—about fifteen, Annie thought—had come up beside her. He was thin and wore the ubiquitous blue jeans and simple T-shirt that teenagers everywhere chose as their uniform. The only deviation in this boy's outfit was the red bandana loosely tied around his neck.

He'd spoken slowly and politely. Annie smiled at him.

"Thank you for asking. I was hoping to see someone

on the tribal council, but I see everyone's gone home, probably for the weekend."

"Yes, nobody's here. We have a receptionist during the week, but the council only meets on certain days. You have to make an appointment. There's a certain procedure, and it's not often easy to get to address our elders."

The boy said this without inflection, as if this were simply the way of the world, which, Annie realized, it was, at least here on the reservation.

"That's too bad. I'm only here for a few more days, and I was hoping someone could answer a question for me."

"What is it?"

The simplicity of his question and his earlier response touched Annie. It was as if he had no guile, no agenda, but simply stated what was true and important. Talking to him was a refreshing change from what she'd encountered with most teenage boys back home.

"It's a bit complicated," she told him, smiling again. "If you have a few moments, I'll tell you. Would you mind if we sat in the shade? I've got a dog in my truck who would love to be outside."

In lieu of answering, the boy simply gestured to a small patio in the back of the council building. There were a few tables and, Annie saw, merciful shade provided by a large overhang.

"Great. Let me get Wolf."

"You have a wolf?" This seemed to interest the boy.

"Just a dog named Wolf. But he can be ferocious if he needs to be. He's come to my rescue more than a few times."

Wolf bounded out of the truck and up to Annie. He eagerly looked at the boy, sniffed his hands, and promptly sat on his haunches in front of him.

"You passed the test," she said, jokingly.

The boy didn't smile back. "I had a dog once. He was killed when I was eight. I called him Roger."

"Roger? I don't think I've ever known a dog with that name before."

"I was watching a lot of cop shows back then. The police would always say, 'Roger this' and 'Roger that.' I thought it was a cool name."

Annie knew she was not going to ask how the dog had died. She didn't want to know.

The two sat in opposite chairs on the patio. The merest of breezes fluttered over the patio. Wolf lifted his head from the concrete pavement where he was resting and let it waft over him, his eyes still closed.

"I'm Annie Carson, by the way," she told the boy, and extended her hand.

"My name's Colin. My tribal name is Sahale."

"Pleased to meet you, Colin. Or would you prefer to be called by your native name?"

"Colin's fine." He sat quietly in front of her, waiting for her to speak.

"I live on the Olympic Peninsula," she began. "Our primary tribes are the Quinault, Makah, and S'Kallam."

The boy nodded. "I have a cousin who's a Makah. He lives on the ocean."

Annie nodded in return. "Colin, I came to your part of the world to buy four horses that are for sale in the feedlot in Loman."

She watched him carefully. She couldn't imagine it, but if Colin supported rounding up wild horses for slaughter, she wanted to know now. But Colin simply inclined his head slightly. He was not giving her a lot of information to go on.

"A friend of mine was supposed to come with me.

He'd flown here earlier to look at the horses. But he was killed in a plane crash coming back, so I'm making the trip alone."

She waited for a response, any response. But Colin was motionless and gave no hint of whether this was news or not.

"The woman who sold the horses to me—to us—wrote a receipt on the back of an envelope." She dug it out of her saddlebag purse and handed the Xeroxed copy to Colin so he could easily see the PRIVATE AND CONFIDENTIAL lettering.

"I want to know what secret business the tribe has with these people." She paused. "It's very important to me."

The boy stared at the Xeroxed copy of the envelope, using both hands to hold it. Annie willed herself to be patient as the boy continued to examine the words, as if they held some hidden meaning he could not yet decipher.

Without warning, the boy suddenly crumpled the piece of paper with one fist. The crackling sound of crushed paper startled her and she involuntarily jumped. She stared at Colin.

"Why did you do that?" Annie felt utterly confused.

"Let me ask *you* something." The boy looked at her defiantly.

"Go ahead."

"What was the name of your friend? The one who died in the plane crash?

Annie's lips felt dry. "Tony. Tony Elizalde."

The boy looked back at her, his eyes softening a bit.

"Come with me," he said, rising from the table. Colin self-consciously handed the crumpled paper back to her and Annie accepted it in silence.

She quickly realized that "come with me" really meant for her to drive Colin and herself to a place he wanted her to see. She wasn't too concerned about her safety. Colin seemed like a nice kid, and his reaction to seeing a letter addressed to the feedlot owners was appropriate—she hoped. Besides, she had Wolf riding shotgun in the extended cab and her own rifle was now firmly affixed to the gun rack above her.

"Hop in," she said, opening the truck with her key. "I'll get the air-conditioning going."

Like Wolf, Colin preferred riding with the window down.

They bumped along the dusty road out of town, backtracking on the same miles Annie had just traversed. Ten minutes of silence passed, until Colin pointed to a small road leading off to the right.

"Turn here," he said.

The road was marked PRIVATE and was accompanied by another sign that cautioned any trespassers that they would be prosecuted and shot, and not necessarily in that order. But Colin seemed unaffected by the warning, and Annie made no mention of it. The going was rough. Hairpin turns made it difficult to navigate the narrow road, and about a quarter mile in, Colin signaled for her to pull over to a small grove to her left.

"It's easier to walk from here," he explained.

Annie nodded and locked her truck. Wolf raced on ahead, following the road. Colin strode ahead of Annie, who'd taken the time to pluck two bottles of water out of her cooler. She could barely see the boy and dog up ahead. They were walking quickly, and the heat made Annie's progress indescribably slow, at least so she thought. Thankfully, the incline turned downward after ten minutes, and for the first time in days, Annie felt as if she was walking in the cool of natural shade. It was wonderful.

She saw Colin and Wolf waiting for her in a small

grove of quaking aspen. When she reached them, she handed one bottle of water to the boy, who accepted it with a quick nod of thanks. Annie was pleased to see him offer Wolf a drink from the bottle after he had slaked his own thirst.

"We have to be quiet," Colin said. "There's not much of a path anymore. Try not to disturb any rocks. The rattlers like to sleep underneath them."

Annie hoped that Wolf had absorbed this advice as well. Letting the boy and Wolf precede her, she left the shade of the trees and began to carefully pick her way through the exposed scrub before her. Going downhill was almost worse than uphill, she thought. There were no branches to hold on to, and the path, such as it was, afforded no level purchase. Once he'd reached the bottom, Colin held out one hand and guided Annie to the edge of a small stream that had largely dried up. He put one finger to his lips, the universal sign for silence. Annie nodded. All she could hear were the click and buzz of insects in the distance and the sound of Wolf's panting breath. Colin walked along the side of the creek, his worn sneakers making no sound. Annie tried to emulate him with less success. Wolf easily trotted alongside them, his big paws noiseless.

When Colin squatted, Annie immediately followed his move while automatically reaching out for Wolf to still him. She held her breath and looked at where Colin had trained his eyes. She knew in an instant that what she was seeing was both sacred and secret.

Before them, in a sylvan glen, grazed a family of horses. The herd was smaller in size than the one Annie had seen streaming through the canyon days before. A black mustang stallion stood vigil on a small rise behind the herd, while several mares and their foals grazed below on nubs of brown vegetation. One of them, a pinto, was clearly pregnant. She was significantly under-weight, Annie saw, and that made her condition more obvious. Her stomach was pendulous in comparison to the rest of her body, and Annie observed hollows on both sides of her tail, evidence that foaling could be only days away. She looked inquiringly at the boy.

"Maybe three, four days at the most," he said with a slight shrug of his shoulders.

"Is she well? Progressing normally?"

Annie had seen two mares give birth in her lifetime. The first time, she had been ten years old and had watched a mare deliver in the field. All had gone well, and Annie had been in awe of how, after a few false starts, the little foal had staggered to its feet and stood, wobbling on its spindly legs. Before she went home that day, the foal was running and kicking up its heels in the field. The second time, Annie had been an adult and responded to the desperate call of a friend whose mare was trying to foal but having difficulty. That birth had not ended as happily.

Annie looked at the pinto again. She seemed perfectly content, but it was so hard to know. She wasn't a vet, nor was she in the breeding business. She turned to Colin.

"Have you seen this before?"

"Many times. I think she will do fine." Colin paused. "I have been protecting her for many months, ever since I knew she was in foal. But now, I am concerned. The men who round up our horses may have discovered my hiding place and will come look for her and the others. I think this is what the letter from our tribe said to the people at the feedlot. That more horses would be coming to the feedlot before the herd is shipped." He paused for a moment. "You know what they will do to the foal."

By now, Annie knew full well, and she was sickened by the thought.

"How did you meet Tony?"

"Through my little sister, Aleisha. We take turns guarding the herd. Tony saw her walking down the road from the village. He was coming to talk to the elders, just as you wanted to. He'd heard what some of our people do to the horses. Aleisha took him to our secret place, and he promised that he would save the pinto and her foal for us. And then he died."

Annie was profoundly moved by the boy's simple yet eloquent words.

"Don't worry, Colin. I'll make sure the pinto is saved. If I can, I'll try to save everyone in the harem." Annie knew this was the term most people used to describe small bands of wild horses. She held out her hand.

"Any promise Tony made extends to me."

Colin solemnly shook her outstretched hand. As always, his response was simple and direct.

"Thank you, lady."

Annie realized that, for the first time since she'd arrived here, she truly trusted someone. And someone trusted her in return.

Driving back to Browning, Annie began to think about the logistics of accomplishing what she'd just assured Colin she'd do. She'd already committed to taking one other horse, the Thoroughbred Eddie, and now she'd told Colin that she'd save the pinto and her foal, not to mention the other four mares and their offspring, as well as the mustang stallion. At this rate, she was going to need more than Jessica's repaired horse trailer to make good on her promises. She was going to need a massive caravan.

The problem was, she thought, the longer she stayed in this town, the more tempting it became to save just one more horse. But who was she to make the decision about which horses to take? The initial decision to buy four feedlot horses had been approved by the board of Alex's Place. Travis, the board chair, was all for the idea, but Annie wasn't sure he'd feel as enthusiastic about bringing home more than twice the original number pledged and paid for, especially several newborn foals. She owed it to Travis to let him know what she'd managed to get herself into and hoped she would not incur his wrath.

Annie had never seen Travis angry, but she had no doubt he could be a fierce adversary if he felt that Annie had gone too far. Which, in fact, she had. She knew this and dreaded the potential backlash from other board members as well. Knowing Marcus, he might be more amused than annoyed at her softhearted promises, but perhaps not. Months before, he'd hired her to help divest his wife's estate of twenty extremely expensive horses trained for dressage and as hunter/jumpers. He probably wouldn't be thrilled to know that a herd nearly matching that number had been spoken for in eastern Washington—and these were horses who would require a lot of work, both to bring them back to health and to train. Tony had intelligently selected four feedlot horses that would best fit the needs of the boys who would be staying at the new ranch. Her selections were made simply on the basis that the horses didn't deserve to die when so much life was left in them. What was she thinking?

Annie flipped on her CD player to distract herself from ruminating any longer about her hasty decision. If worst came to worst, she would take Eddie, the pinto, and her foal and care for them herself. And hope that the tribe was not privy to the location of the remaining members of the harem. Which she ached to save, as well.

It was close to nine o'clock when she rolled into Browning, and on a whim, Annie decided to change motels after all. True, it was only a quarter mile from the scene of the vandalism, but why should she stay in a place that didn't protect its guests from lowlife thugs? She pulled into the town's only competition and walked into the reception area.

"Howdy." The man behind the counter looked like a retired rancher who had decided on a second job to help pay his beer bill. Telltale spidery red lines creased his ruddy nose and cheekbones.

"Got any rooms for the next three nights?"

"How many beds?

"One's fine."

"Well, I got one upstairs, and one on the ground floor. You got a preference?"

"Which is quieter?"

"Upstairs. We got an elevator, too. It's small and sometimes don't work too fast, but it'll get your luggage up there."

"What's your pet policy?"

"If they're well behaved, they can stay for free. If not, we'll ding your credit card after you leave."

"Deal."

Annie completed the transaction and drove the short four blocks to her first motel. It took her five minutes to pack and for Wolf to eat his second dinner. Annie had already shared with him a hamburger she'd procured from a fast-food place on the outskirts of town. She'd have loved to return to the Cattle Rustler Café but remembered just in time that she'd told Mindy she was on her way to Spokane, and she'd told enough fibs for one day.

She entered the small reception area to return her key. The clerk on duty was someone she'd never seen before.

"Anything wrong, miss? You're checking out early. Registration says you've paid up through next Tuesday."

"That was before you let a bunch of rednecks trash my trailer on your property and then denied that you saw it happen."

The clerk drew back sharply. "I wasn't aware of that. Have you reported it to the police?"

"Of course. They've got it well in hand." A deputy's card had been stuck in her door when she returned. She figured she'd drop off the incident report tomorrow. That was, if the cop shop was open on weekends.

"I'm very sorry. I wasn't on shift that night—Brett was." The clerk looked down and Annie could swear his face showed signs of guilt. "Tell you what. I'll just refund the nights you're not staying—after tonight, of course. It's a shame what happened."

And you know exactly what did happen, Annie thought, *just like Bill.* The only difference was this clerk seemed to have a working frontal cortex and felt a modicum of shame.

That transaction completed, Annie drove back to her new temporary home. She eschewed the elevator—it did look old and creaky and was incredibly small—and walked up three flights of stairs. Her new room was a definite step up. It had a real HDTV and even offered HBO. The kitchen accommodations were lacking, but at least she had a brand-new mini fridge and microwave that didn't smell like burning popcorn. With any luck, the coffee would be better, too.

But the landline she'd had in her old room was missing in this one. She trudged back down again to reception to inquire about breakfast hours. Who knew, perhaps eggs Benedict would be on the menu here.

"Six to ten," came the prompt answer from the desk clerk. "Just turn right off that hallway. Breakfast room is on your left."

Annie thanked the man and paused. She now was staying in the motel Tony had checked into over a week ago. She wondered if the desk clerk would remember him.

"A friend of mine stayed here not long ago," she began. "His name was Tony Elizalde. Do you, by any chance, remember him?"

"Sure do. He was a nice young feller. Terrible about him going down in that plane with Danny Trevor."

Annie's heart skipped a beat. She hadn't expected the clerk to be so forthright. She had been getting used to receiving half answers to her innocent questions.

"Yes, we were all shocked by his death back home. I know it's a long shot, but did Tony leave anything in his room? He was only here the one night."

"Not that I'm aware of. Didn't even go up to his room after he registered. Just took the key, turned around, and left. Didn't see him again until the next morning when he checked out. A local gal was with him then." The desk clerk grinned at her.

"Oh? He'd mentioned that he was going to look up a friend when he was here." This was a fib, but just a small one, her Good Angel acknowledged.

"Yup, I recognized her. Maria Hernandez. I've known her all her life, ever since she was a little girl. She came down with him when he checked out on Thursday. That pilot feller was waiting for both of them."

"Danny Trevor was *here*?"

"Yup, said he'd been hired to take the man home across the mountains."

"Did you know Danny very well?"

"Just knew he was one of the bush pilots in the area. Good reputation, I gather. He'd flown up in Alaska for a time, then for one of the big commercial outfits. Have they found out yet what happened to that plane?"

Annie swept aside the question. She had one of her own and knew she had to phrase it carefully.

"How about Tony's friend, Maria? I assume she was meeting Danny Trevor for the first time, too."

"Hell, no. They were old friends, the way they greeted each other. Big hugs, you know, 'nice to see you again' kind of thing. Tony was meeting Danny for the first time, but I got the impression that Maria and Danny went way back."

As Annie trudged back up to her room, she chalked up another point against her new friend. If it was true that Maria and Danny were old friends, then what were the odds that she knew about Danny's work for the tribe?

Annie suspected they were very good, indeed.

CHAPTER 19

It was six o'clock in the morning. Annie's cell had awakened her with a soft vibrating buzz, its signal that a new text had arrived and was awaiting her perusal. She eagerly grabbed the phone, conscious that she was rapidly becoming as addicted to the device as her friends. And she'd ragged *them* for years for their devotion to the stupid things. What was happening to her?

The text was from Marcus, and read:

I'm on my way. In-flight map puts me somewhere over Iceland. See you soon, and stay safe.

Annie hadn't realized how much she'd wanted Marcus with her until she knew that it was actually going to happen. And she was very glad she'd upgraded her motel accommodations. It wasn't quite on the scale that Marcus had provided in Port Chester, but it was the best she could do. She quickly replied with her own text:

Can't wait to see you. Change in address. I'm now in Browning's BEST motel, endorsed by AAA.

She typed in the address and pushed SEND.

Buoyed by Marcus's update, Annie threw back the covers and started her day. To her regret, the dining options here were little better than in her previous lodgings. She walked the two blocks to the local café and, after breakfasting on eggs and toast, braved the icy chill of the overly air-conditioned IGA to raid the deli aisles. There wasn't much to choose from, but she selected the most expensive bottle of red wine she could find, another of sparkling water, a circle of domestic Brie, and a small box of crackers. She would eschew drinking if any driving was to be done, but there was nothing stopping her from enjoying a bit of wine in her room with Marcus, was there? She imagined their happy reunion, now a mere twenty-four hours away, and felt a wave of happiness flow through her. Her body already was anticipating Marcus's first warm kiss.

"Did you find everything you needed?" the grocery checker patiently asked Annie for the third time.

Annie snapped out of her daydream and dug into her purse for her cash, managing to spill all her loose coins onto the checker's side of the counter at the same time.

"Sorry," she said to the clerk, who calmly picked up the change and handed it back to her.

"Have a nice day," the clerk said unenthusiastically when Annie's few purchases were bagged.

Annie gave her a big smile. She certainly intended to try. Especially since she knew the next day would be even nicer.

It was still early enough to walk a few more blocks without fear of sunstroke, so after quickly stowing her

purchases in her room, Annie whistled for Wolf to ac-
company her down to the sheriff's office. As she'd suspected, the front door was locked and the printed
office hours made it clear that any police assistance
over the weekend would require a call to 911. Annie
stuffed the incident report back in her purse and
turned back toward the motel. What could she do for
the rest of the long day that stretched out in front of
her? Maria, she knew, would be at the feedlot, but this
was Tinker's day to help. Then she remembered—
Myrna was back. Presumably, she'd sobered up by now
to handle the feedlot in her usual cruel and tyrannical
way

According to Annie's phone, Maria had not tried to
contact her at all the previous day, and the realization
bothered her. In theory, this meant Maria didn't even
know about the vandalism to the trailer, or Annie's new
living arrangements. It seemed odd for Maria not to
call. She hadn't expected the woman to dog her every
footstep—she knew Maria had a family of her own—but
after the ruckus at the bar, it was strange that she hadn't
followed up to make sure Annie was all right.

Or, perhaps Maria felt the same way about Annie's
failure to check in yesterday. Annie had never spent a
lot of time worrying about what other people might or
might be feeling when it was so much easier to pick up
the phone to find out in person. She did so, now.

But all she got was Maria's voicemail. Very well, then.
She would leave a message. She waited for the familiar
beep, the cue to start talking.

"Hi, Maria, it's Annie. Just wanted to give you an update. You may have heard that I came back to the motel
on Thursday to a thoroughly trashed trailer. I'm assuming it was the work of the bar thugs. It's being repaired
as we speak. I've also switched motels, and am hoping

to leave on Monday along with the trailer and the horses. Oh, and Myrna's back, if you didn't already know. I guess that means the horses are back to being cared for by their wicked stepmother. Call when you can, and please tell me my horses are okay."

Perhaps she should just go to the feedlot herself to check on the horses. But Annie could not forget Myrna's dramatic outcry to Sheriff Mullin yesterday. The woman seemed convinced that Annie was her husband's killer. Either that or, as George's real killer, she was doing a damn good job pretending that was the case. Exactly how would Myrna's accusations affect Annie's ability to take the feedlot horses on Monday? Would she refuse to hand them over to the person she believed had killed her husband even though the horses had been paid for in full?

No, checking up on the feedlot horses alone was a bad idea. She had no idea what weapons Myrna might own, and there was no point in going over if it would just antagonize the woman who held the proverbial reins, particularly if she thought Annie had her own suspicions about her killing her husband. It was far more sensible to wait until Marcus was with her when she did visit. She was sure even Myrna wouldn't shoot her if she was accompanied by a man who exuded the calm strength of character that Myrna clearly lacked, and George had apparently never had.

The ebullience she'd had felt just an hour ago was replaced with a nagging feeling of dread—an emotion that had plagued her too much of the trip. It was so difficult to plan one's life when you were accused of murder and no one would tell you when you could leave or what you could take with you when you did.

She was anxious to know how Andy was faring with the trailer, but thought it only polite to wait a few hours to let him work on the rig before pestering him. That left her with only one place left to go—the county airport. She told herself she merely wanted to find out more about Danny Trevor and his relationship with the local tribe. Deep down, she knew she wanted to know more about why his plane had crashed and who had been so desperate to kill the pilot that he or she didn't mind taking Tony out along with him. Besides, Travis had fully expected her to talk to the airport employees, so why shouldn't she? She knew she was treading on dangerous ground but didn't care. If she was prohibited from talking to Dan about what he'd learned from the FAA and NTSB, then she'd do her best to find out herself.

The county airport sign appeared just where she'd remembered it on her way to Duncan, two days before. She turned left at the sign and drove eight miles down a straight and very dusty two-lane road until she saw a row of tidy hangars before her. A large commercial sign out front that read DUNCAN-LOMAN INTERNATIONAL AIRPORT confirmed that she'd arrived at the right place. The sign amused her. She could see a number of prop planes inside the complex, but suspected they were incapable of crossing the Atlantic without frequent fuel stops. What foreign country were they talking about? Oh, of course—Canada was just a couple hundred miles to the north. *That* foreign country.

She drove in through the open gates in the high chain-link fence that encircled the airport, and pulled into the visitor parking space with the most shade. Stepping outside, she shielded her eyes from the sun and took in the tiny airport. Aside from the row of hangars on the left, she could see only one other building on the place. It was tall, made of galvanized steel, and had two industrial-sized doors that gaped open. It had to be the maintenance shop, she thought, and calling to Wolf, she walked toward it, passing a small hut with the sign CUSTOMS along the way.

Just outside the taller building, she paused. Several banks of commercial lights were overhead, but they were no match for the sun outside. She blinked, trying to regain her normal sight.

"What can I do for you?" A man in industrial overalls was approaching her, a giant wrench in one hand.

"I'm looking for Dave." Annie had decided on the drive over that her best opening gambit would be to thank the man who had suggested calling Andy's Repair.

"He won't be back until Monday. Can I help you with something?"

The man, whose sewn-on name tag identified him as Mack, seemed eager to get back to work but was doing his best to be polite.

Oh, hell, Annie thought. She might as well go for broke. The worst that could happen would be that she was asked to leave.

"My name's Annie," she began. "Annie Carson. I'm a friend of Tony Elizalde, the man who died in the plane crash with Danny Trevor. I'm in the area, and really was just hoping to find out more about the crash and why it might have occurred."

Mack stared blankly at her. This was not going well.

"I realize you've probably already been asked those questions by officials. I've been told that the NS—the NS—"

"The NTSB." Mack was at least kind enough to help her out.

"Right, that the NTSB has been here. I was just hoping someone who works here could give me an update. Since I'm in the area," she finished lamely.

Mack put down his wrench, which made Annie feel slightly more at ease.

"Not a lot to tell. I didn't work on Danny's plane, but the guy who always did the preflight inspection said it was good to go, and Danny always did a once-over himself. Plane took off fine. I was here that day and saw it taxi and take off. As to why a fire would start in the cockpit over Snoqualmie, I haven't a clue. There's a rumor that it was rigged, but it doesn't make any sense. Danny wasn't the most popular pilot here, but as far as I know, he didn't have any real enemies. How about your guy?"

It was a fair question. "Loved by everyone, including children and animals of every size," Annie said sadly. "His death broke everyone's heart."

"Sorry to hear that."

"Did anyone here get a chance to look at the wreckage?"

The man shrugged.

"We do aircraft salvage, but because the airplane crashed so far away, it didn't make sense to haul it back here. The insurance company took what was left of the Cessna and must have found a closer place to part it out."

"I wasn't aware that there was anything left to save."

"Probably wasn't. My guess is the fire destroyed anything that might have been reconstructed. Still, the fuselage was worth something."

Annie was now at a crossroads. She could ask Mack if he knew how the Cessna might have been rigged, but she suspected that if the NTSB knew, it was keeping that information close and only sharing with law enforcement. Even if he knew more than what Dan already had told her, it was unlikely that Mack, a stranger, was going to fill in any of the many blanks in the story. No, it was better to query him about Danny Trevor, someone he definitely had known.

In the few seconds all this had gone through Annie's mind, Mack had been steadily looking at her. Now he gave her an encouraging half smile.

"Look, I met your friend before the flight. He seemed like a nice guy. If you want, you can ask me questions while I work. I'm in the middle of a dynamic prop balance on the Cessna in here, and it has to get done by today. The owner's coming into town tonight and expects to fly it tomorrow."

Annie peered at the airplane she saw parked in the middle of the hangar.

"Is that the same kind of plane Danny Trevor flew?"

"Pretty much. It's a Cessna 182, a slightly younger model. It basically runs just the same, just has a few more bells and whistles."

"What was he like? Danny Trevor, I mean. I know he was supposed to be a good pilot, but that's about all I know."

"You mean as a person? Hard to tell. Wasn't married, I know that. Not sure about any kids. When he first came here, he used to brag about his days as a commercial airline pilot, and all the babes that would fall into his lap. Then someone started the rumor that he'd been canned from the commercial job. The story I heard was he got busted on a random drug test. All I know is Danny stopped talking about the good old days after that."

"Did he? Did he have a drug problem?"

"Not that I could see. He'd toss back a few beers with the rest of us, but I never saw him drunk. You really can't have a drug or alcohol problem in this job. Not if you want to last in it."

"But if Danny failed a drug test, why was he still allowed to fly?"

"Oh, you don't lose your ticket just because you get fired. As long as Danny could pass his annual medical exam, he was good to go."

"Was he close to anyone around here?" Mack had already said the pilot didn't have any real enemies. But did he have any real friends?

"Close buds, you mean? Not really, but then, I only saw him at the airport. Don't recall ever seeing him outside of work. Around here, he was pretty friendly with AJ, the guy who took care of his aircraft and did his annual inspections. I got the feeling that they'd known each other before, maybe in Alaska. That's where Danny flew before coming over here."

"So both the pilot and his plane have to pass a yearly exam in order to keep flying?"

"That's about it, besides a biennial flight review for private pilots. If you fly commercial, it's an annual checkride. Of course, Danny always opted for the owner-assisted aircraft inspections. We call them 'trunk annuals.' They cost a lot less, and if the pilot is good about taking care of his aircraft, they're easy to get through."

"Does AJ still work here? I'd like to talk to him if he does."

"Not since the plane crash. I think he took it hard. He was just a part-timer anyway, and I think he had another business on the side."

"Do you know how to reach him?"

"No, but Dave might. Or Kevin, he's the boss. They'll both be here on Monday."

Throughout the conversation, Mack had been working on the propeller. He now moved around to the left side of the plane and opened the small door to the cockpit.

"Time to see if all my hard work has paid off," he told Annie with a wink.

"Are you going to start it?" Annie asked, a bit alarmed. She wasn't sure how Wolf would react to the simultaneous roar of the engine and the whirr of the propeller.

"Yup. Want to climb in and see?"

Annie hesitated for just a second. "Yes, but let me first put my dog in the truck. He's not used to airplane noise."

"Roger that."

"She was leading Wolf out of the building and instantly thought of Colin and his ill-fated dog. She fleetingly wondered if Colin's secret herd, safe and sheltered for now, would meet the same fate as Roger.

Returning to the building, she heard Mack call, "Climb on in." She looked over and saw him in the left seat of the cockpit, leaning toward her to give her a hand through the copilot's door. Once she was seated, he handed her a set of headphones with an attached mike.

"Might want to put these on."

Annie did as he suggested.

"Can you hear me?" Annie nodded. Mack's voice through the headset came through loud and clear.

"Now I'm going to start 'er up." Mack reached over to turn and pull out a knob on the far left. He pushed it in and locked it closed, then turned the ignition key. The engine roared to life. Annie watched the propeller blades flutter for a nanosecond, then dissolve into a dizzying whirr of motion. Just sitting in the plane while it was pulsing with such power was thrilling, but Annie had no way of knowing if Mack's work had been successful. She glanced at him, and he smiled broadly.

"Look at the instrument panel," he told her through the headset. "See how all the needles are holding steady?"

Annie nodded her assent.

"If the propeller's off balance, it can make the gauges real jumpy," Mack explained. "Particularly in the gyro horizon and the compass." He pointed to both. "The pilot needs to know that the information he's reading from the dash is accurate. Balancing the propeller reduces the vibration that can cause that. Makes for a smoother ride, too."

Annie looked at the dashboard in front of her and the impressive array of gauges. It looked terribly complicated.

Mack turned off the engine and took off his headset.

"I think this old girl is good to go." The propeller was just beginning to lose its momentum, and the blades were nearly visible again.

"Why did you pull out that knob over there?" Annie pointed to the small cylinder to his left that he had pulled out and pushed in.

"That's the primer. Ever drive an old farm truck? It works just like that. Except in a Cessna, the fuel's stored up in the wings. It's gravity fed to the primer. Helps start the engine."

Annie was majorly impressed.

A half hour later, Annie was on the road again, this time headed toward Andy's Repair. She'd thanked Mack for his time, not to mention the small lesson in airplane maintenance, and assured him she'd call the office on Monday for AJ's phone number. She didn't know when she'd have a chance to talk to him, but it wouldn't hurt to have it on hand.

Her cell phone buzzed for the second time that day as Annie was gassing up and considering whether she should buy junk food here or back in Browning. This time, the text was from Dan, and it was a terse **Call me**.

The gas-pump nozzle clicked off, signifying the tank was full. Annie didn't wait for the receipt to slowly spit out of the island station and jumped into her truck to maneuver it to a place where she could talk undisturbed. Wolf was in the backseat, sleeping, oblivious to the vanilla ice cream Annie had just been about to buy.

"What's up?"

"FBI K-9s found the detonator this afternoon."

"Where was it?"

"In some bushes near the lodge. Turns out it was an old cell phone, rigged to go off from a simple phone call. All the miscreant had to do was dial the number, let it ring, and it detonated whatever IED he'd planted on the Cessna. The feds also found a pair of gloves in the same area. Could be coincidental, could be what the killer was wearing when he set it up there. They aren't ski gloves, so we're hopeful."

"What do the feds think?"

"I'm not sure they do think. They just investigate. No one's making a claim that either Tony or Trevor was the intended victim, but it seems pretty clear to me that the pilot was targeted, not our boy."

"Absolutely. I've found out a few things, too."

"Annie! You are not to go around investigating. Listen to your attorney!"

"Hah! I never thought I'd hear those words come out of your mouth. Do you want to know or not?"

"I'm not sure I should. In fact, I know I shouldn't. But go ahead, shoot."

"Trevor was fired from his job as a commercial airline pilot for a dirty drug test. He went to Alaska for a time, then moved here. Not many friends, no family to speak of. His best buddy was the maintenance guy who took care of his plane in Alaska and moved here along with Trevor."

"Okay. So far, that's interesting background, but it doesn't exactly tell me why someone would want him killed."

"I'm getting to that. Last year, Trevor signed a contract with the local tribe to scour their territory for bands of wild horses. Once he'd pinpointed from the sky the areas the horses were using for grazing, it was easy to round them up. I talked to a woman who saw his plane pass her animal sanctuary toward the reservation like clockwork. She knew that was her signal to negotiate the sale of the new influx of horses that would arrive at the Loman feedlot the next week."

"She's hardly providing proof that members of the tribe are doing this."

"Wait, Dan! There's more. I talked to a native boy who knows this goes on for a fact. And the receipt I got to bail out the horses? It's on an envelope from the tribal council to the feedlot owners."

"It's sounding a bit more plausible. But still, Annie—"

"Dan, you can't appreciate it until you've been here a few days, but this is an extremely divided county. One half thinks rounding up wild horses and selling them for slaughter is just fine, it's the way of the Wild West and always will be. But there are just as many people who are sickened by the knowledge that this goes on. People like me. Any one of them could have wanted Danny Trevor dead. He was making it incredibly easy for the tribe to solve their wild-horse problem. In the most horrific and cruel way, I might add."

"Listen to yourself, Annie! 'People just like me.' No wonder you're still a suspect when you say things like that out loud. From now on, we're not talking. Period. It's too damn dangerous. How's the trailer?"

"I thought we weren't talking," Annie said huffily.

"Just answer the question, then I'll let you go. Is it going to be fixed? And where's Marcus? Shouldn't he be there by now?"

Annie was tempted to remind Dan that the man he was so anxious to see come to her aid was the same man he'd arrested for murder a mere six months ago. She decided to restrain herself.

"The trailer's in a shop right now, and the owner has promised to deliver a serviceable product by Monday. In exchange for a lot of money, I might add, but Jessica's insurance will ultimately cover it. I'm headed over to the mechanic's now to check on its progress."

"Good."

Annie knew the word was meant as grudging praise.

"As far as Marcus, he's just seen the northern lights off Iceland and is due to arrive on schedule, which is sometime tomorrow morning."

"So all you have to do is keep out of trouble until then."

"Don't I always?"

CHAPTER 20

Annie decided to let her smartphone's map app lead her to the mechanic's shop. It occurred to her that she was becoming more dependent on the small hand-held device than perhaps she should be. But it was so helpful and so informative. And so far, it had proved a much better navigator than she was by nature. But now, she was sure the bouncing blue ball was leading her far afield. It was instructing her to turn into the most suburban setting she'd seen since coming to eastern Washington.

But, as always, the app was right. Andy's Repair Shop was situated in back of his split-level rambler home, a massive commercial garage nearly the size of his residence. She parked her truck on the grass beside it. Inside, she saw the trailer hoisted several feet off the ground and Andy stretched out on a dolly, working underneath. Old-time country-western music blared from a portable

GARNER

radio on a nearby counter. The shop was festooned with calendars and posters sent by trucking vendors and companies. A vivacious, scantily clad female was the focal point in most. Another sign stating IT'S FIVE O'CLOCK SOMEWHERE! was pinned to the inside of a side door, and Annie noticed a small refrigerator close by. She doubted it contained tools of his trade.

"How's it going?" she called out as she approached the garage. Andy didn't answer. He was intently trying to screw something into the undercarriage that Annie couldn't see. She didn't want to scare him to death, so she cleared her throat and, when that elicited no response, stood by silently and waited for Andy to emerge.

Several minutes ticked by. Annie was getting impatient, but she also was impressed by the man's dedication to a job she'd practically begged him to do. She had no idea what damage had been done underneath the trailer, and knew it might well be the area that most compromised the trailer's restorability.

Finally, Andy pushed himself out, sat up, and mopped his brow with a red kerchief.

Annie stepped forward. "What'd you find?"

Andy yelped and jumped at the same time. The dolly silently slid out from underneath his legs and the mechanic slid ungracefully to the ground.

"I'm very sorry," Annie said, meaning it. "I've been here for a bit but didn't want to disturb you. I had this image of some hydraulic lift failing if I spoke and the whole trailer crashing down on you."

Andy laughed, a bit shakily. "Not likely. I mostly work alone, so I'm pretty good at making safety my first priority. But I appreciate your waiting, just the same."

"I take it the party revelers weren't content to just bash the sides in?"

Annie had reminded herself on the way over that she

had to stick to the story she'd told him. She wasn't sure why it was so important that the mechanic not know that local townsmen had been the real assailants. But for some reason, she felt pinning the blame on transitory visitors to his hick town more prudent.

"Actually, no, it looks pretty clean under there," Andy said, rising to his feet. "I just wanted to make sure the brake system was still intact. It is. That's a lucky break. I'm not sure I could have replaced it by the time you need it."

"Excellent. How's everything else look? I mean, the stuff that's not visible."

"Well, the lighting system needs a lot of work. The party animals managed to break out every light inside and out and screw up the wires. Getting them repaired will take up most of today and tomorrow morning. Tomorrow afternoon, I've got a couple of guys coming over to help me take out as many of the dents as I can."

Annie hoped none of Andy's helpers were related to the men responsible for putting them there.

"How about the windows? Will you have time to replace those?"

"Afraid not. What I can do is make sure all the broken glass is removed. I'll give you the name of a glass doctor I know in Ellensburg. I'll do the research and let him know what he needs to order. He probably can do the job in a day, if you can spare the downtime."

Annie had forgotten she'd told him her next stop was a mere two hours away, and she would be carrying no horses with her.

"No, that's great. I'll make the time. Thanks for thinking ahead."

"Happy to help."

Annie looked critically at the lettering on the side. She wanted it gone.

"And you will be able to remove the graffiti?" she asked anxiously.

"Not a problem. You'll probably want your regular mechanic to restore the finish once you get back home. It'll look a lot better when you take it on Monday, but not brand-new, which this trailer appears to be."

"It is. This actually was its first time out."

"What a shame. Police any closer to catching the people who did it?"

"They say it'll be real easy to find the ringleader. And that should lead to all of them."

"Ringleader? Sounds like someone caught 'em in the act. Did you see anything? I thought you were at dinner or something when it happened."

Annie silently cursed herself for being so stupid but gave Andy a confident smile.

"Yes, I just learned today. Apparently there were several eyewitnesses who could describe the principal players quite well."

Annie told herself she wasn't exactly lying. She knew darn well that if someone would just sit on Deputy Goddard, he could give the names and addresses of everyone else who'd accosted her at the bar.

"I'm not surprised. Whoever took a bat to this trailer had to be making a helluva lot of noise. Anyone walking by would hear it. Be kind of hard not to notice."

There was nothing more to do but let Andy continue with his work. She was delighted to note that the offensive garbage had been removed from the interior and several air fresheners now hung inside. She reminded Andy to go over the horse partitions to make sure everything was still intact and no glass shards remained, but she also was effusive in her praise for the work; as far as she was concerned, Andy was a godsend. They agreed that Annie would come by in the late afternoon tomorrow to review the latest progress he and his helpers had made. She was relieved that Marcus would be spared from ever seeing—and, hopefully, knowing about—the ugly words sprayed on the side.

She pulled out of Andy's enclave, waving good-bye as she did so. Wolf, she'd noticed, had clambered into the extended cab and was once more taking a power nap. He certainly knew how to deal with the heat—take a siesta. Her cell informed her the temperature still was in the mid-nineties. Annie wondered how anyone worked in this weather. The options seemed to be to risk a heatstroke outside or freeze to death in any commercial building. She looked forward to creating a temperate climate in her new motel room. Maybe she'd emulate her blue heeler and take a nap.

The familiar buzz of her cell aroused her from her thoughts. Annie dutifully pulled over and glanced at the screen. It showed Maria's now-familiar number, and Annie felt a rush of relief to connect with the only person she really knew in this town. Or did she? The pleasure she'd felt quickly dissipated as she recalled her earlier thoughts about her friend's apparent duplicity. Could she truly trust no one in this hot, dry, scraggy dust bowl of a town?

"Maria! How are you?" Annie's tone was uncharacteristically cheery.

"Tired. A bit hungover. But essentially fine. What's this about the trailer?"

Annie gave Maria the short version of events, ending with her trip to Andy's.

"I'm hopeful it'll be in good enough shape to hitch to my truck on Monday. Aside from how it looks, the main problem seems to be rewiring the brake lights and interior ones. The windows are gone, but they're not essential. They might make the horses more restless when I first hit the road and the breeze comes in. We'll see."

"Or it might make them happy to be feeling all the fresh air. I've just returned from the feedlot. Thanks for the warning. Myrna is back in full force, ordering around a bunch of workers I've never seen before. She looks in remarkably very fine spirits for someone who's just lost a husband."

"Yes, and I haven't seen any notices for a funeral in the local paper."

"A celebration is more likely in order. Anyway, your five horses are fine. And the mustang is definitely on his way to recovering from whatever he had. In fact, he's looking so good that I don't think it was strangles after all."

Annie noted that Eddie was now firmly attached to the original four horses Tony and she had designated. The woman was good at her job of adopting out horses, that much Annie had to give her.

"What a relief. What did Myrna say about my taking them?"

"Subject didn't really come up. I assumed that because they were still in their separate paddocks that nothing had changed. Why?"

"Myrna showed up at the sheriff's office as I was retrieving my rifle. She screamed at the sheriff that I'd killed her husband, which I'm now thinking may have been a cover-up. She also was three sheets to the wind, so I don't know how seriously Mullin took her, especially since he'd just handed over my Winchester. But I don't need any more snags right now. A friend's coming into town tomorrow, and I want to hit the road on Monday. No offense or anything. It's just this trip's taken longer than I ever expected."

"No offense taken. Is your friend that boyfriend you mentioned, by any chance?"

Annie squirmed in her truck seat. She shouldn't have offered that information. Well, it was too late now.

"It is. I'll be glad to see him." No reason to mention that Marcus was flying all the way from London and would arrive in his private Learjet.

"Well then, it looks like this is the last day we'll have a chance to get together. Are you free tonight?"

Annie had no intention of repeating the drinking party that had ensued the previous evening. But it wasn't as if she had any other plans, and Maria knew it. She'd have to punt.

"I really need to catch up on a bunch of phone calls this evening. Everyone back home thought I'd be back long before now, including a caretaker who's looking after all my animals. And it wouldn't hurt to get a good night's sleep, either. I don't think I slept more than an hour or two at a time last night, worrying about whether someone was going to come crashing through my door."

"I understand. But you'll be safe in your new motel. No one can get to your room without going through reception first. How about getting together now? I've got two hours before I have to pick up the kids. There's a coffee shack between Browning and Loman that's not bad. Want to meet up for iced tea?"

"Sure. I'm practically in Browning now. See you in about ten minutes."

Annie knew she wouldn't be able to hold back from querying Maria on the discrepancies in her stories. She just hoped Maria had good answers to her many questions.

But Maria was decidedly closemouthed.

"Look, I don't care where you work, or *if* you work." Annie's tone was getting a bit testy. "I just want to know why you lied to me about working at your sons' school. I'd also like to know how you really heard about George's accident."

"I can't tell you." Maria had doggedly replied this to every previous question.

"Why not?"

"It's just not possible."

Annie wanted to scream. The one person she'd trusted in this town was obfuscating the truth for no apparent reason. And that put everything Maria had told her in doubt.

"Fine. So what else shouldn't I believe? That you didn't know that Danny Trevor worked for the tribe, tracking down wild herds? Or that you and Tony were as close as you say you were?"

Maria winced and took a small sip of the iced tea in front of her.

"That's not fair, Annie. There's one small part of my life I can't share with you, okay? I have to keep it private. It doesn't mean everything I've told you should be cast in doubt."

"Really?"

"Really."

Annie glared at the woman she had come to consider a friend, and who, despite Annie's insistence, continued to look remarkably at ease.

"Okay, don't tell me. You don't know me that well, and you don't have to. But look at it from my point of view. You come barreling into the feedlot moments after the sheriff shows up and minutes after George is killed. You *say* you heard about the accident on the school's police scanner, but now we know that isn't true. What am I supposed to think? Particularly since I happen to be the person who's been accused of murdering George, so much so that I've even hired an attorney to represent me."

"Annie! Is that really necessary? If Harlin gave you your Winchester back, doesn't that clear you?"

"Apparently not. There are still surveillance tapes that Harlin's hoping will show me using another rifle. The official word is still to stay put until further notice. Although I'm telling you, on Monday morning I plan to be on the road, clearance or not."

Was that wise? Maria was close to Harlin. Would she now tell him Annie planned to take off without the official blessing from law enforcement?

Maria seemed to see the question in Annie's eyes.

"Don't worry, Annie. I won't say anything to Harlin or anyone else. I'll help you load on Monday and make sure Myrna doesn't give you any more grief. And I wish I could tell you more, I really do. But it's safer if I don't. For everyone's sake."

And with those enigmatic words, Maria refused to say a single word more on the subject.

Annie parted from her friend ten minutes later. The two women had managed to chat about other things, mostly to do with horses, but the hug that Maria bestowed on Annie was uncomfortable and awkward. Annie was distinctly disgruntled with the way the conversation had gone. She knew no more now than before. And what she didn't know was driving her nuts.

She pulled into the motel parking lot, turned off the engine, and rolled down the window. Bad idea. A gust of hot air washed over her and awakened Wolf, who lifted his head, whined, and laid it down heavily again on his paws.

"I know, buddy," Annie muttered. "It's too damn hot here. We'll be home soon. I promise."

She heaved herself out of the truck, and trudged inside, Wolf at her heels. She gave a tight smile to the receptionist clerk behind the desk, who started to speak but then apparently thought better of it after he'd seen his guest's set face.

She wearily plodded up the two flights of stairs to her floor. Opening the door, she stepped inside and was just about to turn around to lock it when she stared into the room, disbelief and joy flooding her face. Marcus was reclining in the room's one overstuffed chair. When he saw Annie, he stood up and strode over to her.

"I thought you were over Iceland!" she managed to choke out after he'd enveloped her in a huge hug and a bigger kiss.

"That was twelve hours ago. The text must have been delayed. I'm here now."

"And I am so happy you are."

"Now that I'm here, what's there to do in this godforsaken town?"

CHAPTER 21

Annie gazed rapturously at the rib eye steak in front of her. It was about the size of Texas and grilled to absolute perfection—pink in the middle and charred on the outside. She sighed happily but was aware of Marcus's bemused gaze upon her.

She glanced over at the salmon on his own plate.

"Are you sure you don't want some? I've obviously got enough to share."

"Thank you, Annie, but no. I get more enjoyment watching you tear into a steak than I do eating one."

"You're sounding suspiciously like my half sister Lavender. Although I don't think she particularly likes to watch me eat red meat."

Marcus laughed his deep, husky laugh she loved so much. It almost made Annie want to stop what she was doing and devour the man instead.

"I've just returned from a week in London. I've had more than my share of steak and kidney pie and pub fare. Fresh Northwest salmon is just what I crave right now."

Annie looked skeptical as she raised the first juicy bite of steak to her lips but said nothing. The steak was calling to her and would not be denied.

Between mouthfuls, Annie assured Marcus that the animals she and Tony had selected were sequestered and healthy enough to travel. She also reluctantly confessed her split-second decision to adopt Eddie, the woefully underweight Thoroughbred, as well.

"Why not?" Marcus promptly responded. "Maybe Trooper would like a friend who's the same breed. Anyway, if you think he needs saving, that's good enough for me. We'll figure out where he should reside later, when he's restored to good health."

What a man, Annie marveled. She was touched by Marcus's seemingly unending generosity toward others, both human and animal.

"Thank you, Marcus. I knew you'd understand. And when you see the feedlot—" She felt the telltale pricking behind her eyes that occurred whenever she thought about the hateful place. "When you see it, you'll know why I wish I could simply take every one of the horses with us. What lies ahead of them is unbelievable cruelty. It's unconscionable what people do to perfectly sound horses."

She unconsciously wiped her eyes with her cloth napkin. When she was done, Marcus reached over and took her hand.

"People who care deeply, people like you, are what give me hope for the world. Keep on thinking that way. You may not be able to save them all, but you're making a difference, and that's what counts."

"Stop, or I'm going to start blubbering all over my half-eaten steak."

"Have another glass of wine. And let's look at the dessert menu. I know that will cheer you up."

Bolstered by Marcus's praise, Annie accepted the second glass and wondered when would be a good time to bring up the other herd of horses—the ones sheltered in a secret sanctuary on tribal land, the ones she'd promised Colin she'd save, as well.

After dinner, they strolled along main street, arm in arm. It was a far different scene from Port Chester, where the surrounding bay gave off the fresh smell of salt water, and the breeze was constant and welcoming. At least the sun's rays were no longer drilling down on them, which made walking tolerable. And since Annie was with her very favorite person in the world, it really didn't much matter where she was.

She'd avoided telling Marcus about the damage to the trailer, and he hadn't mentioned it, either. Annie was sure he would have if Dan had filled him in. As they approached the motel, she decided it was time he knew. She dreaded his reaction to the news. But Marcus preempted her with a topic of his own.

Leading her to a bench in what the motel euphemistically called "the garden area," he sat down and waited for her to be seated, as well.

"Now then. Tell me about your meeting with Alvin. Since you're now properly lawyered up, I can't talk to him or you about your case. Lawyer-client privilege and all of that. But at least let me know how eastern Washington's finest criminal defense attorney treated you. Are you feeling more relieved knowing he's looking out for your interests?"

Annie shrugged. "He was pretty swell. I told him exactly what had happened, and he thought there wasn't too much to worry about. And yes, he told me not to talk about the case with anyone—" Annie recalled her recent conversation with Dan, and paused. "He also said that he'd be in contact with both the prosecutor and sheriff and do his best to get me off their suspect list. And thanks to Alvin, I now have my rifle back. He said the sheriff wouldn't have released it if it hadn't tested clean."

Annie had been looking at two geckos chasing each other over rocks as she talked. She could feel Marcus's eyes upon her.

"Why do I feel as if I'm getting about half the story?" His tone was not accusatory, but she did hear concern in his voice.

"Well, because you are. It's a bit more complicated than that."

"I thought so. Tell me everything, privilege be damned. I'll swear we never had this conversation."

"Good. Dan said that, too, when we last talked."

Marcus chuckled. "How'd he feel about your retaining counsel?"

"Believe it or not, he was in favor of it. He doesn't trust Sheriff Mullin, and he's absolutely right not to. The fact is—" Annie took a deep breath. "The fact is last Thursday night, I was threatened by a bunch of local men at a bar. I was there with Maria—she's the woman who helped Tony and is helping me and unfortunately now I don't trust her either. Anyway, I was there with Maria and a bunch of Maria's friends, and a group of guys came up and started accusing me of killing George. One of them was a deputy. He wasn't as obnoxious as the others, but he reminded me I couldn't leave town. Which Dan said was hogwash, I could leave anytime I wanted and he wants me to do so immediately. Then, when I got back to my motel room that night—

the other one, the first one I checked into—Jessica's trailer was all smashed up. It's now at a repair shop and is supposed to be ready to go by Monday. The guy who's doing the work is great. Anyway, I told Alvin all about the trailer's being vandalized, and he said to report it to the police. Dan told me not to bother, which was my clue that he thinks Sheriff Mullin is a dirty cop. So Alvin called Mullin and got him to release my rifle, but I still don't know where I stand as far as being a suspect even though Alvin is telling me not to worry. Just don't talk to anyone, like I am now."

The words came out in one long rush, and Annie suddenly felt exhausted. She also wasn't sure she'd expressed herself as clearly as she might have. She looked at Marcus. His blue eyes were intently focused on her face. To her dismay, she realized she had no idea what he was thinking. Usually, she could tell in an instant. She turned away again and concentrated on the geckos, now barely visible in the fast-oncoming sunset.

"That's quite a story." Marcus's voice was unusually bland. "Let me make sure I've got all the facts right. When did you arrive? Five, six days ago?"

"Six," Annie morosely replied.

"Right. And during those six days, you've been accused of murder, threatened with violence by local hooligans and told to leave town, ordered *not* to leave town by a crooked sheriff, had your trailer vandalized, hired an attorney to protect you, and had to change motels because of threats against your life. Is that it?"

"Pretty much."

Marcus's succinct recap made everything that had happened sound a bit incredible even to her—and she'd been there.

"Pretty much. Oh, yes—Maria. Why don't you trust Maria? I don't think that was in your original narrative."

She had to know what he was feeling. She turned and saw a face suffused with deep solicitude. She sighed and gently leaned against his shoulder. Annie was very much aware that she was resting on a long, jagged scar that ran down the left side of his neck, a permanent reminder of his near brush with death six months ago. It looked completely healed, but Annie still hoped she wasn't hurting him. Draping his arm around her, Marcus gave her a comforting squeeze, as if to reassure her that he was perfectly fine.

"Why is Maria under suspicion?"

"Well, she lied. She told me she worked at a local public school, and that was the reason she couldn't be at the feedlot to help load on Tuesday. It was actually the sheriff who pointed it out. He told me it was a shame Maria was no longer employed by the school. When I confronted her today, she admitted the lie but wouldn't tell me why."

"So she wasn't truthful about her place of employment. What's so bad about that? It doesn't make her entirely untrustworthy, does it?"

"No, it sounds silly when I say it now. But the problem is that Maria did come to the feedlot Tuesday morning, about two seconds after the sheriff's office arrived. And she told me she'd come from school, after she heard the news on the school's police scanner."

"Do schools have police scanners now? I suppose they do, just in case an escaped convict is in the vicinity."

Doctbay?

"Whatever. All I know is that she made a huge point of telling me where she'd just been, and it was a lie. I'm getting so paranoid I'm beginning to wonder if Maria killed George, then hung back until the cops showed up as a kind of alibi."

"Well, if she truly wasn't at school, it isn't much of

one. But I see your point. She went to a lot of trouble to make you think she was somewhere else during the murder."

"Yes, and there's more." Annie snuggled more deeply into Marcus's chest. It felt heavenly. "I found out the pilot was working for the tribe, as a scout for wild herds. He'd find their grazing areas on the rez, then the natives would swoop in to capture them and take them to the feedlot. Maria claims she knew nothing about this. Yet the desk clerk here said Maria and Trevor knew each other pretty well."

"Why would the desk clerk know that?"

Ah. She'd have to reveal Tony's hidden love life. Or what she thought was his hidden love life.

"Well, according to Maria, she and Tony were more than just friends. She's the person who told him about the feedlot horses and suggested he take a look at them for Travis's ranch. She told me she spent the night with him the day he came up here, and that much I think is true. The desk clerk noticed Maria coming down with Tony the morning he checked out. Trevor was waiting at the motel, ready to fly Tony back home. The clerk said Maria and Trevor were obviously old friends."

"Hmm. Maria does seem to be holding something back. And you've met her, and I haven't, although I assume at some point I will. But it's still a stretch to think she's a killer."

"Yes, but—"

"You may recall that there was a lot of circumstantial evidence pointing at me in Hilda's death. Back then, you believed in me when no one else did, except my mother, of course. What you've described to me now sounds pretty similar to my case. Why don't you give Maria the benefit of the doubt until you know more?"

Annie sat up and stared off into the now near darkness surrounding them.

"You're right. I'll try to suspend judgment. It is hard to think of Maria as a cold-blooded killer. Besides, if the plane crash *is* connected to George's death, I can't imagine Maria's being willing to sacrifice Tony along with Trevor. Unless they had a horrible fight the night before or something."

"Stop thinking. It's bad for you."

"Got anything else in mind?"

Marcus did.

The next morning, Annie proudly showed Marcus her new breakfast nook, the small café down the street where she'd first met Maria.

"Welcome to the home of the never-ending cup of coffee," she jokingly told him as a waitress approached their table.

Marcus held out his mug. "Fill 'er up." He took a large sip, put down the mug, and closed his eyes. Annie tried to squelch the vague envy she felt whenever she saw anyone drink their coffee black. She required cream and copious amounts of sugar.

"Are you feeling okay?"

"Fine," Marcus replied with his eyes still closed. "It's merely jet lag. For some reason, I think it's time to go back to sleep."

"We could do that. . . ."

"Yes, but the problem is, I'd really sleep. It's better if I force myself to stay up. I'll probably fade this afternoon, but let's enjoy the morning while I can still prop my eyes open."

Annie was relieved to see Marcus somewhat revived

after a large breakfast of ham and eggs. When her smartphone buzzed from inside her purse, she instinctively grabbed it and trained her eyes on the screen. She swiped, punched out a quick message, and slipped the phone back into her purse in a matter of seconds. The fluidity of her movements did not go unnoticed by her companion two feet away.

"Looks like you've become quite proficient on that phone," Marcus said approvingly. "I take it you're finding it useful."

"Are you kidding? My life now revolves around that device. It tells me what time it is, when I should get up, what the weather's going to be like—not that there's much variation around here—how to get someplace, and the latest news. It's become an indispensable part of my wardrobe. I'm afraid to leave home without it. I don't know whether to thank or curse you for bringing it into my life."

Annie's eyes sparkled as she spoke. Marcus grinned back at her.

"And texting, even. My, my. You're on a slippery slope. The next thing you know, you'll be on Twitter and posting on Facebook."

"Fat chance. One has to draw the line somewhere. But it really has been a great addition to my life. Thank you for introducing me to the brave new world of smartphone technology. As you know, I'd never have done it by myself."

"The pleasure is all mine. Now I know I can reach you just about anytime I want. That was really my diabolical plan all along."

Marcus held out his mug to the waitress, who was walking by. Annie was sure it was his fifth cup.

"Who was in need of your attention just now, if I might ask?" he asked.

"Oh, that was Lisa at the stables. She just wanted me to know that everything's A-OK. She even sent me a photo of Trooper rolling in the pasture. It's pretty adorable. Let me show you."

Annie dug out her phone again. She pulled up the text from Lisa and tapped on the photo to make it full screen.

"What do you think of your boy?"

Marcus turned the screen toward him and smiled. The photo showed Trooper on his back, four legs wildly pummeling the air and twisting slightly to scratch his back.

"The noble horse at play."

"Horses gotta roll."

"So I can see. Have you had a chance to test-drive the camera app yourself?"

"I have, indeed. Just a minute."

Annie pulled up the camera app and stared blankly at it.

"Darn."

"What's wrong?"

"Nothing. I just can't remember how to access photos. I took a bunch of the damaged trailer, and Jessica painstakingly walked me through the process of sending them to her email. But now I can't remember what she told me."

"Don't worry. It'll be like second nature to you before you know it. Let me show you."

Marcus leaned over and showed her an image on the bottom left.

"See this? Just select that and all your photos will come up in sequence. You can swipe to the one you want."

Annie hastily grabbed it back from him. Marcus looked up, surprised.

"What's the matter, Annie?" He sounded a bit hurt.

"Sorry. I just didn't want you to see some of what was done to the trailer."

"That doesn't sound good. Why don't you let me decide if I can stand it?"

She silently handed the phone back to him and watched as Marcus scrolled through the photos she'd taken. She saw his face turn from one expressing natural curiosity to one of stone, his lips tightly compressed.

"It'll all be gone today," she assured him. "Andy promised me."

"That doesn't negate the fact that it was done. I'm glad you took these photos, Annie. Not just for Jessica's insurance purposes. I intend to find the men who did this to you and make sure they're charged to the fullest extent of the law. This is despicable. It's worse than despicable. It's . . ."

"I know," Annie said quietly.

"Every one of them is going down whether they wear a police badge or not. Especially the ones wearing badges."

Annie almost pitied Deputy Goddard. Almost, but not quite.

CHAPTER 22

Marcus continued to fume throughout breakfast. All the equilibrium he'd evinced the night before as Annie recited her litany of troubles had been dispelled.

"I'm calling James Fenton right now," he informed Annie, and reached for his own cell. Annie was sure James would drop everything if Marcus were in need of legal help; he'd done it before. She wasn't so sure he would react as promptly if he knew she was the damsel in distress.

Annie put her arm on Marcus's.

"Wait," she pleaded. "Let's concentrate on getting out of town first. There's not much point in stirring things up the way they are now."

He reluctantly returned the cell to his jacket. But he continued to fume.

Annie desperately wanted to restore the good humor

they'd enjoyed just a few minutes before. She glanced out the window just in time to see a battered, sea-foam-green truck rattle by, going far faster than the local speed limit allowed. And it was heading north. It was precisely the diversion Annie needed.

"Come on, Marcus. Let's go. I just saw Maria heading out of town like a bat out of hell. I want to follow her."

She grabbed her purse and watched a startled Marcus abruptly stand up and throw a twenty on the table.

"Let's go," was all he said.

Annie and Marcus raced out of the coffee shop and back to the motel parking lot in record time. As soon as she yanked open the door of her truck, Wolf greeted her with a sharp bark of hello. Annie had no idea how he'd gotten here—she could have sworn he was in the motel room when they'd left for breakfast. Perhaps the maid had inadvertently let him out and Wolf had discovered her truck's rolled-down windows. In any case, it was too late to do anything about it now. But Wolf intuitively picked up on the immediate nature of his mistress's departure. Without a sound, he jumped into the back and obediently sat down. Yet even her blue heeler couldn't resist the thrill of the chase. By the end of the first city block, he had edged his way toward the console, panting heavily, delighted at being part of this unknown adventure.

Annie was driving. She still hadn't caught a glimpse of the Toyota truck and was beginning to think Maria had too much of a head start for them ever to catch up. If so, it surely wasn't for lack of trying. They'd left so quickly, the poor waitress probably thought they were trying to abscond without paying their bill. She hoped the twenty Marcus had flung down was still on the table in the flurry of their hasty departure.

She glanced over at Marcus, who was completely absorbed in the landscape flying by them.

"Do you have any idea where she's headed?" he asked without taking his eyes off the road ahead.

"She's headed toward the rez. I think. There's a crossroads about ten miles ahead of us. One way goes to the tribal lands, the other up to an animal sanctuary owned by a friend. If we don't catch her by then, we never will."

It occurred to Annie that Maria might very well be on an errand of mercy for Olivia. Perhaps an animal was sick or injured. If that was the case, Annie was going to be more than a little embarrassed by her fool's errand. But if not—if Maria was headed to the reservation, and it had anything to do with Danny Trevor or the roundup of wild horses, she wanted to know what part she played in it. She stepped on the gas and officially exceeded the speed limit by fifteen miles an hour. She prayed that at ten o'clock on a Sunday morning, every local police vehicle was either parked in front of a church or the home of the deputy who drove it. The last thing she needed was to be pulled over for speeding. Somehow, she knew Alvin Gilman would not condone her decision to violate the basic rule of speed.

She was fast approaching the fork in the road and still the road ahead loomed ominously empty. The good news was there were no slow cars to get around. The bad news was that Maria's pickup had seemingly disappeared into thin air.

Then Marcus pointed in front of him. "Up there! I think I see a truck." Annie squinted against the glare of the windshield. As usual, she had forgotten to put on sunglasses. But yes, Marcus was right—she could see Maria's distinctively colored vehicle about a half mile up the road. And fortune was shining down on her. Maria was approaching the place where she'd have to make a decision to turn either right or left, and it was now within Annie's line of sight. She'd soon know if Maria were headed toward Olivia's menagerie or some other destination. She considered easing up on the gas pedal but decided to demur. Unless Maria was specifically looking for her in her rearview mirror, she'd never know Annie's truck was on her tail. And it had taken such an effort to find her. Annie wasn't going to lose her now.

Maria made a large right turn, ignoring her turn signal. Annie was aware that the Toyota had barely slowed down to make the corner. Whatever lay ahead, her friend intended to get there as quickly as possible.

Annie was at the same crossroads a minute later, but Maria's truck was already out of sight. She glanced at Marcus. He smiled and gave her a thumbs-up. Annie returned the smile. At least the chase had eradicated the anger he'd felt at the café.

They passed the road sign marking the distance to the tribal council, and Annie knew that, like it or not, she soon was going to have to adhere to the speed limit. But suddenly Marcus shouted, "Stop! Slow down!" Puzzled, she immediately applied the brakes.

"It's a green truck, right?"

Annie nodded.

"I saw it tucked into a side road about a quarter mile back. She's either parked there because she knows she's being followed, or she's parked there because that's where she's supposed to be."

Annie was impressed.

"Do a lot of surveillance in your spare time?" she asked casually, as she backed onto the shoulder of the road to begin an ungainly U-turn.

"No. I watch too much television. Ask me about DNA analysis sometime. I'm an expert."

Turning around on a narrow two-lane road with two-foot drop-offs on each side wasn't easy, but Annie accomplished this as adroitly as she could. She slowly drove in the opposite direction, looking on both sides of the road for signs of the truck. A few seconds later, Marcus pointed to the right.

"Up there. It should be just beyond that clump of pine trees."

It was. As she coasted by Maria's truck at five miles per hour, the truth suddenly struck her. Annie knew precisely where Maria was going, and why. She found a better turnaround place, made another U-turn, and turned into the rural lane. Parking her truck next to Maria's, she turned toward Marcus. He looked at her inquisitively but said nothing.

"Now I understand everything," she said simply. "Follow me."

The climb up the hill seemed less steep than it had on Friday, despite the medical kits both she and Marcus were hauling. Perhaps it was because the sun was not as high in the sky as it had been the day Colin had taken her here. Or perhaps it was because of the adrenaline that was now flowing through her body and knowing what was happening in the quiet grove ahead.

Annie strode ahead of Marcus, but she could hear his footsteps close behind her. Her dog had opted to crash through the sparse copse of black cottonwood on the right, periodically running across the road to find Annie, only to take off again. She wished she had the energy of the blue heeler. It was taking all she had to get to the grove as quickly as possible in a straight line.

When she reached the dried-up stream, she halted to catch her breath. She wasn't wearing boots, just sandals, and hoped none of the indigenous snakes had awakened as a result of their hasty trek through their territory. Perspiration dripped off her face, and she impatiently wiped it away with her one free arm.

Behind her, Marcus quietly said, "What are we looking for?"

"A small herd of horses. One of them may be in labor."

"Ah." He stood quietly, obviously awaiting her next instructions. He really was a remarkable man, Annie thought fleetingly. She'd dragged him away from the café with little explanation and he had unhesitatingly followed her every move. She wondered if she'd have been as amenable had the situation been reversed. Possibly not.

She turned and held out her hand for the kit he was carrying.

"Wait here just a bit. Let me locate them first, then I'll come back for you, if I can. Try to keep Wolf with you. The mare in foal doesn't need any outside distraction right now."

Marcus nodded and softly whistled for Wolf, who was happy to join him. He took hold of Wolf's collar, and said, "We'll be here. Don't be long. And watch out for rattlesnakes."

She marveled at his prescience as she picked her way along the rocks that lined the empty stream.

Near the opening where she'd peered at the horses with Colin, Annie heard Maria's voice. It was calm but forceful, as if she was issuing orders to someone, but Annie couldn't make out the words. Placing the two medical totes in front of her, she inched her way through the thicket and out onto the small pasture beyond.

Her eyes were immediately drawn to the pinto mare, who showed no resemblance to the quietly grazing horse she'd looked upon a mere thirty-six hours before. Now, the mare was nervously pacing up and down the pasture, occasionally stopping to paw the ground or nip at her flanks. Then it suddenly halted, and Annie knew in an instant that the mare was about to roll. She almost rushed forward to stop it, but noticed Maria standing a discreet distance away from the troubled horse, making no move to intervene. So Annie did nothing, as well, and simply watched as the mare's knees buckled and her body landed heavily on the ground. When the mare had rolled and laboriously heaved herself up again, Annie quietly stepped out onto the shriveled grass pasture in full view of her friend, a medical tote in each hand.

Maria instantly met her gaze, and a long, slow smile creased her face.

"I wondered if you'd caught on," she said, gesturing for Annie to come join her.

Annie walked over, giving the mare a wide berth as she made the short trip. She knew this was the one time when even the most herd-bound animal wished to be left alone. She glanced around the grove to see where the other horses were stationed. The mares and their offspring were grazing on the far side, under motionless aspen trees. The stallion stood on a small rise on the opposite end, flanked by Colin and a young girl who Annie intuited was his sister. Colin was wearing his trademark blue jeans, T-shirt, and red bandana. Aleisha was dressed in an orange jumper and pink cowboy boots.

"How's it going?" she quietly asked Maria.

"Fine, so far. Colin texted me about an hour ago. He'd come up here with Aleisha and found the mare in this condition. Now we're in a waiting game. As you just saw, she's still trying to get the foal into position. I'm glad you're here, Annie. ~~I don't expect anything to go wrong, but it's always good to have another set of hands.~~"

"I brought Marcus with me—my boyfriend. He arrived a day early. When I saw your truck zooming out of the town, I first thought Olivia had called with some animal emergency."

"But then you saw me turn toward the reservation. Colin told me he'd met you a couple of days ago, and you'd mentioned you were Tony's friend. That's the reason he showed you the shelter. We've done our best to keep it a secret for three months now. It's not fair that Olivia has to try to save every pregnant mare the tribe rounds up for the feedlot. Colin and Aleisha are very attached to this one. So I told them we'd do our best to save her. Nobody knows about this place except the four of us. And Tony."

"Yes, but I'm afraid that Myrna does know. Did Colin tell you I found the tribe's return address on the envelope Myrna used to write that receipt for me?"

"No. We haven't really had time to talk about anything other than the mare's progress. What's that all about?"

"I saw it when I was handing it over to my attorney to make a copy. He said it would help bolster my story that I really only came here to pick up the horses. When I got it back, I noticed it came from the tribal council, and they'd written 'private and confidential' on the front. Colin thought this meant they'd found your hiding place and were alerting the Fullmans that a few more horses would soon show up in their feedlot."

"Damn!" Maria spat out the word. Annie was taken aback. She glanced at the mare, once more pacing up and down a well-worn patch of grass. She appeared not to have registered the outburst. All her attention was on getting her foal born, and by the swish of her tail, she wanted it to be done quickly, too.

The foaling process could start any minute, Annie realized. She turned toward the opening that separated the grove from the outside world, then to Maria.

"Listen, I need to go and get Marcus. He's not a vet. He won't be of any use if we do have trouble, but I just can't leave him waiting by the stream wondering what's happened to me. Wolf is with him. But Marcus will make sure he behaves."

Maria nodded, her eyes still smoldering over the news that Colin and Aleisha's herd might be in peril, despite their best efforts.

Annie slowly jogged to the opening, nimbly pushed herself through, and ran along the empty streambed until she saw Marcus, who was sitting on the ground with Wolf's head in his lap.

"How is everything?" He sounded as anxious as if he were awaiting the birth of his own child.

"The mare's in the first stage of labor but hasn't started the birthing process. But that could start anytime. Come with me, and I'll find a good place for you and Wolf to be when that occurs."

"We could stay here."

"You could, but I'd rather you didn't. This herd has been hidden from the natives for several months now, and it's safer for you to be inside their sanctuary than outside, where you might meet someone who asks what you're doing here."

"Got it. Okay, Wolf, up you go. You'll have to continue your long list of grievances against your mother another time. We've just received our marching orders."

Marcus and Wolf rose from the ground, Marcus dusting off his clothes while Wolf simply gave himself a good shake.

"Very funny. That is the most spoiled dog on the planet."

"That's not what Wolf tells me. I think there's still more you can do."

"Well, it'll have to wait. This mare's foal takes precedence right now."

"Hear that, Wolf? Someone else needs your mother more than you do. The nerve."

The trip back to the grove took only a few minutes now that there was less cause for secrecy or silence. Annie sent Marcus and Wolf up to Colin, who was still minding the stallion. The black horse was the second most nervous animal in the grove, but Annie assumed he was primarily concerned with keeping a lookout for predators. Another mare, which Annie assumed was the alpha in the herd, had moved closer to him, just in case the stallion decided he wanted to be invited into the birthing room. Annie knew that, on rare occasions, the stallion in a wild herd would try to harm a new foal, especially if it was male, to eliminate any future competition early on. Annie thought this guy looked more inclined to simply care about the pregnant mare's safety. But it could have been wishful thinking.

Marcus immediately introduced himself to Colin, shaking his hand, then did the same with Aleisha. Colin's sister, Annie noticed, was about half the age of her big brother, only seven or eight years old. She had long brown hair, big brown eyes, and, like her brother, the most solemn face Annie had ever seen on a child. But they both appeared comfortable having Marcus in their company, and Wolf was an instant draw, so Annie jogged down the rise, content that at least the human herd would not require her attention.

When she rejoined Maria, the mare was still pawing the ground, but now her legs were flexed as if she was preparing to void. Sure enough, a rush of fluid suddenly appeared between the mare's legs, and Maria grabbed Annie's arm.

"Her amniotic sac just broke," she breathed. "It won't be long now."

When the stream of fluid stopped, the mare slowly lowered herself until she was lying flat on the ground, her legs sticking out like pegs. Annie watched the mare closely. Sweat had broken out around the pinto's shoulders, and she was breathing more heavily. The mare was trying so hard to help the foal, that much was obvious, but there was no sign of the foal's front feet, the first to emerge from the birth canal.

"We're in the home stretch," murmured Maria. Annie fervently hoped so.

The foal miraculously emerged twenty minutes later. Before that happened, however, the mare had risen, straining to deliver in a standing position, and Maria and Annie had stood poised to help guide the foal to the ground if that occurred. But then the mare had lain down once more. She looked exhausted. Annie looked at Maria, concern and confusion in her eyes.

"She's just resting," Maria told her kindly. "She deserves to. Everything will be all right."

And it was. After a few minutes, the pinto once again strained on the ground, and a moment later, one diminutive hoof and the foal's nose appeared. A minute after that, the foal had fully emerged, its long legs ridiculously splayed in all directions and its head bowed low in a bluish-white liquid. Its mother softly nickered and began to lick the tiny foal's flanks, gently nuzzling it to move. Now Maria seemed ready to intervene, much more than when the mare was so valiantly trying to urge her newborn out into the world.

"I need to check on the umbilical cord," she whispered to Annie, and began to inch her way over to the exhausted mare. But then she stopped and Annie knew everything was as it should be; the wild mare had bitten the cord herself, her last act in separating the filly from her womb. Annie glanced down at the two medical bags beside her. Maria would use her Betadine to disinfect the portion that was still attached to the new foal, but that was all that was needed from her arsenal. At no point had Annie even thought about ripping into one for assistance. Mother Nature had taken care of everything, and quite nicely, too. She knew it wasn't always this way in the wild, but she was thankful beyond words that it was, today.

She glanced up at the rise, and saw Marcus, Colin, and Aleisha all looking down at the now standing mare and the foal resting beside it. She thought she had never seen three happier, beaming faces than at that precise moment.

An hour later, the tiny, exquisitely proportioned filly tottered to her feet for the first time. The spindly legs wobbled, then collapsed, and the foal landed on the ground looking utterly surprised. She nickered to her mother and her mother answered back. Annie was sure the message was, "Don't worry, little one. You'll be walking in no time." It was adorable. Annie knew that before another hour passed, the foal would be standing upright and not long after that, nickering to and nudging her mother to find her source of sustenance. *If only human babies were as advanced at birth*, Annie thought. But then, no animal, of any species, could ever hope to compete with a horse.

* * *

As Annie watched Maria attend to the resting mare, she noticed Marcus in conversation with Colin. She wondered what they were talking about. Both he and Colin were seated on the ground, facing each other. She was struck by the seriousness of their discussion and the attention each seemed to be paying to the other's words. Marcus, it seemed, had a knack for getting anyone to talk. Perhaps it was because he was willing to engage at the young man's level.

Now Annie watched Marcus get up, shake Colin's hand, and begin walking toward her.

"I can't remember when I've had such an exciting afternoon," he told her. "Thanks for arranging it. And here I thought rural eastern Washington had nothing to offer."

Annie grinned at him. She was about to give a sassy reply when she heard an unwelcome sound from far away. Marcus heard it, too, and pulled her to his side. They both stared into the distance. The throb of high-powered vehicles was unmistakable, and the faint swirl of rising dust along the sparse tree line marked their steady movement.

Annie looked behind her. She saw Aleisha and Colin clutching each other in terror. She watched Maria wearily rise to her feet. Her face looked worn-down and haggard. Annie could understand why.

A convoy of three large ATVs rumbled its way across the upper ridgeline. Annie knew the occupants within. It was the tribe's roundup crew, and they had come to collect more wild horses. It appeared her warning to Colin might have come too late.

CHAPTER 23

For a long time, no one moved or spoke. Everyone seemed transfixed by the sound and sight of the ominous caravan bumping along the rough terrain above them. Only when the sound of throbbing motors receded into the distance did Annie let out her breath and try to take stock of what had nearly occurred in their sylvan sanctuary.

She knew, more acutely than ever before, that what Colin and Maria and Olivia had all told her was true. The tribe was aggressively committed to ridding their lands of wild herds. Annie had no doubt its elders claimed a long list of reasons why so many horses running free were a detriment to their environment—and to the horses themselves. She could see for herself the land was overgrazed and the vegetation woefully sparse. The mare that had just given birth was visible proof that there was not enough grass for her to sustain a decent weight. The fact that she'd given birth to a healthy foal was in itself a small miracle. What Annie could not understand, or forgive, was the tribe's ready acceptance to give up the captured horses for slaughter in a foreign country, where the journey from feedlot to slaughterhouse was unbelievably cruel and the method of killing even more so. Euthanizing the horses would be far kinder. But where would the money be in that?

Maria was the first to speak.

"We'll have to move them. We were lucky this time. We won't be the next." Her voice was flat and brooked no dissent. None was given. Nothing was said at all.

But where? Annie had no idea where cubbyholes on the reservation lay and where one might safely stow four mares, four foals, and a stallion. She felt a deep sense of despair settle into her bones. It was impossible to keep up with the machinations of a business machine determined to eradicate, and profit from the sale of, unwanted horses.

Marcus cleared his throat.

"Maria, I don't believe we've formally met. I'm Marcus Colbert, a friend of Annie's. I can see what you're trying to do here, and if there's any way I can help, I will."

Maria gave a tight nod, then granted him a small smile. She walked over to shake his hand.

"Nice to meet you, Marcus. I appreciate the gesture. And I'm grateful for what you and Annie have promised to do with five of the feedlot horses. Every horse saved is a blessing."

Marcus nodded. There seemed to be nothing else to say at the moment. He turned toward Annie.

"Darling, I know you and Maria probably have a lot to talk about. Would you mind terribly if I took your truck and headed back to the motel? If I don't get some sleep, I may not last long enough to look at the trailer with you later on."

How remiss of her. Annie had forgotten all about Marcus's jet lag. It must be hitting him full throttle right now. She dug out her keys from her jeans pocket and handed them over.

"You sure you're okay for driving? I can always take you back and return."

"I'll be fine. This plan assumes, of course, that Maria, you'll be willing to take Annie back later."

"Sure. No problem." Maria seemed a bit puzzled by the conversation but didn't hesitate in her reply.

Marcus gave Annie a quick kiss on the cheek, waved to Colin and Aleisha, and headed toward the small space that separated the glen from the rest of the world. Not for the first time, Annie was impressed by Marcus's physical prowess. For such a big, tall man, he navigated the tangled thicket with the agility of a mountain lion.

"I like the darling part, but an afternoon nap? He looks like he has more stamina than *that*."

Maria said it jokingly, but her remark still irked Annie. They were sitting on the rise alone, except for the quietly grazing herd beneath them. Colin and Aleisha had taken off shortly after Marcus's departure. Before they'd left, Maria had tried to assure them the herd would be moved to safer ground and soon, but the despondency in their eyes had told both women that they had little hope left that the mare and her new foal would survive the roving band of ATVs.

Both the pinto and the foal were now standing. The newborn was still a bit wobbly and valiantly trying to catch a meal from her mother.

"He just came back from London," Annie said shortly. "In fact, he flew directly from Heathrow to here."

"Directly? A big jet airliner landed in our dinky little airport?"

"It was a private plane." Annie didn't feel like expounding. It was nobody's business how Marcus got here. The fact that he was here was enough.

"Aha. Well, looks like you picked a winner, Annie."

A winner? Exactly how did Marcus's appearance of wealth make him a winner? Annie was tired of trying to explain the complex relationship she shared with Marcus to other people, especially when it was still evolving. She wasn't sure she fully understood it herself.

It was time to change the subject.

"So I take it you were here the morning George died, instead of at school?"

"Guilty as charged."

Annie was not going to let Maria off the hook again. She wanted answers she could fully understand, even if she decided she couldn't condone them.

"So why the elaborate ruse?"

"I don't know. Somehow it just seemed easier. I knew you'd half expect me to be around at send-off, and I couldn't tell you about our secret horse haven. I didn't know you well enough. Tony knew, of course, but I swore him to secrecy, too."

Annie remembered that Tony had mentioned the children, but not in any context.

"Well, he kept his word. But you could have simply told me you couldn't be there on Tuesday. It would have been no big deal."

"You say that, Annie, but you haven't seen how hard it is sometimes to wrest those animals away from Myrna. She always finds reasons they can't go just yet, or new fees to tack on. I know of at least two occasions when new owners postponed pickup at Myrna's insistence, then found their horses gone when they returned."

From what little Annie had seen of the crazy feedlot owner, she could believe it. Maria continued her explanation.

"I fully intended to be there on Tuesday, but Colin asked me to check on the horses that morning. He had to take his grandmother to the doctor, and she no longer drives. I'm not sure Colin actually has a driver's license, either, but at least he's safe behind the wheel. Anyway, I couldn't turn down Colin even though it left you in the lurch. I guess I felt I had to give a valid reason of some kind, even if it wasn't true. It was the first thing that occurred to me. The truth is I did work for the school up until four months ago, when I was laid off."

"Sheriff Mullin mentioned that you were a superb reading tutor."

"I am. And I got a call on Friday from the school, asking me to reapply. I'm thrilled. I could really use the extra money."

Annie believed this unequivocally.

"So how did you manage to show up at the feedlot so quickly?"

"The old-fashioned way—someone told me. I really did want to see you off if I possibly could, so I got up at the crack of dawn—"

"I know. And jump-started Donny's car."

"Yup, I got the call at six o'clock and rushed over. She cannot be late for work. Her boss is a fanatic about being on time."

"But when Donny started to say where you were headed, you cut her off. So I assume Donny knows about the horses, too?"

"Absolutely not. After I helped Donny with her car, I told her I had to get to Olivia's to help with a sick animal. But if she'd said that at the bar, you'd have known the school story wasn't true."

"Back to the question. How'd you know about George's accident?"

"I dashed to the grove, checked on the horses, and was barreling through town when I saw the entire police force peel out and head toward Loman. I rolled down my window and asked the last car to leave where they were headed. The nice deputy said the feedlot—George had had an accident. I just followed him there, at a slightly slower rate of speed. It was pretty clear what had happened as soon as I got there."

Annie assimilated all this. It made sense, and she wanted to believe Maria. She needed to feel that someone in this town told the truth. If she really wanted to check, she supposed she could ask for the name of the deputy Maria had spoken to, and confirm that their brief exchange had actually taken place. She didn't much feel compelled to do so. As Marcus had pointed out, Maria did not give off the appearance of a coldblooded killer.

But then there was Danny Trevor. Maria had been just as shocked as she was when Olivia informed them he had been patrolling wild horses from the air.

"Okay, I believe you," she carefully told Maria. "But there's one more thing I have to know."

"Shoot."

Maria had the ability to look always at ease, Annie thought, even under pointed questioning. She wished she'd been so relaxed during the hours Sheriff Mullin had been grilling her.

"Danny Trevor. You knew him. I'm finding it hard to

believe you didn't also know about his contract with the tribe."

"I swear, Annie, I knew nothing about it. Sure, I knew Danny. He spoke at my son's school one day when I happened to be a volunteer. We talked afterwards about where he'd flown and that kind of stuff. But we didn't hang out together. And I honestly thought the tribe was hunting wild herds with ATVs only, like we saw today. If I'd known he was working with the tribe's roundup gang, I would have called him on it. Anyway, Danny's gone, and I doubt any other local pilot would agree to take up where he left off."

"I hope you're right."

The two women sat silently for several minutes. The tension Annie had felt earlier was nearly gone. The ATVs had not returned and Maria had answered most of Annie's questions satisfactorily. She still felt she didn't know the whole story, but she didn't need to. All she had to do was pick up a trailer, load up, and go. And make sure that Eddie was transported ASAP. For the tenth time, she wished she'd asked Jessica for her six-slant instead of the four. But then, the foal probably wasn't quite ready to learn how to load. It probably was better to return with Jessica and pick up Eddie, the mare and foal, and any other horses who happened to land in her lap along the way. Where all these horses would stay during the quarantine period and beyond was too much to think about right now. Annie looked down at the herd, calmly grazing together once more, although the pinto mare and her little one were still keeping their distance. The stallion, Annie was relieved to see, showed no signs of aggressive behavior. He was too busy preening.

"Oh, look! The foal's finally got the hang of latching on." Maria pointed at the bucolic scene before them.

"Excellent. Which reminds me, I haven't eaten lunch."

"Let me get you back to the motel. We've given Marcus enough time alone. In fact, he's probably wondering where you are."

Marcus was just emerging from the shower when Annie entered the motel room. The sight of him wrapped in a scant towel made her want to tear off her sweaty clothes and drag him back into bed. Instead, she gave him a swift kiss.

"Did you manage to sleep at all?"

"I did. The maid came by just as I was coming in, but I told her not to bother cleaning the room. I hope that's okay with you."

"Fine with me. The bed's just going to get mussed up again, anyway."

He kissed her back, this time lingering more.

"Very good point."

Annie felt much revived after her own second shower, and once she'd dressed, she joined Marcus on the small balcony outside the room.

Marcus was scribbling on a notepad, his cell phone close by. When he saw her sit down, he flipped over the pad and smiled at her.

"Company trade secrets?" she asked. "Don't worry—they're safe with me. I couldn't understand them if I tried."

Marcus grinned. "Sorry, Annie. Business seems to follow me even on the dusty trails to eastern Washington."

"So I gather. Fortunately, I've got an angel of a caretaker who is doing all my work for me. All I have to do is write her a check."

"Yes, and I think the nonprofit should reimburse you

for her time. This trip has turned out to be far longer and more complicated than any of us ever imagined."

Annie waved off his suggestion.

"Happy to do it. And aside from Jessica, I am the right board member for the job."

"No doubt about that. So how did things go with Maria? Did you get things sorted out with her?"

Annie frowned. "Pretty much. She owned up to being at the grove instead of the school the morning George died, and said she simply followed the line of cops going out to the feedlot. It makes sense. And it's possible that she didn't know Danny Trevor was involved with the roundup gang on the rez. I don't know. In some ways, I think Myrna's the more likely killer. I just wish I didn't feel that I'm always getting half the story whenever I talk to Maria.

"She's got a right to her own privacy."

Annie considered this for a moment and reluctantly agreed.

"Yes, she does. Whenever she asks me a personal question, I want to clam up, too."

"I'm sure of that. I feel privileged whenever you divulge the slightest tidbit about your misspent youth."

Annie swatted at his arm. "Very funny."

"And I know we're not supposed to talk about it, but I also know you're wondering as much as I am whether or not Tony's death is somehow related."

She sighed. "I think they have to be simply because they both occurred so close in time. That, and the fact that we know both *were* murders. Have you talked with Dan? He just told me the FBI found the detonator near Snoqualmie Lodge. And you'll never guess what it was—a rigged cell phone, can you believe it? Someone definitely wanted Danny Trevor dead. Both Trevor and

George were up to their ears in the horse-selling business. The problem is that the list of people who hated what both did for a living is pretty much endless."

"Which is why Sheriff Mullin would be incredibly happy to find anything that links at least one of the deaths to you."

Annie nodded glumly, then sat up straight.

"Wait, Marcus. There may be something that helps provide ex—ex—you know, the kind of evidence that proves I'm innocent."

"Exculpatory evidence?"

"That's it! Alvin said the test showing my rifle hadn't recently been used was exculpatory evidence, and once the sheriff reviewed the security tapes, it will be, too. But I have photos, ones I took that day. When I first discovered George's body in the feedlot paddock—"

Annie's mind instantly went to that chaotic scene, and the sight of the two horses methodically pounding on what was left of the feedlot owner's body. She unconsciously made a small grimace. Marcus was silent and waited for her to continue.

"Anyway, I thought I would have to remove the body, even though I knew I should wait for the cops to do that. But I had no idea how long it would take for them to arrive, and meanwhile, poor George was being, well, pulverized, and the horses were going nuts. So I took a bunch of photos of the scene just to make sure the sheriff would know how it looked when I first saw it."

"Excellent, Annie! Did you hand them over to Mullin?"

"No. I didn't."

"Why not?" Marcus seemed surprised.

"Frankly, I forgot. Maria showed up a few minutes after the sheriff, and we spent the next several hours just taking care of the horses. They'd been terribly traumatized by all the violence. First, we had to move them, then feed them, and we ended up cleaning all the troughs and doing other things just to make them more comfortable."

"Sounds exactly like something you'd do."

"Yes, well, after that was done, I immediately was escorted into Mullin's patrol vehicle and subjected to several hours of questioning down at the precinct. I completely forgot about the photos, and when I did remember, I didn't particularly want him to have them."

"Why? They might have made a difference in how Mullin viewed your status as a suspect."

"Maybe. But he was so suspicious of me from the start. I worried that if I told him about the photos, he'd think I was simply documenting the murder I'd just committed. Besides, I don't think they show anything but photos of the Kubota and the placement of the body. But maybe there's something on there I didn't see when I was taking them."

"I take it you also haven't shown them to Alvin, either?"

"Again, I completely forgot that I took them. It's weird. I must have wanted to block the bloody scene from my mind."

"So you haven't looked at them since that day?"

"I haven't looked at them at all. Didn't want to. Seeing everything in person was enough."

"Let's take a look at them now."

As Annie feared, she had a strong visceral reaction to looking at all the images she'd captured on her smartphone not so long ago. Once more, she felt the dark terror that had permeated the feedlot that Tuesday morning, when crazed and confined horses had raged against their confinement, desperate to be away from the sight and smell of blood that assaulted their senses. She could tell that Marcus was disturbed by the images, as well. But he continued to scan each one carefully, long after Annie's appetite for revisiting the scene had vanished. Her appetite for food also had disappeared.

"It looks like you used the burst mode on a lot of them," he observed. Annie was still at the patio table, but she was leaning back in her chair, no longer desiring to look at the play-by-play recap she had created.

"Yes. Hannah showed me how, and the horses were moving so fast in the paddock, it was difficult to find a focus. I hoped that one or two might come out this way."

Marcus nodded and continued his silent analysis of the images, slowly swiping each photo aside when he was done. Then he paused, swiped back and forth a few times, and stopped.

"Annie, I do believe you may have captured a significant clue. Come over and look at this."

Marcus had not taken his eyes off her phone while he spoke. Annie reluctantly joined him. She hoped the photo wasn't one of the close-ups of the body. She'd been so numb that day, the full effect of what she had seen hadn't seemed as real as it did now.

She pulled her chair closer, and Marcus pointed at a place to the far left in the image on the screen.

"See that, up there? It's a just a wisp of something red. Up in the corner, near that shack in back of the corral."

Annie peered at it and quickly saw the spot Marcus referred to. It was just a dot of red, visible through the heads and manes of horses flying by. It was merely by chance that it had been captured digitally. Another nanosecond, and the blur of horses would have shielded it from sight.

"Now, let's go a couple of images further." Marcus advanced the roll of images slightly and stopped again.

"Here it is again, the same red dot. Only now it's moved, just a bit. See? We first saw it over by that shack. Now it's closer to that second corral, behind the one you were facing."

Again, Marcus was right. It looked like the small red dot, but it had moved farther back and behind the second paddock.

"You can't tell what it is from these shots," Marcus went on. "It's not red-eye created by the camera; it's definitely part of the physical scene. But in this image—" Marcus swiped the roll once more. "In this one, you *can* see what it is."

Annie looked at the image Marcus had just selected and gasped. The red dot now appeared on the other side of the screen, the far right, where the road leading out of the property began. Except it was no longer a red dot. It was a red bandana, and although the image was blurred, Annie could see that it was draped or tied around someone's neck. One thing was certain. Whoever was wearing the bandana was running fast, and far away from the feedlot.

CHAPTER 24

Annie stared at Marcus, unwilling to say what was racing through her mind. There was only one person they both knew who sported a red bandana, someone who Annie was sure had not shed one tear over George Fullman's demise. Had her photos just proved that he was responsible for that death?

Marcus spoke first, and quietly.

"We don't know if it's Colin, Annie. And even if it is, it doesn't prove he was involved in the murder."

All she could do was shake her head sadly. She couldn't even voice her suspicions; it was hard enough thinking them. She hoped it wasn't Colin. She hoped it was *anyone* but Colin.

"At the moment, I'm glad you forgot to provide these photos to the sheriff," Marcus went on. "But that doesn't mean you might not have to. Tomorrow, I want you to call Alvin and get his advice. It may provide exculpatory evidence for you, you know."

"I don't want to! Not if it implicates Colin!" Annie was surprised at the anger and, if she admitted it, fear in her voice.

Marcus sighed. "You may not have a choice, Annie. But I'm not an attorney. Ask someone who is."

Ten minutes later, they were back in Annie's truck, headed toward Andy's Repair Shop. Both were silent, although Annie continued to think furiously about what the photos might imply. She was sure Marcus was doing exactly the same thing.

Maria had told her she'd subbed for Colin that morning in the grove. Had she done so because she knew Colin planned to murder the feedlot owner? If so, didn't that make Maria complicit in the homicide? Or had Colin really told her that he needed to be with his grandmother and Maria had bought the story? Yet . . . Maria was awfully quick with coming up with her own stories when she had to. Why should Annie believe this one now?

And then there was the matter of Danny Trevor's death. What if it *was* Colin in her photos, and he had killed George Fullman? Did that mean he'd killed Danny Trevor as well? Annie recalled Tony telling her that Rick had left earlier and another pilot, someone local, would be flying him home. It was the last conversation they'd had. What if Colin had rigged Trevor's plane, not knowing that Tony was also going to be on board? If so, Colin must be wracked with grief and remorse right now. Had she noticed these emotions in the boy? No, she had not. But then, he'd barely shown any kind of emotion when she'd been around him. Besides, she didn't know if it was Colin in those images anyway. But then, who could it be? And why, oh why, had she ever shown those stupid images to Marcus in the first place?

"Stop thinking about it," Marcus told her, breaking the silence. "We don't know enough to come to any sound conclusions, and the ones you're reaching now are going to drive you crazy. Let's concentrate on our present task. Which is making sure your local mechanic has done his job, and we can leave tomorrow, as planned."

She turned to him and nodded, trying to smile.

"Cheer up, Annie. You'll soon be reunited with all your horses and be a happy woman again."

"What about you?"

She couldn't believe she'd said that. Neither, apparently, could Marcus.

"What about me? What do you mean, Annie?" There was definitely a tinge of curiosity in his voice.

"I mean, will you have to leave as soon as we get back to the Peninsula?"

"Why, Annie Carson. I don't believe it. You actually prefer my company over your horses'?"

His teasing rejoinder was just what she needed to get her mood back on track.

"Well . . . not quite. But close. In fact, dangerously close, come to think of it. Let's just say I would be happy if you could stay awhile. Besides, you're due for another riding lesson."

"Hmm." Marcus considered her reply. "Well, I didn't bring any riding clothes."

"Not a problem."

"What? You keep an array of men's riding clothes in your closet just in case a stray cowboy wanders by?"

"Hardly. But all you really need are riding boots, and we've got plenty of local stores that carry them."

"I see. Well, then, I believe I can extend my stay a day

or two. <u>Not to ride, necessarily.</u> Just to make sure you're settled in all right, along with all your new horses."

She smiled and continued to drive, waiting for the nice woman inside her smartphone to tell her when to make the next turn. Marcus did a lot of things very well, but she doubted that settling horses was one of them. Then again, she might be surprised.

Country music poured out of the shop when Annie pulled up a few minutes later. Andy saw her drive in this time and had the good courtesy to lower the volume as Annie's truck rolled to a stop.

The trailer was now outside on the lawn and looked considerably more presentable than it had the previous day. The ugly graffiti had been scrubbed off, leaving abrasions in the aluminum finish, but that was far better than the alternative. The tires were fully inflated. And the number of dents had considerably lessened. Annie began to hope that she and Marcus might actually be able to leave tomorrow, after all.

"It looks great!" she exclaimed to Marcus.

"Cosmetically, yes," he replied, opening his passenger door. "I'm more concerned how it handles on the road."

Annie was halfway out her own door when she suddenly remembered the small fibs she'd told Andy about how the trailer became so damaged. Thinking about Colin as a potential killer had completely wiped this little detail from her mind.

Jogging around to join Marcus, she grabbed his arm.

"You need to know something. Andy thinks I'm on my way to Ellensburg to pick up some horses. He knows nothing about the feedlot business. And he thinks I'm a professional hauler. You're going to have to be—" Annie wracked her brain. "You can be my boss, who came over just to make sure the job was done right."

Marcus assimilated new facts quickly, Annie noticed. It probably was what made him so successful in his own business.

"Are we using the same names?"

"Sure. I'm using mine. If he finds out why we're really here, we'll be a hundred miles down the road. If he even cares."

"Sounds good to me. As your boss, however, I have to say that although I understand why you refrained from telling Andy your real reason for being here, it appears Maria isn't the only person spreading stories in this town."

"Shush! Oh—and people at the motel did the damage. You know, visitors from out of town."

"Why'd they do it?"

"I told them to hold down the noise."

"Was this with or without your shotgun?"

"It's a rifle. Very funny."

Andy was waiting for them by the trailer, a broad smile on his face. It was clear he was extremely pleased with the outcome of his rush job.

"Andy, I can't believe the transformation," Annie said admiringly. "It looks like the trailer I came into town with again."

The praise made Andy's eyes light up. "It was quite a job, let me tell you, and I got one or two things left to do. But nothing I can't finish by tomorrow morning. And I called my buddy in Ellensburg. He's already ordered the glass for you and says he'll be able to install it on Tuesday, if that still fits your schedule."

"That's wonderful." Annie intended to whiz by every single Ellensburg exit tomorrow. She'd have to make amends with Andy's glass doctor later.

"Andy, I'd like you to meet Marcus Colbert, my boss. M—Mr. Colbert, this is Andy, the mechanic who's done all this work."

"Pleased to meet you." Marcus shook Andy's hand. Annie noticed he loomed a good six inches over the mechanic. And, of course, he was considerably more handsome.

"Mr. Colbert, is that right? I couldn't believe what your gal here had me haul in a few days ago. This trailer looked like it was headed to the junkyard. I don't know what she said to those noisy neighbors of hers at her motel, but it sure must've ticked them off."

"Ms. Carson has a habit of sometimes speaking before she thinks. We're working on that, aren't we, Ms. Carson?"

Annie wanted to kick him but managed to sweetly smile back.

"Sometimes it's just better to let things go."

"That's right. Well, Andy—if I may call you that—"

Andy eagerly nodded.

"I'd like to go over what you've done, if you don't mind. I'm sure everything's in order, but I'm afraid Ms. Carson was unable to tell me the full scope of the damage. This is mostly for insurance purposes, you understand."

"I sure do. Um—" Andy seemed to fumble for the right words. "Ms. Carson told me she'd be paying for my work up front and getting reimbursed by your insurance later. Is that still the plan?" He sounded a bit anxious.

"Sure thing. I can write you a check or give you a card. Your choice."

Andy beamed once more, and he and Marcus walked to the front of the trailer, where the mechanic began describing how he'd realigned the hitch. Annie followed, but it was clear the two men were talking to each other and not particularly including her in their discussion.

Fine. She decided to check out the horse's quarters inside, which was really her domain, anyway. Annie wanted to be sure the horses would be as safe and comfortable as if the trailer had just rolled off the lot, which, she realized morosely, it had, only a few months before.

She pulled out the ramp and was pleased to watch it fall plumb with the ground. This was essential, since she had no idea how the horses would load, and any uneven jiggle they experienced stepping up might persuade them not to enter the big, scary box. Thankfully, the mats had proved impervious to any damage; they had been built to last and looked good as new. Andy had hosed out the interior from top to bottom, and at least the inside siding looked fairly pristine. The two oscillating fans were a bit bent, but they switched on and off just fine. The protective bars on the missing windows had been straightened and sat tight in their fixtures, all the head ties were in place, and every latch worked perfectly. Only the dome light still needed work; the stripped wires overhead attested to this one job that still need Andy's attention. Aside from this, the interior looked perfect and ready for horse loading. She stepped out, relief washing over her. It was going to be all right. Finally.

She met up with Andy and Marcus in his commercial garage.

"I was just telling Marcus here that it was lucky those tires were deflated with nothing more than a nail. That made 'em easy to repair. I didn't even have to use the spare. If someone had slashed them—" Andy shook his head.

"Yes, that was a lucky break," agreed Marcus. "I wish

they'd slashed the wires, though. It looked like most of them were ripped out. Must have been difficult to put those back together again."

"It was, it was. Fortunately, I got a lifetime supply of just about every kind of wire you'll ever need. Boat, plane, helicopter, truck, you name it, I can wire it."

"How extraordinary, Andy. Where'd you learn to work on such a wide breadth of engines?"

"Mostly Alaska. Lived there for nearly twenty years, and most of the time I was two hours by plane from the nearest hardware store. You learned to do everything and to make everything do."

"I can imagine."

Enough of this bromance chatter, Annie thought, and looked squarely at Marcus.

"You know, in the ten years I've worked for you, you've never let me call you by your first name," she said to him, doing her best to look hurt. "But Andy here gets to call you Marcus the first time he meets you."

Marcus got up from the stool he'd been sitting on.

"True." He looked critically at her as he said it. "But then, I've never called you anything but Ms. Carson."

Andy laughed. "Looks like the two of you get along all right, no matter what you call each other. Well, Annie, did you see anything inside the trailer that still needs fixing? Aside from the dome light, which I already told your boss about?"

Of course he had told Marcus instead of her. Who else needed to know besides him? Annie was beginning to regret the character she'd created. Maybe she should have made Marcus a journeyman truck driver instead.

"Nope, it all looks fine." Annie decided not to hold back. After all, Andy had done a superlative job with what he'd been given. "Actually, it looks more than fine. It looks terrific. I can't thank you enough for going the extra mile on my—our—behalf. It means a great deal to know my schedule won't suffer because of your hard work."

"Aw, it was just the kind of challenge I like," Andy replied. "As I said, it'll be ready to go by eight o'clock tomorrow morning."

"I may not be with Ms. Carson when she comes by," Marcus interjected. "Why don't we take care of the bill now? That is, if you can guesstimate the time you've got left."

"Oh, don't worry about the dome light, Marcus. I'll just throw that in for free."

"That's very kind of you, Andy."

"Might want to wait until you see the bill before you say that. It's in the house. Be right back."

Andy left, and Annie flew over to Marcus, throwing her arms around him.

"Well, Mr. Colbert," she said coyly, exaggerating each word. "Let me know when you're ready to be called by your first name."

Marcus laughed but gently pulled her arms away from him.

"We're still in character, Ms. Carson. Try to hold off until we're out of the driveway."

"I'll try."

The screen door on the main house slammed, and Annie was glad she was demurely sitting on a stool instead of on Marcus's knee when Andy returned to the garage.

"Here it is." Andy handed Marcus the invoice, which Annie noticed ran to more than two pages.

Marcus quickly scanned it and nodded briskly.

"Looks in order to me. Do you prefer credit card or check?"

"Check would be fine."

"I'm afraid I didn't bring my business checks with me—Ms. Carson called me while I was on vacation. Will a personal one do?"

"Sure. As long as there's money backing it, I don't care where it comes from."

"Whom should I make it out to?"

"Andy Johnson Auto Repair will do 'er."

Marcus dutifully wrote out the check while Annie's brain reluctantly set aside thoughts of kissing Marcus. Another thought had taken hold: The mechanic's name was Andy Johnson? Short for AJ? As in AJ who lived in Alaska and followed Danny Trevor to eastern Washington?

"Did you know Danny Trevor?" She'd blurted it out before remembering, as Marcus had just reminded her, she was still in character.

Andy's face suddenly changed. It closed down, and to further the effect, the mechanic turned away from her so she could no longer see it.

"Yeah, I knew Danny." All the joviality in his voice had vanished. "Why? Why do you want to know?"

Annie thought hard and fast.

"Oh, Dave mentioned it. You know, the guy who recommended I call you. He mentioned something about a recent plane crash and said the pilot's name was Danny Trevor. Dave said he didn't know how it could have happened, since his mechanic, AJ, had looked at the plane right before takeoff. When I saw your name, I just made the connection."

Her heart was beating fast, and she dared not look at Marcus, whose face she was sure would be expressing his displeasure over her major gaffe.

"Dave said that?" Andy turned and looked at her. A mask had come over his face, and Annie couldn't read what it was.

She dumbly nodded.

"Well, what do you know. Yeah, I was Danny's mechanic, both here and back in Alaska. I already talked to the boys at the NTSB all about it. Why? Something else you want to know?"

"No," Annie said lamely. "I was just curious, that's all."

"Well," Marcus said with false heartiness. "We don't want to take any more of your time, Andy. Thanks again for all your hard work. Ms. Carson will see you tomorrow morning."

Andy picked up the check, looked at it, and set it on the counter.

"Pleasure doing business with you, Marcus."

He said not a word to Annie as she and Marcus walked back to the truck. All Annie could think about was what her boss, Mr. Colbert, had said. Sometimes she did speak before thinking, and she was furious at herself for so stupidly doing so now.

But miraculously, Marcus did not scold, criticize, or in any other way bring up Annie's gross blunder. As she turned right to exit Andy's suburban enclave, all he said was, "What do you think, Annie? Time to shake the dust off this old town?"

She turned gratefully to him and smiled. She couldn't have agreed more.

CHAPTER 25

Despite Marcus's generosity of spirit in not mentioning her gaffe, he was beginning to irk Annie. Just a bit. It started when they returned to the motel and, after dinner, he declined her invitation to join her in a walk with Wolf. It was a beautiful night. The temperature was actually bearable. And it was their last night together in this miserable town. But Marcus had demurred, telling her he had several business calls to make, and it would be an excellent time to make them while she and Wolf went on a nice constitutional.

When she'd returned an hour later, Marcus had still been on the phone, but had quickly hung up when she and Wolf entered the room. She'd had no quarrel with their nighttime activities—quite the opposite—but this morning, Marcus had again begged off from accompanying her, this time to Andy's to pick up the trailer, pleading more urgent business to attend to by phone.

Really, Annie thought. If this was what life with Marcus was going to be like once they returned to the Olympic Peninsula, he might as well fly back to San Jose, don one of his Armani suits, and make phone calls from his office. She was deeply appreciative of his gallantry in coming to her aid, but frankly, his attention span, at least toward her, had lasted approximately twenty-four hours before it had reverted to its usual all-business mode. This did not bode well for a long-term relationship. Had she spent hours a day talking to Lisa about her horses and flock of sheep? No, she had not. Was it too much to ask that he, too, suspend his business affairs for just a few days, for her sake?

Then again, who had willingly paid for her attorney, not to mention made an extravagant flight to eastern Washington after arriving from a week in London, just to be at her side? She resolved to try to be more understanding. But she was still just a teensy bit irked.

Annie was also more than a little ticked at her own self. Because Marcus had not brought up the subject of what to do, if anything, when she saw Andy, Annie was unsure whether she should apologize to the mechanic for bringing up Danny Trevor or if doing so would just rouse his curiosity more than it already had been.

She was pondering the consequences of both actions as she drove to the mechanic's shop when her phone buzzed. It was Alvin Gilman, returning her voice message from last night. Marcus had insisted that she make the call, over her very strong objections.

"I'm not trying to get Colin into trouble," he'd assured Annie for the third time. "I just think you need to know the legal ramifications of what your photos show. It's the prudent thing to do, Annie, and in your heart, you know it."

She did. But she'd felt like a turncoat as she had left a message with Alvin's answering service, asking him to please call her the following morning. And when morning arrived, Annie had come to her own private decision. She would describe the photos as purely hypothetical evidence to Alvin. She felt quite clever. She was sure no other client of Alvin's had ever thought of this angle before.

"Annie! How are you? Please assure me you're not calling to report another run-in with the locals."

"No, no, I'm fine. And so is the trailer, more or less. I'm actually on my way to collect it right now. It's been at a local mechanic's shop for the past two days, and Marcus and I have deemed it roadworthy enough to haul."

"Oh, is Mr. Colbert with you now? Glad to hear it. We had a nice chat about you several days ago."

"I can only imagine."

Alvin laughed. "Not in that sense. We were both deeply concerned about your status in our local justice system."

"That's a relief. Well, I called for two reasons. First, since Marcus is now with me, we intend to pick up the horses this morning and head out this afternoon. We are not sending out a press release or informing the local constabulary of our imminent departure. We're just leaving."

"Fine. If there's any backlash, I'll handle it. But there's no need to tell me exactly where you'll land. That way I can honestly say I don't know where you are."

"Got it. And you never know—we might decide to take a tour of all the major national parks along the way. Unlikely, but possible."

"If asked, I'll say you're considering a longish vacation to no place in particular."

"Which I always am. The second reason I called you was to ask you a kind of 'what-if' question."

"You mean a hypothetical? Shoot."

Annie felt a bit deflated realizing her ingenious idea had been floated by her criminal defense attorney before.

"Yes. Well, suppose someone took photos of a murder scene, including the victim, and later found out the photos showed someone else at the scene that they hadn't noticed when they were there?"

"You mean, the person who took the photos didn't realize the other person was present until he or she showed up in the roll?"

"Exactly."

"What's the question?"

"If the photographer has a pretty good idea of who's in the picture, does she have to turn over the photos to anyone, like an attorney, or law enforcement?"

"Is the photographer a possible suspect in this murder?"

"You could say that."

"And is the photographer represented by counsel?"

"Thankfully, yes."

"Well, it's entirely the photographer's call. But if she does decide to share them with anyone, it should be with her attorney. But she can choose not to share them at all, if she wants. Although she should think carefully about how the other person in the photos might help resolve her own suspect status."

"Wonderful. Thank you, Alvin. You've made a hypothetical person feel much better."

"We always strive to make our clients happy—even the ones that hypothetically exist."

*   *   *

Annie arrived at Andy's garage at 8:10, much buoyed by her conversation with her attorney. The trailer was still parked outside on the lawn, and Annie maneuvered her truck in front of it, lining it up with the trailer hitch. The orange Chevy pickup she'd seen yesterday was now parked in the interior of the garage, its hood propped up. Annie could see the mechanic bent over the engine, his toolbox beside him on the cement floor.

He looked up after Annie stepped out of the truck to survey the remaining distance between her truck and the trailer.

"Morning," he said, sounding cordial enough.

"Hi, Andy. Any trouble with the dome light last night?"

"Nope, it's wired in and works great. Let me show you."

He unlatched the back doors and walked inside, flipping a switch in the back. Overhead, the dome lit up with a subdued white light, as promised.

"Thanks, Andy. I'm hitched and ready to roll." Annie paused. Marcus had implied he had several calls to make that morning, and she wasn't inclined to return if she'd just be ignored. "Would you mind if I reloaded the hay nets and put some shavings on the floor before I leave? I want to be ready to load as soon as I hit the—the stables in Ellensburg."

Damn! She'd almost said feedlot. What was coming over her?

"Sure. Don't mind if I don't watch, do you? I'm in the middle of a delicate task in this old crate."

"Not at all."

Annie backed up another two feet and carefully secured the horse trailer to her hitch. The operation took a good ten minutes, and she realized she was already sweating from the exertion. As tempting as it was to leave now, she was determined to give Marcus all the precious time he obviously needed to tend to business. So she searched in one of the inside pockets of her purse for the key Jessica had given her, sending up a prayer of thanks that the local goons hadn't jimmied the storage unit when they were bent on destroying the rig.

Annie noticed the mechanic watching her as she unlocked the side unit.

"This'll just take a moment," she told Andy, as she lugged out four hay nets. Thank goodness Jessica had given her an extra set. She didn't know what Andy had done with the first set, which had been in the van when it was trashed, and didn't care. She was sure the garbage flung inside had rendered the hay inedible and the nets permanently reeking of filth.

She began stuffing the first net, thinking, as she always did when on this task, how much she disliked the process of putting unruly hay into nylon mesh bags with fishnet lacing. It was labor intensive and slow going.

But hay nets kept horses occupied on long trailer rides and, back home, on days when the heavens opened with such pounding rain that even the horses headed for the paddock. So Annie continued to stuff, while Andy continued to tinker with his engine.

"Took me a bit by surprise when you mentioned Danny's name," he said casually. Annie had her back to him so could not see his expression. She managed not to flinch and to continue her job. Now she stood upright and faced him.

"I'm so sorry to have brought it up. I only heard his name in passing, and wasn't thinking of how you must feel, losing a good friend."

Andy gave a half nod and turned his face.

"Yeah, Danny was a good friend for a long time."

Was? Annie wondered if the use of the past tense re-

ferred to all or just part of the two men's friendship.
She wanted to say she'd lost a good friend in the plane
crash, too, but knew she couldn't. That would seem like
far too much of a coincidence.

"Must be tough, after working together all those
years," she said tentatively. It was the most uncontroversial
response she could think of at the moment. She grabbed
the next hay net and began to work methodically on fill-
ing it.

"Up in Alaska, you get used to plane crashes in the
bush," Andy told her. "Did you know that it has the highest ratio of pilots to population of any state in the union?
Doesn't mean everyone's an ace, though. Lots of things
can go wrong in the wilderness. Especially if you're an
inexperienced pilot and don't know how to react to
sudden weather changes."

"I can imagine."

"Yup. Sudden wind shear, cloud cover, incoming
storm off the water. If you want to stay alive, you'd better know how to handle your plane in all situations. You
can't be too careful in those old Cessnas."

What was his point? Annie was confused by where
Andy was leading the conversation.

"Are you a pilot, yourself?"

"Me? No. I just work on engines. Although in an
emergency, I could probably take one up. No one knows
the instrumentation better than I do."

Well, that was a bit of hubris, Annie thought. She
said nothing as she grabbed the last hay net, thankful
that it was the last to fill. She decided she could spread
the shavings on the trailer mats when she got back to
the motel. The conversation was getting a bit weird.

She pulled up the drawstrings to the last net, tossed
it into the trailer's storage area, and walked over to
where Andy was working.

"All done," she said brightly. "Thanks again, Andy. I should be on my way."

"Didn't you want to spread some chips or something?"

"Oh, I'll just wait to get to Ellensburg. I'm already late starting out. I should get on the road while the sun's still low."

Annie was walking around the pickup as she said this. The restoration job Andy had performed on the old truck was impressive. Every square inch was immaculate, gleaming, and new.

"Did you keep the original engine?" Annie wanted to leave on a good note, and figured that complimenting him on his handiwork was a surefire way to ensure that.

"Sure did. I replaced parts of the interior where I had to, but otherwise it's the same truck that was built in 1950. Even the radio on the dashboard is the original."

Annie peered inside and saw a small AM radio. She glanced at the floorboard, covered with new grey mats.

"What's the button on the floor for?"

Andy grinned and came over to her, wiping his hands on a big red handkerchief.

"That's the starter. Just pull out the choke—" Andy pointed to a knob on the left side of the dashboard. "Then step on the starter. Let me show you."

Andy hopped into the front seat, pulled out the choke, and put his steel-toed work boot on the button. The engine roared to life. Andy then adroitly pushed the choke back in.

Andy turned to her. "What do you think?"

"I'm thinking they don't build them like they used to."

"You got that right," Andy answered cheerfully, turning off the engine. "Well, take care, Miss Annie. And say hi to your boss when you next talk to him. He's a real nice guy."

"Will do." Annie scrambled into her front seat and slammed the door a little too loudly. She noticed she was perspiring, and it wasn't even nine o'clock yet. That was what a little bit of manual labor could do to you in this climate. That, and seeing Andy maneuver the choke in the pickup truck. It had immediately reminded her of the primer Mack had shown her on the Cessna at the airport, and Andy had certainly had a lot to say about those planes this morning.

She turned the key in her ignition and glanced out the window. Andy was still standing by her truck, quietly sipping his coffee. She waved a cheery good-bye to him and carefully pulled forward, making a large circle as she exited his backyard. As her front wheels hit the asphalt on Andy's suburban street, she glanced in her rearview mirror one more time. Andy was still there, mopping his face with his big red kerchief. It took all of Annie's self-control not to gun the engine and to continue her slow retreat out of the neighborhood.

The decision of whether or not to surrender her photos of the feedlot crime scene was now a slam dunk. Of course she would turn them over to Alvin Gilman. Now that she was sure who George's killer really was.

CHAPTER 26

Marcus was less sure about the wisdom of Annie's decision.

She'd raced up to the motel room and burst in to find Marcus still on his cell phone. Annie couldn't help but feel a bit annoyed. Marcus had promised that he would be packed and ready to check out of the motel as soon as she got back, and it was now nine-thirty. He looked no more ready to go than he had when she'd left for Andy's.

He quickly ended the call and smiled.

"All set?"

"I am. The trailer's hitched, and all I have to do is spread some shavings when we get to the feedlot. But listen, Marcus, I spoke with Alvin—"

"Good girl."

Annie ignored his patronizing approval. She knew he meant well, and she could educate him later.

"And Alvin said I could do anything I want with the photos—share, not share, although if I do share, it should be with him. But that's not my news. I got a very strange vibe from Andy this morning."

"Oh? Do tell." Marcus seemed genuinely curious about what Annie had to report. She inwardly smiled. She had his attention again. All she had to do, apparently, was bring up the subject of murder.

"He went on and on about his time up in Alaska and how often plane crashes happened there. It was just weird. And, listen to this—Andy has a red handkerchief, too! I'd forgotten I'd seen him wipe his face with it on my first visit. He brought it out again today."

For some reason, Marcus did not jump to his feet and compliment Annie on her brilliant deductive reasoning. Instead, he looked as if he expected her to say more.

"Don't you see?" Annie was perplexed at Marcus's inability to see what was so clear to her. "Andy's the killer! He was the last person to look at Trevor's airplane and must have rigged it. Then, a week later, he killed George at the feedlot. It's *Andy's* red bandana that shows up in the photos, not Colin's."

"I see. What's Andy's motive for each murder?"

Annie paused. "I'm not sure."

"Not sure or don't know? Think about it, Annie. As Danny Trevor's designated mechanic, Andy probably made a good income off the pilot. Why would he want to kill the goose that laid the golden egg? As far as George Fullman, we don't know that Andy even knew who he was. It's unlikely their businesses would have overlapped. Even Trevor's connection with the rounding up of horses doesn't make it likely. I doubt Trevor ever had any dealings with the feedlot owners. His only business was with the tribe."

Annie was already feeling dejected, but Marcus wasn't finished.

"The red-bandana theory is tempting, but it's just not enough. I suspect every other male in this rural county has one red bandana in his possession. Around here, red bandanas seem to be the predominant male fashion accessory, especially when paired with red suspenders, which seems to be another hot fashion trend."

She sank down into a chair.

"Damn. I guess I'm back to Myrna as the killer."

Marcus smiled, walked over to her, and kissed her cheek.

"You don't have to solve every murder you come across, you know. Solving mine was enough."

"Okay, fine. I was all set to give Alvin the photos, but now I think I'll hold off."

"I fully support that decision. Give me five minutes, and I'll be ready to go. Your dog has been very good company while you've been gone, but I can tell he's eager to hit the highway."

"Aren't we all."

Seven long days had passed since Annie arrived in eastern Washington. As far as she was concerned, it had been a lifetime. She yearned to return to the abundant green landscape of her native Olympic Peninsula and be with her own herd of horses once more. Every day, Lisa had sent her texts, assuring her that every one of her equines was safe, healthy, and happy—Annie's pre-scribed requisites for every animal she owned—and frequently attached a photo or two as proof of their well-being. Still, it was not quite the same as being there. She was eager to see all her horses and get back to her normal routine.

Although, what that routine might look like in the future with four new horses, and five, counting Eddie, Annie wasn't quite sure. She'd tried to reach Jessica the previous night but only got her voicemail, and was hesitant to try later, knowing her large-animal vet's often early bedtime. She'd settled for a text, informing her of her expected ETA on Monday, and had been relieved to see a return text from her this morning, although it was uncharacteristically terse and devoid of details. All Jessica had typed was, Sounds great. See you soon. Annie assumed that she was supposed to haul the feedlot horses to the ranch Jessica had designated as their place of quarantine several days before. She scrolled through their text thread to review the directions and figured she'd give Jessica a call once she was truly on the road and knew her arrival time better.

Annie was reviewing Jessica's instructions one last time as she waited impatiently in her truck for Marcus to settle the motel bill. The engine was running, and Annie felt an intense desire to get on the road. What was taking him so long? She looked toward the office and finally saw him emerge, once more on his cell phone. Honestly, didn't the man ever think about anything other than work? His behavior was quickly passing the annoying stage and bordering on the infuriating.

She watched him pocket the cell as he approached and gave her a broad smile. It was so appealing that she forgot that their late start time was all his fault. She grinned back and reached over to open the passenger door. Wolf promptly made a nosedive to join him up front, but Annie put up her arm to curtail her dog's effort.

"Sit," she told him, using her alpha voice, then added in her normal voice, "Honestly, Wolf, you were with him all morning. Give me a chance to be with the guy, would you?"

Wolf gave an infinitesimally small whine but obediently sat down.

Marcus sighed. "It's like this all over the world."

"I can only imagine." Annie's tone echoed Marcus's, one of mock resignation, and they turned to each other and laughed. She put the truck in gear and started to ease out of the parking lot, heading south toward Loman. They were finally on the road. They were finally going home.

Annie had resolved to get her visit to the feedlot over as quickly as possible. She didn't know how she'd react to loading four horses when she knew so many others would be left behind. *Stay tough,* she reminded herself, as she approached the road leading into the feedlot. This was not the time to lose her emotional control.

The turnoff to the dusty road approached, and she made a gentle right, using her turn signal to alert other vehicles of her slowness. The trailer noisily banged up and down as she drove the bumpy mile before the turn into the feedlot. Annie hoped it was just the unevenness of the road and that, once four horses were safely ensconced inside, the ride would go more smoothly.

And then the final turn came. Annie made it slowly and carefully. She felt Marcus's eyes upon her and turned to him to smile. Even this effort caused a small quiver in her lips. *Buck up, Annie,* she sternly told herself. *It'll all be over soon.*

She looked ahead for the electric gate, and there, in front of her, was Maria, lounging by the tailgate of her battered green pickup. Annie had never been so happy to see her as now. With renewed hope for a speedy load-and-go, she pulled up alongside the Toyota and leaned out the window.

"Ready?" Maria said only the one word, but Annie knew all that one word encompassed.

"Ready."

"Then let's get the show on the road."

Maria punched in the code, and the electric door slowly swung open. Annie entered and parked her truck where she had the first time, under the line of alders that acted as a wind barrier and paralleled the main paddock—a paddock, Annie reminded herself, that offered no shade or shelter to the animals inside.

"I'll have to deal with Myrna first," Annie explained to Marcus after she'd turned off the engine. "I still owe her money for the quote-extended board-unquote."

"I don't suppose you could negotiate an even trade, seeing as how you took care of her horses for a couple of days?"

"Fat chance."

"I'm sure you're right. Wolf and I will stay here if you don't mind. You don't need any more people to stir the pot, and I know you're anxious to get this portion done."

How true, Annie thought, although she felt a tinge of disappointment that Marcus had chosen not to join her in her last dealing with the feedlot owner, particularly since he knew that Myrna had shrilly and quite publicly accused Annie of killing her husband, and was still high on her own suspect list.

She got out of the truck and saw Marcus immediately pull his cell phone out to make another business call. It flashed through her mind that Marcus might have reached his saturation level for Annie's life, the one that revolved around horses. His dead wife had been just as besotted with equines, although in a different sort of way, and look what had happened to that marriage. Hilda and Marcus had ended up living nearly a thousand miles apart and had been on the verge of divorcing when she was murdered.

But this was no time to worry about the state of their relationship, or why Marcus was so preoccupied with business right now. She had four horses to load and another sale to negotiate. There was no way Annie was going to leave the skinny Thoroughbred in Myrna's care a minute longer than was necessary.

She gave a quick nod to Marcus and walked over to Maria, who was waiting for her by her own truck.

"Where's Myrna?" she asked.

Maria pointed down the aisle that divided the sick horses from the rest of the feedlot herd.

"She's somewhere back in there. I suggest we stay put and let her approach us."

"Where are the horses?" Annie felt anxiety tugging at her and knew she would not be at ease until she knew for certain that the four horses were still here and ready to travel.

"You can just barely see them from here. Look way down on the left."

Maria pointed with one arm, and Annie was relieved to see the herd in the same small paddock, which now included the mustang and Eddie.

"Eddie is going to be unhappy when his new playmates leave without him," Annie regretfully told Maria. "Promise me you'll make sure he's okay until I return."

"I promise. And he'll be fine, Annie. He's a resilient kind of guy, I can tell. He's used to rolling with the punches."

Annie knew this was true. After all, what other choice did Eddie have? She glanced over to the main paddock to take her mind off the hurt and confusion the Thor-

oughbred would feel after realizing he'd been left behind, and noticed a tall black-and-white pinto staring at
her. She was struck by his eye coloring—one was cobalt
blue, the other a typical dark brown. The blue orb was
mesmerizing, almost willing her to come over. Then the
pinto turned his massive head, and she was shocked to
see that three-quarters of his left ear were missing.
Annie wondered whether frostbite had been responsible, or if something worse, something violent, had torn
so much of the ear away. When she saw how the large
white blaze on his face drew apart to create a slightly
off-kilter heart shape on his forehead, she could no
longer resist the horse's almost magnetic pull. Walking
over to the paddock fence, she stood on one of the bars
and reached out her hand. The pinto gazed at her,
sighed, and gently laid one massive check on her palm.

It was too much. Annie knew she was going to start
weeping any second, and there was nothing she could
do about it. She fiercely wiped her eyes with her arm
and stroked the pinto with her free hand. There was
nothing she could do. She was doing all she could.
There was nothing she could do. She was doing all she
could. Annie continued to repeat the words to herself as
her own private mantra. It kept her tears from spilling
over, but she knew she was still crying.

Behind her, she heard the ominous rumble of a van
on the country road outside the feedlot. Annie's heart
sank. Oh, Lord, this couldn't be the transport, could it?
It would be just her luck to see all the horses in the paddock—including the one she was now stroking—piled
into the massive van that would carry them on a long,
hot, waterless ride to their ultimate destination.

She turned her head, prepared to see the worst. But
what she saw made no sense, no sense at all.

It was a caravan of trailers, longer than Annie had

ever seen before in her life, and none of them looked anything like what she'd expect from a slaughterhouse. Gleaming in the sun, the vans looked extraordinarily well built and equipped for horse travel. What was going on? She jogged over to the electric gate to get a better look. The dust the convoy created was intense. Putting her hand to her forehead to better shield her eyes, she focused on the first van coming toward her. When it was twenty feet away, she finally could make out the driver. It was a woman, and she looked astonishingly like Jessica, her large-animal vet. Was she hallucinating?

But no, there was Maria, by the electric fence, waving her through. Her mouth open, Annie watched Jessica send her a cheery wave as she drove by. Annie was too dumbfounded to do anything in return; all her attention was on the second van now coming through the gate. As it rolled in, she recognized Samantha Higgins at the wheel. This time, Annie at least managed to raise her hand in response after Sam threw her a friendly salute. Next in line was a van driven by her good friend LuAnn, who yelled something Annie could not make out over the noise of the caravan. She watched incredulously as more and more trailers rumbled into the feedlot. Annie saw her good friend Sarah, who'd just picked up Layla at her stables, at the helm of the next van. Patricia Winters followed, hauling a spectacularly long trailer with the logo RUNNING TRACK FARMS emblazoned on the side. Annie barely had time to register that the British manager of an elite horse farm was probably seeing a feedlot for the very first time. Next in line was Jessica's six-slant trailer, driven by—could it be?—Kim Williams, one of Suwana's finest deputies. Annie doubted Kim had ever driven a horse trailer in her life—but then, she'd led frightened horses out of a burning barn for the first time only six months ago and done an admirable job. Identifying the driver of the final trailer to enter the feedlot was easy. Annie would have known Dan Stetson's massive head anywhere. And riding shotgun with the sheriff was Travis Latham, chairman of the board of the organization that had authorized adopting—Annie's brain came to a thudding halt. She knew what the arrival of seven trailers implied. But could it really be so?

She raced to the trailer Jessica had driven in and stood panting in front of the driver's side, too wound up to speak. She looked up to her vet, and her eyes begged the question she seemed unable to ask.

"Don't thank me," Jessica said blithely. "Thank the man over there. It was all his idea."

Annie turned and saw Marcus, now out of the truck, standing by Dan and Travis, grinning broadly as Dan slapped him on the back. In fact, they all seemed to have huge grins on their faces. Only Annie, it seemed, was just a wee bit still in the dark. She caught Marcus's eye, and he looked back at her.

"We're taking them all," he said simply.

Later, Annie wondered if Marcus actually had said something more. It was hard to know, since at that moment, and for the second time in her life, she slid to the ground in a dead faint.

CHAPTER 27

MONDAY AFTERNOON, AUGUST 15

Myrna was the one who unwittingly revived Annie. "What the hell are you all doing here?" she snarled at the group as she clumped up the aisle, passing her angry eyes from one group to another.

The harshness of her voice roused Annie, whom Marcus and Maria were now tending to on the ground. She realized her face was wet. And she was incredibly thirsty. Then she remembered. She'd just watched seven trailers roll into the feedlot and Marcus—that wonderful man, Marcus—had just told her *they were taking them all*.

She struggled to get up, but Maria gently shook her head no and motioned that she should go with her over to the aspen trees, where there was a modicum of shade. Marcus stood up, dusting his knees, and looked at Travis. Travis nodded back, and the two men approached the seething feedlot owner, who looked as if she wanted to spit venom at both of them.

"Mrs. Fullman, my name is Marcus Colbert, and the gentleman with me is Travis Latham. We'd like to purchase every single horse now on your property. We're prepared to pay you fifty percent more than what you normally would get for the lot, and we'll pay you in cash. Do we have a deal?"

Myrna gasped and sputtered. From Annie's vantage point by the trees, it didn't appear that Myrna was ready to accept even these remarkable terms.

"Who are you?" Her tone was decidedly suspicious. "Are you from the Department of Agriculture?"

"No, ma'am," Travis interjected. "We're from a non-profit organization in Suwana County. We need horses and hear you often sell them to qualified buyers."

Trust Travis to coat the truth with a few embellishments intended to soften up the old hag, Annie thought. She wondered if it would work. She knew her friends had no intention of leaving the feedlot unless their trailers were filled with Myrna's horses. And Myrna was going to make a load of money, a lot more than she'd get from the slaughterhouse. What was her hang-up?

"Well, that's all fine and dandy, but how do I know you are who you say you are?"

Travis calmly removed an envelope from his blazer's inside pocket and pulled out a number of papers.

"This is our nonprofit certificate from the state, as well as our status from the Department of Licensing." He handed them over to Myrna, adding, "If you'd like to see our articles of incorporation, I can provide those as well."

Myrna squinted at the documents, then roughly pushed them back toward Travis.

"You're not part of the media?"

"No, ma'am," Travis and Marcus said simultaneously.

"You just want to buy these horses." Myrna stated this as a fact, not a question.

"That's right, Mrs. Fullman. We just want to buy your horses—all of them."

"Four of 'em have already been sold."

"I'm glad you remembered that, Mrs. Fullman. Ms. Carson's horses will be coming with us."

Marcus turned his gaze to Annie, now sitting at the base of one of the trees and guzzling water from a plastic bottle Maria had just handed her. Annie nodded emphatically as she swallowed the liquid, which, at the moment, tasted like nectar.

"What do you want 'em for?"

Honestly, thought Annie, for a woman who had no issue with selling horses for human consumption, she certainly seemed overly concerned about their future now.

"They'll be used for whatever horses typically are used for—riding, driving, light farmwork," Travis said. "They'll be very well taken care of, I assure you."

Myrna narrowed her eyes and looked at the stately octogenarian.

"Some of 'em aren't in very good shape," she said. "Might not be up for a lot of riding."

"We're aware of that, Mrs. Fullman. Those horses will enjoy a good retirement."

Myrna shuffled her feet and looked from side to side. She appeared not to know what to do. Travis and Marcus continued to stand patiently in front of her, waiting for her to make a decision.

"Fifty percent more than the Canadian house, you say?"

Annie assumed she was talking about one of the slaughterhouses north of the U.S. border.

"That's right. You tell us what you'd get from your regular buyer, and we'll increase the price by fifty percent. Paid in cash."

Annie's patience was growing thin. She wanted to rush over, grab Myrna by the shoulders, and shake her until her eyes bugged out, and she managed to say one simple word—*Deal*.

Finally, Myrna sniffed. "Suit yourself. You can have them all. Let me figure out how much you owe me. Once I get the money, they're all yours." She stomped off toward her office. One would have thought she was more angry than pleased about the way negotiations had worked out.

Annie felt such a rush of relief flow through her that she felt she couldn't move a single limb. She felt embedded in the ground, too stunned to do anything except exist. And then she started to sob, convulsively. Maria promptly poured the rest of the water bottle over her head. The impromptu tonic had an astounding effect on the patient. Annie stood up and started hugging everyone she saw, starting with Marcus.

Myrna took her own sweet time devising her buyout price for the feedlot herd. Annie wasn't the least bit surprised. After all, the money Myrna made today would surpass anything she'd have garnered on any other one, and Annie had no doubt that Myrna was laboriously trying to figure out how much she could pad the bill and still get away with it. She knew all her friends must appear like the most stereotypical horse-loving, tree-hugging group Myrna had ever encountered, and the feedlot owner would want to take full advantage of their generous natures.

As far as Annie was concerned, Myrna could manipulate the figures as long as she wanted. She knew it would make no difference in the end and that Travis would pay her price. Besides, the longer Myrna fiddled with the numbers, the more time she had to catch up with her friends, all at once. If she'd tried, she couldn't have planned a better party for herself.

Which, Marcus reminded her, was what it actually was.

"As I recall, this is a very special day," he murmured to Annie, once he'd been able to extricate himself from an embrace that had elicited quite a few whistles and catcalls from the audience. For once, Annie didn't care.

"I should say it is! How often are fifty horses saved from a terrible fate, thanks to your remarkable scheming?"

"Well, true. But I was referring to something else. Do you know what day it is, Annie?"

"Monday. It's Monday, August . . ." She tried to count the days she'd been here in her head. "I know I arrived a week ago. That was the eighth. Which makes this—"

She stopped.

"It makes it your birthday. Happy birthday, Annie."

A roar of cheers and applause surrounded her. She was stunned. It *was* her birthday. It had always been easy to remember before. But then, her life usually was a lot less complicated in mid-August than it had been this year. She was now officially forty-four. She vowed to make it the best year of her life, ever. And to spend as much time as she possibly could with Marcus and too many horses to count.

"Did you plan it this way?" Annie asked incredulously. She couldn't believe Marcus could have orchestrated all of this for her birthday.

"No, the rescue team's coming today was just a serendipitous event. It worked out perfectly."

Gazing around her, Annie looked at all the people who were so important in her life.

"But how did you get everyone together?"

"A lot of phone calls. Many, many phone calls. Not to mention about two hundred texts."

Oh. So *that* was why Marcus's cell phone had seemed glued to his ear practically as soon as he'd arrived.

"But why? Why did you decide to do this? I mean, it's incredibly generous and fabulous and wonderful, but just because I said I wished we could take them all—"

"About sixteen times."

"—I didn't imagine you'd take me seriously."

"Well, I did."

Annie let this sink in. Could she really ask any more of this incredible guy? She realized she had to.

"Then I hate to ask this of you, but as long as we're taking the feedlot horses . . ."

"It's already taken care of."

"It is?"

"Maria's bringing Colin's herd over right now. She left as soon as Myrna agreed to take the bait. Don't worry—Jessica knows all about it. We made sure there's enough trailer space for everyone."

After that, Annie couldn't think of anything else to say. She couldn't have, anyway; her heart was so full that words were simply not enough.

Fortunately, someone—Annie wasn't sure who—had been prescient enough to bring food, in the form of

several large pizzas and fizzy beverages. Everyone settled down in the sparse shade to eat. Annie knew that
each and every person here was going to put in a huge
effort to load and transport the horses, and she was
glad they'd be doing it well fed.

Over the early lunch, Annie got a much better idea
of how the plan had been executed.

"It started with a phone call to me," Travis said, trying to pick up a slice of pizza without dropping top-
pings all over his creased khaki pants. Annie wondered
if he'd ever eaten pizza before. He'd seemed momentarily flummoxed when he realized silverware was not included in the box. Travis gave up the effort and spoke.

"I realized that taking this many horses would radi-
cally change the direction of Alex's Place if that was
their ultimate destination. There's a big difference between a working farm with an assortment of farm animals and a horse-rescue facility. Both fulfill the mission
statement of Alex's Place. But Marcus and I knew that
we couldn't make the decision without the full support
of the board."

"We all got a phone call," Dan Stetson continued,
"and agreed, every one of us, that it could and should be
done. Jessica was the lynchpin to the decision. She knew
better than anyone else just how work intensive it would
be to bring this many nags back to health. In the end,
we voted unanimously to switch the focus of the ranch
to rescue horses. Frankly, I can't think of better projects
for the kids. High time they learned to think of someone's needs beyond their own, and taking care of any of
these nags should get their attention real quick."

"Now, Dan. Try to be a bit more humanitarian. A lot
of these kids don't have much of a chance at home.
They learn to take care of themselves because they have

to. If no one else gives them the attention they need, of course they're going to think about their own needs first." The speaker was Kim Williams, a Suwana County deputy and the only African American and one of the few females on the force.

"I suppose," was Dan's response to Kim's gentle request for a bit of compassion. Dan always had been a stickler for behavioral conformity, Annie thought with some amusement. He thought everyone should just adhere to the laws of the land and be happy about it. He certainly was.

"Well said, Kim," Marcus said approvingly. "Our board is greatly enhanced with your presence on it."

"Hear, hear," Travis added.

"Well, this is all great." Annie meant it, but she also was a little stung at being left out of the deliberations. "But why didn't you include me in the discussion? After all, I'm a board member, too."

"We tried, Annie," Marcus said, trying to keep a straight face. "Travis included you on every email he sent to the board. But it seems you don't check your mailbox very often. Fortunately, we had a quorum, so your vote wasn't essential. Not that we wouldn't have loved to have it," he hastened to add. "But we didn't think you would have disagreed with anything we were considering."

Annie was somewhat mollified. And it had been a wonderful surprise—although she would have been happy to bypass some of the misery she'd felt these last few days, thinking that the rest of the herd, save her five horses, was doomed. She sighed. She knew she had email on her new phone. Hannah had set it up for her and even shown her how to use it. But how many things could you recall after a whirlwind training session with an eight-year-old computer maven? Annie had just as-

sumed she'd catch up on what sparse email she'd received the past week when she returned home.

Jessica rose to her feet, a determined gleam in her
eye.

"Well, I don't know what the feedlot owner is doing
in there, but it's time for me to get to work. Annie, do
you still have that medical kit I gave you?"

"I do, plus my own."

"Let's check out the horses who are verifiably sick
and injured. We've decided I'll haul the worst cases,
and Patricia will take the mares and foals. Her trailer is
big enough to load half of the contestants in the Ken-
tucky Derby and has adjustable stalls to accommodate
both mother and foal."

Annie looked gratefully over to Patricia, the most
well-dressed female in the bunch. As always, she was
wearing her trademark English riding breeches and a
hunting jacket, yet she looked right at home with
Annie's more plebeian friends, laughing and joking as
if she'd been friends with all of them since childhood.
For Patricia to bring one of her state-of-the-art trailers
to the rescue party was a truly magnanimous gesture.
Annie was sure only horses of the highest pedigree had
ever traveled in its luxurious interior before today. Now,
it was going to be used by mares and their offspring
who could be carrying any number of diseases and
whose lineage was questionable. Although, Annie had
to admit, every person spread out on the stubby grass
before her had made the same sacrifice with their own
hauling equipment. She predicted a massive cleanup
and sanitizing party following their arrival. But first,
they all had to get the horses home.

But where exactly was home right now? In the exhilaration of knowing that the horses would be saved, Annie had yet to think this question through.

"Where are we going to put all the horses, Jessica? I assume your client doesn't have enough stalls to accommodate the entire feedlot."

Jessica smiled and nodded toward Patricia. "Running Track Farms has agreed to lease a twenty-acre patch to us for the next several months. It's a section of the facility that's seldom used and already has a dozen or so stalls on it."

"And we're building more as we speak," Travis added. "Dan's organized a construction crew that's building new stalls and run-in shelters right now. Fortunately, with the summer weather being as good as it is, we're not in crisis mode. The acreage has a number of orchards and plenty of shade. And a potable stream runs through it."

Trees. Annie could hardly wait to see old-growth trees again. But then her brain clicked in. "How'd you do it so quickly, Dan? Marcus has only been here two days. How'd you manage to get builders so soon, and on a weekend to boot?"

"Well, Travis's late-night phone call to the county commissioners got the ball rolling," the sheriff said. "That got us an expedited building permit."

"I still can pull a few strings in the county when I have to," Travis said modestly.

"And as you may recall, we have a source of fine manual labor right at our fingertips."

"We do? Where?" demanded Annie.

"About three hundred feet from the sheriff's office, in the Suwana County jail." Kim looked extremely smug as she said this. "The men love working outside, and we're paying them handsomely, aren't we, Dan?"

"Yup. Eighty-five cents an hour. You won't make that much in a state penitentiary. My nephew, Bill Stetson, is ferrying them back and forth to work. He's doing a fine job, that boy. A fine job."

Annie hoped so. Not long ago, Deputy Stetson had let a prisoner out on bail without verifying his local address or the ID of the bail bondsman. She hoped the work crew remained intact while they were under his supervision.

Myrna finally emerged from her double-wide, holding a piece of paper in her hand. She looked down at the group still resting in the trees with ill-concealed contempt.

"Forty grand. And that's my final offer. No negotiating."

Forty grand. Annie gasped. She could barely believe what she'd just heard. She looked at Marcus and Travis to see if they were as taken aback as she was. They were not. Either that, or they were capable of hiding their true feelings better than she was.

"One moment, Mrs. Fullman," Travis told the scowling woman, and walked over to the truck in which he and Dan had arrived. He returned a minute later with a large bank bag.

"Shall we conclude our business in your office?"

"If you want."

Travis and Myrna disappeared into the double-wide and silence reigned in their absence. No one seemed to know what to do or say. This was the moment of truth. Nothing could go wrong now, could it?

Five minutes later, Travis emerged. He triumphantly shook the bank bag toward the crowd, showing how much it had been depleted. Annie cheered and applauded with everyone else, then turned to Marcus.

"Thank you for the best birthday gift in the world."

"You're very welcome. Tell me, how exactly do we get all these large animals into those trailers?"

"Think of each trailer as Noah's ark."

"You mean, we'll load them two by two?"

"Precisely."

CHAPTER 28

It was a good thing her friends knew a thing or two about horses, Annie thought later, because it took all of their combined equine acumen and experience to get the trailering job done. It wasn't just that loading the horses took so much time. It was also the time it took to expertly maneuver and align each truck and trailer correctly and in order, then make sure each horse was safely stowed with food and water within easy reach.

And there were so many horses—Annie had counted close to fifty before, but that number spiked after Maria arrived with the small herd from the reservation. The mare and foal were first to unload. Annie was astounded by the change in the newborn in just a single day. She seemed utterly confident tripping behind or running alongside her mother.

"Thank you, Annie," Maria said, when all the horses

had been unloaded from the cattle trailer Maria had appropriated for the job. "You have no idea how much this means to me and Colin and Aleisha."

"Please come visit the horses anytime you want."

"I'll do that, Annie. Maybe later this month, after you get all the horses settled."

Annie hugged Maria good-bye, and for the first time in days, felt as if the embrace was unencumbered with suspicion, or guilt, or any other lingering negative emotion.

"Tell Colin to come, too. And to bring his little sister."

"I will. Now I'd better get this trailer back before the owner knows it's missing." She smiled at Annie, then turned and jogged easily to her truck. Annie didn't know if Maria was telling the truth about the trailer or not. She decided she didn't much care.

For the first hour, Annie and LuAnn assumed the roles of horse handlers. As she'd suggested to Marcus, the easiest way to load the horses was two by two, starting from the back. Clearing the aisle of all debris, they started with Annie's herd, all of which loaded beautifully. In fact, the majority of the rescues were delighted to climb into their designated trailer although their "walk to freedom" down the aisle often turned into a lope or a fast trot, once they'd seen all their equine friends on board. Annie and LuAnn were leading each horse by a halter, which meant they got just as much of a workout as the horse, only many times over.

Marcus and Travis stood to the side, checking off each one as it entered a trailer and making occasional comments to the horse handlers along the way.

"Getting a good workout, Annie?" Marcus inquired politely after she'd led her sixth cantering horse to the caravan. She was breathing too hard to reply and stopped momentarily to catch her breath, placing her hands on her knees.

"My dear girl, you may faint again if you keep up that pace." Travis handed her a pristine white handkerchief, which Annie promptly obliterated with dust and sweat with one swipe across her forehead. This was her show, and she was determined to lead every horse by hand into a trailer. But eventually, wiser heads prevailed.

"You've got a long drive ahead of you," Jessica sternly told her. "If you wipe yourself out now, you'll be no good on the road. Think, Annie. Be sensible for once."

And so Annie reluctantly ceded her role to Samantha, and LuAnn gratefully gave up her own to Kim. The new relay team was just as efficient and, Annie noticed, had far more energy than the original crew. But then, Kim and Samantha worked out. Perhaps she should join a gym sometime, she thought, knowing she never would.

The next issue became evident once two trailers were filled. Dan had maneuvered both to rest under the most shade he could find, and every single trailer window was open, but it was clear that the horses could not remain standing in solid heat for much longer.

"We'll have to start the transport," Jessica announced firmly. "I don't know why I ever thought we could go back the way we came, as one group. We need to get these horses on the road, now."

Sarah and Dan were elected drivers, and after hugs all around, they climbed into their respective cabs and started the long trek back. It occurred to Annie that everyone here, with the exception of herself and Marcus, had been up long before dawn. It was going to be an incredibly long day. She was so grateful for everyone's help and fervently hoped everyone could sleep in the next day. Which reminded her—who was taking care of everyone's horses? Sam, Sarah, Jessica, and LuAnn all had their own herds to tend do. Patricia, she knew, had a small army of workers and a full veterinary staff to care for the equines at her facility. But everyone else was pretty much their horses' sole caretaker. She grabbed Jessica's arm.

"Who's taking care of your clinic horses?"

"Oh—that's all handled. I called Lisa and asked her if she could organize a round-robin of her horse friends to take care of all our horses today. She did an amazing job; you should see her flowchart of who goes where. I knew she was disappointed not being here and helping with the rescue, but she understood she was needed more back home. She's really a great kid. I'd like to hire her myself. I could use someone like Lisa at the clinic full-time."

"Keep your mitts off her. I found her, and she's mine."

Jessica laughed. "Well, maybe we can share her."

"Perhaps." Annie smiled back but realized how much she would miss her stable assistant if she took another job. In three months, Lisa had become an indispensable part of her ranch.

After the next two trailers were loaded, Kim and Sam clambered up into their trucks and headed out. Dan had already called to inform Jessica he'd just cruised by Moses Lake and was headed toward Ellensburg. Sarah's rig was right behind him.

"Good," Jessica told the sheriff. "Please continue to tag team each other all the way back, just in case one of you needs to stop for any reason."

"Ten-four. Over and out."

"Honestly," Annie told no one in particular. "Give Dan a big rig, and he thinks he's a CBer and king of the road. If he starts calling me 'good buddy,' I'm going to have to slug him."

It was now two o'clock, and the sun was reaching its zenith overhead. Annie looked up at the infinitely blue sky and sighed. They were four trailers down but had just as many to go.

Jessica decided the next trailer to be filled was Patricia's, and the driver insisted on helping escort the mares and foals into the box herself. This provided some much-needed comic relief, as many of the foals had never been outside the paddock and, despite wanting to cling to their mothers' sides, couldn't help but want to explore the new world that had literally just opened up before them.

"Come, little ones, we're all going to take a lovely ride home in a very comfortable trailer," Patricia called out, trying to corral a particularly curious foal who had temporarily gone astray. Annie had been laughing so hard at the zigzag procession that her stomach now ached. She was happy beyond words to know that mother and foal would be together as long as they needed, not ripped from each other at the worst possible time, had Myrna had her way.

And where was Myrna? Annie looked around but saw no sign of the woman. She was probably still inside the double-wide, counting and recounting her money, she thought. That was fine with her.

Once the maternity ward was loaded, Annie and Jessica quickly filled LuAnn's trailer and sent the two rigs on their way. They looked at each other. They were down to two trailers, the ones they'd brought. Jessica's would be the hardest because she was transporting obviously sick and injured equines. Annie's trailer would take the rest of the herd. She did a quick head count of the horses left. They were all showing signs of anxiety, even the sick ones, she noticed, wondering whether or not they, too, would leave or be left behind. She counted eight—no, nine horses. Phew. They had just enough room, with one slot to spare.

At three-thirty, the two trailers were filled. At last, it was time to leave. Annie couldn't wait to see the back of the feedlot. If she could have, she would have lit a torch and thrown it over her shoulder in the direction of Myrna's office as she left. But that would be arson, and deliberately setting fires was wrong. She knew Alvin definitely would not approve.

"If you've no objection, I'll take the lead, and you follow." Jessica was already in her truck, with the air-conditioning turned on high in both her cab and horse trailer. Travis, who had insisted on staying when Dan departed with his trailer, was in the seat beside her.

"Fine with us," Annie replied, glancing at Marcus, who nodded in agreement. Her trailer, too, had air-conditioning of a sort—the au naturel kind. Annie hoped the oscillating fans would keep the air inside from becoming too warm for the horses. It occurred to Annie that Jessica had not said a single word about her other trailer, the vandalized one. It looked considerably better than it had a few days ago, but the aluminum siding was still creased and bent, and in truth, the trailer looked as if it had aged ten years overnight. She vowed she would find a mechanic who would make it look as good as new upon her return. She owed it to her friend.

Annie waited for Marcus to emerge from the gas-station store. At his insistence, they had stopped to gas up and stock up on food and beverages before the long trip home truly got under way. Jessica had gassed up, as well, but had passed on the canteen; she'd thought ahead and brought her own foodstuffs from home. Jessica's truck was now off to the side, patiently idling, waiting for Annie's rig to swing in behind her.

Annie could feel the horses moving around in the trailer but wasn't too concerned. She knew that once they were on the open highway and going at a relatively constant speed, they'd settle down into the rhythm of the road. She tapped her finger on the steering wheel, anxious to start the journey. Marcus must be buying out the entire store.

Her assumption had been correct. He came out with a large paper bag cradled in each arm, and Annie had to push open his door in order for him to deposit them before he climbed in himself.

"Did you leave anything for the other customers?" she inquired.

"A couple of bags of chips. I had to think of Wolf's needs, too."

"Wolf has a half container of perfectly good dog food in the back."

"Yes, but once he sees what we'll be eating on the way home, he won't be content with just plain old kibble."

"What did you get?" Annie started digging through the bags to see what Marcus considered adequate road-trip food. She saw bags of pretzels, potato chips, cookies, sandwiches, soft drinks, and at least a half dozen chocolate bars. She looked quizzically at him.

"I didn't know what kind you liked, dark or milk chocolate, nuts or no nuts, so I got them all." Marcus said this apologetically.

"I like all of them. Excellent job. We shall not starve on the way home."

*   *   *

All that horse gathering had made Annie hungry. She dove into a bag of chips a short mile after she'd exited the gas station. Wolf instantly put his panting tongue next to her right check. Wolf was such a subtle dog, she thought, as she alternated feeding herself one chip and Wolf the next. She wondered if Marcus was watching, and when she glanced over, was amused and relieved to discover he'd fallen asleep, his head resting on the passenger window. Poor guy. He probably was still recovering from jet lag. And it wasn't as if she'd given him a lot of time to catch up. He'd hit the ground running ever since landing at the Duncan-Loman Airport.

She saw the sign that said they were four miles from Loman, which offered four blocks of nothing as far as she was concerned. She crumpled the empty chip bag, and tossed it in the back cab. The sound was sufficient to awaken Marcus, who jerked awake, then yawned, rubbing his eyes.

"Are we there yet?"

"Not quite. We've got about an hour of quaint country roads to traverse before we hit I-90. You might as well go back to sleep. There's nothing here to watch except the grass grow."

Annie was obediently following Jessica's rig. A single car separated them, but it soon turned off onto a farm road. She instinctively tapped her brakes, then slightly sped up to ease the gap between her truck and Jessica's. Even so, Jessica's trailer was making better time; her trailer was perfectly aligned while, despite Andy's hard work, the one Annie was hauling still vibrated a bit more than she would have liked. As she saw Jessica disappear over the crest of a small hill, she reminded herself to call her vet once they hit the freeway to tell her to pull back a bit if she expected Annie to keep up with her all the way home.

"How are the horses doing?" Marcus nodded toward the back.

"They're doing fine. I can feel them moving around a bit, but once we hit the freeway, they'll settle down and be quiet. I'll check on them when we pull into a rest stop. But in general, I'd like to keep moving. Judging from the time we left, we won't be at Running Track Farms until nine o'clock. Patricia's facility is an hour north of my place."

"I wish I could spell you. But I'm just not comfortable driving a truck attached to a trailer with four live animals inside."

"I understand. And I'm fine for driving, really. I'll pick up a cup of coffee somewhere along the way. And if I start to fall asleep, you can sing to me or tell me stories."

Marcus laughed heartily. "You obviously haven't heard my voice. Even my mother admits I'm tone-deaf."

"Well, I guess I'll have to settle for the stories."

Marcus leaned over to look at Annie's truck radio.

"Why don't I try to find something for you so I can go back to sleep?"

"Lots of luck. Around here, you're more likely to hear the drone of crop reports on the air than anything else."

He turned the ON button and started to scan. Most of the selections were a variation of static. The rest belted out energetic Mexican music. He switched it off and leaned back in his seat. Within a minute, he was gently snoring. Annie smiled and carefully unwrapped a candy bar, trying to make as little noise as possible. Wolf whined once for a bite, but when Annie refused to give

in, he sighed and joined Marcus in the sleep of the innocent.

Unlike her passengers, Annie was wide awake. Some
small scrap of information was eluding her, and it was
bothersome. She knew it was something she had heard
on her trip to the county airport, but what the devil was
it? The memory simply wouldn't come to the forefront
of her mind. She relived her conversation with Mack a
dozen times, but still it refused to reveal itself. Annie
knew it was seeing the choke on the old pickup that had
pricked her brain, but after several hours of loading
horses, her brain simply refused to fully engage and
give her the pertinent connection.

Her cell phone lit up, and she grabbed it before it
began to ring. It was Kim, who informed her she'd just
passed Annie's alma mater in Ellensburg and that she
and Sam Higgins were making excellent time.

"Great," Annie said sotto voce. "I'll be the last to arrive,
but that's okay. It'll be wonderful to see all the horses that
preceded us at Patricia's farm. Then I'll really know
they're safe."

"If it's still daylight by the time you get there. But I
know what you mean. Why are you talking so softly?"

"The prince is sleeping. I think jet lag finally caught
up with him."

"Or something," Kim said coyly. "But listen, Annie, I
called to tell you something else. I just got a call from
Rick, Tony's pilot friend, who got some interesting news.
Off the record, of course. Technically, the crash is still
under investigation, and Rick only got this because he's
pals with someone on the NSTB."

"Do tell."

"They think they've discovered the cause of the crash."

"An IED. We've known that for ages."

Actually, it had only been ten days, but at this point, the plane crash seemed to have happened a long time ago.

"Sorry. I mean the NSTB has figured out where the fire started. And where the IED was placed."

"The primer. The IED was attached to the primer."

"Annie! Who have you been talking to? I just got off the phone with Rick!"

"I just figured it out. I mean, literally, just this minute. The IED was on the primer barrel. That's why nobody spotted it—who looks behind dashboards before takeoff? And as long as it didn't detonate, Trevor's plane would have flown just fine."

Annie was now thinking fast, trying to envision what would happen once the primer barrel exploded.

"But once it did, all the fuel would feed down from the wings—that's where it's stored—into the cockpit. And because the fire was behind the dashboard, it would be almost impossible to put out. And . . ."

Suddenly, Annie couldn't go any further. She was imagining what it must have been like for Tony to be in a cockpit with the odor of fuel swirling around and smoke surging through the small area before everything erupted into a terrifying fuel-induced fire.

"You are absolutely right. Brilliant, Annie." Kim sounded genuinely impressed. "I continue to say you should consider a career in law enforcement."

"No way. But thanks."

Annie realized that Marcus was now awake and looking at her. His eyes still looked as if he were half-asleep, but there was an urgency about him that Annie couldn't ignore.

"Gotta go, Kim. Let's talk later." She put down the

phone. Just as quickly, Marcus touched her arm holding it.

"Annie! Coming up on your right! There's something in the road!"

Annie's eyes followed Marcus's outstretched arm. She saw a small oil drum about twenty feet ahead, prominently placed in her lane.

"What the hell?" she exclaimed.

Annie knew she couldn't swerve around it. There wasn't time, and it wouldn't be safe with the trailer behind her, anyway. She also knew her truck and the trailer would never clear the drum if she tried to go over it. She'd have to stop, take it out of the road, and proceed.

She looked around her and saw a place to pull over in relative safety. It was a small turn-in to an abandoned barn, a dingy grey, weather-beaten structure that listed at a perilously sharp angle. She put on her turn signal, as well as her brakes, and started to move toward the opening.

"Call Jessica. She should know we're stopping."

Marcus plunged his hand into his jeans pocket and pulled out his cell. Despite her concern about the truck, she was amused to see him simply punch a number and hold it to his ear. He had entered all of her friends' numbers into his phone. And all this time she'd assumed he was attending to his business, not hers. She hoped her friends hadn't shared any of her deepest, darkest secrets with the man during their many extended conversations.

Suddenly, Annie didn't have time to think about what her friends might have said or not to Marcus. She'd just seen Andy Johnson. He was crouched under the falling-down eave on the north side of the barn, shielded by an old, paint-stripped door. A rifle with a mounted scope was drawn up to his shoulder, and it was trained toward the road. But Annie knew Andy wasn't aiming it toward her. He was aiming at the drum. And when the bullet pierced that metal container, she, Marcus, and the horses would be enveloped in a fiery blaze as deadly as the one that had destroyed Danny Trevor's Cessna less than two weeks ago.

CHAPTER 29

Her warning came out as a high-pitched, out-of-control scream.

"Get out! Get out of the truck right now!"

Startled, Marcus looked at her strangely but did what she said. Her hands trembling, Annie brought the truck to a halt, shut off the engine, and wrenched her own door open. She leapt out and jerked open the door to the extended cab.

"Run, Wolf! Run!" Wolf bounded out but refused to leave her side. With a cry of frustration, Annie gripped his collar and dashed across the country road, dragging Wolf with her. She prayed that Marcus was following them and that no other vehicles were on the road. She stumbled into the wheat field on the other side. A moment later, Marcus appeared alongside her and, without stopping, pulled her to the ground.

"It's Andy! I saw him! He's going to shoot the drum

and the whole trailer will blow! It's a bomb, and it's about to go off!" The last sentence came out in a sob. She looked over to the trailer parked on the other side, now a mere ten feet away from the drum. She knew she couldn't save the horses inside. After all she, and they, had been through, they were still going to die. It was so horribly, terribly unfair. She covered her eyes with her hands so she would not see what was about to happen.

And then a long, fearful shriek filled the air, and Annie's head jerked up. She looked through the wheat stalks at the dilapidated barn where she'd last seen Andy. Behind the barn, and at a full gallop, came a black stallion ridden by a boy with a red handkerchief tied around his neck. The rider's face was streaked with bright swatches of color, as if he were a warrior from long ago, and he held a long pole laced with white rags that rippled in the breeze. The stallion was moving so fast that his legs were a blur. As it neared the barn, Annie saw Colin crouch low by the horse's mane. With one more eerie cry, he aimed his pole toward the terrified man, now standing, his body flattened against the barn door. The horse flew by him, and when Colin rounded the corner of the barn, the pole was no longer in his hand. It was now impaled in Andy's chest, the end still quivering. Its tip must have penetrated the wooden door because Andy was still standing, despite the blood dripping down his shirt. Only his head drooped over. Annie saw the hand that had been holding the rifle slowly release its grip and the weapon fall uselessly to the ground.

She watched Colin spur the horse with his bare feet, urging the stallion forward over the disused farmland in a fierce and constant gallop, his warrior cries echoing in the breeze behind him. When they at last faded away, and Annie was sure that the trailer was still intact, she decided to stand up. She was shaking, and she noticed that Marcus had to help her to her feet.

"You stay here," Marcus commanded.

For once, Annie was in no mood to argue. She had no interest in going down to gaze at Andy's lifeless body. What she'd seen from the wheat field had been more than enough.

Jessica arrived minutes later, while Marcus was still investigating the scene. She parked her trailer next to Annie's and ran over to her.

"What is going on?" Jessica cried, grabbing Annie by the shoulders. "Marcus called me, but he never said anything. All I could hear was a lot of noise. What happened to you?"

Marcus's footsteps were so quiet that when he answered Jessica, she gave a small shriek.

"Marcus! What the hell is going on?"

He was holding Andy's rifle with a handkerchief—a bright red one, Annie observed.

"We've had a bit of a delay. By the way, you've just driven by an IED. We need to stop traffic immediately in both lanes. Would you mind calling nine-one-one?"

"I already have. When I couldn't get you to talk on the phone, I figured you were in trouble. The cops should be on their way now."

As if on cue, the screech of sirens filled the air, and Annie watched four sheriff's office vehicles speed toward them. Marcus stepped into the middle of the road to flag them down.

She groaned. The last thing she wanted was another encounter with Sheriff Mullin. But there he was, the leader of the pack, exiting his county vehicle now. It seemed a good time to check on the horses.

* * *

To Annie's huge relief, the horses in the trailer had not suffered. From the number of piles on the floor mats and the sweat on their withers, she knew they'd been frightened by the sound of Colin's war cries, and even a few minutes in the heat without moving ventilation was less than ideal. Jessica had found a better place to park her rig and had engaged the air-conditioning feature in her trailer. It meant keeping her engine running, but at least the infirm horses inside were comfortable. The trailer she'd loaned Annie, however, did not have this luxury. Thick, hot air surrounded the horses, and she knew the temperature inside the trailer could quickly rise.

What was equally troubling was the line of vehicles that was slowly but steadily piling up in both lanes. Deputy's vehicles had immediately blocked the road, and Annie assumed that someone in the department was frantically trying to figure out a detour route now. Considering that most roads around here were two-lane, finding an alternate route for motorists that didn't bog them down just as much was going to be difficult. She willed herself not to think about the possibility that they'd all have to spend another night here. That would be cruel and unusual punishment, especially since everyone else in the rescue caravan would be happily reuniting at Patricia's place over the next several hours.

The wail of another law-enforcement vehicle filled the air, and Annie sighed. This was not a good omen. She wanted the police vehicles to leave, not multiply.

She noticed Marcus talking to a group of deputies who were watching the state patrol examine the oil drum. He seemed perfectly at ease as he engaged in conversation.

Annie wondered if his bonhomie was genuine or based on currying favor with the people who were in control of when they could leave.

"Annie!" Marcus looked a bit concerned seeing her in front of him. *Well, tough darts,* she thought. She was tired of hiding from Sheriff Mullin. She wanted to go home.

"What's happening?" she said in what she hoped was a friendly voice. "Are we any closer to getting the roads cleared?"

A deputy turned toward her. It was Deputy Goddard. Annie felt cold anger wash over her. She noticed that the deputy looked a bit nervous. As well he should, she thought. Marcus obviously didn't realize this was the cop who had tried to intimidate her several days ago. She remembered what Marcus had said about making him pay, along with all of his other rowdy friends.

"Ms. Carson," the deputy said. His tone was exceedingly polite.

Annie did not respond. She was seething, and knew if she opened her mouth, nothing good would come out. And then, behind her, she heard Sheriff Mullin's voice.

"Why, Ms. Carson, fancy seeing you here. I was just about to call you."

Her heart dropped. What could he possibly have to tell her that was good? Sheriff Mullin was the harbinger of bad news, pure and simple.

Annie's head was swimming. She tried to control the emotions that were churning inside her and knew she couldn't. It was too late. She had been here too long. And now, like it or not, Sheriff Mullin was going to get it with both barrels.

She took two steps forward until she was standing

UNBRIDLED MURDER

just a few inches in front of him. And then she began to speak.

"Please step aside and tell your deputies to do the same. I'm leaving."

She turned and made a step toward her truck.

Sheriff Mullin grabbed her arm.

"Hold on a second. I need to talk to you."

Annie flung her arm up, forcing the sheriff to drop it, and resisted the urge to punch him where it hurt.

"I came to your town one week ago to do one simple task—transport four horses from your miserable feedlot back to where I live. I had the very bad misfortune to be present when a murder occurred there. Instead of being treated with courtesy and respect, I have been subjected to the worst possible treatment. I've been considered a suspect when all I did was report the crime. I have been cooperative at every step of your investigation. In return, I've been threatened by local hoodlums and told to leave town. My trailer was trashed. And your response through all of this has been to ignore these crimes and continue to harass me. So no, you can't talk to me. I will not listen to a man who employs people who take delight in bullying people and destroying their property."

Sheriff Mullin let go of her arm. He actually looked somewhat surprised.

"Who's been bullying you?"

Besides yourself, you mean? Annie thought, but didn't say this.

"Your deputy over there. He was part of the crowd that threatened me if I didn't leave town. And undoubtedly trashed my trailer afterwards."

"Ray, is that true? You told me you'd seen Ms. Carson at the bar. You didn't tell me you were part of the crowd that approached her."

Deputy Goddard's face had turned bright pink. "Leroy was just having a bit of fun," he began.

"Leroy was there with his boys? And you were with him?"

The deputy said nothing.

"Why didn't you tell me?"

"I was just trying to help her." Deputy Goddard definitely was becoming a bit sullen. "I was trying to warn her what might happen if she didn't back off. Besides, it didn't come to nothin'."

"Oh, yes, it did," Annie said angrily. "It resulted in thousands and thousands of dollars of damage to my trailer." She pointed to it on the side of the road. "There are four overheated horses in it right now, and if I don't get them on the road soon, you're going to be investigating a case of animal cruelty, and you'll be the one charged with a crime."

Sheriff Mullin looked over at the trailer. His eyes squinted a bit, as if this would bring the damaged vehicle into better focus. He slowly walked over to it and ran his hand along the creased aluminum siding. Then he turned to the silent group. Annie realized that Marcus was now holding her hand. She gave it a squeeze.

"Here's what I'm going to do. Ms. Carson, I'm going to ask the deputies to clear the roadway so you and your friends can leave now. Deputy Goddard here is going to escort you all the way to the I-90 ramp. After that, you're on your own. Ray, I want to see you in my office at oh-eight hundred tomorrow morning. Is that clear, everyone?"

It was. Annie ran back to her truck, where Wolf had been patiently waiting in the driver's seat. The heeler promptly vacated his position when he saw his mistress's face, the one he knew meant no mercy. Annie turned the ignition key to get the oscillating fans going once more in the trailer and waited for Marcus to finish whatever he had to say to the sheriff. She glanced in her rearview mirror and saw Jessica already in her truck. They exchanged waves and smiled.

Sheriff Mullin walked over with Marcus to the passenger side. Once Marcus was in and had his seat belt strapped, the sheriff put his arms on the window and leaned inside.

"Don't you want to know why I was going to call you?"

Not really, she thought, but answered, "Sure."

"I was going to tell you you're free to go."

Annie started to laugh. She couldn't help it. The stress of the past week was catching up with her, and she found it hard to stop.

The sheriff looked a bit puzzled by her response.

"We will need to get a statement from you, you know. About this"—the sheriff nodded toward the crime scene in back of him—"and about that other thing."

That other thing. Annie reached around to get her purse.

"Here's my report. Photos to follow. Not to mention the bill."

It struck her that the trailer had been repaired by the man who had just tried to kill her. She started to laugh again, then stopped.

"One more thing, Sheriff."

He nodded patiently.

"Tell your deputy over there he can activate his lights but no sirens. The horses have been scared enough by all your noise."

Sheriff Mullin tipped his Stetson toward her. "Will do." He walked toward the deputy's car, and Annie began to laugh again.

CHAPTER 30

It took more than an hour for the small procession to crawl past the long queue of idling cars and trucks on both sides of the road. Deputy Goddard had decided to straddle both lanes, and Annie did her best to look straight ahead as she slowly watched the centerline disappear underneath her truck. She wanted to avoid the glares of sitting motorists, who she knew were destined to be there for hours before the road was finally cleared for travel. It was now late afternoon, and Annie mentally calculated their new arrival time. It would be close to midnight before they arrived at Running Track. But at least she was still alive, as were Marcus and the horses. That more than made up for a few extra hours on the road.

"Remind me never to be on your bad side."

It was the first thing Marcus had said since greeting her after she'd approached the group of deputies. He hadn't said a word throughout Annie's harangue of the sheriff, and she appreciated his willingness to let her fight her own private battle.

"Well, he deserved it. I can't imagine you ever doing anything as heinous as he and his henchmen tried to do to me."

"I certainly hope not."

Two cell phones buzzed simultaneously, and both Annie and Marcus each scrambled to find his or her device.

Marcus peered at his phone's screen. "It's Dan."

"Mine's from Jessica."

"Let me talk to Dan first. He's less up-to-date."

Annie nodded, and flashed her outstretched fingers to Jessica in her rearview mirror, indicating she'd call her back in five minutes or so.

"Put it on speaker," she urged Marcus. "And let's be circumspect. We don't want Dan and Kim to come roaring back here, which they will if they know the whole truth."

"Agreed." He pressed a button, and Dan's booming voice filled the cab.

"What in the Sam Hill is going on? I'm about to head up the pass and hear on the radio that there's a bomb scare on a road I passed through just a few hours ago."

Marcus cleared his throat. "Yes, well, thankfully, we missed the worst of it." Annie realized this wasn't far from the truth.

"Well, thank the Lord for that. I'm assuming all roads are closed for the foreseeable future. Where are you now?"

"We're inching our way to I-90. The roadblock set us back a few hours, but at least we're moving."

"Of all the damn bad luck. So what happened? When I first got the news, I thought it might have something to do with Annie or the horses."

"We really don't know much about it. There's apparently an IED in the middle of the road, but that's about all we know."

Annie was impressed by the way Marcus had adroitly not answered Dan's implied question.

"Who's in charge? State patrol or Mullin's gang?"

"It started with Mullin, but the state patrol is now out in full force. We've seen several of their vehicles zooming by in the last half hour. I'm assuming they're in charge of dismantling whatever is in the road."

"Annie, you there?"

"I'm here."

"Keep your head down. The last thing you need right now is for Sheriff Mullin to realize you're in the backup line heading out of town."

She crossed her fingers. "Will do."

"Well, glad to hear you're both all right. I should sign off now. I'm going up a mountain where cell reception is iffy."

"Sounds good," Marcus said. "We'll keep you updated on our progress. And please let anyone else who hears about the bomb threat know that we're perfectly fine."

"Ten-four, good buddy."

He'd done it. He'd actually said "good buddy." At least it hadn't been directed toward her. Marcus, she knew, was far more tolerant of Dan's speech patterns than she would ever be.

Her phone call to Jessica was also on speakerphone, and was short and sweet as well.

"Annie! You know that mysterious rider who came to your rescue?"

Annie had given Jessica a broad outline of what happened. But she'd decided the rider's identity was on a need-to-know basis, and so far, she couldn't think of a single person who needed to know. Besides, Jessica had never met the young man or even known that he existed.

"Yes?"

"Well, I've been seeing a guy on a black horse, a stallion, I think, following our trek out of town. He's on the left, and every so often he appears."

"Is he wearing war paint?"

"Don't be silly, Annie. If it is the same rider, how do you think he knew what Andy was up to?"

"Hard to say. I can't figure out why Andy went after us at all. I guess the IED means he was behind the plane crash, too, but that's as far as I can get. Andy must have thought I knew something—something that persuaded him I had to be eliminated. Pretty terrifying, when you think about it."

"Indeed. Let's just hope he acted alone, and no one else is out to get you."

"Thanks, Jessica. I know I can always count on you to cheer me up."

Both Annie and Marcus kept a lookout for Colin, but neither of them saw so much as a glimpse of the stallion or the boy. And after twenty minutes, their creep to the freeway eased into a more normal rate of speed, which made outside gazing, at least for Annie, impossible. But even though Colin remained hidden from sight, he was very much on both of their minds.

"That young man is going to need a lawyer." Marcus's pronouncement sounded unequivocal.

Silently, Annie agreed. But what she said was different. "How could he be charged with anything? He saved our lives. We would all be blown to smithereens if it weren't for Colin's bravery."

"Sheriff Mullin already asked me what I observed. I didn't name Colin, but I could see where he was headed, and if he asks me point-blank, I'm not going to lie."

"No, I know you won't. Neither will I. I just wish I knew how he happened to arrive in the nick of time."

"That, and the answer to about a thousand other unanswered questions."

The only thing Annie knew for sure at that moment was that fifty-plus horses were about to start enjoying a completely different kind of life. And that made her very happy.

As Annie had predicted, they pulled into Running Track Farm just before midnight. Marcus had phoned ahead, and so Patricia was waiting by the electronic gate, ready to buzz them in. All the other transport vans had preceded them by several hours, and Patricia assured her that after each trailer unloaded she had sent all the weary drivers home. The twenty-acre plot was almost a mile beyond the boarding and training facility Annie and Jessica had visited earlier this year but easily accessible by a well-kept road. Patricia had hopped into Jessica's van for this final step in the horses' journey.

"Wow, it looks fantastic," Annie exclaimed, after seeing the neat white cross fencing that surrounded the pasture. It was about all she could see at this time of night, but it was obvious that even the seldom-used areas of Running Track Farms were kept in immaculate shape.

"Wait until you see it by day," Patricia told her. "The work crew is fantastic. They've already erected six run-in shelters, and their super assures me they'll have a dozen more completed by the end of the week."

Annie was just glad no escapes had been reported.

But then, eighty-five cents an hour was not an income jail inmates would sneeze at. And the scenery was certainly a lot better than what they saw from the confines of the Suwana County pokey.

"At the moment, there are three secure pastures." Patricia extended her arm into the darkness to designate fenced-in areas Annie could only guess were present. "We've put the stallions in one, the mares and foals in the other, and the rest in the biggest portion. That's where we'll unload yours, Annie."

Fortunately, there were three overhead lights constructed on the pasture poles, so leading the horses out of the trailer was not entirely done by feel. She thought the horses must be exhausted after the eight-hour drive, although she knew Jessica's trailer was a far better accommodation than what they would have had if their destination had been to the north instead of west. All of them were shiny with sweat, but thankfully not overheated. They were simply glad to be let out of their giant crate, no matter how much orchard grass had been given them.

Patricia showed her exactly where the horses would stay their first night.

"I've cordoned off that small bit to the right, so none of them have to worry about making friends with everyone else until tomorrow."

"You've thought of everything," Annie said gratefully. Now that the numbing drive was over, she realized just how tired she was, too. She did not look forward to the hour-long drive home, which would be in pitch-darkness. But at least she had succeeded in getting here, and that was the most important thing.

"Patricia, how about my load?" Jessica sounded a bit anxious. "You may recall that I've got the sick and injured horses."

"Oh, how remiss of me." Patricia made a small *tsk, tsk*, as if she were reprimanding herself. "The existing stalls have been allocated for them, so we can keep them separate from the rest of the herd. They're on the other side. Let's get Annie's herd settled, then we'll take them over there."

When the last horses had been shown to their stables, Patricia led the group to the conference room Annie recalled from her first visit here, when she'd first become acquainted with the rich lineage of Hilda Colbert's horses. An assortment of beverages, both hot and cold, were laid out on a cart beside it.

"Please help yourself to refreshments," she told her very tired visitors. "And congratulations on a job well done."

Annie noted that, for reasons beyond her ken, Patricia looked remarkably well rested, considering she'd been up at dawn and had overseen the arrival of several dozen horses over the past several hours. Perhaps she'd popped into the built-for-horses hyperbaric chamber on-site as a pick-me-up. Either that, or there had been a massage therapist on board the Running Truck van who'd soothed away Patricia's aches and pains as she drove. Whatever it was, she looked twice as alert as any normal person had a right to be. Annie reached out to grab a Red Bull. She was going to need it for the drive home.

"Before we go any further, I do insist that all of you spend the night here instead of returning to your own homes tonight."

Jessica and Annie immediately began to protest. Marcus was strangely quiet.

Patricia put up a hand. "I know you're all anxious to see your beds, but it's now nearly two o'clock in the morning, and you're all exhausted. You've all been to

Running Track before and know that we have guest accommodations ~~at the~~ ready. So, please, think about it
rather than heading off in the middle of the night. Besides, I've already been in touch with both your care-
takers, and they've happily agreed to stay at your
clinic, Jessica, and your stables, Annie, for another
night. So if you went home now, you might not find an
empty bed to sleep in."

"Excellent idea, Patricia." Marcus reached around to
the beverage cart and selected a beer from a local mi-
crobrewery. "I accept your gracious hospitality with
heartfelt thanks."

Annie eyed her companion, put back the Red Bull,
and reached for a microbrew herself.

The cabin given to Annie and Marcus was close to
the pasture where most of the horses had been unloaded. Walking outside in the crisp but clement summer air, Annie craned her neck over the fence line to
see if she could espy the four horses she and Tony had
originally agreed to save, or Eddie the Thoroughbred,
or the horse with one blue eye and one-and-a-quarter
ears, whom she'd secretly named Lefty. She could not.
It was simply too dark to make out anything but the
shape of horses clustered together. But she could hear, if
not see, horses quietly munching on rich, green grass.
This might be a new experience for many of them, she
thought. Green grass was a rare commodity where they'd
just been. A breeze floated through the trees, and the
smell of Douglas fir wafted over her. It was good to be
home.

EPILOGUE

"It's about time we did this," Jessica told Annie, who was dragging all of her mismatched lawn furniture over to her new barbecue pit. The pit had been a surprise gift from Travis Latham, to thank Annie for her above-and-beyond efforts in bringing fifty-eight horses safely back to Alex's Place. Annie really thought Travis was the one who deserved the honors since it had been his forty thousand smackers that had bailed out the equines, but she wasn't going to argue whether she liked the gift or not. It was a sight better than the small Coleman grill that she'd used for the past two decades.

"I agree." Annie was now casting a critical eye at her two picnic tables, recently purchased at a garage sale, and trying to decide how to prop one up a half inch to make it level with one another. Or not.

It was a lovely September afternoon, warm and dry and utterly devoid of the prescient air of autumn that often appeared this time of year. After eyeing Annie's new outdoor pit, Dan had suggested she host a party for all the members of the rescue team, to "get the official update," as he put it, on everything that had unfolded in all the homicide cases since they'd left eastern Washington, and she'd happily agreed. Marcus had flown in yesterday and was now picking up Travis at his home. All of Annie's friends had accepted her invitation on the spot. Even Maria Hernandez would be here; she was driving down from Browning at that very moment. And Kim Williams, Dan's new second-in-command at the sheriff's office, had said she wouldn't miss it for the world.

Annie had gone all out on the menu. It was easy to do, since she knew she wouldn't be cooking most of it. Barbecuing was man's work. You couldn't pry a grilling fork out of a guy's hand if you tried. And who would want to? But at least she'd contributed a succulent assortment of pork, beef, chicken, and sausage for them to work with—them meaning Marcus and Dan, who she suspected would turn into dueling chefs over their coveted rubs. Marcus had brought several he'd purchased from Williams-Sonoma. Annie knew that Dan would be fiercely defending his own personal concoction, made up of who knows what, but definitely good. She'd tasted it before at the annual community barbecue the sheriff's office hosted each July.

Eddie the Thoroughbred had been renamed Eduardo, in honor of Tony's Hispanic heritage, and was now living at Annie's ranch. He'd been a mess when Jessica had first inspected him; his hooves had looked as if they hadn't been touched in a year, he'd badly needed a dental, and every single one of his ribs had been visible to the naked eye. Annie's farrier was doing her best to reconstruct feet that any Thoroughbred would be happy to walk on, but for the moment, he usually wore therapeutic boots to protect his soles and frogs from deteriorating further. It would take several months, her farrier warned her, before he was truly sound and could be ridden.

In regard to the weight issue, Eduardo was doing fine. He zealously cleaned his feed bucket morning and evening and was now munching on good Timothy hay. No longer starved, he looked more like the lean racing machine he'd once been, although that part of his life was over forever, in Annie's book. Examining his teeth had been a rather fraught experience for both Jessica and Annie. They'd quickly learned Eduardo did not like to be tied. Period. He also was nervous about having anyone touch his face. But Annie was working on both of these issues, and she could now stroke his cheek without him flinching. Best of all, Trooper and Eduardo had turned into best pasture buddies almost upon meeting. Their combined high energy was a lovely sight to behold, although Annie realized the time she now spent grooming these two tall horses was twice what she spent on the rest of the herd. The boys just wanted to be boys, and dirt, apparently, was their friend.

Annie's guests had started wandering in around midafternoon, and by six o'clock, the party was in high gear. Marcus and Dan had outdone themselves on the grill, and just seeing the meat piled high on several platters made Annie's mouth water. Everyone had dug in with gusto, and although the levels on the platters had been greatly diminished, Annie was content to see that several days of good leftovers were in store for her, Marcus, and, of course, Wolf.

Completely sated, Annie sprawled on her one good chaise longue. She tried to reach for another beer, but the effort was simply too difficult. Her stomach was strongly urging her not to move for several hours. Fortunately, Marcus swooped in with a replacement before sitting down beside her, so the need for any exertion of energy was thankfully thwarted.

"Thank you, darling," she said. The phrase was becoming easier to say every time she used it.

"My pleasure."

"Have you seen Colin?"

Colin was the surprise guest who'd accompanied Maria today. Yes, school was officially in session, but, as Maria had reminded them, she *was* the tutor for Colin's sophomore class, and she planned to grill him on Washington state history all the way back to Browning tomorrow. Colin had disappeared after feasting on barbecue and hadn't been seen since. Annie suspected he was off in the field, communing with the horses. Patricia had promised to show him and Maria their rescued herd tomorrow, before they left. All the horses were at the tail end of their quarantine experience. They'd be transported to Alex's Place before winter officially began, when the barn and stables would be complete.

Out of the corner of her eye, she saw Colin wending his way back to the crowd. He was essentially a shy boy, Annie knew, not unlike herself at that age. But he interacted well with adults, far better than she had as a gangly, tongue-tied adolescent. And she was glad that he was here today. He was such an essential part of the story that Dan was about to reveal. Dan could be a great storyteller at times, but Annie knew that Colin, who'd lived through his experiences, could best express them.

Sunset was spreading over the ranch. It came more quickly these days, and Annie realized, with a tinge of sadness, that soon the nights would be nearly as long as the days, and the amount of sun seeping through would often be fleeting. Hadn't some poet written "gather ye rosebuds while ye may," or some such line? That was how she felt about today.

Dan gave a large, ungainly harrumph, apparently his vocal indication that the tales were about to begin. It took another five minutes for people to seat themselves with a suitable beverage, but at last Dan had his audience together, and he stood up, ready to begin.

"The secrets to the cases I am about to unfold . . ."

Boos and napkins were thrown in his general direction. Dan glared at his critics and began again.

"All right, all right! I'll cut to the chase. This is one of the most interesting cases I've ever seen. I just wished it had happened in my jurisdiction. I would have cleared it up a lot sooner."

Sporadic laughter broke out, but it was not unkind.

"Here's the mystery. Why would a run-of-the-mill mechanic kill a deputy of the peace, an airline pilot, and a feedlot owner? What possible motive could he have for all these killings? They had to be related, but how?"

"Personally, I'm just glad the killer didn't turn out to be a horse rescuer," Maria said, glancing over at Annie. "That would have been bad for the cause."

"And I'm just happy there was only one killer, period, and he didn't succeed in killing me, Marcus, and the horses." Annie cast a meaningful glance over at Jessica, who smirked.

"Well, for heaven's sake, don't keep us in suspense, Dan. Tell us. Hopefully, in two thousand words or less." Kim Williams had recently been promoted to undersheriff. Annie could tell that she felt a lot more comfortable telling her boss how she felt. *Good for her*, she thought.

"Yes, start with the first murder. Why did Andy kill George?" This was Marcus's contribution.

"Well . . ." Dan said, then stopped. "Oh, hell, Colin, you know this better than I do. Why don't you tell us about the friction between the mechanic and the feed-lot owner?"

Sheriff Mullin had tried to talk to Colin the day after Andy's death. The weapon Colin had used against Andy was widely recognized as his. And everyone knew Colin's black stallion; the two were inseparable. But he found he was unable to talk to the boy, for the simple fact that by then Alvin Gilman was Colin's attorney of record. Marcus had seen to that the next morning, while he and Annie were still luxuriating in bed in Patricia's pasture-side cabin.

Colin had been forthcoming with his new attorney, who, in turn, had related the facts of the case to the sheriff and local prosecutor. Coupled with Annie and Marcus's statements and phone interviews, the prosecutor felt he had no option but to decline to bring charges. Annie personally thought Colin deserved a medal. That, sadly, had not yet been bestowed.

Colin stood up now. Annie was sure he'd grown two inches since she'd seen him four weeks ago.

"I knew about Danny Trevor a long time ago. I would hide in the rocks and watch him fly over our land. One day, I found a place he sometimes landed. Another man was with him, Andy, the mechanic. They argued about what Danny was doing."

"You mean Andy actually thought what Danny was doing was wrong?" Annie couldn't believe this.

"No. They were arguing about money. Andy thought he should get money from the tribe, too, because he took care of Danny's airplane. Danny said he got paid enough and wouldn't get any more. This made Andy mad. So when the plane crashed, I knew that Andy had to be involved."

"Which, of course, was absolutely right," Dan interrupted, looking at the boy with real respect. "And it was perfect timing for Andy. The bomb went off while Trevor was still in the clouds, and as we all know, he was flying VFR."

"We do? *I* don't know what you're talking about," Samantha Higgins shot out, while several people around her nodded in agreement.

"Visual flight rules." Dan said this as if it he'd known it all his life. "The pilot doesn't rely on instrumentation, just what he sees around him. Well, that day, there was a big cloud bank over the pass, and the bomb went off just when Trevor's Cessna was about to go into the murk. Which meant Trevor couldn't see squat outside the plane and, because of the smoke inside the cockpit, couldn't even see his instrument needles plunging. There was no way he could have gotten down quickly. He picked the wrong day to punch into the clouds."

Annie almost wanted to laugh about Dan's self-importance over his newfound aeronautical knowledge, not to mention his new vocabulary. But whenever she heard the story, she thought of Tony and his unexpected and sudden death. Many glasses had been raised today in honor and remembrance of the fallen deputy. Annie had no doubt that they would continue to be raised for years to come.

"But while killing Danny might have made Andy feel better, it wasn't bringing in any money," prompted Maria.

"Yes," continued Colin. "So I started to watch Andy, to see what he'd do next."

The crowd unconsciously settled into the chairs. This was where the story was becoming interesting.

"One day, not long after the plane crash, Andy called George on the phone from his shop. He wanted to meet with him. George must have said okay because Andy was real happy after that."

"Hold on! Wait a minute! How did you manage to pick up on that phone conversation?" Jessica was slightly indignant. "I mean, did you put a bug on his phone, or what?"

Maria smiled benevolently at the vet. "No one pays attention to a fifteen-year-old boy, Jessica. If he's not making trouble, he's invisible. Colin was a good tracker from the time he was just a toddler. You'd be having this private conversation, or so you thought, and realize that Colin was quietly watching you from a corner of the room."

Jessica still looked skeptical.

"That first night you were in town, Annie, and saw the horses on the ridge," Maria began.

"I never told you I went there!"

"No, but Colin did. He was watching you from behind a rock, along with his sister. You never even knew, did you?"

Annie shook her head. It seemed incredible to her that she could have been so unaware. But then, she'd been totally engrossed in the flight of the wild horses.

"So where were you hiding, Colin? When you heard Andy talking to George on the phone?" Jessica now seemed to accept the boy's tracking prowess.

"In the rafters. Where the pulleys are for cars. If Andy was working on a car on the ground, he never looked up."

Ten pairs of eyes looked at Colin, all admiringly. The kid clearly knew what he was doing, even if it was at a high risk to himself had he been caught.

"The next morning, I was supposed to watch the herd. So I asked Maria if she would do it for me so I could wait at the feedlot. She said yes. I got there about six o'clock.

Andy showed up around seven-thirty. He banged on the door, and George finally opened it. They argued, too. It was the same thing. Money. Andy wanted to take over Danny's job and wanted George to convince the tribe. It was hard because while Andy worked on airplanes, he didn't fly them. But he told George he knew everything about flying planes even if he didn't have a license."

Annie remembered Andy's telling her he knew more about airplane instrumentation than anyone else. She'd thought it was an outlandishly boastful statement at the time. She hadn't known then that he knew enough to turn a plane into one massive incendiary device.

"So George told Andy to leave. And then he got on his Kubota and went to feed the horses. Andy returned to his truck and shot him in the back. Then he ran around the corral and out the back."

"Where was Myrna all that time? Didn't she hear the argument? Or the gunshot?" Kim was asking all the questions a good undersheriff should ask.

Dan cleared his throat. "According to Sheriff Mullin, Myrna was having an affair with the fertilizer salesman in Loman. She was barely at the feedlot anymore, let alone home."

"Apparently old George was so blitzed most of the time, he never knew if Myrna was coming or going," Maria added. "But then, I didn't have a clue, either, and I was at the feedlot every week."

Annie found it difficult to believe that Myrna could hold any attraction for another human being, but then, she reminded herself, she hadn't met the fertilizer salesman.

She also knew an inside detail about the case that she and Marcus had decided to keep to themselves. As her last act as Alvin Gilman's client, she'd turned over the photos she'd taken on her smartphone to her attorney, who'd duly passed them on to the police—after carefully looking at them first himself. After enlarging the photos showing the red dots, Alvin had discovered that the first two photos were of Colin, wearing his red bandana, from behind the horses' rear paddock. This was where he'd been hiding, as he later told Alvin. But the third photo—the one of a person fleeing the property wearing red, was of Andy. The enlarged photo even gave pretty good detail of the gun he was carrying—a Marlin lever-action rifle, the same caliber as Annie's Winchester, only Andy's had a mounted scope.

"Why didn't you tell anyone, Colin?" Kim was sympathetic but obviously curious as to why the young man would not report a crime.

"I thought about it. But I didn't like George, and two of the men Andy had killed were killing the horses. So even though Andy was doing it for money, I wasn't sure the killings were a bad thing."

Western justice, Annie thought. There was a certain honesty about it even if it was no longer the prevailing law of the land.

"But I probably would have," Colin continued, "except that I met Annie. And I thought, what if I tell the sheriff what I saw, and he gets mad at me, not Andy? Then Andy could come after me. Or Annie."

"Why would Andy want to hurt Annie?" Patricia was genuinely flummoxed. "She's such a good person."

"Good to dogs and horses," Dan said ominously. "The rest of us take what she dishes out."

Much-needed laughter filled the air. There was something about Colin's solemn delivery about the practical points of witnessing murder that was a little bit off-putting.

Colin did not laugh, Annie noticed. He was always so serious. She hoped someday she'd see the boy laugh—

sheer, spontaneous laughter that came from his gut over something that was spectacularly silly.

"Yes, Annie is a good person," Colin agreed. "But I know the men who damaged the trailer. Andy knows many of them, too, and is friendly with them. When I saw him working on the trailer in his garage, I knew that Annie was in danger."

"But why? Even if Andy knew the men who vandalized it, he was still making a pile of dough off their bad act. How could that put her in danger?" Kim was digging into detail that most other listeners would just let slide.

"Because of what Annie told him."

Annie wracked her brain, trying to think of what incriminating thing she had said that might have set Andy off. She came up with nothing.

"She told Andy that there were eyewitnesses, people who saw who was destroying the trailer. This worried Andy because he was one of them."

A gasp went around the circle, the biggest from Annie. The mechanic had seemed so completely taken in by her story. And he'd done such a good job fixing the trailer. It seemed off-kilter that he would take so much trouble to repair something that he had tried to destroy. But then, he probably thought he was really scoring one over Annie—first, trash the trailer, then profit from repairing it. It still didn't explain why he might want to harm her.

"Then Annie told him that Dave at the airport had talked about the crash. That made Andy really worried."

"Why?" Annie was dying to know.

"Because Dave thought Andy was behind the crash, and Andy knew it. And so Andy called Dave to ask why he had told this total stranger about it, and Dave said he hadn't. That got Andy really suspicious. So he called the motel where Annie had been staying and found out she had checked out earlier than she was supposed to. So Andy told Leroy—"

"He's the top goon in Browning," Annie explained to her friends.

Colin nodded. "He's a bad man. And when Andy told Leroy that Annie wasn't telling him the truth, Leroy told him to watch her because she might be investigating the plane crash and other stuff."

So that was it. Andy had been convinced she was working undercover for the FAA or, more likely, Jessica's insurance company.

"But even if I had, killing me wasn't going to make any difference."

Colin nodded once more. "Yes, but Andy is the kind of person who thinks he has to get rid of anyone who might hurt him. After I heard him talk to Leroy, I knew that he was going to try to kill you, too."

The words sounded so stark coming out of the boy's mouth. But it was true. Andy had tried to kill her, and had failed, only because Colin, her guardian angel on earth, had protected her. What could she possibly do to thank him?

Wolf came trotting around the corner, wearing a bright red bandana. Annie had decided her blue heeler needed sprucing up today in front of so much company and could think of no greater compliment to Colin than for the dog to wear his trademark neck attire. Colin smiled. The smile got even broader when he saw that Wolf was carrying a half-rack of pork spareribs in his mouth. He set it down in front of Annie, pawed the ground three times, and looked up at her.

how do these come into the story?

"What? Do you need another napkin?" she asked. Her tone of voice gave the dog the encouragement he needed, and he promptly buried his teeth into the meat.

Everyone around her began to laugh, even Colin. It wasn't quite the belly laugh she'd hoped to hear, but it was a laugh.

"Roger that," Colin said, grinning, as Wolf enthusiastically began to gnaw away.

ACKNOWLEDGMENTS

A huge debt of gratitude goes to Chuck Perry, chief pilot for Kenmore Air, who not only made sure all the aeronautical bits and language in this book rang true, but also significantly helped shape the plot and turned out to be a very good line editor. His knowledge of old Chevy trucks also should be noted and applauded. My big brother Steve gets full credit for introducing me to this great line of farm trucks, one of which he restored for my husband and painted atomic orange. Other heartfelt thanks go to my agent, Paige Wheeler of Creative Media Agency Inc., Dr. Cary Hills of Sound Equine and vet tech Vicky Carter, ace attorney Ken Kagan, criminal defense attorney par excellence Jeff Kradel, bomb technician Alex Kaye of the U.S. Navy, Sandy Dangler, the best mentor one could ever have, and the many friends who read the book and thoughtfully provided suggestions on how to make it better. I am eternally grateful to Fern Michaels for her continued support and frequent atta-girl's, Robert Schwager for his always insightful comments, and to my husband, who thinks being married to a writer is just swell. Finally, thank you to all the people who rescue horses from feedlots. At some time, every one of these horses was loved. Those who choose to give them new and better lives have earned, as my mother would say, their stars in heaven.

If you enjoyed UNBRIDLED MURDER, be sure
not to miss Leigh Hearon's

SADDLE UP FOR MURDER
A Carson Stables Mystery

At first, horse trainer and Carson Stables owner
Annie Carson blames the random losses of local livestock on feral animals stalking the Olympic Peninsula's farms and ranches. But when one of her own
flock is found savagely slaughtered, it gets personal.
Then it turns dangerous when Annie discovers the
body of a young woman hanging in her new hay barn.
Suddenly, she's up to her neck in complicated myster-
ies—one involving her private life. But her sleuthing
skills aren't exactly welcome by the sheriff. And as she
uncovers a clue to the killer's identity, Annie fears she's
leading a deadly trail straight to her door.

Turn the page for a special look!

A Kensington mass-market and e-book on sale now.

PROLOGUE

TUESDAY, APRIL 26

Ashley Lawton dug into her jacket pocket and pulled out a key, a single strand of green yarn fluttering from the top. She turned to the woman beside her and said proudly, "Mrs. Carr lets me have my own. It's not strictly company policy, but she can't move around very well and it takes her a long time to get to the door."

Her companion nodded appreciatively. She was a willowy brunette dressed in an old-fashioned jumper. Ashley acknowledged her friend's tacit approval with a quick return nod and inserted the key into the lock in front of her. The knob turned, and she leaned inside, calling out, "Mrs. Carr? It's Ashley. I've brought a friend."

They stepped into a small vestibule and a tropical climate. Spring may have arrived on the Olympic Peninsula, but Mrs. Carr's comfort apparently required a higher temperature. Ashley rushed to the thermostat on the wall and peered at the setting.

"She must have forgotten to turn it down." Ashley gave a small, embarrassed laugh. "She gets cold a lot."

"How old did you say she was?" Ashley's friend was still standing by the door, hesitant to venture farther.

"She'll be ninety-six on her next birthday. And still has every one of her brain cells. She's amazing."

"Wow. I want to meet her."

"Right this way." Ashley walked through a hopelessly cluttered living room, picking up dog-eared magazines and crocheted blankets along the way and throwing them onto a sagging love seat. She navigated as someone who knew the house and the habits of its occupant.

"Mrs. Carr? I'm coming into your bedroom. It's ten o'clock. Time for your pills."

The two women walked down a hallway crowded with old family photos long faded from the passage of time.

Ashley pushed open the bedroom door. "Mrs. Carr?" Her friend stood on tiptoe to look over her.

Mrs. Carr's form was barely discernable in the large four-poster bed that took up most of the bedroom. The bed was piled high with comforters in a rainbow of colors. A reasonable person might wonder whether the woman was there at all.

"That's odd. Usually she's sitting up by now." Ashley walked quickly over to the side of the bed and lifted one comforter, then another. Mrs. Carr was now visible, at least from the neck up. But there was no vitality left in her face. Her wide-open eyes had sunk deep into the sockets, and the pallor of her skin was pasty white. Ashley tugged at the comforter, and a clawlike hand emerged, grasping the edge of the cloth, seeming to resist any attempt to take away her last bit of warmth.

"She's dead." Ashley's voice registered astonishment.

Behind her, her friend slid to the floor in a dead faint.

CHAPTER 1

Monday, May 2

A piercing shriek brought Annie Carson out of her reverie. Not to mention her rear firmly back down on her saddle.

She'd been standing in her stirrups to get the maximum view of her sheep pasture. It was a panoramic view—her mount was a 16-hand Thoroughbred, which already put her more than five feet off the ground. The sight of seventy-five ewes and as many lambs in the grassy lea reminded Annie of a Constable painting she'd once seen in a museum. Even the billowing clouds overhead looked painted.

Now she wheeled Trooper around and nudged him forward. The horse took off at a hard canter, turning abruptly in response to Annie's rein onto the trailhead of an old logging road. She pulled the horse up short a few seconds later.

"Hannah! Thank God you're safe!"

"Shhhh!"

If Annie thought it odd that an eight-year-old who'd just issued an earsplitting scream was now telling her to be quiet, she didn't say so. Instead, she calmly walked her horse closer to Hannah's. Bess, fortunately, was not making any noise. She was munching grass, very quietly.

"What's going on?" Annie kept her voice neutral.

"I saw someone in the woods! A man! I think he had a gun."

Annie scanned the thick trees in front of her. It was early May, and the Pacific Northwest was in the full flower of spring. She saw nothing but a suffusion of ferns and undergrowth forming a luxuriant pillow against densely packed Douglas fir.

"What was the man doing?"

"Hiding! He was behind a tree. Then I saw him run to another one. I didn't scream until I saw his weapon."

Hannah's father ran a security business that included transporting Loomis trucks filled with cash from local businesses. She was well acquainted with different caliber handguns and shotguns.

"What kind of weapon?"

"I'm not sure. I think it was a pistol. But I screamed, and then he ran away back there." Hannah pointed with her left arm into the woods.

"Why did you scream? Were you afraid?"

"Just a little. But I thought if I screamed, he'd go away. If he started to shoot at me, I figured I'd just gallop away. Maybe."

Annie was sure Hannah had every intention of galloping away. The problem was Bess, Annie's twenty-five-year-old Morgan who thought indulging in anything beyond a stately walk did not befit her dignified age.

"What did Bess do when you screamed?"

"Grazed."

So much for Hannah's fast getaway from the bad guy. But Annie was more concerned about Hannah's near encounter than she let on to her little companion.

The sound of shifting leaves caught both riders unawares. They started and whipped around in their saddles. Hannah clapped her hands over her mouth to make sure another scream wasn't forthcoming. From the dark forest floor, a fawn emerged, almost perfectly camouflaged against the lush, green backdrop. Walking carefully on its long and spindly legs, it wended its way through the thicket and out of sight. Hannah and Annie remained motionless on their saddles.

"A fawn!" breathed Hannah. "A baby deer! I thought I was going to jump out of my saddle, Annie, but I didn't! Even Bess jumped. A little."

"That's because you're nice and relaxed in your seat, Hannah," Annie replied. "So when something like this happens, it's easy to stay balanced."

Annie was a stickler who told all of her riding students not to grip the horse's ribs with their knees. It didn't help their equilibrium, and it impacted their horse's ability to move freely.

Hannah looked thoughtfully at Annie and nodded. "Do you think the fawn will find its mother?"

"I'm sure it will. The fawn isn't going to move far just because a couple of horses are passing through. I wouldn't be surprised if we saw a deer clearing in the next hundred feet."

"Let's go find it!"

"Nice try, kiddo. Fawns only want to be found by their mommies. Besides, hot chocolate awaits us."

This was the traditional ending to Hannah's riding lesson, and afterward Annie had driven the little girl to her doorstep. Usually, she let Hannah walk back to her home through a well-worn path; after all, the Clare household was only a quarter mile away. But now Annie recalled recent news stories of young children who'd been abducted just a short distance from their own homes, and she had no intention of taking unnecessary chances.

Taking care of her own safety was just as important. When Annie had opened Carson Stables, her training facility for equines, every man she'd encountered had flat out told her that a single woman who weighed a mere 125 pounds would never be able to handle the workload, let alone adequately protect herself from things that went bump in the night, both animal and human.

"Don't expect me to come to your rescue every time you hear a scary noise in the woods," Suwana County Sheriff Dan Stetson had grumbled after she'd dismissed his advice for the tenth time.

Annie had merely laughed. "I won't," was her breezy reply.

That conversation had occurred fifteen years ago. In the intervening time, she'd proven Dan and everyone else wrong. Not one of her detractors knew how hard she worked to make sure no harm came to her or her animals. She'd learned that the best way to keep danger from coming to her doorstep was to meet it head-on.

After dropping off Hannah, she parked her F-250 near the stables and called for Trooper, now contently munching on a flake of orchard grass in the paddock. It was time to find out exactly who had been lurking off the old logging road. If the man Hannah had seen was simply taking a shortcut through her property, he'd be long gone by now. She certainly hoped so.

As usual, the thoroughbred was up for another trail ride. She slipped a hackamore over his nose and, using a rail post, hopped on his back, deciding to eschew his saddle on this trip. At forty-three, Annie was less enthused about playing leapfrog over a horse's back to mount as she'd been in her twenties, but the joy of riding on a horse, sans saddle, still held a certain thrill. The connection with the animal was undeniable. After whistling for Wolf, her Blue Heeler, she cantered the short mile back to the sheep pasture and entered the now-familiar logging trail.

What she found in the interior brush was not a deer clearing, but rather one made by a human, or humans. True, the rough campsite was on the edge of Annie's property, but it looked as if it had been recently used, and for all she knew would be occupied again that evening. The folded army bedroll and cigarette butts littering a small fire pit were enough to confirm that no one had broken camp yet. The only item that was incongruous to the site was a small stuffed animal scrunched partway under a blanket. Annie slid off Trooper to take a closer look, and discovered it to be a very worn, and therefore presumably very much loved, toy lamb. Annie looked it over carefully, then back at the campsite. There was nothing else to intimate a child had been sleeping or living here—just a person who enjoyed inhaling carbon monoxide. She positioned the lamb in the vee of a nearby tree. She figured it wouldn't hurt for whomever was staying here to know that their secluded home had been busted. And for some unknown reason, she felt like keeping the inanimate toy safe. Maybe it was the remnant of a homeless person's former life that he or she carried with them.

Maybe Dan knows who might be living here. Annie snorted as soon as the thought came into her head. Fat chance. The county abounded with homeless people, and the only transients the sheriff knew were the ones who landed in the county jail. However, there was no sign of a man in the vicinity, armed or otherwise.

Annie clambered onto Trooper's back, turned her reins toward the horse trail paralleling the sheep pasture, and headed for home. She waved to Trotter, her donkey of indeterminate age, still fully capable of keeping any would-be predator out of the electrified barriers that encased him, her ewes, and their offspring. When summer ended and the sheep returned to Johan Thompson's farm where they wintered, Trotter would rejoin the rest of Annie's horses. The rotation would begin again in the spring, just before birthing season. Annie kept her sheep for their prized wool, not their taste. She had nothing against meat but preferred that anything she ingested had not first been fed and sheltered by her. It was a specious rationale, but Annie didn't spend too much time worrying about it.

When the barn and tack room loomed ahead and her four horses nickered to her from across the pasture, Annie put the makeshift campsite out of her mind. She leaned forward slightly, Trooper's cue to canter. Normally, Annie wouldn't let anyone canter a horse back to the barn—it was a bad habit and hard to break—but Trooper, bless his equine soul, was a perfect gentleman and knew exactly how far he could go and when to stop.

Annie quickly ushered the horses into the paddock, which adjoined the row of stalls inside the stable. Everyone was ready for dinner and a warm stall, and each horse knew his or her place, although Rover, a once-starved horse Annie had rescued, predictably veered toward Trooper's stall, which held a flake more of Timothy hay than his own. It took one quick sideways look from the thoroughbred to convince Rover he'd made a mistake.

Watching each equine politely enter its stall, she thought smugly, *My horses behave better than most children.* Annie was more than satisfied with playing big sister to

Hannah and other youngsters who loved horses. She was less than thrilled at playing the same role to her real half sister, Lavender, who'd trekked out from Florida earlier this year and temporarily found refuge in Annie's home. Lavender had left their father's home after learning he intended to marry a woman younger than she was. Annie couldn't have cared less about her father's marital exploits; he'd divorced her own mother more than twenty years before, and she hadn't had contact with him in years. But Lavender, despite being a full-fledged adult—at least in age, if not maturity—had always relied upon their father's financial support. Annie had discovered that her half sister now expected her to provide the same level of care and feeding she'd enjoyed in Florida. There were so many things in her own universe to explore, she explained to Annie, she simply didn't have time for a paying job. Annie noticed that Lavender still had plenty of time to criticize the way she lived, however. Fortunately, the situation had remedied itself, and Lavender now lived a safe three miles away. Annie had made sure Lavender returned her extra house key.

Before turning off the stable light, she stepped inside each stall and quickly ran her hands down each horse to make sure all was well. Normally, she would have lingered by them, inhaling and loving the smell of their manes and quietly grooming them as they munched their dinners.

But tonight she had a phone date with Marcus Colbert, the man who had given her Trooper. A few months earlier he'd mysteriously disappeared after his wife, Hilda, was murdered, and he resurfaced—by way of a cryptic postcard—only after the case was solved. The entire world had been convinced that Marcus was on the run from the crime of killing his wife, but Annie's faith in Marcus's innocence had never wavered and she'd been proven right when the real killer was apprehended. Tonight, she would speak to him for the first time in almost two months. His personal assistant in San Jose had set up the phone appointment last week and had promised that Marcus would answer all her questions. And she had a bucketful.

Connect with Us